The
PATRIOTS' CLUB

christopher
REICH

D1033634

headline

First published in Great Britain in 2005
by HEADLINE BOOK PUBLISHING

First published in paperback in 2006
by HEADLINE BOOK PUBLISHING

1

ISBN 0 7553 0629 5 (Super A format)
ISBN 0 7553 3201 6 (A format)

Typeset in Palatino by Avon DataSet Ltd,
Bidford-on-Avon, Warwickshire

Printed and bound in Great Britain by
Mackays of Chatham plc, Chatham, Kent

Headline's policy is to use papers that are natural, renewable
and recyclable products and made from wood grown in
sustainable forests. The logging and manufacturing processes
are expected to conform to the environmental regulations
of the country of origin.

HEADLINE BOOK PUBLISHING
A division of Hodder Headline
338 Euston Road
London NW1 3BH

www.headline.co.uk
www.hodderheadline.com

To Richard Pine
With gratitude

Acknowledgements

I would like to thank the following individuals for their assistance. Detective First Grade (retired) Thomas McKenna, NYPD, Dan Starer of Research for Writers.com, Dr Doug Fischer, Special Agent with the California Department of Justice, Special Agent-in-Charge (retired) Thomas Sloan of the United States Secret Service, Dr Gregory Piatetsky-Shapiro, Dr Raghu Ramakrishnan, Richard Brookhiser, Jeffrey Kroessler, Bob Friedman at Blackstone Group, Tom Flanagan at Lehman Brothers, the kind folks at the Fraunces Tavern in Manhattan, and my good friend, Niklaus Leuenberger of The Peninsula Hotel New York.

At Bantam Dell, I offer my thanks to Irwyn Applebaum, Nita Taublib, Michahlyn Witt, Susan Corcoran, Betsy Hulsebosch, and most especially to my editor, Bill Massey.

Every author owes a huge debt to his family. My wife, Sue, is a partner in every aspect of my work. Words are not enough . . .

Finally, I'd like to thank my agent, Richard Pine, to whom this book is dedicated, and his colleagues at Inkwell Management, especially the indefatigable Lori Andiman.

Past

A warm wind blew off the East River, gathering dust, dander, and droppings off the street and swirling the noxious mix into the air. The two men turned their faces from the gust, before resuming their conversation.

'As always, you exaggerate,' the general was saying. 'Really, you must calm down. Your temper will be the end of you.'

'I hardly think so,' replied his colleague, shorter by a head. 'Look around you. The country's being torn apart. Gangs of ruffians storming courthouses in the West. Farmers in Pennsylvania lobbying day and night to cut taxes, and King Cotton in the South wanting nothing to do with us at all. We're being drawn and quartered.'

'With time, we'll sort out their grievances.'

'With time, the republic will cease to exist! The country's already grown so large, so diverse. Walk up Broadway and all you hear are foreign tongues – German, Russian, Spanish. Everywhere you look, there's another immigrant. I'll give you a dollar for every native English speaker you can find.'

'I do recall something about your being from abroad.'

The shorter man had long ago learned to ignore the ugly facts of his parentage. He was a lawyer by trade, trim and compact with a Roman senator's nose and pale blue eyes. 'We've lost our sense of purpose. The war brought us together. These days, it's every man for himself. I won't stand for it. Not after all we've sacrificed. We need a firm hand to set things right. One voice. One vision.'

'We have the people's voice to guide us.'

'Precisely the problem! The vox populi cannot be trusted. They're a rabble.'

'They are Americans!' protested the general.

'My point exactly,' came the disgusted reply. 'Have you ever known a more quarrelsome bunch?'

The general began to pace, his gaze fleeing down Wall Street and landing on the busy docks. Every day more ships arrived. More new souls treading down the gangway to populate this boundless land, each with his own customs, his own prejudices, his own traditions. Each with his own priorities; priorities that were, by nature, selfish. What could they bring but discord? 'And so?'

The lawyer beckoned him closer. 'I have an idea,' he whispered. 'Something to help you.'

'To help *me*?'

'The Executive. The country.' He laid a hand on the general's arm. 'A way to get around the vox populi. To maintain order. To see your will be done.'

The general gazed down on his associate. They had been friends for nearly twenty years. The younger man had served as his aide during the war. He had shown himself to be courageous under fire; his counsel wise. He was to be trusted. 'And what might that be?'

'A club, sir.'

'What kind of club?'

The lawyer's eyes flickered. 'A patriots' club.'

Chapter 1

Thomas Bolden checked over his shoulder. The two men were still a half block behind. They'd kept the same distance since he'd noticed them soon after coming out of the hotel. He wasn't sure why they bothered him. Both were tall and clean-cut, about his age. They were respectably dressed in dark slacks and overcoats. At a glance, they appeared unthreatening. They could be bankers headed home after a late night at the office. College buddies hurrying to the Princeton Club for a last round before closing. More likely, they were two of the approximately three hundred guests who had suffered through the dinner given in his honor.

And yet . . . they disturbed him.

'I'm sorry, sweetheart,' said Bolden. 'What were you saying?'

'Where are you going to put it?' Jennifer Dance asked. 'You know . . . in your apartment?'

'Put it?' Bolden glanced at the large sterling-silver plate cradled in Jenny's arms. 'You mean I'm supposed to keep it on display?'

The plate looked like the one awarded to the women's singles champion at Wimbledon. This one, however, was engraved with the words, 'Thomas F. Bolden. Harlem Boys' Club Man of the Year.' He'd won plaques, medals, scrolls, and trophies, but never a plate. He wondered what joker at the club had thought it up. Curling an arm over Jenny's shoulders, he drew her close and said, 'No, no, no. This beautifully crafted hunk of lead is going straight into the closet.'

'You should be proud of it,' Jenny protested.

'I am proud of it, but it's still going in the closet.'

'It doesn't have to be the first thing you see when you walk in. We'll put it someplace discreet. Maybe on the side table in the hall leading from your bedroom to the bathroom. You worked hard for this. You deserve to feel good about yourself.'

Bolden looked at Jenny and grinned. 'I feel fine about myself,' he said. 'I just don't want to be reminded how great I am every time I go take a leak. It's so . . . I don't know . . . so *New York*.'

'It ain't bragging if you can do it,' Jenny said. 'Those are your words.'

'I was talking about dunking a basketball. Now, that's an accomplishment for a thirty-two-year-old white male who fudges about being six feet tall. Next time get a picture of that, and I'll put it on the table leading to the bathroom. Framed even.'

Nearing midnight on a Tuesday in mid-January, the narrow streets of the city's financial district were deserted. The night sky hung low, gray clouds scudding between the skyscrapers like fast-moving ships. The temperature hovered at forty degrees, unseasonably warm for this time of year. There was talk of a major storm system hitting the Eastern seaboard, but the meteorologists looked to have it wrong this time.

The annual gala benefiting the Harlem Boys' Club had ended thirty minutes earlier. It had been a ritzy affair: white tablecloths, champagne cocktails, a four-course meal with fresh seafood instead of chicken. Bolden had been too nervous about giving his speech to enjoy the event. Besides, it wasn't his style. Too much backslapping. Too many hands to shake. All that forced laughter. His cheeks felt like a punching bag from all the busses he'd gotten.

All in all, the event raised an even three hundred thousand dollars. His cheeks could take a little roughing up for that kind of change.

A drop of rain hit his nose. Bolden looked up, waiting for the next, but nothing followed. He pulled Jenny closer and nuzzled her neck. From the corner of his eye, he saw that the two men were still there, maybe a little farther back, walking side by side, talking animatedly. It wasn't the first time lately that he'd had the sensation of being followed. There'd been a night last week when he'd felt certain someone had been trailing him near his apartment on Sutton Place. And just today at lunch, he'd been aware of a presence hovering nearby. A nagging feeling that someone was eyeing him. On neither occasion, however, had he been able to put a face to his fears.

And now there were these two.

He glanced at Jenny, and caught her staring at him. 'What?'

'That's my Tommy,' she said, with her all-knowing smile. 'You're so afraid of letting it go.'

'Letting what go?'

'The past. The whole "Tommy B. from the wrong side of the tracks" thing. You still walk as if you're on the mean streets of the Windy City. Like a mobster on the lam or something, afraid someone's going to recognize you.'

'I do not,' he said, then forced himself to push his shoulders back and stand a little straighter. 'Anyway, that's who I am. It's where I come from.'

'And this is where you are now. This is your world, too. Look at yourself. You're a director at the snobbiest investment bank on Wall Street. You have dinner all the time with politicians and big shots.

All those people didn't show up tonight for me . . . they came for you. What you've achieved is pretty damned impressive, mister.'

Bolden dug his hands deep into his pockets. 'Not bad for a gutter rat.'

She tugged at his sleeve. 'I'm serious, Thomas.'

'I guess you must be if you're calling me Thomas.'

They walked a few steps, and she said, 'Come on, Tommy. I'm not saying it's time to join the Four Hundred. I'm just saying it's time to let the past go. This is your world now.'

Bolden shook his head. 'Naw, I'm just passing through.'

Jenny raised her eyes, exasperated. 'You've been passing through for seven years. That's long enough for someone from Swaziland to become an American citizen. Don't you think it's enough to make you a New Yorker? Besides, it's not such a bad place. Why don't you stay awhile?'

Bolden stopped. Taking both of Jenny's hands in his, he turned to face her. 'I love it here, too. But you know me . . . I like to keep my distance. I just don't want to get too close to them. All the guys at work. The stuffed shirts. You gotta keep your distance, or else they suck you in. Like body snatchers.'

Jenny put her head back and laughed. 'They're your friends.'

'Associates, yes. Colleagues, maybe. But friends? I don't recall getting too many invitations to dine at my *friends'* homes. Though that may very well change after the looks I caught a couple of those sleazebags giving you tonight.'

'You jealous?'

'Damn straight.'

Jenny smiled, disarmingly. 'Really?'

She was tall and blond, with an athlete's toned

body, and the best skyhook since Kareem. Her face was open and honest, given to determined stares, and crooked smiles. She taught seventh, eighth, and ninth grade at a 'special ed' school in the Village. She liked to say that it was just like the school in *Little House on the Prairie*, all the kids in one classroom, except that her kids were what the system labeled high-risk teens. High-risk teens were the bad eggs: the boys and girls who'd been expelled from their ordinary schools and were doing time with Jenny until they could be reformed, remolded, and reassigned to a public school that would take them. They were quite a bunch. Drug dealers, thieves, hustlers, and hookers, and not one over the age of fifteen. She wasn't a teacher, so much as a lion tamer.

'By the way,' she said, nonchalantly. 'Dinner's been over awhile and you still have your tie on.'

'Do I?' Bolden's hand shot to his neck. 'It's begun. The body snatchers have me. Pretty soon, I'll be wearing pink shirts and white loafers and putting on tight black bicycle shorts when I hit the gym. I'll start listening to opera and *o-pining* about wine. I may even join a country club.'

'They're not so bad. Our kids would love it.'

'Kids!' Bolden stared at her, aghast. 'You're one of them, too! I'm done for.'

They walked in silence for a while. Jenny tilted her head on his shoulder and laced her fingers through his. Bolden caught their reflection in a window. He was hardly a match for her. His neck was too thick, his jaw too wide, and his dark hair receding quickly at the temples. What remained was thick and peppered with gray and cut close to the scalp. Thirty-two was definitely not young in his business. His face was stern, with steadfast brown eyes, and a directness of gaze that some men found intimidating. His lips were thin, rigid. His chin split by a hatchet. He looked like a man on equal terms with uncertainty. A reliable man. A man to have at your side in the lurch. He was surprised how natural the tux looked on him. He almost felt natural wearing it. Immediately, he yanked off his bow tie and stuffed it in his pocket.

A New Yorker, he said to himself. *Mr Big Shot with a silver plate on the way to the pisser.*

No. That wasn't him.

He was just Tom Bolden, a kid from the Midwest with neither birthright nor pedigree, and no illusions. His mother had left when he was six. He never knew his father. He grew up as a ward of the state of Illinois, a survivor of too many foster families to count, a graduate of Illinois's most notorious reform school, and, at seventeen, a felon. The conviction was sealed under court order. Even Jenny didn't know about it.

Arm in arm, they continued up Wall Street. Past number 23 Wall, the old headquarters of J. P. Morgan when they were the world's most powerful bankers. Not ten feet away, an anarchist's bomb had gone off in 1920, killing three dozen employees and bystanders, and upending a Model T. The chinks in the wall from the shrapnel had never been repaired and were still visible. Across the street stood the New York Stock Exchange, a huge American flag draped across the Corinthian columns, nothing less than a temple to capitalism. To their right, a steep flight of stairs led to Federal Hall, the seat of government when the nation's capital had been situated in New York City.

'You know what today is?' he asked.

'Tuesday the eighteenth?'

'Yes, it's Tuesday the eighteenth. And . . .? You mean you don't remember?'

'Oh, my God,' gasped Jenny. 'I'm so sorry. It's just that with the dinner and finding a dress and everything else . . .'

Just then, Bolden dropped her hand and vaulted up a few stairs. 'Follow me,' he said.

'What are you doing?'

'Come on. Up here. Sit down.' Turning, he indicated for Jenny to take a seat.

'It's cold.' She eyed him curiously, then climbed the stairs and sat. He grinned, loving this part. The *before*. The wind blew stronger, tousling her hair around her face. She had wonderful hair, thick, naturally curly, as many colors as a field of summer wheat. He remembered seeing her for the first time. It was on the basketball court at the Y. She pulled off a between-the-legs dribble followed by a twenty-foot jumper that hit nothing but net. She'd been wearing red athletic shorts, a baggy tank top, and Air Jordans. He looked at her now, dressed in a chic black cocktail dress, her makeup just so, and felt his breath catch. Miss Jennifer Dance cleaned up nice.

'What's the world coming to when the man's got to remember the big dates?' Delving into an inside pocket, he pulled out a slim rectangular box wrapped in royal maroon paper and handed it to her. It took him a second or two to find his voice. 'Three years. You've made them the best of my life.'

Jenny looked between him and the box. Slowly, she unwrapped it. She hadn't even cracked the thing, and she was already getting teary. Bolden blinked rapidly, and looked away. 'Go on,' he said.

Jenny held her breath and opened the box. 'Tommy, this is . . .' She held up the Cartier wristwatch, her expression stranded between awe and disbelief.

'I know. It's vulgar. It's gauche. It's—'

'It's beautiful,' she said, pulling him down to sit beside her. 'Thank you.'

'It's inscribed,' he said. 'I didn't want you to feel bad that I was the only one getting something tonight.'

Jenny turned the watch over, and he observed the play of her features as she read the words. The dollar-sized eyes, the bold, chiseled nose still hiding a few freckles across its bridge, the wide, expressive mouth curling into a smile. Lying close to her at night, he often studied her face, asking himself how it was that he, a man who had never depended on anyone in his entire life, had grown to depend so entirely on her.

'I love you, too,' she said, reaching a hand to touch his cheek. 'For ever.'

Bolden nodded, finding it impossible, as ever, to say the words. He'd written them, that was a start.

'Does this mean you're not scared any longer?' Jenny asked.

'No,' he answered solemnly. 'It means, I'm scared, but I'm getting ready. Don't you go running anyplace.'

'I'm not going anywhere.'

They kissed for a long time like a couple of teenagers going at it.

'I think this calls for a drink,' he said, afterwards.

'I want something silly with an umbrella,' said Jenny.

'I want something serious without one.' He hugged Jenny. The two of them laughed, and his grew louder when he saw that the men were no longer behind them. So much for his sixth sense.

Holding hands, they walked up the street to Broadway. It was a night to celebrate. A night to cherish with the woman he loved. It wasn't a night to allow distrust, worry, and suspicion – the dependable, hard-earned habits of his youth – to ruin. Jenny was right. It was a night to bury his past once and for all.

'Taxi,' he yelled, because he was feeling happy and full of himself, even though there wasn't a yellow cab in sight. 'Where should we go?'

'Let's go dancing,' Jenny suggested.

'Dancing it is!'

Spotting a cab, he put his fingers in the corners of his mouth and whistled. It was a five-alarm whistle, capable of spooking visiting sluggers from the upper deck at Yankee Stadium. Bolden stepped into the street to hail the cab. The taxi flashed its lights and slid over a lane. Turning, he stretched out an arm to Jenny.

It was then that he saw them. At first, they were a blur. Figures moving fast, approaching aggressively along the sidewalk. Two men running. He recognized them at once. The two that had followed them from the hotel. He rushed toward Jenny, jumping onto the sidewalk to shield her with his body. 'Get back!' he shouted.

'Tommy, what is it?'

'Watch it! Run!' Before he could get the words out, the larger of the two men collided with him, a shoulder to the sternum knocking him into the street. Bolden's head struck the concrete. Stunned, he looked up to see the taxi bearing down on him. It braked hard, tires squealing as he rolled toward the kerb.

The other man grabbed Jenny.

'Stop it,' she screamed, flailing her arms at her attacker's head. She caught him with a roundhouse to the jaw and the man stumbled. She stepped forward, swinging wildly. The man blocked the punch, then slugged her in the stomach. Jenny bent double and he held her from behind, locking her arms to her sides.

Woozy, Bolden forced himself to a knee. His vision was mixed up, clouded. His head reeling. He ordered himself to get to his feet. *Jenny needs you!*

The man who had knocked him down grabbed Jenny's wrist, and turned it upright, so the new watch buckle pointed at the sky. Bolden saw his hand rise. He was holding something silver, angular. The hand descended. Blood spurted as the knife cut her forearm and sliced through the strap of the wristwatch. Jennifer cried out, clutching her arm. The bigger man pocketed the watch and ran. With a shove, the other man released her, stooping to snatch the silver plate. Then they were gone, charging down the sidewalk.

Bolden was at her side a moment later. 'Are you all right?' he asked.

Jenny stood with her right hand clamped over her wrist. Blood seeped between her fingers, dripping to the sidewalk. 'It hurts.'

'Let me see.' He peeled back her fingers and examined the wound. The gash was four inches long and deep. 'Stay here.'

'No, it's just a watch. It's not worth it.'

'It's not about the watch,' he said, and something about his tone caused her eyes to open in fright. He handed her his phone. 'Call a cop. Have him take you to NYU Emergency. I'll find you there.'

'No, Thomas, stay here . . . you're finished with all that.'

Bolden hesitated a moment, caught between past and present.

Then he ran.

Chapter 2

The men crossed Fulton against the light, slowing to dodge an oncoming car. Bolden followed a few seconds later, sprinting blindly through the crosswalk. Somewhere, brakes howled. Tires locked up. A driver leaned on his horn. Maybe he even shouted something out the window. Bolden heard none of it. His head throbbed with a single thought. *Catch them.* It beat like a tom-tom, drumming out every other sound.

The thieves weaved through the pedestrians as if they were pylons on a driving course. They had a half block on him, maybe seventy feet at most. They moved fast, but they weren't sprinters and he closed half the distance before they looked back. He saw their eyes widen, heard one of them swear. Thirty feet dwindled to twenty. He stared at their backs, deciding which to go after. Rule 1: Always take the biggest guy down first.

Bolden followed the track set by the slower man. He saw himself racing through the back alleys of Chicago. Blue jeans. Stones T-shirt. The lanky kid with the wild crown of hair. Mean-spirited. Unsmiling. Unreachable. No one ever caught Tommy B.

At Delancey, the men hugged the corner and headed right, down the cross street. The block was dark, less crowded than Broadway. He was gaining on them and he tried to pick up the pace. *Come on,* he urged himself. He pumped his arms, pushed out his chest, but the gas wasn't there. Seven years behind a desk had softened his legs. Weekly games of half-court basketball were hardly enough to keep his lungs in any kind of real condition. Half a minute and already they were burning. The back of his mouth was dry, his breath scratching his throat like a match striking flint.

An alley opened to his right. Dumpsters lined the walls on either side. Steam rose from a grate. Water dripping from a broken pipe had formed a puddle in the asphalt. The men ducked into it. Bolden turned the corner a second behind them. With a last burst, he closed the distance. If he could just stretch out his arm, he could grab one of them by the collar . . .

And then, the two men stopped and turned to face him.

The bigger man was Hispanic with a broad, simian face. The bridge of his nose had been flattened more than once. His hair cut short on the sides with plenty of greasy kid stuff on top, his glaring eyes screaming for a fight. The other man was blond and angular, his pale gaze as placid as the other's was violent. He carried the sterling-silver dish under his arm like a football. A star-shaped patch of scar tissue pinched his cheek. A cigarette burn. Or a bullet wound.

Bolden realized it was a trap. He also realized that it was too late to worry about traps, and that he'd committed himself to this course the moment he'd left Jenny.

Always take the biggest guy first.

Bolden crashed into the darker man, shoulder lowered like a rugby half. He hit him solidly and followed with a jab to the solar plexus. It was like slugging a block of cement. The man retreated a step, grabbing Bolden's fist, then his arm, using his momentum to flip him over his hip onto the ground. Bolden rolled to the right, avoiding a vicious kick. Skittering to his feet, he raised his hands. He jabbed once, twice, connecting with the jaw, then the cheek. The Hispanic man took the punches, and moved closer, batting away Bolden's hands. His own hands, Bolden noted, were meat cleavers. Bolden clutched at his shirt collar, ripping it, then fought his shoulder free and threw an inside uppercut. Suddenly, the man was no longer there. Bolden's fist struck air. And then, his world was turned upside down. His feet were at his head, the ground had taken a flyer, and the sky was doing a barrel roll over his head. For a moment, he had the sensation of falling, and then his shoulder hit the ground.

He lay on his back, fighting for breath. He struggled to pick himself up, but by then both men were standing above him. Their arms hung easily at their sides. Neither appeared winded or in the least fatigued. The knife was gone. A silenced automatic took its place.

'Okay,' said Bolden, taking a knee. 'You win. But that watch is engraved. There'll be a police report filed on it by morning. You won't be able to pawn it anywhere worth a damn.' He was speaking in bursts, like a telegraph operator sending Morse code.

The Hispanic man tossed Bolden the watch. 'Here you go. Keep it.'

Bolden held it in his palm. 'Am I supposed to thank you?' Mystified, he looked past the man's shoulder as a Lincoln Town Car pulled up to the mouth of the alley. The rear door opened, but no one stepped out. 'What do you guys want?'

The blond man with the scarred cheek lifted the nose of the pistol. 'We want you, Mr Bolden.'

Chapter 3

The five men had gathered in the long room, and now stood around the stout, burnished table waiting for the clock to toll midnight. Meetings were to begin with the new day. The new day offered hope, and hope was the cornerstone of the republic. No one drank or smoked. Both were forbidden until the meeting had adjourned. There was no rule, however, against speaking. All the same, the room was silent as a crypt. A problem had arisen that none of them had foreseen. A problem unlike any the committee had ever faced.

'Damned clock,' said Mr Morris, shooting an irritated glance at the ormolu ship's clock set on the mantelpiece. 'I'd swear it's stopped ticking.'

The clock had come from the *Bonhomme Richard*, John Paul Jones's flagship, and remained in its original condition. Jones, in his ship's log, had lamented its tendency to run slow.

'Patience,' counseled Mr Jay. 'It won't be but another minute, and we can all speak our conscience.'

'Easy for you to say,' responded Mr Morris, testily. 'I suppose court is out of session. You can sleep all day.'

'That'll do,' intoned Mr Washington, and it was enough to quiet them both.

They came from government, industry, and finance. They were lawyers, businessmen, politicians, and policemen. For the first time, a member of the Fourth Estate had been offered a place at the table: a journalist with close ties to the Executive and a Midwesterner's unvarnished honesty.

They knew each other well, if formally. Three of the five had been sitting, standing, and, as was often the case in this room, arguing, across the table from one another for twenty-odd years. The newest among them, the journalist, had been inducted three years earlier. The last – by tradition their leader, and as such *prima inter pares* – had guided them the past eight years, the longest period the Constitution permitted one in his position.

Tonight, they had convened to discuss his successor.

Just then, the antique clock struck the hour. The men took their seats around the table. When the final chime had rung, all heads were lowered and the prayer read.

'We now make it our earnest prayer,' said Mr Washington, 'that God would have these United States of America in His holy protection, that He would incline the hearts of the Citizens to cultivate a spirit of obedience to Government, to entertain a brotherly affection and love for one another, for their fellow Citizens at large, and particularly for their brethren who served in the Field, and, finally, that He would most graciously be pleased to dispose us all, to do Justice, to love mercy, and to command ourselves with that charity, humility, and pacific temper of mind, which were the Characteristics of the Divine Author of our blessed Religion, and without a humble imitation of whose example in these things, we can never hope to be a happy Nation.'

'Amen,' murmured the collected voices.

It was given to Mr Washington to preside over the meeting. He stood from his place at the head of the table and drew a breath. 'Gentlemen,' he said. 'I bring the meeting to order . . .'

'About time,' murmured Mr Morris. 'I've got a six A.M. flight to New York.'

Chapter 4

'What's this all about? You got me. Now, tell me what's going on.'

Thomas Bolden leaned forward, picking at a shard of glass embedded in his palm. His pants were torn where he'd slipped on the sidewalk, the flesh peeking out raw and bloody. The blond man sat to his right, the pistol resting on top of his leg. The Hispanic man took the jump seat. Tinted windows blocked out all view of the passing cityscape. A partition separated them from the driver.

'Mr Guilfoyle will answer your questions as soon as we arrive,' said the Hispanic man. His shirt hung open where Bolden had ripped it, revealing a tattoo on the left side of his chest. A rifle of some kind.

Guilfoyle. Bolden tried to place the name, but it meant nothing to him. He noted that the doors were locked. He considered kicking out the windows, but then what? He turned his mind to the men around him. Neither had been the least bit winded after leading him on a six-block chase. The larger man was obviously a master of judo, or a related martial art. He'd thrown Bolden to the ground as if he were as light as a feather. And, of course, there was the pistol. A Beretta 9 mm. Standard issue to army officers. The silencer, however, was nonstandard. He had no doubt that the blond man knew how to use it. He observed their bearing, their upright posture, their steady assured eyes. He guessed that they were ex-military. He could hear it in their clipped voices. He could sense the soldier's rigid discipline.

'Sit back. Relax,' said the darker man.

'I'll relax when I get back to my girlfriend,' Bolden snapped, 'and see to it that she gets to a hospital.'

'She's being taken care of. You don't have to worry about her.'

'And I'm supposed to believe you?'

'Irish, make a call.'

The blond man seated to Bolden's right pulled a cell phone/two-way radio from his jacket and put it to his ear. 'Base One to Base Three. What's the status on Miss Dance?'

Miss Dance. They knew Jenny's name, too.

'Base One,' growled the response, amid a burst of static. 'This is Base Three. Subject en route to NYU emergency room with an NYPD cop. ETA three minutes.'

'How bad is the wound?'

'Superficial. Ten stitches at most.'

He slipped the phone into his pocket. 'Like Wolf says, you don't have anything to worry about. Put your mind at ease.'

Wolf and Irish.

Bolden looked from one man to the other. Who were these two well-trained, capable thugs? How did they know his name? Who was Guilfoyle? And what in the name of Christ did any of them want with him? The questions repeated themselves endlessly. 'I need to know where you're taking me,' he said quietly. 'What's this all about?'

Wolf stared back at him. His eyes were yellowing and faintly bloodshot, flickering with a barely controlled animosity. The will to violence radiated

from him. It was a force as bracing and impossible
to ignore as a slap in the face. 'Mr Guilfoyle will
explain everything to you,' he said.

'I don't know a Mr Guilfoyle.'

'He knows you.'

'I don't care if he knows me or not. Where do
you get off attacking my girlfriend and forcing me
into this car? Who the hell are you guys, anyway? I
want an answer!'

Wolf bolted out of his seat. Fingers pressed
tightly together, his arm shot forward and speared
Bolden in the chest. 'I said to relax. Are we clear?'

Bolden bent double, unable to breathe. Wolf had
moved so fast that he hadn't had time to react, to
even register the assault.

'There's no mistake,' said Irish. 'You, sir, are
Thomas F. Bolden. You serve as a treasurer of the
Harlem Boys' Club Foundation and sit on the club's
board of trustees. You were awarded that silver
plate right there on the floor earlier this evening for
your work with the club. Am I right so far?'

Bolden couldn't speak. His mouth was open but
his lungs were paralyzed. Far away, he heard the
citation being read, the words a dying echo. *Thomas
Bolden began his work at the Harlem Boys' Club six
years ago, taking part in the Wall Street Mentoring
Program. Blessed with a natural rapport and genuine
affection for our youths, he soon became a regular
volunteer at the club. Three years ago, Mr Bolden, in
cooperation with the Gang Intervention Unit of the New
York Police Department, founded "Brand New Day" to
offer positive lifestyle alternatives to youths living in
problem areas. Through an integrated course of
counseling, mentoring, and academic and vocational
instruction, Brand New Day provides young men and
women in the Harlem area a way out of gang-related
activities and a means to break out of the "circle of*

destruction" that claims so many of the neighborhood's youth.'

Irish continued, 'You graduated summa cum laude with a double major in math and economics from Princeton University. You were captain of the rugby team, but you broke your leg in a game against Yale your senior year, and that was that. You wrote an investments column for the newspaper called "Common Cents". You worked twenty-five hours a week at Butler Dining Hall. After that, you attended the Wharton School on a full scholarship. You turned down a job with the World Bank, and passed on a Fulbright scholarship to take a job at Harrington Weiss. Last year, you were promoted to director, the youngest to make it in your hiring class. Are we good?'

Bolden nodded.

Wolf slid forward and tapped Bolden on the cheek. 'Irish asked, "Are we good?" '

'We're good.' It was a whisper.

We want you, Mr Bolden.

The car drove at a steady pace. Bolden guessed that they were heading north either on the West Side Highway or FDR Drive. They were still in Manhattan. Had they crossed a bridge or passed through a tunnel he would have noticed. He sat as still as a rock, but his mind was doing the hundred-yard dash. He had no grievances outstanding, past or present. He hadn't violated anyone's trust. He hadn't broken any laws. He settled into the soft black leather and ordered himself to wait, to cooperate, to be ready for a chance.

Bolden lifted the silver plate off the floor and placed it in his lap. A program from the dinner had fallen out of its protective wrap. Irish read it, then handed it to Wolf, who gave it a perfunctory look and threw it back onto the floor.

'Why do you do it?' asked Irish. 'Think you make a difference?'

Bolden studied the man. His face was lean to the point of being gaunt. His cheeks were sunken, the skin drawn tight across his jaw. His complexion, ruddy, windburned. The reckless eyes, a flinty blue. It was the face of a climber, a triathlete, a marathoner; someone who enjoyed testing the limits of his endurance. Bolden decided the scar on his cheek was a bullet wound. 'You guys were in the army?' he asked. 'What, Rangers? Airborne?'

Neither man protested, and Bolden noted a change in their bearing. A camouflaged pride.

'What's that saying of yours?' he went on. ' "No man left behind." That's why I do it. The kids up there don't have someone looking after them to make sure they don't get left behind.'

He looked out the window, hoping for a glimpse of the street, but caught only his own reflection. *Why did he do it*? Maybe because his life had grown settled and routine, and with the kids, nothing was ever settled or routine. Every decision – from what color shirt to wear to school to which fast-food joint to do their homework in afterwards – was liable to have a profound impact on their future. It was an existence lived on a razor's edge, and it required the skill of a tightrope artist just to stay out of trouble. Maybe he did it for himself. Because he'd been one of them. Because he knew what it was like to live day by day, to think of the future as what might happen the week after next. Maybe he did it because he'd been the lucky one who got out, and you never forgot your brothers.

Wolf checked his watch. 'Call ahead. Tell them we're two minutes out.'

Irish made the call.

'Quite an operation,' said Bolden.

'No more than was necessary to complete the objective,' said Wolf.

'And I am that objective?'

'That's affirmative.'

Bolden shook his head. It was ridiculous. Insane. Despite everything they might know about him, they had the wrong man. But there was nothing ridiculous about the gash on Jenny's arm, or the silenced pistol four inches away. He looked at the tattoo on Wolf's chest. 'What's that artwork? A gun? You used to run with some guys?'

Wolf pulled the torn shirt over the tattoo and buttoned his overcoat. 'If you're so gung ho to talk, tell me this: what exactly did you plan on doing when you caught up to us back there?'

'I planned on getting the watch back and smacking you in the head.'

'You?' An unbelieving smile stretched across Wolf's face. 'You're a little out of practice, but at least, you've got a positive attitude. Tell you what. You got the watch back. Why not try going two for two? Go on. Give it your best shot. Come on. I'm ready.' The smile vanished. He leaned forward, the eyes taunting him. 'Come on, Bolden. Your best shot. You want to smack me in the head. Do it!'

Bolden looked away.

Wolf laughed. 'What do you say, Irish? Could we use him on our team?'

Irish shook his head. 'This guy? You've got to be kidding. We took him six blocks and he was ready to puke. Totally unsat. I'd say he's NPQ.'

'Not physically qualified,' added Wolf, for Bolden's edification. 'You, sir, are unsat.'

But Bolden couldn't care less about his unsatisfactory rating. Something else he'd heard had sparked his attention. 'What team is that?' he asked.

'You know the answer to that question,' said Irish.

'Help me out,' said Bolden.

'We're the good guys,' said Wolf. He rooted inside a canvas bag at his feet and pulled out an antiseptic towelette. 'Get yourself cleaned up. Mr Guilfoyle doesn't like blood.'

Bolden took the towelette and dabbed at his knee. Irish's phone crackled. A voice said, 'ETA ninety seconds.' The car slowed and began an extended left-hand turn.

'Some advice?' said Irish. 'Give Mr Guilfoyle what he wants. Don't mess around. Remember, we know all about you.'

'*Your team?*'

Irish nodded. 'Give the man what he wants. You see, Mr Guilfoyle, he's special. He's got this thing, this talent. He knows about people.'

'What about people?' asked Bolden.

'Everything. Don't even think of lying to him. It makes him upset.'

'So if I just tell him the truth, then he'll know it.'

'Bingo!' said Irish, touching the barrel of the gun to his knee.

Wolf reached into his canvas bag and came back with a knit hood. 'Put this on and keep it on.'

Bolden turned the hood over in his hands. It was a black balaclava with patches sewn over the eyes. A death's hood.

Chapter 5

On December 4, 1783, after eight years of campaigning against the British, George Washington gathered his top commanders together at the Fraunces Tavern, a popular ale house one block south of Wall Street, to formally discharge them from their country's service, and to offer his gratitude for their years of dedication and sacrifice.

The Paris Peace Treaty had been signed on September 3, formally declaring an end of hostilities between the two nations, and giving in writing Great Britain's recognition of the United States of America as a sovereign republic. The last British soldier had left New York eight days earlier. The Union Jack had been lowered a final time from Fort George at the southern tip of Manhattan and the Stars and Stripes raised in its place. (Though not without difficulty. The departing Redcoats had greased the flagpole with tallow, making it impossible for even the most able-bodied seaman to reach the flag. Finally, iron rungs had to be nailed into the pole so a man could climb to the top and take it down.)

Washington and his officers met in the Long Room, on the tavern's second floor. Over tankards of beer and wine, they talked of their victories and defeats. Lexington. Concord. Breed's Hill. Trenton and Monmouth. Valley Forge. Yorktown.

Together they had defeated the most powerful

nation on earth. From thirteen wildly different colonies, they had forged a country united by a common and enlightened belief in the rights of man and the role of government. Never again would they take up arms for so noble a cause. The eyes of history had been upon them and they had acquitted themselves with honor.

It was a sentimental farewell.

Two hundred and twenty-odd years later, the room had been re-created from top to bottom on the second floor of a Virginia country estate. From the aged wood floor to the chiffon yellow paint. From the woodburning fireplace to the Quaker chairs, everything was as it had been that night. Even the table was said to be a replica of the one Washington had sat at that momentous evening, when one after another, he had shaken his loyal officers' hands and bid them a tearful good-bye.

'Has there been any change?' asked Mr Washington. 'Is she willing to join our ranks?'

'None,' said Mr Jay. 'Senator McCoy refuses to reconsider. The woman is as stubborn as a deaf mule.'

'But it's not a matter of choice,' said Mr Hamilton, his cheeks reddening. 'It's an obligation. A God-given duty.'

'You tell her that,' said Mr Pendleton. 'She's made a career telling people like us to go to hell. For some reason, the voters seem to like her for it.'

Six men sat round the table. It was a tradition for each to take the name of one of the six founders. Oil portraits of their namesakes hung on the wall, staring down at them like moody ancestors. George Washington. Alexander Hamilton. John Jay, first chief justice of the Supreme Court. Robert Morris, the gentleman financier who had paid for much of the Continental Army's rifle and grapeshot out of his own silk-lined pockets. Senator Rufus King of New York. And Nathaniel Pendleton, distinguished jurist and Alexander Hamilton's closest friend.

'Does she really know who "people like us" are?' asked Mr King. 'I'm wondering if you made yourself sufficiently clear.'

'As clear as I can until she joins us,' said Mr Jay. 'There's only so much we can tell her without jeopardizing our position.'

'It's the same approach you made to me,' said Mr Washington. He was a tall and distinguished man with thick silver hair, the envy of other sixty-year-olds, and an inquisitor's black gaze. 'Most people would take it as an honor. That isn't the problem. She's made her name as a renegade. It's what got her elected. To join with us would go against everything she stands for.'

'And if she doesn't join?' asked Mr Pendleton.

'She will,' said Mr King, hopefully. 'She must.'

Mr Pendleton dismissed the younger man's idealism with a grunt. 'And if she doesn't?' he repeated.

When no one answered, he looked toward a glass cabinet in the corner. Inside were relics left them by their predecessors. A locket of Hamilton's hair, the color of honey. A splinter from Washington's casket (obtained by an earlier member when the Father of His Country was disinterred and reburied at Mount Vernon). A Bible belonging to Abraham Lincoln. Like him, they had been realists, wedded to the possible.

'It's symptomatic of the times,' said Mr Jay. 'The people aren't used to their government stirring things up. They like America to settle things down. To put out fires, not start them. Senator McCoy looks at us and believes that we've caused the problems.'

Mr Washington nodded. 'Two oceans don't separate us from the rest of the world like they used to. If we want to protect our interests, we have to act, not react. God didn't put us on this map to bow and scrape at the hem of every second-rate dictator.'

'Not problems,' said Mr Pendleton. 'Opportunities. For once, we're in a position to shape the world in our image. It's a question of manifest destiny. It's time we made the most of it.'

'"You are the light of the world; a city set on a hill cannot be hid,"' said Mr King. A journalist and historian, he had written a Pulitzer-prize-winning biography of John Winthrop. At forty, he was the youngest of the group, or the Committee, as they called themselves. Only one man in their history had been younger: Alexander Hamilton, who had founded the club in 1793 at the age of thirty-eight.

'How much does she know?' asked Mr Pendleton. 'Any names? Any specifics? Did you get around to discussing any of our initiatives?'

The mood in the room changed as dramatically as a shift in the wind. The yardarm had swung from reconciliation to confrontation.

'Nothing specific,' said Mr Jay, pushing his horn-rimmed spectacles to the bridge of his nose. He was a short man, and rotund, sparse white hair crowning a pinched, sour face. 'But she knows we exist, and, I would gather, that I'm a member. I assured her that we view ourselves as being entirely at the President's disposal. To help out in those times when extraordinary actions are needed. Actions best not mentioned to the public.'

'Wasn't she curious?' asked Mr King. 'I mean, didn't she want to know who exactly we were? What we've done in the past?'

'Make no mistake, Mrs McCoy was curious.

I talked to her about a few things we'd helped out with. The Jay Treaty.'

'Did you tell her everything?' Mr King appeared shocked at the prospect.

'What I didn't tell her, I let her guess. She's a smart woman.'

Mr King exhaled slowly. In their history, only one President had refused to join. John Adams. But then, he was a President in name only. While he closeted himself away in Braintree, Alexander Hamilton was pulling all the strings, through his close friends in Adams's cabinet. Mr King's palms grew moist and clammy. The entire state of affairs made him more than a little uncomfortable. He was a journalist. It was one thing to report on momentous events. It was another to bring them to pass.

On the desk in front of him lay an aged, leatherbound volume in which the minutes of each meeting were recorded. The newest member of the club, King had inherited the job of 'secretary'. It fell to him to faithfully continue the record. He had studied the minutes – in this volume, and in the five others that preceded it – with an interest bordering on the feverish.

The Jay Treaty. Yes, he thought, it was the only place to begin.

In the summer of 1795, the country was in an uproar. America was caught between its allegiance to France, its ally in the war for independence, and itself in the throes of a wild and violent democratic revolution, and its hatred of England, which had reneged on many of the main points of the Paris Treaty signed twelve years earlier. Britain had brazenly boarded over 250 US merchantmen in the past year, seizing their cargoes and impressing their sailors. ('Impressment' was the practice of forcing captured seamen into the service of one's own military – in this case, the British navy.) British ships had even been so arrogant as to station themselves in a picket at the mouth of New York harbor and had seized four ships in a single day. Up and down the eastern seaboard, there were calls for war with Britain. Riots broke out in Philadelphia and New York. The country was aflame with patriotic fervor.

Hoping to quell the dispute between the two nations, George Washington had sent John Jay, recently retired from his post as the first chief justice of the Supreme Court, to England. The treaty he negotiated reconfirmed an alliance between England and the United States, but was viewed by many as traitorous because it failed to force Britain to repay the debts it had earlier promised. Angry voices claimed the Jay Treaty returned the United States to its role as subordinate to England and that the United States might as well be a colony all over again with George III its king.

The issue was discussed during a meeting held in June of 1795.

June 12, 1795

Present: General Washington, Mr Hamilton, Mr Jay, Mr Morris, Mr Pendleton, Mr King.

Mr Hamilton states that signature of the Jay Treaty is a necessity and of paramount concern to the Union. Friendship and trade with Britain are crucial to the country's growth as an economic power and to its future strategic position.

General Washington concurs. War with Britain is certain should he not sign the treaty.

Mr Morris dissents, stating that Britain must be forced to live up to its obligations as specified in the Treaty of Paris. He notes that he personally is owed over fifty thousand dollars for impressed goods.

Mr Hamilton points out that fifty thousand dollars is a 'trifle'. War with Britain will cut off the English market for American goods and restrict import of raw materials. The resulting economic hardships will divide the country between manufacturing and agrarian interests. The Union will not survive.

Mr Pendleton believes that Mr Elias X, publisher of the _____, is the main impediment to ratification.

Mr Hamilton concurs. Mr X is a rabble-rouser who plays to the base instincts of the crowd for his own aggrandizement. His charisma is sufficient to ensure a widespread rebellion should the President sign the treaty.

General Washington promises to speak with him to express the urgency of the country's plight. A report is promised for the next meeting.

The next meeting, held on June 19, 1795, summarized the outcome.

June 19, 1795

Present: General Washington, Mr Hamilton, Mr Morris, Mr Jay, Mr King, Mr Pendleton.

General Washington reports that his conversation with Mr X was fruitless. Further, Mr X promised to amplify calls for insurrection should he (General Washington) sign the bill.

General Washington states his growing conviction that his failure to sign the treaty will result in open warfare with Britain.

It is agreed that unless Mr X is removed from his position of prominence, the future of the nation is at risk.

Mr Hamilton proposes that grave measures be taken.

The vote is unanimous in favor.

Grave measures.

And then a chilling entry, three weeks afterwards:

A prayer is offered on behalf of Mr Elias X, killed this past Wednesday by 'highwaymen' returning to his home from the City Tavern.

Mr King drummed his fingers on the ledger. The smell of old leather drifted to him, as intoxicating as Kentucky bourbon . . . these ledgers . . . *The True History of the United States*.

Washington signed the Jay Treaty later that July of 1795. The House voted funds for its enforcement by the barest of margins, 51–49. The United States had staked its prosperity on the strength of the British fleet. It was a wise decision. In the next eighteen years, the country's landmass grew twentyfold, with the acquisition of Louisiana and lands west of the Mississippi. Manufacturing capability tripled. Population grew by fifty percent. More importantly, five elections had passed. The country had a history to bind it. When war with Britain arrived in 1812, America fought as a unified populace, and earned a stalemate against a far stronger country.

A silence had settled over the Long Room. The men traded glances, none liking what he read in the others' faces. Finally, Mr Washington looked to Mr Pendleton. 'And Crown?'

'The plan's been drawn up. It's a matter of moving everyone into place. I need the go-ahead to complete the arrangements.'

'I don't like it,' said Mr Jay. 'It's a rule never to interfere in elections. General Washington expressly stated that—'

'The election's over,' said Mr Pendleton, slapping an open palm onto the table. 'The people have chosen.'

'We can't afford to wait eight years to continue,' agreed Mr Hamilton.

'Eight years,' said Mr Morris, with a glance toward Mr Jay. 'That's a damn long time to keep in the shadows. You, yourself, said she was curious. What if she decides to look into our past? It would be just like her to try and unmask us. Another of her crusades.'

'There are still two days until the ceremony,' said Mr Washington. 'I have a courtesy meeting with Senator McCoy tomorrow. Show her around her new living quarters and all that. I'm sure we can find a few minutes alone.'

'And in the meantime?' asked Mr Pendleton. 'This matter can't wait any longer.'

'In the meantime, we vote.' Mr Washington placed his palms on the table and stood. He spent a moment looking at each man. It was not necessary to state the motion. 'All in favor?'

One by one, the men seated around the table raised their hands. For a sanction to be binding, it had to be unanimous. Mr King hesitated, then lifted his hand into the air. When it was his turn, Mr Washington did the same. The sleeve of his gray blazer fell to reveal a round cuff link emblazoned with the seal of President of the United States.

'The decision carries. Mr Pendleton, you have the green light to make the necessary arrangements. But nothing happens until I let you know. I suggest we reconvene tomorrow evening.' He added, 'We owe it to ourselves to make that last approach. Some people believe this office still carries a wee bit of power with it. If I can't convince her . . .' A sad look darkened his face.

No one spoke.

The Patriots' Club stood adjourned.

Chapter 6

'Head down,' ordered Wolf.

The car jerked to a halt. The door opened. A palm on Bolden's head guided him out the door. An iron hand gripped his arm and led him inside a building, his shoulder colliding with something . . . a wall, a door. Objects littered the floor. Several times, he tripped, hearing the clatter of wood or the clank of a pipe rolling across concrete. They stopped suddenly. A grate slid open. A hand pushed him inside a confined space. Wolf and Irish crowded in next to him. The grate banged closed. For ten seconds, the elevator whirred upward. His ears popped. The doors opened. The hand guided him forward. He smelled fresh paint, glue, sawdust. Another door opened, this time quietly. Carpet ran beneath his feet. A hand gripped his shoulder, turning him ninety degrees to the right, then shoved him against a wall.

'Wait here,' said Irish.

Bolden stood still, his heart pounding. The hood was tight and cloying, the coarse filaments brushing his lips, getting into his mouth. Someone entered the room. He could feel the change in pressure, a presence circling him, sizing him up as if he were a slab of beef. Reflexively, he stood at attention.

'Mr Bolden, my name is Guilfoyle.' It was a confident voice, smoke-cured and reassuring.

'I'm sorry for any inconvenience. All I can say is that it's necessary for us to speak and we can't have anyone being privy to our conversation. Wolf, take off that hood, will you? Mr Bolden must be getting a little uncomfortable.'

Wolf removed the hood.

'So, here's our gadfly,' said Guilfoyle. 'Persistent, aren't you?'

He was a short, unattractive man in his fifties with narrow shoulders and a hunched posture. His thinning black hair grew in a widow's peak that he combed away from a lined brow. His eyes were dark, cupped by fleshy pouches, his skin sallow, cheeks sagging, a turkey's dangling chin. The smell of tobacco hung on him like a cloud.

'Come with me.' Guilfoyle led the way into another room. The décor was suited for a clerk or other menial labor: cheap carpeting, white walls, acoustic tiles on the ceiling. A veneer desk sat in the center of the room, along with two office chairs. There were no windows. 'Take a seat.'

Bolden sat down.

Guilfoyle dragged the other chair closer. Sitting, he craned his neck forward, his eyes riveted to Bolden's face. Mouth tight, lips pushed up at the corners, he looked as if he were studying a painting he didn't like.

He knows things about people.

'I'd like you to keep still,' he said, in a doctor's patient, disinterested tone. 'Movement makes things very difficult for me. It will only delay matters. I've only got two questions. Answer them and you're free to go.'

'Easier than *Jeopardy!*'

'This is no game show.'

Bolden took in the almost decent suit, the cheap necktie, the ease with which Guilfoyle launched into his interrogation. The guy had cop written all over him. He folded his hands. 'So?'

'Surely, you know what I'm curious about.'

'No clue.'

'Really? How could that be?'

Bolden shrugged, and looked away. 'This is crazy.'

Fingers like steel pinions grasped Bolden's jaw and guided his face back to the fore. 'You will kindly remain still,' said Guilfoyle, relaxing his grip. 'Now then, let's begin again. Tell me about "Crown".'

'Crown?' Bolden opened his hands. 'Crown what? Crown Cola? Crown Books? Crown Cork and Seal? Give me something to go on.'

'I guess I should have expected that kind of answer from a man who earns his living on Wall Street. Try again.'

'I'm sorry, but I don't get it,' said Bolden, earnestly.

The eyes flitted over Bolden's face. Forehead, eyes, mouth. 'Sure you do,' said Guilfoyle. 'But let's keep going. Play it fast and loose. How about Bobby Stillman? When did you see each other last?'

'Never. I don't know anyone named Bobby Stillman.'

'Bob-by Still-man.' Guilfoyle spoke the name slowly, as if Bolden were deaf, as well as plain stupid. His gaze had acquired a weight. Bolden could feel it like a cold hand on his neck.

'Don't know the name. Who is it?'

'You tell me.'

'I can't. I don't know a Bobby Stillman.' Two questions. Two answers. He'd failed the test brilliantly. He remembered Irish reciting the facts of his life as if he were reading from a book. It was a mistake. All that work for naught. They had the wrong man. 'Is that it?' he asked. 'Is that why you brought me up here?'

Guilfoyle smiled briefly, showing dingy, tobacco-stained teeth. 'There's been no mistake,' he said, almost lightly. 'We both know that. You're very good, by the way. I'll give you that.'

'*Good?*' Bolden sensed what he was driving at. 'I'm not lying, if that's what you mean. You said, "two questions". I answered them the best I could. I told you I don't know what you're talking about. That's not going to change anytime soon.'

Guilfoyle remained still, the unblinking eyes ever searching. Suddenly, he shifted in his chair. 'You can't really think you'll get out of this so easily. Not you . . . of all people. You know who we are; the resources at our disposal. What with all the digging you've done . . . Come now, Mr Bolden.'

'It sounds like you're the one who did the digging and it was for nothing. I'm sorry that you made a mistake, but I'd like to go. This bullshit has to end sometime and I think now's the right moment.'

Guilfoyle exhaled and sat straighter, as if taking a new and harsher measure of the situation. 'Mr Bolden, I had you brought here for the express purpose of learning what you know about Crown. I won't leave until I have my answer. I'd also like you to tell me how you came by the information – and by that, I mean a name. You see, we're very much like an investment bank, ourselves. We don't like our people divulging inside information. Now then, I'd appreciate some answers.'

'I can't help.'

'I think you can. Crown. Bobby Still—'

Suddenly, it was too much. The confined space. The questioning. The insistent eyes boring into him like ice picks. 'Jesus, would you get off of it!' said

Bolden, bolting from his chair, sending it tumbling. 'How many times do I have to say it? I don't know. Got it? I don't know anything about your resources or who you work for. I haven't been doing any digging. You're the one who's mistaken, not me. Look, I've tried to be patient, but I can't give you what I don't have. I don't know who you are, Mr Guilfoyle, or why you're asking me these questions. And frankly, I don't want to know. One last time: I have no idea what Crown is. As for Bobby Stillman, what do you want me to say? We met for tea at the Palm Court in the Plaza last Thursday? The name means nothing to me. It's a blank. That's the truth.'

'That would be impossible,' said Guilfoyle. He remained seated, his voice collected, untroubled.

'What would be impossible?'

'We know the two of you are working together.'

'On the same team,' Bolden suggested, throwing up his arms.

'I haven't heard it put that way before, but yes ... *the same team*. Crown,' repeated Guilfoyle. 'Bobby Stillman. You will tell us, please.'

'I have no idea what the hell you're talking about!'

With surprising speed, Guilfoyle stood and pulled a snub-nosed .38 Police Special from his jacket pocket. Taking a step forward, he pressed the muzzle against Bolden's forehead. 'Wolf,' he called, without unscrewing his gaze from Bolden. 'Some assistance.'

Massive hands clutched Bolden's arms, pinning them to his sides. Guilfoyle opened a door at the far end of the room. Wind howled from the darkness beyond. 'Looks like the storm's on its way.'

'Walk,' said Wolf.

Digging his heels into the carpet didn't help. Wolf lifted Bolden off his feet as if he were no heavier than a case of beer and carried him outside. He set Bolden down on a wood platform twenty feet by twenty, spread across two girders. The door flapped noisily against a metal wall and Bolden realized that he'd been in the construction foreman's temporary office. Above him, the skyscraper's unfinished exoskeleton rose another ten stories or so, the taut girders clutching at the sky like a drowning man's hand. He was facing north, the view over Harlem and into the Bronx obscured by fast-moving clouds.

This was bad, he thought. This was definitely lousy.

'Now, listen . . .' Bolden turned his head to look behind him. A kidney punch dropped him to a knee.

'Stand up,' said Guilfoyle. He waved the pistol toward the opposite side of the wooden platform.

Bolden raised himself to his feet. Haltingly, he crossed the platform. A girder extended from beneath the wood, and beyond the skyscraper's superstructure like a diving board. A heavy chain was anchored to its end. A pulley of some sort.

'As I said, you're quite good, but my patience has worn thin. It's your choice. Tell me about "Crown", and your relationship with Bobby Stillman, and you're free to come back inside. We'll all go downstairs together and I'll see to it that you get home safely. It's a matter of security. I can't leave here until I know for certain the full extent of your involvement.'

'And if I can't?'

'You can't, or you won't?' Guilfoyle shrugged, and his eyes dived over the platform to the ground, seventy floors below. 'Even you must know the answer to that question.'

Glancing down, Bolden saw only a void, the

building's empty guts, and far below, the reflected white of the wooden fence surrounding the construction site. A street ran parallel to the building. Tail-lights sprinted from block to block, stopping at red lights. A gust lashed his face. The wind unsettled the platform, and Bolden's knee buckled, before he regained his balance.

Wolf walked confidently across the platform, a lead pipe in his hand. 'Now's the time, Mr Bolden. Talk. Tell Mr Guilfoyle what he needs to know.'

Bolden took another step back, his heel dipping into air, then finding the wood. It came to him that Guilfoyle did not want to shoot him. A body that fell from the seventieth floor was a suicide. Add a bullet and you have murder.

'Crown. I want an answer. Three seconds.'

Bolden racked his brain. Crown. Crown of England. Crown Cola. *The Thomas Crown Affair*. He'd always thought Steve McQueen in that glider was the coolest guy on the planet. *The Jewel in the Crown*. Wasn't that some book he'd been force-fed in college? Crown . . . crown . . . What was the use?

'Two,' said Guilfoyle.

'I don't know. I swear to you.'

'Three.'

'I don't know!' he shouted.

Guilfoyle raised the gun. Even in the dark, Bolden could see the tips of the bullets loaded in the firing drum. A spray of orange erupted from the pistol. A terrific heat blasted his cheek. The gun roared. Too late, Bolden covered his head. And then there was silence. Seventy stories up, a gunshot is no more than a clap of the hands.

'Bobby Stillman,' said Guilfoyle. 'This time's for keeps. Count on it. One . . .'

Bolden shook his head. He was sick of saying that he didn't know.

'Two.' Guilfoyle turned to Wolf. 'Give our friend something to jog his memory.'

Wolf took a step forward, swinging the pipe as if he were trying a saber. Bolden inched backward, one foot on the girder, then the next. Another inch, then another, until he was three feet from the platform, balanced on a steel toothpick, and he couldn't retreat any farther.

'It's a mistake,' he said, keeping his eyes on Guilfoyle. 'You screwed up.'

'All right then. Have it your way.' Guilfoyle took a last look at him, then turned and walked back into the office. Irish followed, closing the door behind them. A few seconds later, the elevator began its descent to the ground. Bolden watched its controlled fall. He kept imagining bodies tumbling through the air. Twirling slowly, gracefully, silently.

Wolf put a foot onto the girder, trying his weight on it. He held the pipe in front of him and advanced along the eight-inch-wide beam. 'If you've got any wings, now's the time to put 'em on.'

'Why are you doing this?' Bolden asked. He refused to look down.

'It's my business.'

'What do you mean? You mean killing people?'

'I mean solving problems. Doing what's necessary.'

'For "your team"? Who are you guys, anyway?'

'It's our team, actually. Yours. Mine. Everyone's.'

'Who's everyone?'

'Everyone. The country. Who else?' Wolf's mouth hung open, shadows melting his features into a dark, vengeful mask. He stared at Bolden. 'Jump.'

'Ladies first.'

'Smack me in the head, eh?' Wolf swung the pipe. Bolden spun away, the lead scraping his chest. Wolf came closer, too close to miss. 'Long way down,' he said, drawing his hand back. 'Enjoy the trip.'

Bolden launched himself at the larger man, wrapping his arms around his chest, squeezing him as tightly as he could.

'Sonuvabitch, you'll kill us both,' Wolf muttered angrily. His eyes were open very wide now. He dropped the pipe, his massive hands seizing Bolden, prying him off his body. Bolden clutched the muscled torso harder. For a moment, he felt his feet leave the girder. He managed to extend a leg. His foot touched steel. With his last bit of strength, Bolden tipped himself over the edge. Gravity did the rest.

He fell headfirst, the icy wind whipping at his eyes, streaming tears across his cheek. He felt Wolf near him, but it was hard to see. A silence louder than any scream flooded his ears. He couldn't breathe. He was falling backward, arms flailing, his heels turning him around. Below him was blackness, and above him, too. Falling. Falling. He opened his mouth to yell. He gave a terrible, desperate effort, but nothing would come.

He was caught by a slack safety net three stories below. Somehow he'd managed to land on top of Wolf, striking him in the head with his elbow. The man lay still, eyes closed, a web of blood running from his nose.

Bolden crawled off the net to a girder. He lay there for a moment, the steel cold and rough against his cheek. He'd seen the net in the half-light. He'd thought it was closer. He got to a knee, his elbow aching badly, and figured that was what had hit Wolf. Pure luck.

The work elevator was situated in the center of the superstructure. Arms raised like a tightrope artist, he negotiated the steel beams, moving slowly at first, faster as his confidence built. A control box hung by a cable at the elevator. He snatched it in his hands and punched the green button in its center. The cables whirred efficiently, the elevator rising. Wolf hadn't budged. He lay still as a shark caught in a drift net.

The elevator arrived. Bolden rode down in darkness. Guilfoyle was gone. He knew that much. There was no reason for him to stick around. Not when he had someone like Wolf to finish the job. But what about Irish? Irish would be waiting for the body to fall. He would be waiting for his partner.

Through the mesh grate, Bolden peered at the ground below. Because the elevator ran up the side of the building, and because there was only a cage and no doors, he had a good view of the entire construction site. The Town Car was parked inside the gates. No sign of the driver. He spotted Irish standing near a forklift at the opposite side of the site. The ember of his cigarette glowed and dimmed like a firefly. As the elevator approached the ground, he didn't move. The elevator was quiet, but Irish had to be wearing headphones or earbuds not to hear it come to a halt.

Bolden slid open the grate and ran across the dirt, dodging piles of cable, stacks of pig iron. The fence surrounding the work site was ten feet high and topped by a coil of barbed wire. The gate at the vehicle entrance was lower – maybe six feet – but there was still the barbed wire to contend with. He checked behind him, seeing Irish's blond head begin to turn. Just then the front door of the Town Car swung open. A head rose from the driver's seat staring at him.

'You! Stop!'

Bolden threw an upraised palm into the driver's jaw, snapping his head ferociously. The driver hit the door, and fell backward across the seat, one foot inside the car. Bolden heard steps coming from behind. He shoved the driver across the seat, and squeezed in next to him. A keychain dangled from the ignition. Door still open, he turned over the motor and threw the car into drive.

The gate didn't stand a chance.

Chapter 7

Jennifer Dance stood from the examining table and gingerly probed the latticework of stitches running along the top of her left forearm. 'How long do they have to stay in?'

'Seven days,' answered Dr Satyen Gupta. 'Provided there is no infection. It looked to be a clean cut. Very easy for doctors like me to stitch. Can you flex your fingers? Everything feel all right?'

Jenny curled the fingers of her left hand. Thankfully, the blade hadn't damaged any nerves. 'Just fine.'

'I'm going to bandage it now. I want you to keep the arm dry for five days. Rub Iamin gel on the wound twice a day. No sports, no strenuous activity until you come back to have the sutures out. Expect some soreness, but that should be it. Do as I say, and there's a good chance you won't even have a scar. I do first-rate work.'

And you're modest, too, added Jenny silently. She stood still as the doctor wrapped the forearm in gauze and applied a length of tape. Her last visit to a hospital had taken place a year ago. Her mother was suffering from terminal lung cancer and Jenny had flown to Kansas City for a final good-bye. There were no bruises to patch up, no long-simmering grudges. It was just a daughter's chance to say, Thank you. I love you.

Instead of driving directly to the hospital after landing, she'd stopped at her brother's house first. It was on the way, and, frankly, she was scared of seeing her mom. The two drank a beer, and finally, she felt ready. When she arrived at the hospital, she found that a priest was leaving the room. Her mother had died ten minutes before she'd arrived.

'All finished,' said Dr Gupta, cutting the tape.

'Thank you.' Jenny grabbed her purse and headed to the door.

'One moment!' Dr Gupta finished scribbling onto a sheet and ripped the paper from its pad. 'Go to Room Three Fifteen and give this to the nurse. You'll need a tetanus shot.' He groped in the pocket of his jacket and came out with a smaller prescription pad. 'Take this to the pharmacy afterwards and have it filled. Antibiotics. Infection is our worst enemy. You're not taking anything else, are you?'

'Antivert. Just one a day for the last two months.'

'There should be no problem, then. Off you go.'

The police officer who had escorted Jenny to the hospital was waiting to take a description of her assailants. 'Do you have any word from Thomas, uh . . . Mr Bolden?' she asked, afterwards, as the policeman folded up his notepad.

'As of ten minutes ago, no one of Mr Bolden's description has come by the crime scene or the precinct house. I'm sorry.'

She took a step down the hall, then came back. 'Why didn't they take my purse?'

'Excuse me, ma'am?'

'Why didn't they take my purse? It was just dangling there. He didn't need a knife. He could have just grabbed it.'

The officer shrugged. 'I guess they only wanted the watch. You never know with these guys. What's important is that you're all right.'

But Jenny was unconvinced. She knew a little about thieves. She had a half dozen of them as students. Not one of them would have left the purse behind.

Jenny thanked the officer, then made her way to the waiting room. It was a calm night and half the chairs were empty. Besides the legitimate cases, she was quick to pick up the usual lost souls. People with no place else to go who congregated in any heated room during the winter. She scanned the room for Thomas, but he wasn't there. She caught an older woman wearing a Yankees jacket and cap giving her a long look. Jenny smiled, and the woman averted her eyes.

The admitting nurse was no help, either. No one had been in asking about her.

The clock on the wall read 2:15. Over two hours had passed since Jenny had been mugged, or assaulted, or whatever you wanted to call it. She told herself not to worry. If there was anyone who could take care of himself in the big bad city, it was Tommy. Still, she couldn't help but be concerned. She had seen something in his eyes that scared her. Something vicious. Something from the part of him he kept hidden from her. She felt certain that he'd been hurt. She took Tommy's phone from her purse and began to dial, then saw that the batteries were dead. She'd already left a half dozen messages for him. That would have to do.

There was a line running out the door of Room 315. A young Puerto Rican mother stood in front of Jenny, cradling an infant in her arms, singing to him sweetly. Jenny recognized the song. 'Drume Negrita'. In front of her stood an elderly African-American man clad in a dashiki, sporting a leopard-skin Shriner's hat. All he was missing was the royal flyswatter and he could have passed for Mobutu Sese Seko.

Farther down the corridor, she spied the woman in the Yankees cap again, loitering at a water fountain. Was she following her? Jenny tried not to stare, but there was no doubt that the woman was staring right back at her. The gaze was frightening. Dark, accusing, and utterly paranoid.

New York City certainly didn't lack for variety.

Jennifer Dance had moved to the city ten years ago, a junior transfer from the University of Kansas to Columbia University, an English major hoping to become the next Christiane Amanpour. And, if that didn't work out, Katie Couric. She had all the qualities to succeed. She was a decent writer, curious, willful, attractive, with a yen to travel. Hardship didn't scare her. She had no qualms about living in faraway places without running water, regular electricity, or indoor plumbing. She enjoyed spicy food.

She was also polite. Ruthlessly, unfailingly, sickeningly polite. Jenny was congenitally unable to be rude. She wasn't meek. God, no. The bruised knuckles on her right hand attested to that. But when someone told her, 'No, dammit, I have no comment,' she could not bring herself to ask again or to demand that they change their answer. The thought of having to stick a microphone in someone's face and scream your questions at them made her ill.

She left Columbia with a degree in American history and few job prospects. She spent a year giving private tours around the city and working as a guide at the natural history museum. Every few months, her parents would call and ask when she was coming home. The thought of returning to Kansas City – of Saturday afternoons quilting with

Mom, and Sunday church suppers, of babysitting her brother's twins and a job at Daddy's bank ('We'll start you in the trust department at twenty-eight thousand a year. Buy you a little Ford to get around town. How's that sound, sugarplum?') – was too much. She did not want a life that had already been decided for her, with rites and rituals carved in stone, obligatory friendships, and prescribed duties. She was through with Hardee's, the Chiefs, and *A Prairie Home Companion*. The only things she liked about home were crisp green apples sprinkled with salt, and pork tenderloin sandwiches with a dollop of mustard and a slice of raw onion on top.

She earned her teaching credential from Columbia a year later.

Her first job was at a parochial school in Greenwich Village, St Agnes. In those days, she'd still been a good Catholic, and the small classes and promise of order appealed to her. But a twenty-three-year-old with a zest for life didn't last long at St Agnes. The sisters did not approve of Jenny's fast lifestyle – 'fast' being defined as missing Friday-morning mass, drinking margaritas after work, repelling Father Bernadin's all too frequent passes.

She was not asked back for a second year.

With no savings, no reference, and no thought of returning to Mom and Dad in Kansas City, Jenny took the first job she could find. She'd been at the Kraft School ever since.

Officially, the job called for Jenny to provide instruction in math, science, and the arts. Given her students' variance in schooling and abilities, that was impossible. Jenny saw it as her job simply to show the kids that following the rules wasn't such a bad thing. That if you just gave the system a chance, it might work for you. That meant showing up on time, dressing appropriately, and looking someone in the eye when you shook their hand.

One day in five, bedlam ruled in the classroom. Students argued with one another. Rulers were thrown like boomerangs. A bong had been reported seen, and yes, marijuana had been smoked on the premises. It wasn't exactly the high school from *Fame*. But on those days when the classroom grew quiet, and the eyes that weren't too red actually focused on Miss Dance, Jenny felt as if she was getting through. Making a difference even. Corny, maybe, but it felt good.

'Miss Dance,' came an authoritative voice.

'Yes.' Jenny stepped forward, her heart catching a beat. She craned her head, hoping it might be news of Thomas. A nurse stood at the entrance to Room 315, waving a clipboard high in the air. 'We're ready for you, hon.'

She was out three minutes later with a Band-Aid and a stick of licorice to cheer her up. The elevator arrived. Jenny got in and pressed the button for one. *What kind of mugger left a purse?* The question refused to go away. If he could use a knife to snatch a watch, why not take an extra second and grab the purse, too? And that question begged another. Why wasn't Thomas at the hospital? Why hadn't he, at least, found a phone to call? It had been two hours, for Pete's sake!

She remembered the look in Thomas's eyes. It wasn't anger. It was something beyond anger. A blood lust. She rubbed at her own aching eyes. *Don't be hurt, Thomas*, she prayed silently. There was so much she didn't know about him. So much he refused to tell her.

*

They had been introduced at a Y-League basketball game, and afterwards had gone to dinner with a whole crew of friends – some his, some hers – at a Mexican cantina uptown. All of them had saddled up to the bar and ordered margaritas – except for Thomas, who ordered a shot of tequila and a Budweiser. Half the group were attorneys. Fearing a barrage of lawyer talk, Jenny changed her order to the same and grabbed a stool next to him.

She would never forget their first conversation. She wasn't sure how they got on the subject of nature versus nurture, but Thomas began preaching about how everything in life is hereditary. Nature over nurture. You were either born with it or not. All the practice in the world couldn't make him a pro ballplayer, he said. And it wasn't just limited to sports. People, he argued, are born who they are. It didn't matter a lick where you were brought up, in the city or the country, rich or poor, you couldn't escape who you were at birth. You were branded.

Jenny was horrified by his words. As a teacher, she witnessed on a daily basis how environment shaped character. It was her job to help kids overcome the obstacles of their birth. Thomas said she was wasting her time. What she did was no different from painting a car. Only by looking under the hood could you see what someone was really made of. Sure, she might help the kids in the short run – spiff 'em up, polish 'em a little – but in the long run, they would revert to their true selves. You couldn't upgrade from four cylinders to eight.

'I'm sorry, but you're wrong,' she said.

'Oh yeah?' he'd responded, full of himself. 'How many kids have you saved? How many have you gotten back into a regular school?'

'Well . . . none, but that's beside the point,' Jenny answered. The kids had already been adversely affected by their home lives, their families, the whole oppressive blight that came with growing up poor in New York City. You couldn't just give up on them!

His answer was a sigh and a shrug.

Incensed, but willing to let the topic slide, Jenny had bought them a second round and moved on to a more pleasant topic. Basketball. She said she played a little, too. He asked if she played, or if she *played*. To this day, she was proud of herself for not slapping that smug look off his face. Instead, she answered that a hundred bucks was his if he could beat her in a three-point shoot-out. He accepted, if he could set the rules. Each would take ten consecutive shots from anywhere behind the line. He'd spot her a three-basket advantage. Hating him more by the minute, Jenny declined.

The group moved to the table. Happily, Jenny found herself seated at the end opposite Thomas. But try as she might, she couldn't keep from looking at him. He was handsome in his way, hardly her version of Mr Right, yet there was something undeniably compelling about him. When she caught his gaze, his wine black eyes seemed to lock onto her. For lack of a better word, he was magnetic. A raging, sexist egomaniac. But magnetic.

And when he insisted that the lawyer seated next to her change places with him – he'd practically picked him up out of his chair and deposited him on his feet – she was flattered and decided to give him a second chance. Mesmer had nothing on those eyes.

But the evening didn't really fall apart until she informed him that the '84 Lakers were the best team in NBA history. Magic. Kareem. The Coop-a-

Loop thunderdunk. And don't forget James Worthy! The '84 Lakers ruled.

His look could have turned her to stone.

'Ninety-five Chicago Bulls,' he said, offering no further explanation.

When she tried to get into it with him, he held up a hand and looked away. Case closed.

That was when the fireworks started. No one . . . *absolutely no one* . . . held up his hand in Jennifer Dance's face. She called him every four-letter word in the book, then told him he could go to hell in a four-horse carriage, for all she cared. As for his three-point contest, he could take it and . . .

It was then that Peter, Thomas's friend, interceded, and asked Jenny if Bolden had told her about his work at the Boys' Club. He explained that Thomas was setting up a gang-intervention unit in coordination with the NYPD to offer the kids something else to do other than hang out on street corners and get into trouble. He was up there three nights a week, and on weekends. Maybe Jenny could tell him some stories about her kids. Give him a few pointers.

Peter left, and an awkward silence filled the air between them.

'Why do you do it, if you're so sure they haven't got a chance?' Jenny asked, finally, leaning closer to see if it was all bullshit, or if there was something there.

'I'm an idealist. Screwed up, I know, but it's the way I was born.'

She was more confused than ever.

That Saturday they met at the Y for the first of many three-point-shooting contests. She kicked his butt, winning 10-4. In the three years since, he had never beaten her. He could, however, dunk with two hands.

*

The elevator door opened and Jenny stepped into the corridor. In the time it took to descend three stories, she had gotten herself sick with worry. Her born survivor should have checked in by now. She knew she'd be able to track him down at work, but she couldn't wait that long. It was time to start checking hospitals.

Chapter 8

Thomas Bolden was studying the dregs of his coffee when the door to the interrogation room opened and a tall, bleary-eyed man walked in. 'I'm Detective John Franciscus,' he said, a mug in one hand and a sheaf of files under his arm. 'How ya doin'? Need some more coffee? Or is it tea?'

Bolden looked up. 'What happened to Detective McDonough?'

'Little out of his league.' Franciscus pointed to the Styrofoam cup in front of Bolden. 'You okay?'

Bolden crumpled the cup and tossed it into the wastebasket. 'Out of his league. How do you mean?'

'Quite a tale you spun. Robbery. Abduction at gunpoint. Assault. We're talking three felonies right there. You've got a lot of us interested.' Franciscus pulled out his chair and froze halfway between standing and sitting. He was lean and rickety and on the wrong side of sixty, with lank gray hair that hung across his forehead and an alert, angular face. He wore a .38 snub nose strapped to his waist and a badge pinned to his belt to show that he knew how to use it. 'Sure you don't like the brew? I can run downstairs, get you a Coke, iced tea, whatever.'

Bolden shook his head. 'What about the guy I brought in?' he asked. 'Detective McDonough said you were running his prints. Any idea who he is? You check out the construction site yet?'

'Slow down a second,' said Franciscus, dropping into his chair. 'I need a little time to get things all set up.' He arranged the folders on the desk. He unclipped his cell phone from his belt, checked that it was on, then set it down within arm's reach. He dug into his breast pocket and fished out a pair of bifocals and set them down next to the phone. And then, he brought both of them a little closer.

'Construction site was a goose egg. Nobody there. Gates were locked.'

Bolden dug at his palm. He wondered how the gates could be closed and locked when he'd crashed through them two hours earlier. 'Did you send someone up to look? There's a safety net and . . .'

'Like I said, the gates were locked. We saw no sign of intrusion. Tell you what, I'll go by there in the morning . . . have a look around. That all right?'

'That's fine.' He hadn't exactly expected Wolf to hang around anyway. He eyed the clock and yawned. Four-thirty. Since arriving at the precinct house, he'd been fingerprinted, photographed, questioned, and kept isolated in an interrogation room. He'd given his name, social security number, address, home phone number, his work, cell, and BlackBerry numbers, too. He'd showed them the bruises on his back and sides. An officer had taken a look at his cheek and informed him that the grains of gunpowder had been blown so deep into the flesh that they would take months to work themselves clear. They wanted cooperation. He gave it to them in spades. Now, he wanted a little cooperation himself. 'Mind if I use your phone?'

'Sure thing.' Franciscus tossed him the phone, low and fast. 'You're quick.'

'Reflex.'

'Like how you took down that bruiser?'

'Something like that.'

'Think you might have overreacted?'

'No,' said Bolden. 'Not unless you think I blow off rounds an inch from my face to get my jollies or jump from a couple hundred feet up in the air. In fact, Detective, I'd say that given the circumstances, my instincts saved my life.'

Franciscus thought about this for a second. 'I'd say you're right. I'd also say you're lucky. Anyway, your story checks out. Miss Dance's description of the two men who mugged her, um—' He ran a fingernail across the topmost paper in his folder. ' "Irish" and "Wolf" – matches yours. I just got off the phone with the doctor who's looking after the guy you roughed up. He had a tattoo just like the one you said "Mr Wolf" had. A little rifle high on his chest. That's not all. He also has a parachute on his arm with the words "Death before Dishonor" below it. Popular with Airborne troops. We sent his prints down to Bragg and to Fort Campbell, Kentucky. Negative on both counts. How do you figure? First thing they do when you show up for Basic is take your prints. Take 'em again when you join the division. I was there. I know.'

'And so?'

'All these army hotshots. "Unsat" this. "NPQ" that. Rangers . . . Green Berets . . . whatever. Sounds a little weird, don't you think? I'm not one for coincidence. What about you?'

Bolden shook his head.

'I have a call in to the provost marshal's office at Benning,' Franciscus went on, 'and to Army HQ to forward any photographs of soldiers between the ages of twenty-one and thirty-five who meet a description of the men who abducted you earlier. "Wolf" and "Irish", you said their names were. But I wouldn't hold out much hope.'

'And the other guy? Is he talking?'

'Not likely. He's getting his busted teeth fixed as we speak. We're booking him for possession of stolen property and a firearms violation.'

'The gun was stolen?'

'Don't know. Serial numbers were filed down. We can bring them back up if we try hard enough, but seeing as how you weren't killed, I don't really see the point. It doesn't matter anyway. Possession without a permit earns you one year in the slam. No questions asked. It's the cell phone that was stolen. A woman reported the theft yesterday afternoon. The phone was taken from her handbag at a place close to where you work. Balthazar. You know it?'

'Yeah.' Bolden dropped his eyes. 'I had lunch there today . . . um, I mean yesterday.'

'Did you now?' Franciscus made a note, his salt-and-pepper brows arched behind the reading glasses. ' 'Bout time we're getting somewhere.'

'Would you excuse me a second?' Bolden turned in his chair and tapped in his cell number. His answering machine picked up on the second ring. Either the phone was off, or it had run out of batteries. Next, he tried his home. When there was no answer, he left a message saying that he was all right, and that he would be back to shower and change before going to work. Earlier, Jenny had left him a message from the hospital saying that she was fine and was about to be released. He tried her place, and when the machine picked up, he hung up. He'd already left word saying that he was fine, and would call later. He slid the phone across the table. 'Thanks.'

'No problem. We'll just add the charges to your city tax bill.' Franciscus eyed Bolden over the rims of his bifocals. 'That, sir, was a joke. A pleasantry. You may now smile.'

Bolden forced a smile. 'Happy?'

Franciscus set down his pen and folded his hands on the table. 'Actually, Mr Bolden, I'm anxious to learn more about you.'

'What about me?'

'Just a few personal details.'

'I went over this already. What do you want me to add?'

'Look, Mr Bolden, I'm here to help. We don't have to be best friends, but I think it's a good idea for me to know a little about you.'

Bolden was too tired to argue. 'I'm a banker. I work at Harrington Weiss. Born in Iowa. Grew up in Illinois. Went to college at Princeton. Business school at Wharton. Came to the city after I finished. No, I don't know anyone who dislikes me. And, no, I don't believe Miss Dance has any enemies, either.' He drew himself closer to the desk. 'Look, I told all of this to Detective McDonough. I've never seen any of these men before.'

'But they knew all about you. Even where you were eating lunch.'

And that he'd worked twenty-five hours a week at Butler Dining Hall.

Bolden nodded. He knew he would have to get his arms around all that later. Right now, he just wanted to go home.

Franciscus looked down at his notes again. 'And this guy "Guilfoyle", he was sure you knew about something called Crown, and someone named Bobby Stillman?'

Again, Bolden nodded. 'I don't have a clue who, or what, they were referring to.'

'That's what we're here to find out,' said Franciscus. 'I am curious about one thing. Just where'd you learn to hit a man like that? You knocked out three of his teeth. Part of me's wondering who assaulted who. I don't know who I should be feeling sorry for.'

'Don't know. Just something I picked up.'

'No, you didn't. That's not something you just pick up. It's something you're taught. Something you practice. Tell me, where does a bright, well-educated kid like yourself learn to take down two pros?'

Bolden looked at the stack of papers Detective Franciscus had brought in with him. By now, he imagined that they'd run his prints through the system, too. It was the law that the court seal a minor's files when he turned eighteen. 'Don't your papers tell you?'

'That what you're so worried about?' Franciscus closed the folder. 'Nothing in here 'bout you. Anything you want to tell me . . . anything you think might help . . . you got my word it'll stay between me and you.' When Bolden didn't answer, he said, 'Let's start with that artwork on your shoulder. I couldn't help but notice it when you changed shirts. Who are "the Reivers"? Oh, and I especially liked the second part: "Never Rat on Friends."'

Bolden fought the instinct to look down at his shoulder. The Reivers were family. The Reivers were friends who looked out for one another. The Reivers were all he had had when things had gotten tough. 'Just some old friends,' he said.

'Friends who need a few lessons in using a tattooing needle. Where'd you get it? Prison? Reform school? That why you worried if you're checked out? Don't worry, I'm not going to say a thing to your employer.'

Bolden dropped his eyes. He felt himself draw back, the old distrust of police – of authority, in general – take over.

'It's not a crime to have belonged to a gang, Mr Bolden,' said Franciscus. 'It might help me with my work.'

'It wasn't a gang,' Bolden explained. 'Just some guys I used to run with. That was over fifteen years ago. It's got nothing to do with what happened tonight.'

'And what about the gangs you work with in this neck of the woods?'

'The gang-intervention program? It's run out of the Boys' Club. I just help organize some of the events. Raise money. That kind of thing. We held a chess match last weekend. One of the kids beat me in the second round. I didn't make any enemies there, either.'

'So you don't believe that there's a connection between your work at the Boys' Club and what happened tonight?'

'No.'

Franciscus removed his bifocals and laid them on the table. 'And that's your last word?'

'It's the truth.'

Franciscus laughed tiredly. The truth, his eyes said, was a very tricky thing. 'I'm going to level with you, Mr Bolden. I'm not entirely sure you're the innocent you make yourself out to be. I think there's a lot more going on here than you're letting on.' Franciscus moved his chair closer and threw his hands on the table, so that he and Bolden were face-to-face, two opponents ready to arm wrestle. 'I'm going to let you in on a secret. These guys who took you for a ride, made you walk the plank . . . I've met men like them before. There are more and more of them these days. I call it a shadow mobilization. All kinds of special agencies cropping up. These guys come creeping through our offices every now and again, getting a pat on the back from the chief, promises of cooperation, that kind of stuff. Makes you a little scared after a while. I've been on the force thirty-odd years. I know a thing or two about bureaucracy, and I'm asking myself just who in Jehovah's name is supposed to be looking after all these guys? It's my experience that guys who've had their prints zapped from the systems, their pasts erased, are one of two things: spooks or contractors. Now, if they're spooks, it's okay. All part of the game. After all, if I can look 'em up from the Three-Four, you can be sure that someone in Iran or France or India can look 'em up, too. But that dirtbag you took apart is not affiliated with the Central Intelligence Agency, the NSA, the DIA, or any of those Joes. I can tell. My guess is that the goons who came after you tonight are either now, or once have been, civilian contractors.'

Civilian contractors. It was a term that had been all over the news lately. 'Like who? Kellogg Brown and Root? Halliburton? They're builders, right? Oil work, construction, cafeterias, dry cleaning, that kind of stuff.'

'I'd look more on the more active side of things. Security work. Bodyguards. Military trainers. You know the big players? Tidewater. Executive Resources. Milner Group. There are about twenty thousand of them over in the Middle East right now, providing security to our marines. Beefy guys in sunglasses and Kevlar vests. Weapons out the wazoo.' Franciscus shook his head. 'Civilians looking after the military? Go figure that one out. Makes you wonder which side of the donkey his ass is.' Finally, he shrugged. 'My question is, why are guys like this coming after you?'

Bolden hadn't stopped asking himself the same thing since he'd been thrown into the back of the limo downtown. He decided he didn't like

Franciscus's tone much. He was like the rest of the cops he'd known. One hand stuck out to help you up, the other to throw the cuffs on your wrists. 'But you're going to hold him?'

'That we are. Once his mouth's cleaned up, we'll ship him downtown to One PP, give him a B-number, take a picture of him that he can give to his mother. Like I said, illegal possession of a firearm in New York State draws a mandatory one-year sentence. Throw in the cell phone, he'll get to know the Department of Corrections better than he'd like.' Franciscus looked at him a moment longer. 'You aren't afraid these men are going to come after you?'

'I can look after myself.'

'Sure? We're here to help.'

'Yeah,' said Bolden, with more certainty than he felt. 'They know they got the wrong guy. I don't think they'll be coming after me any more.'

Franciscus pushed back his chair and stood. 'If there's nothing else you'd like to add to your statement, you're free to go. One of the officers downstairs will give you a lift home. Anything else comes to mind, give me a call. Here.'

Bolden took the business card and slipped it into his pocket. He wasn't sure whether to say thanks, or screw you. All he knew was that he was happy to leave the police station.

'And Mr Bolden,' said Franciscus, so quietly that he almost didn't catch it. 'Be careful. I don't know what game you're mixed up in. But it ain't patty-cake.'

Chapter 9

It was still night when Thomas Bolden left the Thirty-fourth Precinct. At six A.M., the sky was somber and dark, daylight not due for another hour. Seated in the front seat of a police cruiser, he rolled down the window. An icy gust lashed his cheeks, bracing him. The temperature had dropped while he'd been inside the station. The air had a bite to it. Scattered snowflakes drifted past. The long-promised storm was on its way.

They traveled down Columbus Avenue, then cut through the park at Ninety-fifth Street. Bolden stretched, then pulled his jacket tight around himself. His body was sore, his muscles groaning from the beating he'd taken. But his mind was alert, resilient, tracing a path back through the events of the night: the interrogation at the police station, the fight on 145th Street, Guilfoyle's questioning, the ride with Wolf and Irish, all of it beginning with the attack itself. Somewhere a million years ago, he'd been standing on a podium inside a packed ballroom, accepting the most meaningful honor of his life. Closing his eyes, he could feel the audience's applause – not hear it, but *feel it*. Three hundred pairs of hands. A tidal wave of appreciation.

Nothing happens without a reason, he was thinking.

Six years he'd worked for the Boys' Club. In that time, he'd spent countless evenings and Saturdays at the facility. He'd raised over a million dollars in contributions. He'd started a successful gang-intervention program. It wasn't in any way arrogant to say that he deserved to be named Man of the Year.

It was a rule of his that nothing happened of its own accord. That things happened that were meant to happen. It had nothing to do with fate or predestination or karma, and everything to do with cause and effect. A real-world application of Newton's Third Law. There was no action without a reaction.

Conversely, there could be no reaction without an action.

If he was in trouble now, it was because he'd done something to deserve it.

And yet, he could think of nothing he'd done that might have brought him to the attention of Guilfoyle, and the organization he worked for. *Civilian contractors*, Detective Franciscus had said, *the more active side of things*.

Several of Bolden's clients were active in the defense industry, but they were hardly the type to send out armed crushers to do their bidding. They were large, multinational investment firms peopled by the superstars of the financial world. Corporations whose boards of directors boasted former heads of state, Nobel laureates, and corporate chieftains of companies like IBM, GE, Procter and Gamble – companies that functioned as states within a state. In six years, he'd never known their conduct to be less than strenuously scrupulous. To the best of his knowledge, none owned any companies that could be labeled contractors.

Come on. Think.

Bolden sighed. They had the wrong man. That was all there was to it.

He sat up. He was no longer so tired. 'Wired', was more like it. His eye wandered to the bank of hardware installed beneath the car's dashboard. Some kind of computer equipped with a keyboard, a color touch screen, and a two-way radio that looked powerful enough to pick up the Reykjavík PD.

'Pretty nifty,' he said to his driver, a Sergeant Sharplin. 'What do you got in here?'

'It's a Triton Five-Fifty. She's a sweet piece of work. A mobile data terminal's the heart of the system. It connects me to whatever law-enforcement database I need. I can plug in a name, a vehicle-identification number and see if my man's got a warrant outstanding, or if a vehicle is stolen.'

'Just local databases or does it go national?'

'We're tapped in at the federal level, too. Just think of it as an Internet terminal. We got access to TECS, that's the treasury department, DEA, even the National Crime Information Center. If you've got the right clearance, you can even tap into the FBI.'

'All from this car?' It was a far cry from the last time he'd ridden in a cop car. But then his view had been from the back seat.

'You betcha.'

Bolden wondered what he'd get if he punched in Guilfoyle's name. There was no point. Guilfoyle. Wolf. Irish. All of them were aliases.

Bolden yawned, and looked back out his window. *Nothing happens without a reason.*

He wasn't just thinking about his present circumstance, but about the past.

It was ten o'clock and the bell for second period had already rung, but Tommy Bolden, fifteen, a tenth grader at Oliver Wendell Holmes High, was nowhere near school. Sitting at a table in Burger King, he took a bite of his double-cheese extra onions and chased it down with a gulp of Coke. It was Thursday, and he was serving the second day of a three-day suspension.

One by one, he counted the cigarette burns decorating the tabletop. The knuckles of his right hand were covered with scabs, his lower lip swollen from where he'd gotten hit. Next time, he'd go for the knees earlier, he decided. It was stupid to trade punches with a guy who outweighed you by fifty pounds.

'Dude, you're sitting on our bench. Move it!'

This time it had been a bench. Last time it was a locker. Everyone had their turf, and the new kid had to learn a lesson. *Screw 'em all*, he thought. He would sit where he wanted. He would use the locker assigned to him. If they wanted to fight about it, that was their problem. The thought of Kuziak, lying there on the ground with his jelly belly and his jarhead's crew cut, whimpering about his busted knee, made Bolden even angrier. Served the Polack right. Yet, it was Bolden who had been suspended because he wouldn't walk away from a fight.

He slammed his fist on the table, and when the manager came over, he stared at him until he went away.

A kid could learn to count going through all the schools he'd attended. River Trails. Aurora Elementary. Jackson Middle School. Frazier Heights. Birmingham. Eighteen schools between second and ninth grade.

Prior to second grade, he'd been home schooled by his mother. Every morning he'd sit at the kitchen table and do his reading, writing, and arithmetic, his mother coming in every half hour to check on him. It was just the two of them, and he liked it that way. Liked the attention. Being the man of the house. He also liked how she tickled his feet when they lay together on the couch watching TV. He didn't want to share her with anyone.

They moved constantly, not from county to county, which is what happened when you were in foster care, but from state to state. California, Arkansas, Missouri, New York. Often, they'd leave in a rush, packing quickly and driving off in the middle of the night. Once they didn't even have time to gather up his toys, not even his Green Beret GI Joe.

The thought of his mother left him unsettled. He remembered her energy: she was always on the move, constantly in motion. He wasn't even sure what she looked like any more, other than that she had long auburn hair and pale skin that was soft to the touch. He'd lost all his pictures of her, along with his clothes, his comic books, and his hockey cards, during a messy escape from one of his foster dads. Mike, the auto mechanic, who liked to wrestle a little too intensely for a ten-year-old's taste. He couldn't remember the color of her eyes, or how she smiled, or even the sound of her laugh. The years had left her hardly more than a blur, a shadow dashing out of arm's reach.

Scarfing the rest of his burger, Bolden left his wrapper and what remained of his drink on the table and went outside. He was finished with school. Finished with foster care, too, for that matter. He'd had enough of the quarreling and the fights. He was sick of 250-pound men who got hard-ons when they played tackle football.

Tiny Phil Grabowski was waiting at the corner. 'Hey, Tommy!' he called.

Bolden gave him a high five, then wrapped his arm around his neck, and brought his head to his chest. 'Noogie, dude. Noogie,' he said, razzing his hair.

'Cut it out, man,' said Philly, fighting his way loose. 'You're embarrassing me.'

Phil Grabowski was a sad kid, way short and skinny, and always in some kind of funk. He didn't look old enough to have such a terrible case of acne, but the guy's face was one big zit. His personality wasn't much to write home about either. Mostly, he pouted about his parents getting divorced, or talked about what he was going to eat when he got his braces off. Still, he was here – and not in school, where he was supposed to be – and that made Phil Grabowski his friend.

'We really gonna do it?' Philly asked. 'I mean, you're not serious, are you? It's too hairy, even for you.'

'How else you plan on earning a hundred bucks? Concert's Friday. I, for one, am not missing the Stones.' Bolden started playing the air guitar, singing 'Brown Sugar'. He was dressed in Levi's and a Rolling Stones T-shirt, the one with the pair of flaming lips that was the logo for the '74 North American tour. His jeans were pressed. The shirt was old and fit snugly, but it was clean. Bolden did his own laundry, made his own meals, and generally looked after himself. His newest foster mom had said from the start she wasn't there to 'be no one's slave'.

No, thought Bolden, she was just there to collect her four hundred dollars a month from the state for giving Tommy a cot to sleep on in the same room as six other kids. White trash. Soon she'd be nothing more than a figure in his rearview mirror. Her and everybody else in the Land of Lincoln. He didn't need the money to go see the Stones. He needed it to get the hell out of Dodge. He was leaving Chicago, once and for all.

Nodding his head, he led the way up Brookhurst.

The sky was overcast, threatening rain. A chill wind blew a crumpled pack of cigarettes down the sidewalk. Bolden scooped it up to check if there was anything inside. 'Dud,' he said, and chucked the pack over his shoulder.

A few miles away, he could see the red-brick towers of the Cabrini-Green projects. He knew well enough not to cross Martin Luther King Boulevard. You didn't go north of MLK if you were white. His own neighborhood was bad enough. Clapboard houses in varied states of disrepair lined both sides of the street. This one missing a front window, that one with a hole in its roof, the next needing new front stairs. Every one of them painted in the same shade of neglect.

It was mid-April, but the last snow had fallen three days earlier. Patches of the stuff mottled with mud and grime dotted the sidewalk. Bolden made a game of hopping from one to the next, calling out the names of islands in an archipelago. Midway, Wake, Guadalcanal, Tulagi. Or the central provinces of Vietnam. Quang Tri. Binh Dinh. Da Nang. He thought a lot about joining the marines.

'My mom will kill me if she finds out I'm ditching again,' Philly Grabowski said, hopping behind him.

'I can't believe you're scared of your mom,' said Bolden. 'You're fifteen. You should be telling her what to do.'

'What do you know about it?'

'A lot. Like everything there is to know. I've had like thirty moms.'

'Not real moms.'

'They must be pretty real, because they sounded a lot like yours.'

'It's just because she cares about me.'

'Then stop complaining,' Bolden said, angrily,

stopping in his tracks to confront his friend. 'Maybe she's not so bad.'

'Maybe not,' said Philly. 'At least she didn't dump me.'

'My mom didn't dump me either.'

'Why did she take off on you? You never told me.'

'She had stuff to do.'

'Like what?'

'I don't know, but she said it was important.'

'How do you know? You were six.'

' 'Cause I do.'

'Maybe you were just a royal pain in the ass. That's what my mom says.'

Bolden considered the remark. There wasn't a day that passed that he didn't ask himself what he might have done to make his mother stay. If he could have been more lovable, more obedient, more playful, smarter, taller, faster, more handsome, more helpful, more anything that might have convinced her to hang around. He shrugged. 'Probably.'

Bolden shoved his hands in his pockets. They walked for another twenty minutes. Only when they neared the spot did he slow down and lay out his plan.

'The guy gets to the house every day at eleven,' he said, 'and he leaves at eleven-oh-five. Just enough time to run inside, pick up the cash, and run out again.'

'He's alone?'

'Always alone.'

'How do you know?'

'Because I know. Do you think I just sit around wasting my time all day?'

'And the guy has money?'

'That's what he's doing there. Collecting from the dopeheads who've been there all night long.'

The man Bolden intended to rob was a drug dealer, and the place he ran in and out of was a crack house that had been the subject of several frightening stories at school. Some said it was a flophouse for Mob hit men, others that an exorcism had taken place there. Bolden had cased the house for a week, and come to a less threatening conclusion. Between thirty and fifty people visited the place each night. Some bought at the door. Others disappeared inside to get high. Hits of crack cost ten bucks a pop. He guessed that each customer bought between ten and twenty hits. Any way you looked at it, there had to be upwards of three thousand bucks inside that house.

'What do we use?' Phil asked.

'Fighting sticks,' said Bolden.

'*Sticks?* What, are you kidding? All drug dealers carry guns. Everyone knows that.'

'They're fighting sticks,' he said. 'They're all you need if you know how to use them.'

Lately, Bolden's identity had become a source of increasing concern. This stemmed in part from his inability to fit in with any one group at school, and in part from his confusion about his heritage. His mother had left when he was six. He had never known his father, or even seen a picture of him. He wasn't black, Latino, Chinese, Jewish, or Polish. If anything Bolden was an English name. In Chicago, where everyone was from somewhere, that left Irish as the closest viable ethnic group to which he might reasonably attach himself.

Perusing the stacks of the nearest public library, he had come across a book about Irish Stick Fighting. The book had convinced him that when properly used, fighting sticks could be every bit as lethal as a gun. He knew he had to take into account the fact that the book had been written a hundred years ago, but he believed surprise would give him the advantage he needed.

Reaching behind his back, he pulled a pair of ten-inch batons from his waistband. The sticks were cut from oak, as hard and as heavy as pig iron. 'Hit him on the neck or on the kidneys. He'll go down like a rock.'

Philly stared at the smooth stick as if it were a hand grenade with its pin pulled.

'Just watch me and do what I do.'

The house was easy to spot. Even among a neighborhood of eyesores, it stood out: a one-story shake with wrecked gray siding, and its every window boarded up. A spindly hedge ran around the house and a fractured walkway led up to it.

Bolden directed Philly to a spot on the kerb a few houses down. 'Red BMW,' he said, sitting down, his head turned up the street. 'Keep a sharp eye.'

'But he'll see us,' Philly protested.

'So? We don't exactly look like Mr T. and Hulk Hogan.'

'What if he's got a gun?'

Precisely at eleven, the red BMW rolled into view. The car parked in front of the crack house. A man dressed in jeans and a hip-length leather jacket got out. He was thirty with shaggy brown hair, and he walked bent forward, as if he were fighting a strong wind. Bolden waited until he was inside, then dashed across the street. Thursday was trash day and the two squatted behind a six-pack of battered garbage cans.

The drug dealer emerged a few minutes later. Bolden let him get close to the car, then jumped from his hiding spot and ran at him. The man barely had time to notice him – this tall, lanky kid charging at him like a crazed Mohican – before Bolden brought the baton down on his neck and shoulders.

With every blow, Bolden promised himself that it was the only way that he would ever be free.

The man crumpled to the sidewalk with hardly a whisper.

'Philly, get over here!'

Phil Grabowski remained glued to the spot. 'I c-c-c-can't.'

Bolden struck the dealer in the kidneys, then kicked him in the stomach. Falling to a knee, he searched the man's pockets. 'Bingo!' he said, coming up with a wad of grimy bills. He tried the other side and found a hash pipe, car keys, and the pistol Philly had sworn every self-respecting drug dealer carried. It was a small-caliber automatic, hardly bigger than the palm of his hand. He put it in his pocket.

'Come on,' he shouted, standing and waving Philly over. 'Let's jam!' He ran around the car and slid into the driver's seat.

'Wait,' cried Philly. 'Here I come.'

The limp form of the drug dealer lay between him and the car. As Philly jumped over him, a hand rose up and grabbed his leg. 'Where you goin'?'

'Tommy!'

Bolden looked out the window. The dealer was trying to stand, using Philly as a crutch.

Bolden lowered the window. 'Hit him! Hit him harder!'

Philly thrashed wildly with the baton. 'He won't let go. Tommy!'

At that instant, the front door of the house flew open. Drawn by the shouts, three men bounded down the stairs. Bolden took in the situation. He had the money. He had the car. He had the gun. He could be down the street in a minute and out of the city, ten minutes after that.

'Harder!' Bolden yelled. 'On the head!' Philly had

gotten himself into the jam. If he'd come when Bolden asked, none of this would be happening.

'Tommy!'

Bolden was out of the car a half second later. He did a Starsky and Hutch, sliding over the hood and landing with both feet on the sidewalk, the compact silver pistol extended in his right hand. 'Stop!' he shouted. 'Hold it.'

The three men froze in their tracks. Two of them raised their hands.

'Get in the car, Philly.'

'He won't let go.'

'Let go!' shouted Bolden.

The dealer had his hands locked around Philly's ankles. 'A lighter,' he said, squinting at Bolden. 'The gun. It's a friggin' lighter. You two punks are fucked.'

Bolden stepped toward the dealer. He'd never handled a gun before. He studied the pearl handle, the finely tooled barrel. It felt like a real gun. It had a weight to it. A heft that he liked. This thing was a lighter? A toy? Suddenly, he felt cheated. Pointing the gun at the dealer, he pulled the trigger. The gun bucked, the shot cracking like a bullwhip.

'I'm shot! I'm shot! Oh, Christ! I'm shot!'

A plume of smoke rose from a tear in the leather jacket near his shoulder.

Philly screamed. The three men took off in different directions.

'Go,' said Bolden, calmly. 'Get out of here.'

Philly remained rooted to the spot. 'What about you?'

Bolden gazed at the wounded man. A trickle of blood emerged from his back and snaked down the sidewalk. The trickle grew wider, then wider still. 'I'm staying.'

'But . . .' Philly's eyes blinked madly, and he began to cry. 'But . . .'

'Just go. I won't tell your mom. Go now.' Then he jumped at him and shouted, 'Get out of here!'

Philly turned and ran.

Bolden knelt by the drug dealer. He stuck the bills back in the pocket of his leather jacket. It was cold. His fingers were numb. He opened the man's jacket, then removed his Stones T-shirt, crumpled it into a ball, and pressed it very hard against the wound.

'That was stupid to say it was a lighter.'

'You're crazy, kid.'

In a minute, he heard the first siren. A second joined in, and then another. Soon, the entire world was crying out for Tommy Bolden's arrest. He began shivering. He'd realized that he'd exchanged one jail for another, and the new one was going to be a lot worse. The Dungeon, they called it. The Illinois State Home for Boys.

All of which brought him back to the present.

Why had Guilfoyle come after him?

Nothing happens without a reason.

Chapter 10

The man who had taken the name of Nathaniel Pendleton sat at his desk, his eyes glued to the ship. 'Marvelous,' he whispered to himself. 'A god-damned masterpiece.'

Housed in a custom-built glass case rested a 1:300 scale model of a United States second-class battleship originally constructed by the New York Naval Ship Yard and launched in 1890. The hull was shaped from wood and painted white, with an armored belt below the waterline to protect it against torpedoes. The ship boasted four 10-inch guns in revolving armored turrets. The secondary armament consisted of six 6-inch guns, fifteen small rapid-fire guns, and four 14-inch torpedo tubes. Even the pennants were authentic, and according to Pendleton's painstaking research, the same that were flying that fateful February eve just over a hundred years ago.

He closed his eyes, and for a moment caught the smell of the harbor fresh in his nostrils: frangipani and diesel oil, the scent of fried chicken wafting from the officers' mess, and from far away the acrid hint of a fire burning in the cane fields. The boat rocked gently, moaning as she tugged at her mooring lines. From land drifted the merry sounds of a mariachi band. Laughter. Catcalls. Closer, a sailor called out, 'Lieutenant. Vessel off the starboard bow!'

And then the explosion.

Pendleton jerked in his chair, eyes wide open. But in his mind, he saw the blinding flash, felt the deck buckle beneath him, the boat pitch hideously to starboard on her journey to the bottom of Havana Harbor. He shook himself and the room came back into focus.

He'd been there. By God, he was sure of it.

Standing, he walked to the model, letting a hand graze the glass enclosure. The reason for her sinking was still officially a mystery. He knew better. A limpet mine attached to the forward bow had ripped through the ship's hull and detonated the ammunition bunker. It was a pity, but necessary all the same. She truly was a beautiful boat.

He felt a presence stir behind him. 'Well?' he asked. 'How did he find out? It was Stillman, wasn't it? They'd recruited him.'

'No,' said Guilfoyle. 'He's a blank slate.'

Pendleton turned. 'Come again?'

'Bolden didn't know a thing.'

'But he had to know. His tracks were all over our reports. He was a Class Four offender. You said so, yourself.'

'My guess is no.'

'I take it you questioned him?'

'That's what you bring me in for.'

'And?' demanded Pendleton.

'I've never had a more innocent responder. He was forthcoming. Didn't play any games. Wasn't afraid to get steamed. I gave him the test. Genuine all the way.'

'What about Stillman?'

'The name meant nothing to him.'

'It's in the reports. There's a trail . . . a nexus.'

'We have to examine the possibility that Cerberus kicked out a false positive.'

Pendleton returned to his desk and sorted through a sheaf of papers. Suddenly, he slapped his hand against them. 'There! Look! Phone calls. Wednesday, Thursday, Friday. Don't tell me Cerberus made a mistake. The system's cost the government eight hundred million dollars and counting. It doesn't make mistakes.'

Guilfoyle held his position. He stood placidly, hands clasped behind his back. 'It could be a question of faulty data. You know, "garbage in, garbage out". We've only been fully operational for a few months. There's plenty of—'

'Faulty data?' Pendleton shook his head. 'Cerberus took the information directly from Ma Bell. We didn't tell the damn thing where to look. It found it by itself. A Class Four offender. That means four indications of hostile intent. Cerberus didn't make a mistake. It can't.' He took a breath, rubbing a finger across his lips, studying Guilfoyle. 'Maybe, it's time to admit that a machine knows better than you.'

Guilfoyle said nothing.

Sometimes he stood so still, Pendleton thought he was embalmed.

Pendleton walked to the floor-to-ceiling window. Looking north he gazed down upon the Potomac, a dark, steely snake, and beyond it, stretching toward the horizon, the Lincoln Memorial, the Reflecting Pool, the Washington Monument, and at the far end of the Mall, its dome nearly obscured by cloud, the Capitol. The view stirred him. The seat of the greatest empire in history. A reach that would have made the Romans envious. Pendleton was here, at its center. A player. A force, even.

Arms crossed over his chest, attired in a three-piece charcoal suit, his lace-ups spit shined, he was the model of the patrician class. He was sixty-seven years old, tall and lean, with the stern, skeptical face that in films belonged to diplomats and spies. He had been both in his time, as had his father, and his father before that, all the way back to the Revolution. He would have been handsome, except for his eyebrows, which were gnarled and unruly as a briar thicket, and gave him a wild, unpredictable air. His hair was thinning, its once dictatorial black yielding to gray. Slick with Brylcreem, it was meticulously parted, and combed to the right. It was the same haircut he'd kept since 1966, when he was a young marine infantry lieutenant in the Republic of Vietnam. He'd seen no reason to alter it since. Good memories.

He swung around and looked at Guilfoyle. 'What seems to be the problem?'

'There's been a glitch.'

'I should have known it. You're the only man on my payroll who prefers to give me good news on the phone and bad news face-to-face. And so?'

'Extraction went perfectly. Solutions got messy.'

'Elaborate, please.'

'Bolden messed up one of my men pretty badly. As soon as he's fixed up, he'll be transferred downtown to Police Plaza.'

'You mean he's in jail?' Pendleton blinked quickly, feeling his heart jump a beat. 'That's no glitch. It's a nuclear meltdown.'

'We have a team on it. Our man will be clear by noon.'

'You're telling me a banker from Harrington Weiss got the better of a Scanlon contractor graded "Solutions capable"?'

'That's correct.'

'But we're talking trained killers. Special Forces. Green Berets.'

Guilfoyle nodded and lowered his eyes. It was

as close as he ever came to offering an apology. 'All the same, I'd advise you to let it go,' he said. 'Bolden's a busy man, as you well know. Like I said, he's a blank slate.'

'Not any more, he's not,' said Pendleton. Shock had given way to fury. He couldn't allow this kind of cock-up. Not on his watch. The others wouldn't stand for it. 'I'd say he knows everything.'

'A few words, that's all. They're meaningless to him. In a week, he won't give it two thoughts.'

'I'm not concerned with a week. I'm more interested in two days from now. We can't have someone snooping after the fact.'

'It's more complicated than that.' Guilfoyle explained once more about the Scanlon employee sitting in a New York City jail, and the fact that both Bolden and his girlfriend had filed police reports that included descriptions of two other Scanlon men, Walter 'Wolf' Ramirez and Eamonn 'Irish' Jamison. 'Should anything happen to Bolden, the police might be suspicious. It would be difficult to control a homicide investigation. I imagine Bolden's given the police a fairly sharp description of me, too.'

'There's a girl mixed up in this, too?' Pendleton frowned.

'She's a nobody,' said Guilfoyle.

Pendleton rocked in his chair. It was a problem, but one that could be contained. He certainly had the means.

'Freeze him out. Discredit him. Take his life away. You know what to do. If we can't kill Bolden, we can do the next best thing. We can make him wish he were dead. Oh, and the girl . . . let's take her out of the equation. It'll be a lesson to Bolden to keep his mouth shut.'

Guilfoyle stared at him, not saying anything. Finally, he nodded.

'All right, then,' said Pendleton. 'It's decided.' He banged on the desk, then stood and walked toward the model battleship. 'See this?'

Guilfoyle joined him alongside the glass case. 'Very sharp.'

'Take a closer look. She's perfect. Made by a Dutchman in Curacao. A real master. Cost me ten thousand dollars.' Pendleton raised a hand toward the model, as if wanting not only to reach into the case, but into the very past itself. 'Went down with two hundred and fifty souls. They were good boys: well-trained, enthusiastic, ready to fight. They gave their lives so America could take her place on the world stage. Hawaii, Panama, the Philippines, Haiti. Five years after she went to the bottom, they were ours. Sometimes, the only way to get something done is to spill a little blood. Damned shame, really.'

Guilfoyle bent lower to read the name off the battleship's bow. 'Remember the *Maine*!' he whispered.

Chapter 11

Yoda was waiting on the kitchen counter when Bolden stepped through the door. 'Awake, are you? Did you not sleep?'

The giant orange tabby stared at him and yawned. Bolden walked past him, into the small kitchen, and turned on the light. 'Want milk, do you?'

Yoda raised his paw and kept it there.

Bolden set a saucer on the floor and poured in some milk. 'May the Force be with you, too.'

There were eleven messages on his answering machine. The tenth said, 'Thomas, um, hi. It's three-thirty. I've checked all the hospitals for you, but you're not there. I'm at home. Call me as soon as you get this. Love you.'

Bolden dialed Jenny's house. She answered on the first ring. 'Thomas? Where are you?'

'Hi, it's me,' he said. 'I'm at home. I'm okay.'

'Where have you been? I was worried.'

'It's a long story, but I'm fine. Sorry I didn't call sooner.'

'It's okay. I got your last message. Where'd you go, anyway? I waited on the street for twenty minutes, then the police officer insisted I go to the hospital.'

'I got your watch back.'

Silence. Bolden heard a sob, then a muted laugh.

He sighed, pinching the bridge of his nose with his thumb and forefinger. He wanted her there with him, instead of at her place.

'Let's have lunch,' he suggested. 'We can talk about it then.'

'I can come over now.'

'I've got to be at work by eight. There's that Jefferson deal I told you about.'

'Don't go,' Jenny said. 'I'll take a day, too. Come over to my place.' She dropped into her Russian-secret-agent voice. '*I make it vorth your vhile, comrade.*'

'Can't do it,' he said, hating how he sounded like an uptight jerk.

'I need you,' she said, and her voice had dropped into another tone altogether. 'Come over. Now.'

'Jen, it's a big deal. People are coming in from D.C. There's no way I can miss it.'

Jenny sighed. 'Okay, lunch then,' she said, too soberly. 'I've got something to tell you, too.'

'Hint?'

'Never. But I'm warning you. I may hijack you afterwards.'

'If things go well with Jefferson, I may let you. Lunch. Twelve sharp.'

'Regular place?'

'Regular place,' he confirmed. 'And you? Your arm? Only ten stitches.'

'How did you know?'

Bolden turned on the television. The channel was tuned to CNBC, the sound muted, and for a minute, he just sat there and stared at the numbers scrolling across the bottom of the screen. The long bond was up. North Sea crude down a dollar. The Nikkei had closed up fifty.

His vision blurred.

Crown. Bobby Stillman.

Bolden closed his eyes, forcing the words from his mind, turning the volume on Guilfoyle's lifeless voice down to zero. The fact that five hours ago a man had aimed a pistol squarely at his face and fired a bullet that missed him by a few inches, the fact that he had been made to stand on a naked girder seventy stories above the ground, the fact that he had attacked a man on that girder and toppled into a net sixty feet below it that in all honesty he hadn't been sure was there – all of this seemed impossible and distant. It couldn't *really* have happened. Not during the same day that had begun with him eating breakfast with clients at the Ritz-Carlton in Boston and continued right through his donning a tuxedo for the gala dinner and giving Jenny her anniversary present on the steps of Federal Hall.

He opened his eyes and stared at the numbers scrolling on the TV screen. If gold cost $460 an ounce in London, he could be sure it was the truth. If the long bond was trading at five and three teenies, he could believe that, too. The numbers were real. He could trust them. It didn't make any sense that someone would try to kill him because they believed he knew something that, in fact, he did not. *Crown. Bobby Stillman.* He couldn't trust what he couldn't understand, so he had to forget it. To wipe the events from his mind. Bolden knew how to forget.

After a while, he decided he had better try to eat something. It was going to be a busy day, and an important one. Responsibility tugged at him like an undertow, something he couldn't see, but was powerless to overcome. He shuffled to the refrigerator and took out some eggs, pepper jack cheese, diced ham, and a half gallon of orange juice. From the pantry, he doled out five thousand milligrams of vitamin C and four extra-strength Advils.

He sat down on his piano bench and shoveled the eggs into his mouth. Yoda jumped up next to him and he fed the cat a sliver of ham. Finished, he set the plate on the floor. Yoda was on it in a flash. A cat who liked eggs and pepper jack cheese. Maybe that explained why he weighed twelve pounds.

Forget it. Forget it all.

Twisting on the bench, he hit a note with his index finger. The piano was a beaut, an antique Chickering upright. Above it hung an original poster of *Yankee Doodle Dandy*, Jimmy Cagney winking at him from the haze of seventy years. He ran his hand along the ivory keyboard. 'Chopsticks' was as far as his talent went. Once he'd made his bundle, he'd take some lessons. He wanted to be good enough to play three songs well: that music from Charlie Brown, the 'Maple Leaf Rag' by Scott Joplin, and the *Moonlight Sonata*. Tommy Bolden playing Beethoven. Even now, half exhausted, the idea made him smile.

The clock on the oven read 6:10 as he deposited the plate in the sink and ran some hot water over it. He walked into the living room and collapsed onto the couch, staring out the window at the East River. Beyond it, the concrete flats of Queens huddled like a cellblock beneath the gray sky. He looked around the apartment that he'd moved into four years ago. At the time, all his possessions had fit into three suitcases and a half dozen moving boxes, not including his Naugahyde La-Z-Boy recliner, his Lava Lamp, and his framed poster of Zeppelin jamming at Madison Square Garden.

That stuff was long gone.

Jenny's first crusade was to give him taste. Taste was not innate, but was learned. Taste was a burgundy sofa and an art deco wall mirror. Taste was an original Eames recliner and a seven-foot Kentia palm. Taste was the Cagney poster, which had once hung in the lobby of the Biograph Theater in Times Square. Taste was afternoons trawling Greenwich Village's countless antique shops and furniture dealers in search of . . . *the right thing*. Taste, he had learned, was spending lots of money to make it look like you hadn't spent lots of money at all.

One soggy fall Saturday, after a visit to an antique store he was sure they'd visited the week before, Bolden rebelled. It was his turn, he said. That day taste was a Macintosh receiver with two hundred watts per channel, a pair of JBL studio monitors to blow them back to the Stone Age, and the Stones cranking out 'Midnight Rambler' (live) at eighty decibels. Taste was a bottle of cheap Chianti, spaghetti with Ragu tomato sauce, a loaf of hot garlic bread dripping with butter, and his old college comforter spread across the living-room floor on which to enjoy it all. Taste was making love as the lights of Manhattan came to life around them, and crowding into a steaming-hot bathtub afterwards.

Bolden's eyes walked the floor where they had lain curled up under his frayed, all-purpose comforter, and came to rest on the candle she had made for him out of the Chianti bottle, the kind with straw wrapped around the bottom and wax drippings down the sides.

'Terrible taste. Terrific memory,' Jenny had said.

He missed her.

Thinking of the kiss that had accompanied the

candle, he closed his eyes and laid his head on the cushion. He needed to rest. Just for a few minutes. Ten or fifteen . . .

Bolden dreamed. He stood in the center of a large room, surrounded by a circle of boys, teenagers really. He knew them all. Gritsch, Skudlarek, Feely, Danis, Richens, and the rest of them from the Dungeon. They were stamping their feet on the wooden floor, chanting his name. He looked down and saw the body on the floor in front of him. He bent down and turned it over. It was Boyle. He was dead, his neck grotesquely twisted, his eyes and mouth open. 'It was an accident,' a sixteen-year-old Bolden shouted. 'An accident!'

The circle of boys closed in on him, chanting his name. All were holding pistols. The same gun that Guilfoyle had pointed at his head. They raised their arms. Bolden felt the barrel pressed to his forehead. They fired.

The gun!

Bolden woke with a start. It was then that the image came to him. A memory from the night just passed. He rushed across the living room to his desk, a nineteenth-century secretary. A legal pad sat on top of it. He found a pen and began to sketch the tattoo he had seen on the chest of the man who had wanted him dead. The first drawing was terrible and looked like a misshapen dog bone. He tore off the paper, wadded it up, and chucked it into the wastebasket. He started again, working slower. A sturdy stock led into a long, tapered barrel. Finished with the outline, he colored it in. Still terrible, but he had captured the idea more or less. He held up the drawing for examination.

An old-fashioned rifle, circa 1800. Something

Daniel Boone would carry. A frontiersman's rifle. No, not a rifle, he corrected himself for the second time.

A musket.

Chapter 12

Detective First Grade John Franciscus couldn't believe his eyes. About ten yards away, a tall, black guy, maybe forty, nicely dressed, was standing with his Johnson in his hand taking a leak on the side of St Thomas's Episcopal Church. The sight incensed him. Here it was, barely eight in the morning, and this guy's letting go on a house of worship like he's watering the roses.

Slamming on the brakes, Franciscus pulled his unmarked police cruiser to the sidewalk and threw open the door. 'You!' he shouted. 'Stay!'

'Whatchyou—' The man didn't have time to finish his sentence before Franciscus ran up and slugged him in the mouth. The man tumbled backward over his feet, his right hand still firmly clamped to his exhaust pipe, the pee flying all over him. 'Shit,' he moaned, his eyes fluttering.

Franciscus winced at the smell of the booze wafting up at him. 'That, sir, was a lesson in attitude adjustment. This is your neighborhood. Take better care of it.'

Shaking his head, Franciscus headed back to his car before the guy could get a better look at him. The kind of behavior that Franciscus called preemptive action, or an attitude adjustment, was strictly frowned upon these days. Some called it excessive force, or police brutality. Even so, it was too effective a policy tool to be discarded entirely. The way

Franciscus saw it, he was just doing his duty as a resident.

Harlem was his neighborhood, too. Coming up on thirty-five years, he'd been policing out of the Three-Four and Manhattan North Homicide. He'd watched Harlem pull itself up by its bootstraps and turn from an urban war zone where no man was safe after dark – white, black, or any shade in between – to a respectable, bustling community with clean sidewalks and proud citizens.

You let the small things slide and people get the idea that no one gives a darn. No sir. You have to bust the homeless guys who spit on your window and want a dollar to clean it off; the winos who demand tips as doormen at ATMs; corner crack dealers; farebreakers; grafitti artists. Anybody and everybody who made the streets an ugly, difficult place. He was not about to stand for some knucklehead peeing in public, and on a church, to boot.

It was policing this kind of low-grade delinquency that had reclaimed Harlem from the thugs and the thieves, and made greater New York the safest big city in the world.

A mile down the road, Franciscus pulled his car over and slipped the 'Police Business' card onto the dash. Craning his neck, he stared up at the highrise. Hamilton Tower, after Alexander Hamilton, who'd built his 'country' house, the Grange, just up the road. What someone was thinking building a luxury office tower around here was beyond him. The building looked to be about twenty percent finished. He surveyed the building site. The only vehicle on the premises was a Ford F-150 pickup. He looked around for some hard hats, checked if the crane up top was moving. The site was as quiet as a morgue. Franciscus knew what that meant. No *dinero*. Just what Harlem needed. Another white elephant, excuse the pun.

Franciscus checked both ways, waiting for a hole in traffic. Strictly speaking, he was off duty, but he had a few things he needed to clear up, or he'd never get to sleep. Home was not a place he cared to be when his mind was jumping through hoops. It was a nice enough place, four thousand square feet, two stories, white picket fence, and a lawn out back up in Rockland County. But it was lonely as hell. His wife had passed away three years earlier. His sons were living the life of Riley out in San Diego, both of them sheriffs, God bless 'em. These days it was just him and the radiator, each of them ticking away, waiting to see who was going to give out first.

A car passed and he jogged across the street. Five strides, and he could feel the sweat begin to pour, his heart doing the Riverdance – and this with the mercury barely clawing its way above zero. He slowed to a walk, and wiped his forehead.

At the supervisor's shack, Franciscus knocked once, then stuck his head in the door. 'Anyone here?'

'Enter,' answered a gruff voice.

Franciscus stepped inside and flashed his identification, keeping it there good and long so there wouldn't be any questions afterwards. The badge wasn't good enough any more. Every Tom, Dick, and Harry had a fake. 'I'd like to take a look around. You mind?'

'Not if you're interested in building a new precinct station here. We got plenty of floors open. One through eighty. Take your pick.'

The construction manager was an older guy with a beer belly and a beet red face. He had a copy of the *Post* in his lap, a cigarette burning in the ashtray next to a supersize mug of coffee, and a bag of Krispy Kremes in arm's reach. Franciscus took a look at him, wondering how this guy's heart was holding up.

'I need to get up to the foreman's shack,' he said.

'Go ahead. Gate's open. Elevator's running. Not much to see up there. Don't get too near the edges, ya hear?'

'Don't worry about me. I don't feel like taking a dive any time soon.' Franciscus nodded toward the work site. 'Mind me saying, I don't see many guys around.'

'You and me both. The suits are waiting to see if anyone's actually gonna move in, before they plunk down any more dough. If you need anything, just holler. Loud!'

Franciscus chuckled. It was weak, but at least the guy was trying. 'You said the gate's unlocked. You keep this place open all night?'

'Tell me you're kidding and you'll restore my faith in city government.'

'Who has the keys?'

'Me. And about twenty other assholes. Don't tell me you want their names.'

'Naw. Just yours. You look familiar. Ever carry a badge?' It was a line. Something to puff the guy up a little. Win him over.

'No sir. Did a year in 'Nam, though. That was enough time in a uniform for me.'

'Same here. Nice memories.' Franciscus rolled his eyes.

'Alvin J. Gustafson at your service.' He reached into his pocket and found a business card. 'Call me Gus. I guess I better ask what this is about. What exactly are you looking for?'

'Anyone asks, Gus, I'm just checking the view.'

*

Franciscus found the foreman's shack as Bolden had described it. He strolled to the door and opened it. The view faced north toward the Bronx, just like Bolden had said. No question this was the place.

Franciscus stuck his hands in his pockets and leaned against the wall. He didn't have much on his mind, no suspicions, no ideas, really. He'd come up to run Bolden's story through and imagine what had happened here.

It was the man he had under watch at the hospital who bothered him. He had no doubt he was a veteran, but so far his prints had come back negative. He hadn't been carrying any identification and refused to give his name. In fact, he didn't even want to use his phone call. He just sat there quiet as a lamb. He was, Franciscus concluded, a serious player, and Franciscus had every intention of learning who had sent him uptown to do bodily harm to Thomas Bolden.

Franciscus looked at the doorway and the chairs, trying to figure out where Bolden had been standing, where he hit the floor. As his eyes skimmed the carpet, he spotted a sterling-silver collar stud lying near the base of the desk. He picked it up. From Tiffany, no less. 'Wasn't Bolden the big muckety-muck?' he mused, dropping the metal sliver into his pocket. A little physical evidence never hurt.

After a few minutes, he headed back to the elevator. On the trip to the ground floor, he reviewed the facts, as he knew them. Unbeknownst to him, Mr Thomas Bolden is followed from his office to lunch at Balthazar yesterday at one o'clock. The suspect steals a cell phone that he can use anonymously later in the day. That night, Bolden's girlfriend is mugged by two men in their mid-to-late twenties. Her watch (an anniversary gift valued at six thousand dollars) is stolen, along with a large sterling-silver plate. Bolden gives pursuit and is forced at gunpoint into the rear of a limousine. The watch and plate are returned. During the ride uptown, one of the assailants hints at having served as a Ranger in the army. The limousine deposits Bolden and the two assailants at a deserted building site in Harlem sometime around 12:30 A.M. The gate's open. The foreman's shack has been prepared, right down to ripping the construction plans off the wall. Everything has been arranged beforehand with care and precision. He is interrogated by a man named Guilfoyle about something called Crown, and whether or not he was acquainted with an individual named Bobby Stillman. Bolden says no, whereupon Guilfoyle forces him outside, onto a platform seventy stories up and about the size of a postage stamp. When Bolden still refuses to play ball, he fires a gun next to his cheek to make sure he's not lying.

At this point, Franciscus paused in his reconstruction of the events to reflect. In short order, he decided that if someone put a gun to his head, he would admit to knowing Chief Joseph of the Nez Percé Indians. *Note to self: Mr Bolden has himself some brass ones.*

Franciscus continued. Guilfoyle gives his associate, Wolf, instructions to kill Bolden, then leaves the building. Bolden manages to wrestle Wolf off the girder. The two fall sixty feet into a safety net. Bolden descends to the ground, surprises the driver, whacks the hell out of him, and takes off with the car, crashing through the gates. Two hours later, when the site is checked, no sign is found of Wolf or of any crazy business, whatsoever.

It was one wild-ass story, thought Franciscus, as he crossed the construction area. It had to take a lot to bring someone like Bolden into the police station. He made a note to run a check on him, if the budget could stand it. Tossing the shirt stud in his hand, he decided everything Bolden had said was true. What he wasn't sure of was whether Bolden was hiding a prior association with Guilfoyle. It seemed like an awful lot of work to get the wrong guy.

'Still here, Gus?' he said, knocking on the door of the supervisor's shack.

'Busy as ever.'

Franciscus stepped inside. ' 'Fraid I'm going to need the names of the people who have a key.'

'Knew it.' Gustafson tore a sheet of paper from a notebook and handed it to him. A list of names numbered one through six filled the left-hand side of the page. 'Be prepared, my father taught me. Turns out I couldn't think of twenty. Only six. Otherwise, you can call the head office.'

'Where's that?'

'In Jersey. Atlas Ventures.'

'Never heard of them. Why don't they have a sign up?' Franciscus didn't know of a construction site that didn't boast ten signs advertising every tradesman working on the project.

'They did. They took it down a few days back.'

'Kids spray it with graffiti?'

'No. People don't mess with us too much. The building's considered good for the neighborhood and all that. Maybe they thought it was looking beat-up or something.'

'Could be,' said Franciscus, giving a shrug to show he didn't really care one way or the other. 'Heckuva view, by the way.'

'Ain't it though?'

*

Franciscus had driven fifty yards down Convent Avenue when he slammed on his brakes. He looked out the window to his right at an old Federal-style house painted pale chiffon yellow. The house was immaculately cared for. An American flag flew from the porch. A National Park Service sign declared it a national monument. The Grange had been the last home of Alexander Hamilton, built in the years prior to his death. At the time, it was considered a country house, and the ride to lower Manhattan took over an hour. It had been moved once already to its present location and another move was scheduled. It was flanked on one side by an aging brownstone, and on the other, by an uncared-for church.

Why here?

That was the question that continued to nag at him. Why kidnap a man near Wall Street and drag him all the way uptown? Professionals who were patient enough to case a victim for days before grabbing him could have taken him anywhere. If someone wanted Bolden killed, then that someone had wanted him killed here. In Harlem.

He stared at the flag flapping in the brisk wind. For some reason, he thought of the musket tattooed on the man's chest.

Chapter 13

The firm of Harrington Weiss occupied the eighth through forty-third floors of an unexceptional gray granite building two blocks down the street from the New York Stock Exchange. Founded in 1968, Harrington Weiss, or HW, as it was referred to familiarly, was a newcomer on the Street. Compared to its competitors, many of whom had first opened their doors one hundred years before, it had no history. Nor could it compete in terms of size. With assets of three billion dollars, the firm counted just over two thousand employees spread across offices in New York, London, Shanghai, and Tokyo.

But Solomon Henry Weiss had never wanted his firm to be the biggest. He preferred to be the best. A native of Sheepshead Bay, Brooklyn, Sol Weiss had left school at the age of fourteen to take a job as a runner at the New York Stock Exchange. He was hardworking, smart, and congenitally skeptical. He moved up the ranks quickly, earning his stripes as a trader, specialist, and, finally, market maker. Dissatisfied with brokering other people's trades, he founded his own firm to run whatever money he had saved, and the little he could raise from family and friends.

It was the sixties, the age of the conglomerate, and Wall Street was in the thrall of the 'Nifty Fifty', the fifty or so companies who seemed to be solely responsible for powering the Dow Jones Industrial

Average's move from 300 to nearly 1,000. But Weiss was never one to follow the herd. His goal wasn't to beat the Industrial average by a few percentage points. He wanted to kick its ass and leave it begging for mercy on the ticket-littered floor of the Exchange.

Weiss hung out his shingle as a 'stock picker'. It was his practice to place enormous, highly leveraged bets on the shares of only two or three companies at a time. Some called him a gambler, but he thought it the other way around. Weiss knew the companies he invested in, inside and out. It wasn't a gamble, so much as a well-calculated risk. The first year he made fifty percent on his investments, the next year forty-five. It wasn't long before word of his impressive track record spread. Within ten years, the firm of Harrington Weiss had grown from five employees to five hundred, and his assets under management from one million to one billion dollars. That was just the beginning.

In fact, there never was a Mr Harrington involved in the firm's day-to-day business. The man didn't exist. Weiss chose the name because of its phonetic similarity to 'Harriman', Brown Brothers Harriman being the epitome of the well-heeled 'Waspish' firm. Or as he put it more eloquently, 'No blue-haired society matron is going to hand over her grandson's inheritance to a bunch of pushy New York Jews.'

Weiss was a character only Wall Street could create. He was short, fat, and homely with large, tragic brown eyes, great sagging jowls, and hair the color and texture of a Brillo pad that he unsuccessfully camouflaged with gobs of gel. He was given to wearing bold pin-striped suits with even bolder striped shirts. A four-carat diamond stickpin held his necktie in place. He wore his solid gold Breguet wristwatch over his French cuffs, in the manner of Gianni Agnelli, the late Italian billionaire and chairman of Fiat. It didn't matter that Weiss didn't know Agnelli, that he didn't speak Italian, or that he'd never been to Europe. Weiss knew class when he saw it. And that went for the seven-inch Romeo y Julieta cigar he clasped between his fingers ten hours a day, seven days a week.

And yet, for all his flamboyance, Weiss was the picture of discretion. Soft-spoken, sincere, deeply religious, at the age of sixty-six, he had assumed a near-mythic stature in the investment community. Weiss was the last honest man, integrity personified, and, as such, the 'consigliere' of first choice among America's most prestigious corporations. Over the years, he had received many offers to sell his company, a few at wildly inflated sums. He'd turned them all down. The company was family, and family counted for far more than money. He was addressed by one and all as Sol.

Harrington Weiss concentrated on the high end of the business: institutions, banks and brokerages, the larger family trusts. The minimum balance set for managed accounts was ten million dollars, but those valued at fifty million and above were preferred. The investment-banking arm specialized in mergers and acquisitions advisory and corporate finance work to a handpicked coterie of firms.

On the Street, HW had a reputation for steering winning deals to its clients i.e. deals that were nearly always profitable. Some talked about Weiss's 'golden touch', but there was no luck involved, thought Bolden, as he lowered his shoulder and passed through the revolving doors. Just hard work. Long hours taking apart balance sheets and P and Ls and figuring out what made a company tick.

And then, more hours figuring out what needed to be done to make it hum.

Bolden slid his ID card over the scanner and pushed his way through the turnstile. 'Morning, Andre,' he said, with a nod of the head to the security guards. 'Morning, Jamaal.'

'Hey, there, Mr B.'

Bolden hurried across the crowded lobby to the bank of elevators that serviced the thirty-fifth through forty-fifth floors and squeezed into a packed car. He was dressed in a charcoal suit, blue chalk-striped shirt and navy tie, a trench coat to ward off the cold. He carried a worn but polished satchel in one hand, and an umbrella in the other. He glanced at the faces surrounding him. The men fatigued, dark circles beneath the eyes, preoccupied. The women resigned, overly made up, anxious. He fit right in.

He got out on forty-two and waved a hello to Mary and Rhonda at the reception desk. Copies of the *Wall Street Journal* and the *New York Times* were fanned across the counter like a deck of cards. Bolden didn't bother picking one up. Reading a newspaper at your desk was a firing offense. You'd be safer keeping an open bottle of Jack Daniel's in plain sight and a spliff burning in the ashtray.

The office was richly decorated in English Regency style: wooden floors covered with plush maroon runners, muted silk wallpaper the color of antique ivory, and polished nineteenth-century tables lining the halls. Prints of gentlemen riding to hounds, old American warships, and pastoral landscapes adorned the walls. Somewhere there was even a bust of Adam Smith.

At seven-thirty, the place was still coming to life. As Bolden walked the hall, he saw that most of the executives were in, sitting at their desks answering e-mails, sorting through offering memorandums and analyst's reports, writing up call reports, and generally figuring what ploy they might devise that day to earn the firm a few greenbacks. Harrington Weiss was a partnership. Revenue was strictly recorded, and bonuses were meted out accordingly. In the lingo, you ate what you killed.

'Hey, Jake,' he said, ducking his head into an office. 'Thanks for coming last night. The donation . . . it was too much. Really, I can't say enough . . .'

A dark, mousy man worked busily at his computer. 'You da man, Tommy,' he answered in a booming voice, without ever taking his eyes from the screen.

Jake Flannagan. Head of investment banking. Bolden's boss.

Six years had passed since Bolden had begun work at HW. He'd started as just another galley slave, one of a class of twenty, paid an even hundred thousand dollars a year before bonus. His first assignment placed him in mergers and acquisitions where he spent endless hours tinkering with financial statements to arrive at a targeted company's true market value. What if revenue increased by two percent? Three percent? Four percent? What if expenses decreased? An infinite string of permutations calibrated to match the exact depth of the client's pockets.

From M and A, he'd moved to capital markets, where he'd learned how to price securities, IPOs, mezzanine debt, junk, you name it. And then, on to investment banking proper, where he'd jumped a flight three days a week to visit companies and pitch them ideas about what they needed to buy, the divisions they should divest, and the benefits of doing a secondary stock offering. Thomas Bolden: the Fuller Brush Man in a thousand-dollar suit with something in his satchel to fit every CEO's taste. When it was decided his smile needed work, the firm paid to have his teeth whitened.

'Adam, Miss Evelyn,' he said, to two assistants, making way for them to pass.

Bolden knew everyone's name. He made a point of it.

Passing the cloakroom, he deposited his trenchcoat and umbrella, then moved across the corridor to grab two cups of coffee, one for himself, and one for his assistant, Althea.

A year ago, he'd been promoted to director and given a spot in the special-investments division. The special-investments division was tasked with maintaining the firm's relationships with the growing rank of private equity firms. His clients were the crème de la crème: the Halloran Group, Olympia Investments, Atlantic Oriental Group, and Jefferson Partners.

Private equity firms, or financial sponsors, as they were known in the trade, made it their business to buy companies, fix whatever ailed them, and sell them at a profit a few years down the road. To do this, they raised pools of capital from investors, called funds. The funds ranged anywhere in value from five hundred million to six or seven billion dollars. His most important client, Jefferson Partners, was due to close the industry's first ten-billion-dollar fund any day now. Bolden was due at a swank dinner in DC that night to help Jefferson convince the last holdouts.

It was Bolden's job to keep his ear to the ground for news about companies that were looking to be sold and whisper his discoveries in his clients' ears. The companies could be publicly traded or privately held. Textiles, finance, consumer goods, or oil. The only thing they had in common was their size. The private equity firms Bolden worked with didn't buy anything valued at less than a billion dollars.

The special-investments division was the equivalent of the all-star team. Shorter hours. Fewer clients. World-class boondoggles. And of course, the bonuses. No one earned more than the fat cats in SID. And for good reason: the tight relations forged with their clients resulted in at least one executive leaving HW each year for the greener, and infinitely higher-paying pastures, of private equity. A partner at HW stood to earn anywhere from five to twenty-five million dollars. The same position at a sponsor paid five times that. Real money.

'You're in late,' announced Althea soberly, her suspicious brown eyes giving him the once-over.

Bolden set her coffee on the table, then slipped by her into his office and took the hanger off the door. 'Shut the door,' he said.

'In or out?' she asked, meaning should she come in or stay out.

'In.'

'What's wrong?' she asked, stepping into his office. 'You don't look so good.'

'I've got a small problem. And I need your help.'

Althea closed the door. 'Uh-oh.'

Chapter 14

It was five minutes past eight. The telephone repairman looked up from his wristwatch and watched as the night doorman left the building and crossed the street toward the corner of Sutton Place and Third Avenue. The old Irishman was weaving slightly and the repairman knew it wasn't just from a long night on the job. He waited until the doorman had disappeared down the block, then left the cozy, heated confines of his truck and entered the lobby of 47 Sutton Place.

Waving to the day man, he was quick to present the work order for his examination. He was dressed in a Verizon uniform. A tool belt hung low on his waist. All the same, he did his best to avoid eye contact and spoke with his face lowered, as if, despite his size, he was congenitally shy. He didn't want the doorman to spend too much time checking out his swollen nose, or the fresh cuts that striped his chin and his neck. After some small talk, he took the elevator to the basement and checked the junction box where the phone lines entered the building. It took him less than a minute to isolate the line for apartment 16B. The eavesdropping device he'd installed a few weeks earlier remained in place. All calls were transmitted to a base station cached up the block, and relayed via satellite to the organization's op center in DC.

Leaving his tools on the floor, he retraced his steps to the elevator and rode to the sixteenth floor. The two Schlage locks were easily defeated. He was inside Thomas Bolden's apartment a minute later. He removed his work belt and set it on the floor, then slipped on a pair of surgical latex gloves. Paper 'galoshes' stretched over his boots prevented the Vibram soles from squeaking on the parquet floor. Carefully, he wiped down the doorframe and doorknob for fingerprints.

Mrrr-owww.

Wolf spun on a heel, a double-edged assault knife bared between his knuckles. Perched on the kitchen counter sat the biggest damn tabby cat he'd ever seen. He lowered his knife and felt his heart rate slow. The cat raised a paw in greeting and cocked its head.

'Lord almighty,' muttered Wolf, as he slid the knife into its sheath. No one had told him about the cat. He spent a minute petting it, though as a rule, he didn't like cats. No loyalty. That was their problem.

He was born Walter Rodrigo Ramirez in Ciudad Juárez, Mexico, but he'd called himself Wolf for as long as he could remember. To his way of thinking, a wolf was the noblest creature on earth. He hunted only when he needed food. He looked after his family first. He was loyal to the pack. And he was the baddest motherfucker in the woods.

A full-color, full-face tattoo of a wolf, ready to pounce, covered every square inch of Wolf's back. If you looked deep in the wolf's eye, you could see his prey, a hunter standing with his hands in the air. The hunter was pure evil. He, Walt Ramirez, was the wolf.

Protect the weak. Defend the innocent. Strike down thine enemies and vanquish all evil by the right hand of God.

That was Wolf's credo.

And Bolden was at the top of his list. Bolden was the hunter. Bolden was evil. Soon, he would have his hands raised, begging for mercy. None would be shown. No quarter would be given. No one humiliated the wolf.

Beginning at the point farthest from the entry and working his way back, Wolf searched the apartment. Bathroom. Bedroom. Living room. Kitchen. For a big man, he moved quietly and with sure feet. He had learned his trade at installations with names like the Covert Warfare Training Center and the Special Warfare School. He had honed it to a razor's edge in places like Kuwait, Bosnia, Colombia, and Afghanistan during sixteen years of military service. His specialty was elegantly termed enemy extraction. Less elegantly, he was known as a body snatcher.

It had been three years since he'd worn a uniform, yet he had never left his country's service. At the urging of his superior officer, he'd retired from active duty to work for a company with close ties to the top ranks of government. The company was called Scanlon Corporation, and it did much of the work that the armed forces could not be seen to do itself. The pay was four times what he'd earned as a sergeant, first class, and the company offered a 401(k). There were also excellent health-care benefits and a $250,000 life-insurance policy. Taken together, it went a long way toward compensating for the retirement on full pay he'd been four years from earning. Wolf had a wife and three kids under the age of seven to keep clothed and fed. Most important, the work was essential to keeping America strong at home and abroad.

For the past two years, Wolf had hunted terrorists in the purple mountains of the Hindu Kush:

Afghanistan, Pakistan, and the lawless borderlands that separated the two. Finding a bad guy, he'd call in his team of 'wolverines', set a perimeter, and hunker down until nightfall. Out came the iPod, in went the earbuds, and on went Metallica. When Wolf hit a target, he was fuckin' pumped, mainlining adrenaline.

But capturing the bad guys was only half the job. The other half was interrogating them. Time was critical. Ten minutes meant a player escaping or being captured. It meant an American soldier living or dying. That was the way Wolf saw things. Black and white. He didn't hold with any of this bullshit about torture not working. It worked, all right. A man would give up his infant daughter when he was being skinned alive. You cannot lie when a superheated Bowie knife is flaying you strip by strip. Sometimes, he still heard the screams, but they didn't bother him too much.

Duty. Honor. Country.

That was also his credo.

America had given his father, a Mexican immigrant with no money, no education, and no skills, a chance. Now, his papa owned a successful dry-cleaning business in El Paso, and had just opened a second store across the border in Ciudad Juárez. He drove a red Cadillac. American doctors had operated on his sister's cleft palate, leaving hardly a scar, and giving her a beautiful face. Now, she was married and had children of her own. The American military had taught him the value of sacrifice for a greater cause. It had made him into a man. The day Wolf received his American citizenship was the proudest of his life. He prayed for the President every morning and every evening.

And now, an asshole like Bolden was trying to fuck everything up. Putting his nose where it didn't belong. Associating with a bunch of left-wing kooks who thought they knew better than the men in Washington. He looked around the apartment, at the fly furniture and the kick-ass stereo and the unbelievable view. Bolden had it much too good to be badmouthing the system. The Wolf would not permit it.

Seventeen minutes later, he had scoured the apartment. He found only one item of interest: a scrap of paper lying in the wastebasket. The drawing on it was crude, but he recognized it right away. He called Guilfoyle to tell him what he'd found.

'The man's a snoop,' Wolf added, before ending the call. 'He ain't one to forget what's been done to him.'

Chapter 15

'I need a list of all companies my core has bought and sold in the last twenty years,' said Bolden, once Althea had taken a seat.

'You want what?'

'A list of companies my clients have bought and sold. The information's in the offering memos. It's just a question of going through them and writing it all down.'

'Why are you asking me? Don't you have an associate you can call, one of those boys who likes to work even harder than you?'

'I'd like you to do it.'

'Sorry, Tom, my morning's all booked. I've got about three of your expense reports to get through first, then—'

'Althea!' The burst escaped from Bolden before he could stop it. He blew out through his teeth. 'Just get it done. Please.'

Althea nodded, but he could see that she was angry.

Like half the assistants in the office, Althea Jackson was a single mom working ten-hour days to give her son a better life. A native of St Barts, she spoke fluent French and just enough Spanish to swear at the cleaning crews when they didn't leave Bolden's desk just so. She stood five feet one inch in her stockings and made it a point not to wear heels. Even so, she walked the halls like a queen. She was imperious, haughty, and temperamental as hell. She was also whip smart, efficient, and loyal. In a perfect world, she should have gone to university and graduate school herself.

'Start with Halloran, then go on to Atlantic Oriental, and Jefferson Partners. Find the offering memorandum for every fund the companies have raised. At the back, there's a listing of all prior transactions. Name of company, what they paid for it, what they sold it for, and the rate of return to investors. All I'm interested in are the names of the companies and their principal business activities.'

'What exactly are you looking for?'

'I'll know it when I see it.'

'If you'd tell me, it might make my work a little easier.'

Bolden leaned forward. 'Just do what I asked. I'll explain it to you later.'

Althea rolled her eyes and exhaled. One more indignity visited upon her. She stood and opened the door. 'Your meeting with Jefferson Partners has been moved to the forty-second-floor conference room. Eight o'clock.'

'Who's confirmed?'

'From Jefferson, Franklin Stubbs, and "la Comtesse", Nicole Simonet.'

'Your favorite,' said Bolden.

'Too bad she doesn't look as pretty as her name. That child was just born ugly.'

'Be nice, Althea,' said Bolden.

'Now, I have to be nice, too? You know where she's from? Bayonne, New Jersey. And her thinking she can speak French better than me.'

'You have a very capable network of spies. I'd hate to think what you've dredged up about me.' Bolden began gathering together the papers he'd need. 'What else is going on?'

'Meeting with the finance committee at ten. Interview with that boy from Harvard at eleven. Conference call with Whitestone at eleven-thirty. Lunch with Mr Sprecher at twelve. Then—'

'Call him and reschedule. I've got other plans.'

Althea raised her eyes from her notepad. 'You're not missing lunch with Mr Sprecher,' she said in a no-nonsense voice. 'No one stands up the head of the compensation committee two weeks before bonuses are handed out.'

'I've got a lunch date with Jenny.'

'Not any more you don't. This has been on your calendar for a month. He's reserved a table at Le Cirque and told Martha to clear his schedule until four, and then book a massage at his club at six. He's planning on having a real good time.'

Bolden tapped his desk. There was no way out of it. Althea's bonus came straight off the top of Bolden's. If he didn't go, she'd never let him forget it.

'Okay,' he said, checking his watch. Jenny would just be starting class right now. He'd catch her in an hour, when she had a break. 'Remind me to call Jenny when I get out of the Jefferson meeting.'

Althea was still shaking her head as she left his office. 'Oh, and Tommy,' she called, pausing at the door. 'You got something on your cheek. Newsprint or something. I'll get you a wet tissue to wipe it off. Must have been a *real* late night.'

Taking a breath, Bolden pulled the piece of paper with the drawing of the tattoo out of his pocket and put it on the desk. He wrote the words 'Crown' and 'Bobby Stillman' below it, then refolded the paper and put it in his pocket.

It was officially time to stop thinking about what had happened last night and get his head into the job.

'Althea,' he called. 'I'm due to fly down to DC tonight for that Jefferson dinner. Can you double-check my flight details? What time am I set to leave?'

As Bolden gathered his materials for the meeting, he looked around his office. It wasn't too big, maybe fifteen by ten, one of five lining this side of the forty-second floor. A window looked out over Stone Street, and directly into another office building. If he pushed his cheek to the glass, he could make out the East River. Pictures of Jenny, and some of his success stories at the Boys' Club, lined the shelves. There was Jeremiah McCorley, currently a senior at MIT, who, Bolden had learned the night before, had just been offered a fellowship at Caltech in Pasadena. Toby Matthews, who was playing base-ball on a full scholarship at the University of Texas at Austin, and an academic all-American. Mark Roosevelt, who was finishing his first year at Georgetown's School of Foreign Service, the finest diplomatic school in the world. Not bad for a bunch of foster kids from Harlem. Bolden kept in touch with them all, writing e-mails, sending care pack-ages, making sure they had plane tickets to get home for the holidays.

And then there was a picture of Bolden with one who hadn't made it out. Darius Fell. Chess cham-pion. Punt, Pass, and Kick finalist for the state of New York, big-time crack dealer, hardened criminal, and major-league gang banger. Darius was the one that got away. He was still out there braving it in the wild. Bolden gave him another year before he was dead or in prison.

To the business at hand . . . Jefferson Partners . . . Trendrite Corporation . . . a five-billion-dollar deal. Concentrate, Bolden.

He picked up a copy of the bound memorandum.

It was two inches thick. A code name was written on the cover, which was standard practice for deals involving publicly traded companies. The target company, Trendrite, was the nation's second-largest processor of consumer data, handling requests for more than a billion records a day. Whenever someone bought a car, Trendrite learned about it. Whenever someone sold a house, Trendrite got the details. Miss a mortgage payment, delinquent with credit-card debt, increase your life insurance, Trendrite made it its business to know that and more; specifically, your name, age, social security number, annual income, place of employment, salary history, driving record, and legal history, plus seventy other points of personal data. Every person in the company's database – and that meant ninety-eight percent of all Americans – was classified into one of seventy 'lifestyle clusters', among them 'Single in the City', 'Two Kids and Nowhere to Go', and 'Excitable Oldies'.

It sold this information to its customers, which included nine of the country's top ten credit-card users, nearly every major bank, insurance company, and automaker, and lately, the federal government, which used Trendrite's personal-profiling systems to check out airline passengers. And for all this, it earned three billion dollars a year in revenues, and four hundred and fifty million in profit.

The deal was Bolden's baby. He'd come up with the idea. He'd contacted the company. He'd pitched it to Jefferson. Supervised the road show. Overseen financing. Everything was all set to go. HW's fees were estimated to top a hundred million dollars. It would be his first big payday.

RM. Real money.

Just then, he spotted Sol Weiss's leonine gray head; the man was loping along at the far end of the hall. He was dressed in a double-breasted blue suit, a silk hankie overflowing his breast pocket, the unlit cigar leading the way. With him was Michael Schiff, the firm's CEO.

'Althea,' he called again. 'What about those flight times?'

He peeked his head out the door and saw her sitting at her desk, crying. 'What is it?' he asked, rushing to her side. 'What happened? Is it Bobby? Is he okay?'

But she refused to look at him. 'Oh, Thomas,' she sobbed.

Bolden laid a hand on her shoulder and was shocked when she knocked it away. He looked up. Weiss and Schiff, and two uniformed security officers, were powering down the hallway. Stone faces all around. It was impossible to mistake their intention. These guys were out for blood. He wondered what poor sucker had got his ass caught in the ringer this time.

'Tommy!' It was Sol Weiss, and he had his arm outstretched and his finger pointed directly toward him. 'We need to talk.'

Chapter 16

Five stories beneath the frozen Virginia landscape, Guilfoyle sat listening to the recording of Thomas Bolden's phone call to Jennifer Dance that had been made shortly after six o'clock that morning.

'Don't go,' the woman said. 'I'll take a day, too. Come over to my place. *I make it vorth your vhile, comrade.*'

'Can't do it,' replied Bolden.

'I need you. Come over. Now.'

'Jen, it's a big deal. People are coming in from D.C. There's no way I can miss it.'

'Okay, lunch then. I've got something to tell you, too.'

'Hint?'

'Never. But I'm warning you. I may hijack you afterwards.'

'If things go well with Jefferson, I may let you. Lunch. Twelve sharp.'

'Regular place?'

'Regular place. And you? Your arm? Only ten stitches?'

'How did you know?'

The recording ended.

Guilfoyle was seated at his stainless-steel desk on the upper level of the Organization's command and control room. The room was the size of a college lecture hall and bathed in dim blue light. Technicians manned broad computer consoles on three descending levels. All were men. All held PhDs from top universities in computer science, electrical engineering, or other related fields. All had worked for Bell Labs, Lucent, Microsoft, or a firm of equivalent stature before joining the Organization. The pay was equivalent. It was the toys that lured them, the prospect of doing pioneering work on the most advanced, and certainly the most secret, software array in history.

A dull rumble shook the floor as the air-conditioning kicked in. It might be thirty degrees up top, but the massive array of parallel-linked supercomputers combined with a lack of natural ventilation meant that temperatures were much higher down here.

'Do you want to hear it again?' a tech named Hoover asked, from his console.

'Thank you, Mr Hoover, but I think that's enough.' Guilfoyle drummed his fingers on the desk, his eyes glued to the crude drawing that had been found in Bolden's apartment. He sighed, and reluctantly admitted that Mr Pendleton had been right. Maybe a machine did know better than him. Three large screens occupied the wall in front of him. One showed a projection of a Manhattan city map. A sprinkling of blue pinlights spaced at even intervals from one another formed the outline of a bell covering the lower half of the map. Every few moments, the pinlights advanced along well-marked streets, like some type of newfangled electronic game. An array of three letters glowed beneath each pinlight. RBX. ENJ. WRR. Each pinlight represented one of his men, his location broadcast by an RFID chip (Radio Frequency Identification) implanted in the soft flesh of the upper arm. Besides the recipient's name, the RFID chip stored his blood type and full medical history.

In their midst, a sole red pinlight flickered faintly.

It was the red pinlight flashing at the corner of Thirty-second Street and Fifth Avenue that interested him. The light jumped erratically from block to block, then disappeared for a moment, only to reappear a few seconds later a half block away. The profusion of skyscrapers combined with the sheer volume of cellular traffic in Manhattan made it difficult to track the weak GPS signals emitted from a cell phone, or in Thomas Bolden's case, his BlackBerry personal assistant.

The regular place.

'Mr Hoover. Bring up a record of Bolden's credit-card transactions for the past twelve months please.'

'All of them? He's got a Visa, a Mastercard, and two American Express cards, one personal, one corporate.'

'Leave out the corporate Amex. We're not looking for a business expense.' In his short time with Bolden, Guilfoyle had pegged him as a straight-up individual. Not the type to put a lunch with his girlfriend on the company's tab.

'What are we looking for?' asked Hoover.

'Isolate all dining establishments in New York City south of Forty-eighth Street. Drill down to the time of charge. Bracket eleven A.M. to two P.M.'

Though the command and control room was cooled to sixty-eight degrees, he felt hot and unsettled. He removed a handkerchief from his pocket, and drew it across his forehead. A few moments later, a record of all the lunches Bolden had charged in downtown Manhattan flashed onto the screen. There were twelve transactions in all – fewer than Guilfoyle had expected – and they were spread across ten establishments.

Ten years earlier, the Organization had purchased the nation's largest processor of consumer loans: credit cards, mortgages, auto loans. Though it had sold the company in the meantime, it had not forgotten to install a 'back door' inside the firm's software to allow unfettered, real-time access to all their customer records.

'Let's go to Bolden's ATM records. I'd appreciate it if you'd map them.'

A minute passed. The blue and red pinlights disappeared, replaced by a sprinkling of green pinlights dotting lower Manhattan. Guilfoyle was quick to notice a cluster near Union Square.

'Bring up all restaurants on Union Square.'

Six lights appeared around the perimeter of Union Square Park.

'Did Bolden use his credit card to pay for lunch at any of these?' Guilfoyle asked.

'Negative.'

'Let's keep looking. Run through all stored phone communications since we began surveillance, ditto for e-mail, run the web addresses he's been frequenting.'

Hoover grimaced. 'That may take a while.'

'Make sure it doesn't. He's due to have lunch with Miss Dance in three hours and we're going to be there.'

When word of Sol Weiss's death, and more important, of Bolden's escape, had reached him, Guilfoyle had been reviewing Bolden's file with an eye to discovering how Cerberus had kicked him out as a Class 4 offender. Cerberus was the Organization's watchdog, a parallel-linked supercomputer programmed to search for clues indicating activity that might be detrimental to the cause. It drew from phone records, flight logs, insurance databases, credit histories, consumer profiles, bank logs, title companies, and many other repositories of sensitive information – all of it, officially, in the private domain.

Over the years, the Organization had purchased companies active in all these fields. And though it was the Organization's modus operandi to restructure them for a quick and profitable sale, it made every effort to build in a permanent access to the companies' databases. Only after 9/11, however, did the Organization begin to assemble these companies with any coherent strategy, and then it was at the government's request.

Following the terrorist attacks on the World Trade Center and the Pentagon, the United States Department of Defense established the Information Awareness Office to create a network of integrated computer tools that the intelligence community could use to predict and prevent terrorist threats. The program was officially named Total Information Awareness, but after a public outcry about government intrusion into its citizens' privacy and charges of Big Brother and an all-seeing, all-knowing Orwellian state, the name was changed to Terrorist Information Awareness. Its motto remained the same, however: *Scientia est potentia.* 'Knowledge is power.'

Terrorist Information Awareness brought together a host of technologies being developed to help law-enforcement authorities track down terrorists around the globe and effectively guess what their targets might be. Data mining, telecommunications surveillance, evidence evaluation and link discovery, facial- and gait-recognition software: these were a few of the tools harnessed. The hue and cry of civilian-privacy advocates caused the government to dismantle the program. The Organization volunteered its help to rebuild it.

In secret. No one, it argued, was better suited to the task. The government accepted.

The result was renamed Cerberus, after the vicious three-headed hound that guarded the entrance to Hades. And though the project remained ostensibly under government control, the Organization had made sure to build its own portal to access the system when necessary. While the threat to the United States came from abroad, the Organization had threats of its own to monitor, and these threats were domestic in nature. To charges that the Organization was using Cerberus to violate the average American citizen's sphere of privacy, it replied 'nonsense'. It was a case of the greater good and the informed minority.

The threat assessment concerning Thomas Bolden cited four hostile indicators. Three hostile indicators were needed to earn a positive reading – 'positive' meaning that the subject merited attention as a potential danger. Four indicators called for the establishment of an electronic-surveillance perimeter. And five mandated immediate intervention with a copy of the assessment to be sent automatically to Solutions.

Guilfoyle reviewed the indicators one at a time. The first was drawn from a cell-phone transmission between Bolden and a business associate. The second from an e-mail he had sent to a friend at another investment bank. The third from a scan of his residential computer's hard drive. The fourth from an intra-company memo he had forwarded to Sol Weiss discussing the firm's investment policies.

Highlighted in yellow were the keywords Bolden had used that had drawn Cerberus's attention. *Distrust. Conspiracy. Illegal operation. Trendrite. Antigovernmental. Monopolistic.* And, *Crown.* 'Evidence extraction', the process was called.

Finding clues hidden in disparate mediums and tying them together.

By isolating each indicator and reading it in context, Guilfoyle was able to identify where Cerberus had made its mistake. When Bolden had used the keywords near, or in conjunction with, the Organization's corporate name, Cerberus had drawn a false inference about a pending threat. It was a software program, after all. A powerful one, to be sure. But it couldn't be expected to reason out its programmer's mistakes. At least, not yet.

It was the last indicator, however, that left Guilfoyle stymied. The one taken from Bolden's residential phone bill. On three successive nights a week earlier, Thomas Bolden had placed calls from his home to a residence in New Jersey that was later discovered to have been used by Bobby Stillman. Guilfoyle double-checked the dates. There was no doubt that Stillman had been occupying the premises at that time. And yet, Guilfoyle was certain that Bolden had not been lying. Thomas Bolden did not know Bobby Stillman. Nor did he have a clue about Crown.

It was Guilfoyle's gift that he was able to discern with uncanny accuracy not only a person's intentions, benign or hostile, but also whether that person was lying or telling the truth. He had always been able to sense when a person was less than forthcoming, but it wasn't until his second year as a police officer in Albany, New York, that he'd learned to trust that sense and to hone it into a skill.

On that particular day, he and his partner were rolling in their police cruiser through Pinewood, conducting a routine neighborhood watch, when they noticed a homeless man dressed in a khaki trench coat, pantyhose, and combat boots, stomping along the sidewalk. There had been a complaint about a man matching his description harassing a woman out walking her dog. Stopping beside him, they rolled down the window and asked his name. At first, the man didn't respond. Like many homeless people, he appeared mentally ill and mumbled to himself constantly. His hair was long and unkempt. His beard was matted and scraggy. He continued walking, shooting them strange glances. There was no indication that he was armed or possessed of hostile intent. Until that date, there had never been an incidence of a street person or vagrant assaulting an Albany police officer. Albany was not New York City.

Guilfoyle, who was driving, called through the window for the man to stop. Finally, the man complied. Guilfoyle's partner opened his door and asked, 'What are you doing?' 'I've got something to show you guys,' the vagrant said. He approached the car, still mumbling and addressing the invisible personalities who peopled his world. He was smiling. Most people would have taken him for nothing more than a harmless nutcase. But when Guilfoyle looked into this man's eyes, he knew at once that he intended to kill the police officers. With no hesitation, Guilfoyle, aged twenty-three, drew his service revolver, forced his partner back against the seat, and fired twice into the homeless man's chest. When the vagrant collapsed to the ground, his trench coat fell open to reveal a jury-rigged flamethrower. The nozzle was threaded down the arm of his coat and cupped in his palm. In his other hand, he held a Zippo lighter. A search of the vagrant's belongings kept at the Catholic rescue mission turned up a journal in which he wrote about his desire to 'send cops back to hellfire'.

Two months later, Guilfoyle responded to a domestic-violence complaint. When they arrived at the address, however, the woman who had called was no longer there. Guilfoyle questioned her husband, who said that she had gone out for a drink. The man was calm and forthright, explaining that his wife was simply angry with him for gambling. Suspicious, Guilfoyle and his partner searched the apartment, but found no trace of the woman. The apartment was clean and in good order. There was no sign of a struggle, no evidence of mayhem. Yet, Guilfoyle was certain that the man had murdered his wife. He didn't know exactly why, just that his brief interrogation of the man had left him convinced. *He knew.*

Guilfoyle returned to the husband, and standing very close to him – close enough to see only his face and nothing beyond it, close enough to smell his breath, to register every twitch of his mouth, to see that his brown eyes were flecked with green – he asked where he had hidden his wife's body. The man's calm dissolved like a thunderclap. Breaking into tears, he led them to a closet in his bedroom where he had stuffed his wife's strangled, lifeless body into a steamer trunk.

Word of Guilfoyle's extraordinary talent spread quickly. In short order, he was promoted to detective and brought in to handle the more difficult interrogations. Behavioral scientists arrived from the state university at Binghamton to study his skills. They had him watch endless reruns of *To Tell the Truth*. Guilfoyle never failed to guess the impostor. They showed him copies of the FBI's 'Ten Most Wanted Criminals' circular and he was able to assign each the offense for which he was wanted. A team from DARPA (Defense Advanced Research Projects Agency) arrived to ask for his assistance with something they called the Diogenes Project, Diogenes being the ancient Greek who went from house to house shining a lantern in every man's face, seeking a truly honest man. For months, they worked with him to catalog the taxonomy of human expression. Together, they scoured medical texts and identified every distinct muscular movement that the face could make, a total of forty-three in all. But no matter how hard they tried, they could not teach the skill to others.

The human face was a canvas on which man painted his every thought and emotion. Some strokes were deft, lightning quick, others long and lingering. Look close enough, however, and you could see them all. A knitting of the brow, a tightening of the mouth, a narrowing of the eyes: Guilfoyle was able to process all of this instantaneously and know a man's state of mind. It was his gift.

And so he had known that Thomas Bolden was telling the truth.

Yet to believe that, Guilfoyle had to also believe that Cerberus had kicked out a 'false positive', in the parlance, meaning that the system had identified the wrong man. He could not do that. There was the matter of the phone calls Bolden placed to Stillman. If Bolden had called Bobby Stillman, he had to know her.

Guilfoyle fingered the drawing of the musket. In his mind's eye, he was looking at Bolden. The two were back in the room on the seventieth floor of Hamilton Tower. He traced every line of the man's face, recalled every twitch of his lips, the direction of his eyes. He decided that he very much wanted to speak with him again. He had a disconcerting feeling that for once, he may have been wrong, and that Thomas Bolden had bested him. He did not enjoy being made to look like an idiot.

*

'Hoover,' he called.

'Yes, Mr Guilfoyle?'

'How's it coming?'

'Slowly, sir. We have a lot of conversations to go through.'

'Hurry it up. We've got to get our men in place before he arrives.'

Grasping the paper with his left hand, he folded it dexterously into quarters and slipped it into his jacket pocket. As a boy, he'd practiced long hours to be a magician. He became adept at sleight of hand, and, when working alone, was able to master the most difficult illusions. Yet, everyone agreed that he was a terrible magician. One fault doomed him from the beginning. He couldn't smile. People preferred to watch his hands instead of his face.

Chapter 17

The crew pushed past Bolden into his office, all four of them. One of the uniformed security men closed the door and took up a position with his back against it.

'Tommy, please take a seat in that chair,' said Michael T. 'Mickey' Schiff, the firm's chief executive.

'I think I'd like to stand, Mickey. What's the deal?'

'I said take a seat. Your wishes are no longer a matter of concern to this firm.'

'Please, Tom,' said Sol Weiss. 'Take a seat. The sooner we're done here, the better.'

'Sure, Sol.' Bolden allowed the chairman to guide him to one of the armchairs normally reserved for guests. 'What's this about?'

'This is about you, mister,' said Schiff, every bit as aggressively as before. 'About your disgraceful predilections. About bringing dishonor upon the reputation of a venerable institution and shaming the man who gave you a chance to make a place for yourself.'

The CEO of Harrington Weiss was a slight man, wiry, and proud of his fitness, his skin tanned the color of polished oak. Schiff was the firm's Mr Inside, the ice-blooded technocrat who had overseen HW's successful forays into derivatives and the private equity market. As was his custom, he was dressed in a tailored navy chalk stripe with plenty of cuff showing. His hair was colored a brassy auburn. Bolden noticed that his gray roots were showing. Must have been a busy week.

'Stop it right there,' he said. 'I've never done a thing to hurt HW.' He appealed to Sol Weiss. 'What's he talking about?'

A crowd was gathering outside the office. Secretaries, assistants, and a smattering of executives formed a semicircle of aggrieved onlookers. At its center, her chin held high, stood Althea.

'Thomas, we have a situation here,' said Weiss, in his tacks-and-gravel baritone. 'Diana Chambers contacted us this morning to inform us about the misunderstanding that took place between you two last night.'

'What misunderstanding was that?' asked Bolden.

'The gist of her complaint is that you assaulted her in the men's room of the hotel last night after she refused to perform oral sex on you. I'm sorry to be so blunt.'

Schiff cut in impatiently. 'Is it your practice, Tom, to slap around women who won't have sex with you? Are you one of those freaks that needs to feel like he's in control to be a man?'

'Diana Chambers said what?' Bolden asked, dumbfounded. Like him, Diana Chambers worked as a principal at HW. She was a pretty, prim blonde, proud of being a Yalie, short and athletic with blazingly white teeth and brown eyes that bugged out when she smiled. She worked in Capital Markets so he saw her regularly. They were friendly, but not friends. 'It's not true. None of it. Not a word. I talked to Diana for maybe two minutes last night. I certainly didn't go into the men's room with her. I didn't ask her to have sex with me and I didn't hit her. Where is she? I can't believe she said this. I'd like to talk to her myself.'

'I'm afraid that's not possible,' said Sol Weiss. 'She's at the hospital.'

'At the hospital?'

'That punch you saw fit to give her left her with an orbital fracture,' said Schiff.

'This is nonsense,' said Bolden, looking into his lap, shaking his head.

'I wish we could say that we agree with you, Tom,' said Weiss. 'But we've got a sworn affidavit alleging your behavior. There are two detectives waiting downstairs to take you into custody.'

Schiff removed a photograph from a buff envelope and handed it to Bolden. 'This was taken last night at the battered-women's unit at Doctors' Hospital. Care to explain?'

Bolden examined the photo. It showed a close-up of a woman's face. Her left eye was swollen horribly, colored black and blue. There was no question it was Diana Chambers. The insinuation ... no, the *accusation* that he had done this incensed him. A lump of anger rose in his throat, choking him. 'I didn't do this. Christ, I'd never . . .'

'She swears you did,' said Sol Weiss. 'What can I do, Tom? My hands are tied. You know Diana. She's a good girl. I can't imagine her lying any more than I can you doing this to her.'

'But she *is* lying,' said Bolden.

'That'll be for a court to decide,' said Schiff. 'Now, you're going to have to leave the premises. Didn't you hear Sol? There are two detectives downstairs waiting to take you in.'

'Give me a break,' said Bolden. 'Sol, I was at your table last night. So was Jenny. I could barely move ten feet there were so many people stopping by. Did you see me talk to Diana Chambers?'

'Look, Tommy, it was a big place,' said Weiss.

'Did you see me talking to her?' Bolden demanded.

Weiss shook his head and grunted irritably. 'I like you, kid. You know that. But I don't have any choice but to go by what Diana's telling us. If it's nonsense, then we'll forget all about it. But, first, we have to get to the bottom of it.'

Bolden looked from one face to the next, then exhaled a long breath. Once he left the office, he'd never be back. HW wasn't a white-shoe firm; it was more like silk-stocking. The taint of wrongdoing was enough. Once word got out, Bolden would always be the guy who beat up Diana Chambers. His ability to attract business would effectively be nil. The mere charge was tantamount to industrial castration.

Sol was the one to deal with here. He was the boss. He'd come up from the streets. He'd know how Bolden was feeling. 'Did you talk to her?' he asked him. 'She told you this herself?'

'No, I did not,' said Sol. 'Her attorneys have contacted the firm. If it makes you feel any better, we've decided to place both you and Diana on paid leave until the matter's settled.'

'I can't take leave right now,' Bolden protested. 'We're about to close the Trendrite deal.'

'Jake Flannagan can take it.'

Bolden swallowed, the hairs on the back of his neck bristling. And his bonus? Would Flannagan take that, too? This was the biggest deal of his career they were talking about. 'This is crap!' he said, bolting out of his chair, throwing his arms in the air. 'Utter bullshit!'

Schiff stepped forward to deliver the coup de grâce. 'Miss Chambers's attorneys have informed us that she will be pressing criminal charges against you, and against the firm. Besides the events of last night, she's talking about some past violations that took place right in this office.'

'This is a mistake,' said Bolden, his eyes searching the office as if he might find the answer hidden in his books or papers. 'Diana must be covering for someone.'

'It's no mistake,' said Sol. Suddenly, he looked bored and annoyed, and Bolden could see that he was against him. 'Look, Tommy, let's do this nice and easy. Mickey's talked to the special victims unit of the police department and he's convinced them not to arrest you on the premises.'

'Arrest me? For what? I already told you I didn't do anything.'

'If you'll just gather your things and go downstairs . . .'

'I'm not going downstairs or anywhere else,' argued Bolden. 'I don't know what's going on . . . why Diana would make these insane accusations, but I'm not just going to stand here and take it. You've all known me for six years. Look at the work I've done at the firm. At the club. I'm not some kind of animal.' But when he looked at the two men, he met a stone wall. 'You have my word that I did not touch Diana Chambers.'

'Tommy, we've got the letters,' said Weiss. 'The lovebird stuff you and Diana were exchanging by e-mail.'

'There are no e-mails,' said Bolden. 'I've never written Diana Chambers a flirtatious e-mail in my life.'

Weiss shook his head, his mouth pinched uncomfortably. 'As I said, Tom, we have a record of your correspondence.'

'You have no such thing.'

All the while, Schiff had been holding a sheaf of

papers rolled up in his hands. Now, he raised the papers and extended them to Bolden. 'You're denying you wrote these?'

Bolden read through the e-mails. It was standard soap-opera script. I love you. I need you. Let's go screw in the washroom. Exactly what you'd expect from a pair of egocentric young bankers in love. 'I know what kind of software the firm uses,' he said. 'It records every keystroke of every computer in the place. If I wrote those records from my computer, it will show it. Time. Date. Everything. Show me the records.'

'There are ways around that—' said Schiff.

'Get an expert in here right now,' said Bolden, approaching Sol Weiss. 'Someone who can take apart my hard drive and tell us who hacked into it. Then we'll have some idea of who engineered this . . . this . . . setup. Come on, Sol. Put a stop to this. Someone's framing me.'

'Who?' Schiff cut in. 'Answer that. Who did all this? Who busted up Diana's face? Who wrote all those e-mails? Come on.'

Bolden wasn't sure how to go about describing his suspicions. Where to begin . . . what to say . . .

And in that instant, he lost them. Weiss's face clouded over. Schiff's brow tightened. Bolden's momentum was spent. The temperature in the room might as well have dropped ten degrees.

'Nobody's taking your computer apart,' said Schiff. 'We know that you were conducting a secret affair with Diana Chambers. You had a couple of drinks under your belt, you felt the blood running, so you took her to the bathroom. She didn't deliver the goods, so you belted her.' He turned to Sol Weiss. 'Come on, we've wasted enough time on this. It doesn't matter what Bolden says in here, anyway. We're all fucked. It's going to end up in court and the firm's reputation will be indelibly tarnished.'

Weiss laid a hand on Bolden's shoulder. 'Look, Tom, unfortunately everything Mickey's said is true. There is going to be a criminal complaint lodged against you and the firm. I, personally, would appreciate it if you'd allow these gentlemen to accompany you to the lobby.'

Bolden looked at the guards, and realized that he didn't recognize them. He, Thomas Bolden, who went out of his way to talk to every employee, to know their names, and a little about them, had never before laid eyes on these two hulks. They sure as hell weren't your average Argenbright employees. They weren't affable or easygoing. No weight problem, lousy vision, or snaggletoothed grins, here. These guys were pumped. They were fit. Like Wolf and Irish, they were capable.

'Who are they? I don't know them.'

'Come on, sir,' said one of the guards, reaching out for him. 'Let's do this the right way.'

Bolden shrugged off the hand. Belatedly, it came to him that this entire charade was an extension of last night's events. Guilfoyle was not finished with him. Bolden backed up a step. Suddenly, he was going on about what had happened the night before. The mugging, the ride to Harlem, the intense interrogation about subjects on which he was totally and blessedly ignorant. He pointed at his cheek, demanding that they all take a closer look. 'It's a powder burn. Someone tried to kill me. That's what this is about. It's about something called Crown. About some guy I never even heard of. Check their chests,' he said heatedly, pushing his way past Schiff toward the uniformed guards. 'They have tattoos. A musket. Look for yourselves.'

Sol Weiss clutched at Bolden's shoulder. 'Tommy, calm down. Get ahold of yourself. We're listening.'

'No, you're not,' said Bolden, turning on him, knocking Weiss's hand off his shoulder. 'You haven't listened to a word I've said. You've made up your minds and you're wrong.'

He hadn't meant to be so aggressive, but somehow Weiss lost his balance and toppled to the floor. The sixty-eight-year-old chairman of the last pure partnership on Wall Street uttered a plaintive cry and tumbled backward into the corner. A billionaire had been assaulted by a hysterical executive. A violent, unstable criminal had taken his hand to the head of the firm.

Bolden kneeled to help Sol Weiss to his feet. Mickey Schiff struggled to get past him and offer assistance to the fallen chairman.

A billionaire had been assaulted!

'Goddamn it,' said Schiff, over his shoulder. 'Get Bolden out of here. Now!'

One of the two guards, the one who'd done the talking, unsnapped his holster and drew his pistol. 'Mr Bolden. You will come with us now, sir.'

Until then, Bolden had kept his emotions under control. One look at the gun changed all that. They had missed him once, he told himself. They wouldn't miss him again. His escape had been a matter of dumb luck. No one had expected Bolden to be able to look after himself. The sole advantage he'd enjoyed was gone. He was sure that the men downstairs were not police officers, and that this had nothing to do with assaulting a woman. *Nothing happens without a reason.* It was about a setup. And in that instant, all his old talents came back to him in a rush: his distrust of authority, his reckless violence, his fine-tuned paranoia, and most important, his hard-earned instinct for survival.

Mickey Schiff stood next to him. Bolden grabbed him by the shoulders and shoved him into the guard holding the gun. Bolden followed close behind, keeping an arm on Schiff's back, sandwiching the guard between Schiff and the wall.

'Stop it, Tommy. No!' yelled Sol Weiss.

Pistol held high, the guard fought to slide past Schiff. Bolden clubbed the outstretched hand. The gun fell to the floor.

The second guard was working his pistol free.

Bolden knocked Schiff aside and scooped the gun off the floor, as Sol Weiss rushed to get in between the parties. 'Put your guns away,' he shouted, waving his hands. 'This is Tommy Bolden. I won't have it. I won't.'

'Gun!' shouted the first guard.

'Drop the weapon!' shouted the second guard, raising his pistol.

'Stop it! All of you!' shouted Weiss.

And then amid the disorder, a gunshot exploded.

A kaleidoscope of blood and gore splattered the window.

Sol Weiss turned unevenly. For a moment, he stood shaking, trembling violently, his mouth working like a fish's, a choking noise rising from him, his eyes dreamy, unfocused.

'Sol!' cried Bolden.

Weiss slid to the floor, a ribbon of blood streaming from the crater in the center of his forehead.

Chapter 18

Bolden shoved his way past the stunned onlookers into the hall. Past Schiff, past Althea, past the other decent, familiar faces he'd worked with for the past six years. No one said a word. No one tried to stop him. The silence lasted five seconds, before a woman screamed.

Bolden started to run. To his left, glassed-in offices like his own ran to the corner of the building. To the right, the floor was divided into cramped two-person work areas that housed the firm's analysts and associates. Between each was a small nook filled with filing cabinets, copying machines, and occasionally, a space for an executive secretary. The philosophy was to force employees at all levels out of their offices and into common spaces where they could work on projects together. Crosspollination, they called it.

Everyone on this side of the floor had heard the gunshot. Those that hadn't gathered outside Bolden's office were either standing or cowering by their desks. Every other person had a phone to their cheek. They knew the drill. Gunshot. Call 911. One more red-blooded American gone postal.

A few came after him, timidly at first. Seeing the guards in pursuit, several more joined the fray. Bolden could feel rather than see them. He wasn't taking time to look.

Damn you, Sol, he cursed silently. *You had no*

business acting the hero. What were you thinking getting between me and a man with a gun?

Turning a corner, he ran down the corridor that bisected the forty-second floor. The hallway was dimly lit. He passed the coatroom, the snack area with its array of upscale vending machines, the shoeshine closet, and finally, the washrooms. Whatever else happened, he knew that he would never work at Harrington Weiss again. He hadn't shot Weiss, but it didn't matter. Just like it didn't matter that he'd never laid a hand on Diana Chambers. The fact that Weiss was killed in his office was enough. Bolden was tainted.

Ahead, twin white doors separated the work area from the public area. He passed through them and emerged into the firm's reception.

By now, security had been notified and the elevators had been taken out of service. Every redcoat in the building would be waiting for him downstairs. An interior flight of stairs curved in a graceful spiral down to forty-one – the trading floor and the directors' fitness room. From forty-one, the stairs descended one more flight to the executive dining area. Harrington Weiss took up ten floors in all. Sol Weiss and the top brass were on forty-three. You could access the floor only by an internal elevator on forty-one and forty-two. From the lobby, you needed the proper key.

Bolden bounded down the stairs three at a time. Hitting forty-one, he bumped into two traders from the derivatives desk. 'Sol's been shot!' he said, breathlessly. 'Get up there. He needs help.'

The two men ran up the stairs and Bolden could hear shouts of confusion as they collided with his posse.

Forty-one was a universe unto itself. The trading floor was an unboundaried work area spanning the width of the building. Desks ran in parallel lines like yardage markers on a football field. Corps of traders sat, stood, argued, bantered, joked, and cajoled, but never loitered. No one ventured out of sight of their trading screens and their telephones. It was just after eight, so added to this mix was a wandering band of vendors, peddling breakfast burritos, energy bars, bagels, lox, fruit, and plenty of Red Bull and Diet Coke.

Bolden dived into the throng, running with his head down, his shoulders hunched. A few of his friends laughed at him, others pointed. Most paid him no attention whatsoever. They'd seen stranger things in their time.

The trading floor was organized according to instruments traded. Skirting the edge of the floor, he passed the desks for US stocks, foreign stocks, then currencies. Bonds were divided up among corporates, convertibles, or 'converts', and municipals, or 'munis'. Spotting Bolden, several men called out to him, but Bolden didn't answer. An old saw said that if a guy hadn't found a living trading bonds, he'd be driving a truck on the Jersey Turnpike. From the foul language shouted at Bolden, you'd think it still held true. In fact, ninety percent of the men and women on the floor held MBAs from Ivy League schools.

Bolden ran past the derivatives desk, where no one paid him any heed at all. The derivatives team was made up of the firm's quant jocks and rocket scientists. MBAs weren't the norm, but PhDs in quantum physics and pure mathematics. Human life forms didn't register for these guys. Just numbers. Most of them were Indian, Chinese, or Russian. So many, in fact, that their patch of the woods had been dubbed the UN.

The good thing about trading was that the hours

were civilized. You started at seven and went home at five. The bad thing was that you started at seven and went home at five *without leaving the trading floor*. Lunches outside the building were a rarity. Many a trader had passed nearly every daylight hour of a thirty-year career walking the same ten-by-ten square of carpeting. Bolden preferred his fourteen-hour days, weekly plane travel to visit target companies, and twice yearly boondoggles with clients to St Andrews, the island of Nevis, or helicopter skiing in the Bugaboos. That life was gone, he reminded himself.

Glassed-in offices reserved for department heads lined the interior wall. To a man, the executives were engaged on the phone or in meetings. Just then, he spotted Andy O'Connell, who ran 'converts', dropping his phone and rushing out of his office. O'Connell stood in the center of the corridor, waving his arms as if to distract a charging bull. 'I've got him,' he shouted, pushing his glasses up on the bridge of his nose. Bolden lowered his shoulders and straight-armed the slight trader. O'Connell tumbled to the carpet.

News of Sol Weiss's shooting had hit the floor like a tidal wave. One second, no one knew a thing. The next, a wild silence leveled the place, everyone sharing shocked looks, whispering, holding back tears while reaching for their phones to confirm it was true.

Bolden wasn't sure where he was going, only that running was preferable to stopping. Stopping meant getting caught. And getting caught was not an option for an innocent man. He needed distance. Distance and time.

'Thomas!' It was Mickey Schiff. The man had a voice like a bull-horn. He stood back a ways, by the corridor leading to the elevators. He placed his hands on his hips. 'Come now, Tom. Don't run!' The stance said it all. The elevators were blocked off. The entrances to and from the building secure.

Bolden turned long enough to meet Schiff's eyes, and read the anger painted in them. Ahead, a wood-paneled wall partitioned the floor. The directors' gymnasium sat behind it. He followed the wall to the glass doors that led to the gym. Inside, two young women seated at the reception desk looked at him in surprise.

'Sir, may I help you? Please, sir . . . you can't . . .'

Bolden skirted the desk and found himself in the main exercise area. He'd never been in the directors' gym. For all the talk about 'crosspollination', there were strict rules about mixing with the proles. A row of Lifecycles occupied one half of the room, parked next to the floor-to-ceiling window. In case the view toward Battery Park and the Statue of Liberty wasn't inspiring enough, each bike had a television. Every TV was on and tuned to CNBC or Bloomberg Television.

Running machines occupied the left-hand side of the room. Treadmill after treadmill after treadmill at ten grand a pop, and not a soul to be found. He ran to the end of the floor. A second room housed a fully equipped weight room. It, too, was empty. He slowed to check for an exit, then moved down the corridor. He negotiated the locker room, steam room, checked inside two massage rooms. A clock on the wall read 9:05.

'Sir, please . . .'

He turned to face one of the attendants. 'Is there a stairwell?' he asked, hands on his knees, fighting for breath. 'I need to get downstairs.'

'Yes, of course.' She pointed to an unmarked white door a few feet away. 'But where are you going?'

Bolden opened the door and ran down the stairs. A dim light burned overhead. The staircase descended one flight before coming to a dead end. Bolden emerged into the executive kitchen.

Like any self-respecting bank, HW maintained its own kitchen. Or two kitchens, to be exact. There was a cafeteria on thirty-eight, and the dining room on forty that served lunch for directors and above, and catered formal gatherings. Smaller, more intimate rooms existed on forty-three, for those occasions when secrecy was of the utmost importance.

A few chefs were unpacking the morning's deliveries. Otherwise, the place was empty. Settling to a brisk walk, Bolden made his way through the stainless-steel counters, searching for a service entrance. He'd never seen a chef outside the kitchen, so he knew that they must have their own entry. He checked the pantry, then the meat locker. He came to a sliding door built into the wall. He pushed it open to reveal a dumbwaiter. The space was tight, but he might fit inside. He leaned his weight on it and the tray dipped perilously. He stepped back and looked to either side of him. A stainless-steel door opened to the garbage chute. He looked inside. It was a long way down and pitch black.

And then he saw it. Across the room was a fire alarm, a red metal box with a white T-pull.

Since 9/11, the firm had practiced evacuating the building twice a year. Every floor had its assigned fire marshal. When the alarm was activated (silently), everyone knew to gather in lines at the elevator and calmly leave the building. Once downstairs, each floor would make their way to a preordained meeting point one block from the building. Roll was called and when all floors were accounted for, the firm trooped back into the building. No one joked. No one complained. Fire alarms were serious business.

'Danny, search the area. Hey, chef, you seen anyone come through here? You did? Where'd he go? Thank you.'

Bolden heard the voices echoing inside the kitchen. His eyes darted from the alarm to the entry. Dashing across the room, he pulled the alarm. Immediately, water sprayed from the overhead nozzles. A siren buzzed and the wall-mounted strobes began to flash. Bolden rushed back to his spot. Grabbing a stack of plates, he threw them into the dumbwaiter, then pressed the lift button. He stepped to the left, pulled open the garbage chute, and climbed inside. The door slammed shut behind him. The chute was four feet by three, stamped from reinforced aluminum. Like a climber negotiating a couloir, he wedged his feet against opposite walls. Every few seconds, he slipped. An inch. Two inches. The darkness was total. The chute might drop to the basement.

'Security says the alarm was pulled in the kitchen.' It was Schiff again, and closer. 'Fan out, gentlemen.'

Footsteps echoed above Bolden's head. His hands were slippery with sweat and exertion. He tensed his muscles, but pushing too hard was as bad as not pushing hard enough. He slipped again.

'Mr Schiff, the dumbwaiter's going up.'

'Say again?'

'Bolden's in the dumbwaiter. Goes to forty-three, that's it.'

Schiff shouted for his men to go to forty-three.

Bolden held his breath. He waited a minute, then inched his way up. His right shoe caught and came loose. He struggled to hold it, but a moment later, it tumbled into the darkness. Reflexively, he jammed his foot against the wall, but the sock was nearly worn through.

Bolden felt himself going. Inch by inch. Falling. In desperation, he reached for the sill of the entry. His fingers grasped only air. He dropped in stages, four inches, six, twelve, gathering speed. He pressed his palms to the wall, but his palms bounced off. Suddenly, he was in free fall, his stomach pressed high in his chest. A moment later, his feet hit something soft. He landed in a pile of rancid garbage. Yesterday's meals. He kicked at all four walls. A door opened and he stepped into the custodian's chambers.

Thirty-nine was not officially a floor. No elevator stopped there. It was a floor between floors, a technical work space crammed with over three thousand miles of cable and wire from the trading floor, servers, mainframes, Liebert air conditioners to keep the firm's IT infrastructure operating at a perfect sixty-four degrees, and most important, an uninterruptible power supply.

He looked around the cramped foyer, walls on two sides. A service elevator faced him.

Bolden waited two minutes before pressing the call button.

Over a thousand people crammed the lobby and the promenade that surrounded the building. Bolden exited the freight elevator and walked into the milling masses. He let the crowd dictate his pace, never hurrying, never pushing, content to keep his head lowered and let the flow carry him. Nearby, there was a commotion. One of the downstairs security guards pushed past him, then abruptly stopped and took a step back.

'You Thomas Bolden?'

'No,' said Bolden. 'Jack Bradley.'

The guard stared at him a second longer. Bolden was just another white face. 'All right, Mr Bradley,' he said. 'You go ahead, sir.'

A minute later, Bolden passed through the massive glass doors.

The temperature had dropped further. The air crackled with cold. The day was gray and frigid.

Chapter 19

His name was Ellington Fiske, and he stood beneath a driving rain in front of the Ronald Reagan Building at the corner of Pennsylvania Avenue and Fourteenth Street. Rain funneled off the hood of his poncho and onto his shoes, it sluiced from his shoulders, and dripped from the ends of his sleeves. Though the word 'Police' was stenciled in block letters upon his back, he was, in fact, a member of the United States Secret Service. The assistant director for National Special Security Events, he was in charge of all security measures surrounding the inauguration of the forty-fourth President of the United States.

Fiske strode into the center of the street. He was a small man, standing five feet seven inches in his brogues, and wiry; 141 pounds according to his wife's digital scale. He looked both ways, careful to avoid being run over by a piece of heavy machinery. Though Pennsylvania Avenue had been closed for nine hours, the four-lane boulevard was a hive of activity. Forklifts rumbled across the sidewalk, removing the more than three hundred concrete casements that lined the street in front of any federal building. Teams of laborers threw up scaffolding to erect bleachers that would line the parade route. The air rang with hammers knocking home bolts and pinions. A few feet from Fiske, a large crane ground to a halt. Chains were attached to a traffic signal positioned in the center island. The crane's arm lurched skyward. The traffic signal was uprooted and deposited onto the flatbed of a waiting truck. The process was to be repeated twenty times up and down Pennsylvania Avenue by four o'clock that afternoon.

In the space of twenty-four hours, the length of Pennsylvania Avenue from Fourth Street to the White House would be transformed from one of the busiest thoroughfares in Washington, DC, to a 'sanitized', or 'threat-free', parade route with seating for fifty thousand spectators and standing room for several hundred thousand more. The rain would dampen the crowds, but not by much.

Staring east toward the Capitol, Fiske felt a shiver rustle his spine. It was not from the cold. Fiske had dressed for the occasion and wore his best thermal underwear and heated shoes. It was a warning. *Be on your guard.*

Senator Megan McCoy was the first woman to be elected to the office of President of the United States. Though she'd won in a landslide, there were all too many people not yet ready to have a woman govern them. They were the same kind of people who didn't want a black man on the Supreme Court, or Ellington J. Fiske as the third-ranked official in the Secret Service. In the run-up to the event, Fiske and his deputies had questioned and detained three times the usual number of nutcases boasting about their plans to kill the President.

There was more to it than that. Fiske had a feeling something was up. He'd run over the plans a hundred times. A thousand. Still, he was certain he was missing something. Maybe he always felt that way before a big event. It would go a long way toward explaining how the son of a North Carolina garbageman had risen to so high a position by the age of forty-four.

A column of trucks drove past, dousing Fiske with a curtain of water. He swore audibly, but restrained himself from raising a fist. The trucks were loaded with scores of waist-high iron barricades to be placed exactly three feet from the sidewalk. Other barricades would be placed one block to the rear of either side of the parade route, thus creating an access-controlled perimeter. Nine 'choke points' would regulate entry into the parade area. At each, spectators would pass through a magnetometer and have their belongings searched. An additional six choke points would regulate entrance for those holding tickets to the White House reviewing stands.

Fiske walked over to a cluster of police officers huddled inside a covered forecourt of the Reagan Building. One by one he checked their credentials. 'If you control the credentials, you control the event.' That was Fiske's working motto. To that end, every law-enforcement agent assigned to the inaugural had been checked and double-checked prior to receiving a color-coded pass that not only indicated his branch of service, but also governed access to the varied function areas.

Though officially the Secret Service acted as agency-in-charge, it was hardly alone in its efforts. The FBI, the Metropolitan Police Department, the US Capitol Police, the United States Park Police, the army, and the Presidential Inaugural Committee all held jurisdiction over some or all parts of the inaugural route, or the Capitol building, where the President was to be sworn in at noon, Thursday.

It was not, however, the professionals he was worried about.

An event of this magnitude required bringing in hundreds of temporary employees. Of these, some were retired cops, some event personnel, some volunteers, and some private security companies. If he had less control over this group, he made sure they stayed farthest away from government officials he was paid to protect.

Just then, a navy blue Suburban, doors emblazoned with the seal of the Secret Service, drove up. Fiske climbed inside.

'How are things coming, chief?' asked Larry Kennedy, his number two, a beefy redhead from Boston.

'Colder than a witch's tit out there,' said Fiske, shaking the rain off him like a wet cat. 'What's this I hear about an electrical malfunction?'

'A mike on the podium shorted out. We've got some techies coming in to take a look at it.'

'The presidential podium?'

Kennedy nodded, seeing a storm far worse than the one pounding them at that moment brewing in Fiske's eyes.

'Who are they?'

'Not to worry, chief. They're all squared away. They're with Triton.'

Fiske did not like that answer. 'Triton Aerospace? I thought they made missiles. What the hell they doin' messing with my podium?'

'Missiles, anti-aircraft systems. Hell, sir, they make everything. They made the commo system we got in this car. A Triton Five-Fifty. Guess they make PA systems, too.'

'I don't like it,' said Fiske, scowling. 'Get me over there.'

'Your party, boss.'

'Say that again.' He looked at Kennedy. 'Tell me you brought me some coffee!'

Chapter 20

It was nine o'clock, and the senior executives of Jefferson Partners had gathered in James Jacklin's spacious office for the morning meeting.

'Morning, Guy,' said Jacklin, Jefferson's founder and chief executive, as he crossed the office. 'Morning, Mike. Everyone here? Good. Let's get started.'

'Bob's in New York,' said Guy de Valmont. 'This is it, then.'

'So he is. Well, I'd say we have a quorum nonetheless.' Jacklin descended a step to the seating area. 'Today's the day,' he said. 'Dinner starts at eight. I want all of you there a little early. We don't want our guests wandering around like lost sheep. And black tie across the board. I don't want to see any white dinner jackets. We're not showboats. Spread the word.'

Jacklin sat down in his lacquered Princeton chair, the only one in the office that didn't torture his back. 'So, then . . . tell me, people, everyone's clients coming?'

'Coming? We're overbooked,' said de Valmont, the firm's cofounder, a tall, elegant man of fifty. 'We'll be sending half of President McCoy's cabinet to the inauguration with a hangover. It's the hottest ticket in town.'

'Should be,' said Jacklin. 'We're serving enough caviar to gut the Caspian Sea for a decade.'

Fifty pounds of beluga caviar, to be exact, grumbled Jacklin, followed by mixed summer greens, capellini with shaved white truffles (another mind-numbingly expensive delicacy), dry-aged prime New York steak, and chocolate mousse. When his back had forced him to give up golf, he'd taken up cooking instead. He'd planned the menu himself.

The dinner was to take place at his estate in McClean, Virginia. Officially, it was a fund-raising affair. For the first time in the private equity industry, a company had raised ten billion dollars in a single fund. (Or at least said they had. The fact was that they were more than a billion short. Jacklin had to do everything in his power to close the gap by the time supper was put on the table.) The press had gotten wind of the proceedings and dubbed it the Ten Billion Dollar Dinner.

Jacklin smiled inwardly. You couldn't buy that kind of publicity.

A short, brown-skinned man in a blue jacket, gold braided epaulets at his shoulders, approached. 'Yes, Mr Jacklin, may I take your order for breakfast?'

'Thank you, Juan. I'll have an egg-white omelet, with some smoked salmon, and a rasher of that applewood bacon. Crispy. Very crispy.'

'Mrs Jacklin tells me your doctor said, "No bacon." Your blood pressure, sir. Too much salt.'

Jacklin took his Filipino steward's arm and patted it gently. 'To hell with him, Juan. A man's got to live a little. Oh, and don't forget my Bloody. You know how I like it. It's going to be a busy day.'

'Yes, Mr Jacklin. Coffee? Chef has a new blend from Sumatra. Very good.'

'Fine idea, Juan. There's a good boy.'

Jacklin's office was divided into two functional areas, and ran in an L shape anchored by the northeast corner of the twentieth floor. The working quarters ran up the north side of the building, and comprised his desk, an ornate mahogany monstrosity that had belonged to Georgie Patton when he'd been governor of Bavaria following the second war, chairs for partners or principals, and shelves adorned with the dozens of de rigueur tombstones. 'Tombstones' were Lucite trophies commemorating completed deals. Somewhere in there, he'd placed photographs of his family. Sneaking a look, he'd be damned if he could find them.

His fellow partners had taken up their spots in the 'guest quarters', and sat on the comfortable, low-slung couches that faced one another over a travertine coffee table. There was Joe Regal, who'd spent thirty years at Langley in operations. And Rodney Bridges, who'd done twenty years as a Wall Street lawyer before jumping the fence and playing top cop at the Securities and Exchange Commission, and who had now jumped back. There was Michael Remington, recently retired Secretary of State, and aide to three presidents.

And then there was Jacklin, himself. The pictures adorning his wall counted as an illustrated record of his rise to power. There was Jacklin, age twenty-four, fresh from Naval Flight at Pensacola on the deck of the *Enterprise* in the middle of the South China Sea backed by his A-6 Intruder. There he was, at thirty-two, being sworn in as congressman, and ten years later, taking office as Secretary of Defense. More recent pictures showed him recreating with the last three presidents – playing tennis, fishing for striped bass, and attending an event at the Kennedy Center. The pictures never failed to elicit the requisite oohs and aahs. Yes sir, ole J. J. was connected.

If there were a class system to every industry,

Jefferson belonged to the aristocracy of finance. 'Private equity' was just the newest name for an old game. The English called it merchant banking way back when Britannia ruled the seas, and the East India Company owned everything worth having. Junius Morgan, J. P.'s father, had perfected the game and brought it back with him from London. Jacklin had helped tweak it, introducing the concept of 'leverage' to give the investor more bang for his buck. Twenty-five years earlier, when Jacklin set up shop, Jefferson was called a leveraged buyout firm, or LBO for short. And the tone used was more fitting for freebooters and buccaneers than royalty.

Time, and an unrivaled track record of success, had tempered any criticism. Since its founding, Jefferson Partners had invested some $185 billion in over three hundred deals, and delivered returns averaging a phenomenal twenty-six percent per year. Ten million dollars invested with Jefferson back at the beginning was worth a billion-two today. By contrast, the same amount invested with the Dow Jones Industrial Average would have brought you barely $200 million. Chump change.

Pension funds, college endowments, corporate treasurers, and the larger family trusts comprised the backbone of Jefferson's clientele. For years, they had fairly begged to invest their money with Jefferson. There was a $100 million minimum and the line started at the door.

The last years, however, had seen a surge in the number of private equity firms. With the market in the doldrums, investors began seeking out 'alternative instrument classes' where their dollars could work harder. Foreign markets? Too risky, and who could forget Russia in '98? Derivatives? One word:

'longtermcapital'. Then there was Jefferson, quietly buying and selling companies, not making any waves, and all the while raking in the chips. What had everyone been thinking? The answer had been there all along.

From the outside, private equity looked like an easy way to make a buck. After all, what did it take? A few smart guys with a little experience and a Palm filled with the names of their nearest and dearest. Drum up some money, find an undervalued company, do a little pruning, and you were off to the races. Best of all, there was no need to have the costly infrastructure of a bank behind you. Ideas were the equity investor's capital. Brainpower. Savvy.

It only got better from there. The profit structure was set up to reward those with the ideas. This was no fifty-fifty split. Most funds promised a certain return on the clients' investments. They called this return the hurdle rate. Usually, it stood at around twenty percent. While the return wasn't guaranteed, Jefferson could not take a profit itself until it had paid its investors their twenty percent.

The rule was that once the hurdle rate had been met, and the clients paid out, the rest was divvied up according to an eighty-twenty split, with the equity firm getting the lion's share. What made this all the more irresistible was that the private equity firm, or financial sponsor, as they were referred to within the industry, put up the least amount of money, usually just five percent of the purchase price.

Say a company cost one billion dollars. The equity firm would put twenty percent down and use the services of a friendly bank to finance the remaining eighty percent through a debt underwriting. But look closer at the twenty percent, or two hundred million dollars, that the equity firm pledged. Of that amount, $160 million, or eighty percent, was paid out of the fund. The firm, itself, chipped in just forty million dollars of its partners' money. Come time to sell that lump of coal turned diamond, it was the firm's turn to shine.

If in a year, they sold the company for two billion dollars, the profit would be divided up thusly: investors in the fund would receive their investment back plus the twenty percent on top of it, a total of approximately $192 million. They would then receive another twenty percent of the remaining $968 million, or $193 million, bringing their grand total to $386 million earned on an investment of $160 million. In one year! A home run, to be sure. But it was nothing compared to what the private equity fund earned.

The remaining eighty percent of the $968 million profit, some $774 million, less twenty or thirty million dollars for fees to investment banks, lawyers, and accountants, flowed directly into the partners' pockets. Remember, the equity firm only put up forty million dollars of its own money. One year later, they wrote themselves a check for $774 million, and, of course, another forty million for the money they'd invested originally. These were profits on a biblical scale.

Jefferson had kept its position as an industry leader by virtue of its record, and its constant drive to close bigger and bigger funds. A few years back, one had topped out at five billion dollars, making it the first to be called a mega-fund. Tonight, they would gather to toast Jefferson Capital Partners XV, which was set to close with over ten billion dollars committed. No one had thought of a name yet for a fund that big.

*

'A word?'

Guy de Valmont took Jacklin by the elbow and led him to a corner of the office. 'See the article in this morning's *Journal*?'

'No,' said Jacklin. 'Didn't get a chance yet.'

'It's about Triton. It claims that if the appropriations bill doesn't pass, Triton will have to declare Chapter Eleven.'

Jacklin tugged at his chin. Triton Aerospace was a manufacturer of anti-aircraft systems that Jefferson had purchased eight years earlier. Eight years was an eternity in private equity. Speed was the name of the game. Buy a company, turn it around, ratchet up the free cash flow, then sell the thing. That was the ticket. Jefferson's average holding period of four years led the industry.

'Company's really in the shitter. We're never going to find a buyer unless that ass Fitzgerald signs off on that bill.'

'That ass Fitzgerald' was Senator Hugh Fitzgerald, chairman of the Senate Appropriations Committee, and the bill being bandied about was the $6.2 billion Emergency Defense Funding Bill, of which $270 million was earmarked for the Hawkeye Mobile Air Defense Units manufactured by Triton.

Jacklin gazed down at the Potomac. In the sodden, gray morning, the river looked lifeless, dead. He thought of the dinner planned that evening, the care and preparation expended to ensure that it was the event of a lifetime. Not to mention the expense. Truffles. Caviar. Peter Duchin's big band was setting them back a hundred thousand dollars alone. Word that one of Jefferson's companies was due to declare Chapter 11 would be a fly in the soup. A goddamned hairy Texas horsefly! Jacklin tightened his hand into a fist. He'd be damned if Hugh Fitzgerald would single-handedly shut down Triton.

'I'm due to testify on the bill later this morning,' he said, with a glance over his shoulder. 'I'll have a word with the senator afterwards, and see if I can't convince him to recommend its passage.'

'Fitzgerald? Good luck, J. J. The man's left of Gandhi.'

'I know. I know,' said Jacklin, with a wave of the hand. 'But, the senator and I go way back. Just a matter of having him reconsider his career options. He's seventy-four years old, after all. Time he did something else with his life.'

'And if he doesn't?' De Valmont yanked out his silk pocket square and began to carefully refold it.

'I'm sure we can find a way to convince him. Either with a carrot or a stick.'

De Valmont nodded, but his eyes said he wasn't convinced.

Jacklin returned to the center of his office and sat down in his Princeton chair. It wouldn't be easy, he admitted, but it could be done. It was no coincidence that many of the senior partners at Jefferson had served in high government positions. Some called it access capitalism. J. J. Jacklin preferred 'good business'.

'Gentlemen,' he called to his partners. 'Shall we get down to brass tacks?'

Chapter 21

Thomas Bolden sat in the back of the taxi, his cheek pressed to the cold metal doorframe. Traffic moved in fits and spurts. The sky had hardened to a steely gray, the clouds fused into a solid, darkening wall. The taxi came to a halt. Pedestrians hurried along the wet sidewalks, one eye for the sky wondering when the hesitant snowflakes would yield to the real McCoy.

Bolden glanced at his lap. His right hand trembled as if palsied. *Stop*, he ordered it, silently, but the shaking didn't lessen. He took a breath and placed his left hand on top of it, then stared back out the window.

Until now, it had all been a terrible mistake. The mugging, his abduction and interrogation, the botched attempt to kill him. He'd been willing to consign all of it to the trash. Guilfoyle had the wrong man. It was that simple. Yet, as they drove up Fifth Avenue, his hand shaking, his eyes aching in their sockets, his trousers stained with cooking grease and yesterday's veal piccata, he realized that he'd been wrong. It didn't matter if he could forgive and forget. They would not.

'They' had followed him into his workplace.

'They' had gotten to Diana Chambers.

'They' had killed Sol Weiss.

It didn't matter that he had no knowledge of 'Crown' or a man named Bobby Stillman. The fact that he knew of them was enough.

'They' would not go away. Not now, Bolden told himself. Not ever.

He thought of Jenny.

If Diana Chambers was fair game, she might be next.

'Driver,' he said, tapping his knuckles on the Plexiglas screen that divided the cab. 'Take me to Fourteenth Street and Broadway. The Kraft School. There's a twenty in it if you can make it in ten minutes.'

Chapter 22

Of course, they couldn't stop talking about the mugging.

'Calm down, you guys,' said Jennifer Dance. She sat on the front of her desk, legs dangling. 'One at a time. Remember, once someone else starts talking, keep your thoughts to yourself until they've finished.'

'Yo, Miss Dance.' A tall, fleshy Hispanic boy with a crew cut and a green tear tattooed at the corner of his eye stood up.

'Yes, Hector, go ahead.' Then, to the rest of the class: 'It's Hector's turn. Everyone give him your attention.'

'Yeah, like shut up,' added Hector, with real venom, casting his eyes around him. 'So, Miss Dance, like I'm wondering, if it was this razor-sharp knife, why didn't it cut right through your arm? I mean, like deep, like you guttin' a cat or somethin'.' He shot his buddy a glance. 'Ten stitches, man. I could do better than that.'

'Thank you for your comment, Hector, but I think I've already answered that. I don't know why he didn't hurt me worse. Just lucky, I guess.'

' 'Cuz you good-lookin',' a voice rumbled from the back of the room. 'Them boys wanted to slam yo' ass.'

Jenny stood and walked briskly down the aisle. It was a normal-sized classroom, one student per desk, blackboards running the length of each wall, map cartridges she'd never even thought of using, hanging behind her desk. She stopped in front of a hulking young man seated in the last row.

'That's enough, Maurice,' she said firmly.

Maurice Gates shrugged his massive shoulders and dropped his eyes to the floor as if he didn't know what the big deal was about. He was a huge kid, well over six feet, at least 220 pounds, braided gold necklace hanging outside his football jersey (in defiance of school rules against jewelry), his baseball cap turned halfway to the back.

'Jes' the truth,' he said. 'You a good-lookin' woman. Wanted to get him some gash. 'At's all. Know'd you'd like it, so he didn't want to mess you up real bad.'

'Stand up,' said Jenny.

Maurice looked up at her with sleepy eyes.

'Stand up,' she repeated, softer this time. The classroom was all about control. Lose your temper and you'd already lost the battle.

'Yes ma'am.' Maurice rose to his feet with enough moans and grimaces to do Job proud.

'Mr Gates,' she said, 'women are not bitches. They are not "ho's", or "gashes". Is that clear? We, females, do not live in a constant state of arousal. And if we did, we wouldn't require the attentions of a crude, chauvinistic musclehead like yourself.'

'You go, girl,' said one of the students in the back row.

Maurice shifted on his feet, his face a blank, as Jenny continued. 'You have been in my class for two weeks now,' she said, standing toe-to-toe with him. 'At least once a day, I have asked you to refrain from using offensive language. If I can't teach you algebra in this classroom, I would, at least, like to teach you respect. Next time I have to waste a

second of the class's time keeping your butt in line
– *one second* – I'll have you kicked out of school.'
She delivered the last part on her tiptoes, her mouth
a few inches from Mr Maurice Gates's ear. 'Your
attendance here is a condition of your release from
Rikers. So unless you want a ticket right back there,
you'll sit down, shut up, and keep your comments
about the superior sex to yourself.'

Jenny stared into the boy's eyes, seeing hate flare
in the way his eyelids twitched, sensing his anger
at being humiliated in front of his classmates. The
kids called him Mo-fo, and they used the words
with all due deference. Make no mistake, he was an
angry, volatile young man. His case files pretty
much came out and said that he'd been a player in
several unsolved homicides. But Jenny couldn't
worry about that. She had a class to teach. Order to
keep. She owed the kids that much. 'Sit down,' she
said.

For a second or two, Maurice Gates remained
standing. Finally, he bunched his shoulders and sat.

The hush in the classroom lasted ten seconds.

'We were discussing what an appropriate
punishment might be for mugging someone,' Jenny
said, retaking her place at the head of the class.
'Remember, I got my watch back. All I got was a
little cut and very scared.'

'You popped one of 'em, too.'

'Yes, I did,' said Jenny, adding a little swagger to
her step. 'A right hook.' A few of her knuckles were
swollen and painful to the touch.

She checked the clock. Nine-thirty. Her school
planner called for her to teach math and English
before recess. Math was a goner. She still had hopes
for salvaging English. She was reading the class
'The Most Dangerous Game', the story where a mad
hunter sets men loose on his private jungle island

to track down and kill. There were plenty of metaphors in the story that the kids could relate to, especially at the end when 'the Man' gets his comeuppance.

'Twenty years,' someone shouted. 'Sing Sing.'

'Nah, ten, but no parole.'

'Ten years?' asked Jenny. 'For grabbing a watch and giving someone a little cut? Don't you guys find that kind of harsh?'

'Hell no.' It was Maurice Gates. 'How else you think they gonna learn?'

'Excuse me, Maurice, do you have a comment?'

The supersized teenager nodded. 'You got to teach those muscleheads a lesson,' he said, eyes boring into Jenny. 'You got to be tough. No mercy. Unnerstand? Less'n you want 'em to come for you in the middle of the night. They mad enough, they even cut you in your own bed. Door locked. Don't matter. They gonna get in, they want to bad enough. Take care of bidness. You be sleepin' alone. They gonna get in. Cut you good. Ain't that right, Miss Dance? You got to put 'em away.'

Jenny held his eyes, wondering if she might have to go to security on this one. *Don't you dare come after me*, her look said. *I can take care of myself.*

'Ten years,' said Hector, banging his feet on the ground.

In no time, the class raised a chant. 'Ten years. Ten years.'

'Enough!' said Jenny, patting the air with her hands. She looked from face to face. Hector had robbed a bodega in his neighborhood. Lacretia had gotten into 'the life' when she was twelve. For the most part, they were a decent bunch of kids. They weren't angels, but she hoped she could just drive home what was right and what was wrong.

'Miss Dance?'

'Yes, Frankie.'

Frankie Gonzalez walked up alongside her and put his head on her shoulder. He was short, and skinny, and rubbery, the class runt and self-appointed clown. 'Miss Dance,' he said again, and she knew he was making his wiseass smile. 'Yo, I kill them muthafuckers they touch you.'

The class cracked up. Jenny patted his head and sent him back to his desk. 'Thank you, Frankie, but I think that's a bit extreme, not to mention against the law.'

She dropped off the desk and walked to the chalkboard. She wanted to make a list of appropriate penalties and take a vote. Crime and punishment passed for reading and writing.

Just then, the door to her classroom opened. A tall, rangy man with close-cropped gray hair and a weathered face peered in. 'Miss Dance, may I have a word? Outside, please.'

Jenny put down the chalk. 'I'll be right back,' she said to the class. She smiled as she entered the corridor. A parole officer, she thought, or a cop come to tell her about one of her new charges. 'Yes, what can I do for you?'

The man approached her, the smile bleeding from his face. 'If you ever want to see Thomas Bolden alive again,' he said, his voice hard as a diamond, 'you'll come with me.'

Chapter 23

'Look who's back,' said Detective Second Grade Mike Melendez as John Franciscus walked into the squad room. 'Night shift ain't enough for you, Johnny? Hey, I got a shift you can take.'

'Short Mike. How you doin'? Tell you the truth, heating's going berserk at the house,' Franciscus lied, stopping at Melendez's desk, rapping his knuckles twice as if knocking. 'Place is like a sweatbox. Got a guy coming at noon to take a look at it. Just what I need. Put another C-note into the house.'

Melendez stood up from his desk, stretching his six-foot-eight-inch frame, and headed toward the hall. 'You doing a four-to-one? Didn't see you on the roster.'

'No. Figured in the meantime I'd take care of some paperwork, maybe catch a few Zs in the duty room.'

Melendez gave him a look as if he were certifiable. 'Make yourself at home.'

Franciscus walked to the back of the squad room, saying his hellos to the guys. A New York City detective's day was divided into three shifts: 'eight-to-four', 'four-to-one' (which actually ended at midnight), and the night shift. Twice a month you did a 'back-to-back', meaning you did a four-to-one and an eight-to-four the following day. Since most of the cops lived upstate, they'd fitted out the duty room with a couple of cots and plenty of fresh sheets.

The detectives' squad room for Manhattan North was located on the sixth floor of an unmarked brick building on 114th Street and Broadway. They shared the building with SVU – the special victims unit, child protective services, and the local welfare office. It was a real crowd of jollies from morning till night. But the squad room, itself, was a haven: large, clean, and heated to a pleasant sixty-six degrees. A row of desks ran down each side of the room, separated by a wide aisle. The floor was old freckled linoleum, but spotless. The walls were standard-issue acoustical tile. A bulletin board covered with shoulder patches from visiting cops hung on one wall. Franciscus preferred it to the pictures that hung across the room. There in a row were the ranking policemen in the New York City Police Department. The big muckety-mucks. The commissioner, his deputy, the chief of police, and the chief of detectives. Once he'd dreamed of having his picture up there too, but things happened.

Just then, Melendez sauntered over.

'Pickup already go through?' Franciscus asked. Every morning at eight, a paddy wagon stopped by to haul the night's take down to 1 Police Plaza, or 'One PP', for formal booking and arraignment.

'Half hour ago. Your boy went along nice and easy.'

'Still not talking?'

'Not a peep. What's up with that?'

'Don't know. I'm heading over to see Vicki. See if she can dig something up for me.'

'You got a name?'

'Not his, unfortunately. Something else the complainant was talking about.'

'Who? Mr Wall Street?'

Franciscus nodded. 'Amazing a kid like that can make it. You see his body art. "Never Rat on Friends." You love it? I had something nifty like that on my shoulder, they would have kicked my butt out of OCS.'

'Doesn't matter where you come from any more. It's what you can do. How you handle yourself. Look at what Billy did with his GED.'

Melendez's kid brother, Billy, had worked as a trader with a foreign exchange firm doing business out of Tower 2, eighty-fifth floor. No one above eighty-four made it out. 'God bless, Mike.'

'Amen,' said Short Mike Melendez. 'Oh, the lieutenant said something about seeing you later. He's in his office, you feel so inclined.'

'You want to take odds on that?' As union trustee, Franciscus was in constant demand to answer questions about health care, retirement, and the like. The lieutenant had his thirty in, and was set to retire in a month's time. For weeks, he'd been harping on how to take his pension.

Franciscus had hardly sat down and gotten comfortable when he saw Lieutenant Bob McDermott amble from his office. McDermott raised a hand. 'Johnny. A word.'

Franciscus labored to his feet. 'You still thinking of taking insurance? Don't.'

McDermott shook his head and frowned, as if he wasn't interested in talking about himself. 'Got a sec? Need to tell you something.'

'Actually, I'm just on the way to IT. Got a lead I want to check on.'

'It'll just take a minute.' McDermott put a hand on his shoulder and walked with him toward his office. Given the lieutenant's easygoing nature, it might as well have been a stickup at gunpoint.

McDermott shut the door behind him and walked to his desk. 'Got a report here from your doctor.'

'Yeah,' Franciscus said, lightly. 'Saw him last week.' But inside him, his gut tightened.

'You didn't tell me.'

'Nothing to tell. Just the usual.'

'That's not what it says here.'

Franciscus waved away the report. 'Ah, that's bullshit,' he said. 'Just some minor blockage. He gave me a load of pills. No problem whatsoever.'

'EKGs don't lie.' McDermott settled his gaze on Franciscus. 'Johnny, did you know that you had had a heart attack?'

'It wasn't a heart attack. It was just a . . .' Franciscus tried to keep up the bluster, but couldn't quite bring it off. The thing about the lieutenant was that he was truly a good guy, probably better suited to the clergy than the police. 'To tell you the truth I didn't have a clue,' he said, at length. 'I just took it for another lousy day. You know . . . the job.'

'Says here you have an eighty percent occlusion of five of your principal arteries. Eighty percent! Johnny, your heart's a walking time bomb. Why haven't you scheduled a procedure?'

'A procedure?' Franciscus pulled a face. 'Come on. I quit smoking five years back. I haven't had anything stronger than a beer in ten years. I'll be okay.'

'Look at you. You're gray as a ghost,' said McDermott with genuine concern.

'It's friggin' winter. What do you expect, George Hamilton? Besides, you don't look so hot yourself.' Franciscus looked away, feeling miserable for the cheap shot.

McDermott tossed the manila folder that held Franciscus's future onto his desk. 'Sit down.'

Franciscus took a seat. 'Look, Bob, let me ex—'

'Please, John.' McDermott rocked in his chair for a moment. The two men exchanged glances. Franciscus shrugged. McDermott said, 'I looked at your file. You got thirty-four years in, plus three military. Some people would call that a career. You should be following me out the door.'

'And then what? You got a job lined up at OTB for me, too?'

'I'd be happy to. You know that.'

'Don't bother. I don't want to be a fink, looking over a guy's shoulder making sure he's not slipping an extra twenty out of the till.'

'Here's what you do. Have the procedure. File for disability. You retire on four-fifths pay for life. Nontaxable. You know the rules, Johnny. No police officer is allowed to work with a life-threatening condition.'

'This ain't the balloon the doc was talking about,' said Franciscus. 'It's the friggin' chain saw right down the middle. No cop's allowed back on the job after open-heart surgery.'

'You got eighteen months to go before mandatory retirement. What are you trying to do to yourself?' McDermott twirled in his seat and threw a thumb toward the window. 'You want to die out there?'

For a few moments, the two sat in silence. Franciscus listened to the sounds of the office: the clicking of the computer keyboards; the sudden, raucous laughs and catcalls; the constant opening and closing of doors. All of it added up to the rattle and hum of a vibrant, necessary organization. He'd always thought that being a detective was the greatest job in the world. God had to have invented it, it was so much fun.

'You're telling me it's over,' he said, hardly a whisper.

'You're sixty-two years old, John. Think of the rest of your life.'

'I got more to give.'

'Of course you do. Give it to your family. Give it to your kids. Your grandkids. I want to see the paperwork requesting surgery by this afternoon. Something happens to you now, with you knowing about your condition and not doing anything about it, you'll be on your own. Insurance won't touch you. This can't wait.'

'I've got something else that can't wait,' said Franciscus. Rising from his chair, he felt more like a hundred than sixty. 'Excuse me, Lieutenant.'

McDermott pushed back his chair and pointed a finger at the retreating figure. 'I want those forms on my desk by five!'

Franciscus made his way to the rest room and splashed cold water in his face. Yanking a few paper towels free, he dried his cheeks, his forehead, his chin, while studying himself in the mirror. Funny thing was that he couldn't see the disease that was ravaging his heart, robbing the muscle of its precious blood supply, causing its very walls to decay. He was gray, but then he'd always been that shade. It wasn't a question of eating badly. If anything, he was too skinny. For six months, he'd been following that low-carb diet, and now, like half the other guys in the squad, he was bone thin, his eyes looking like Super Balls ready to pop out of their sockets, his face angular, if not gaunt. He didn't even feel too bad, not counting getting a little more winded climbing the stairs than he used to, and the way he sweated like a racehorse at the drop of a hat.

Franciscus chucked the towels into the trash and stood up straight. Shoulders back. Chin up. Like a cadet on graduation day. He felt something in his back pop. Grimacing, he let his shoulders fall where they wanted. He sure as shit wasn't a cadet any more. He smiled sadly at his reflection. He'd been lying about not noticing the heart attack. In fact, he'd had two of 'em. Both times, he'd been aware of a sharp, piercing pain radiating from his chest up the side of his neck, extending down his left arm, making his fingers tingle. The pain had been fleeting, lasting maybe a minute or two. He'd written it off as a pinched nerve, or a bout of bursitis. But he'd known. Somewhere inside him a voice had whispered the truth.

He left the rest room and walked to an office down the hall. 'You in, Vick?'

A pretty, generously bosomed Hispanic woman answered from her seat at a bank of desktop computers. 'Oh, hi, Johnny. Always open for you.'

Vicki Vasquez was the class of the squad. She wasn't a cop, so to speak, but a data administrator, meaning it was her job to deal with the deluge of paperwork Franciscus and his fellow police officers generated. As usual, she was dressed nicely, wearing gray slacks and a neatly pressed white blouse with a string of pearls at her neck.

'Got a name I need you to run.'

'I'm all ears.'

'Bobby Stillman.'

'One *l* or two?'

'Try either way.' Franciscus pulled up a chair and sat down next to her. He could never get enough of her perfume. Rosewater and almonds. He loved the stuff. There was a time when he and Vicki had been hot for each other, but nothing ever came of it. Franciscus had been married at the time. As much as he wanted to jump Vicki's bones, he couldn't do it to his wife and kids.

'I'm not expecting anything. Just a name a guy mentioned last night. Made me curious.'

Part of Vicki's job was to run prints, B-numbers, and aliases through the mainframe at 1 Police Plaza downtown. People kept talking about installing a system where the detectives could do it on their own, but Franciscus figured that was a long way off. They were still getting used to e-mail.

'Nothing with one *l*,' said Vicki. 'I'll try two.' She typed in the name a second time, chatting all the while. 'Did you hear that the lieutenant is retiring? Isn't that a shame? Maybe it's time you took his place. Can't be a first grade for ever.'

'Yeah, I heard. Bob's been chewing my ear off for a month about what kind of pension he should take. Either standard or with—'

'Oh my,' said Vicki Vasquez suddenly, putting a hand to her mouth.

'You got a nibble?'

'Oh my,' she said again. 'It's an alias. Bobby Stillman, a.k.a. Sunshine Awakening, Roberta Stillman, Paulette Dobrianski . . .'

'Sunshine what?' Franciscus scooted closer, his nose up in the air like a bloodhound who'd caught a scent.

'Sunshine Awakening.'

'You mean we're talking about a woman?'

'Roberta Stillman, yes,' said Vicki Vasquez. 'Open warrant in connection with a capital homicide. You really hit the jackpot here.' She read from the screen. ' "Sought for questioning in connection with the murders of Officer Brendan O'Neill and Sergeant Samuel K. Shepherd. July 1980." ' She spun in her chair, practically pushing her boobs into his face. 'Don't you remember? Bunch of leftover hippies that bombed some computer company in Albany. They called themselves the Free Society. There was a big shoot-out. They killed the officers who'd come to question them. SWAT came and trapped them in this house. The standoff was on TV live. I sat in my kitchen eating ice cream the whole time. I think I gained five pounds.'

'You shittin' me? Pardon my French.'

Vicki Vasquez shook her head. 'Your Bobby Stillman is a cop killer. Reward's still open. Fifty thousand dollars.'

Franciscus brushed the hair off his forehead. A cop killer with fifty thousand dollars on her head. No kiddin'. He was done feeling like an old man. He was back to twenty with a wild hair.

'Thank you, Vick,' he said, taking her face in his hands and kissing her forehead. 'You're a beaut!'

Chapter 24

Bolden threw open the door to Jenny's classroom without knocking. He stepped inside and met a sea of gaping faces.

'Yes? May I help you?' asked the teacher, a slight Chinese woman.

'Jenny.' Bolden looked around the room. 'This is Jenny Dance's class. Where is she?'

'You are?'

'He's Thomas,' volunteered one of the students. 'He's her squeeze.'

'Her main man,' came another voice, to a crescendo of chuckles and wisecracks.

'Yo, Tommy, you lookin' all a mess,' shouted someone else.

Bolden didn't acknowledge any of them. 'I'm Tom Bolden,' he said, stepping inside the classroom. 'I need to speak with her. It's important.'

The teacher took in Bolden's clothes and motioned for him to join her in the corridor. She shut the door behind them. 'Jenny's not here,' she said, visibly agitated.

'Didn't she come to work?'

'Yes, she did. But she left the class twenty minutes ago and she hasn't come back since.'

'She didn't tell you she was leaving?'

'She didn't tell anyone. The students said a man came to the door asking for her. She told them to wait quietly while she spoke with him. No one said anything when she didn't come back in. These kids . . .' – the slight woman shrugged – 'well, they're not exactly scholars. Finally, one of them came and got me.'

'Did they see who it was?'

'Just that he was black. He must have been respectably dressed, because a few thought he was an administrator. Is there anything we should know about? Is something wrong?'

Bolden began to walk back down the hall.

'Is there anything wrong?' the teacher called again.

'Mr Guilfoyle, I have something that might interest you,' said a nasal, South Asian voice.

Guilfoyle rose from his chair and walked down the stairs to the work area. It was Singh, a young Indian they'd picked up from Bell Labs. 'Yes, Mr Singh?'

'I was doing a cross-check on Bolden's insurance records to see if he might have visited a pharmacy in the area regularly. I drew a blank, then I checked this Dance woman's records.' Singh leaned closer to his monitor, his eyes narrowed. 'Her medical insurance records indicate that she's recently had a prescription filled at a pharmacy on Union Square once a month. On Wednesdays, around twelve o'clock. Like today.'

'What's the prescription for?' asked Guilfoyle.

'Antivert.'

'Never heard of it. Any idea what it's for?'

'Why yes,' said Singh, swiveling his chair so he faced Guilfoyle. 'The active drug is meclizine. It combats nausea. As a matter of fact, my wife used it, too. It's for morning sickness.'

'Thank you, Mr Singh.' Guilfoyle crossed the room and put a hand on Hoover's shoulder. 'Bring up the pharmacy, would you?'

A light appeared on the corner of Sixteenth Street and Union Square West.

'Get me the phone number of all restaurants within a four-block radius of that pharmacy. Then, I want you to cross-check them against Bolden's phone records. Cell, private, and business.'

Hoover pursed his lips and looked over his shoulder at Guilfoyle. 'This will take a few minutes.'

'I can wait.'

At Canal Street, Bolden purchased a pint bottle of orange juice from a corner vendor and guzzled it in ten seconds. Tossing the container into a garbage can, he caught sight of something dark and mottled on his sleeve. He looked closer, touching it with his fingers. It was blood. Sol Weiss's blood. He dropped his hand as if he'd been shocked. He looked down the street as memories of another day flooded his mind. There was blood on his sleeve that day, too.

'Come to Jesus. Come to Jesus.'

Chanting.

Bolden heard it building in his ears, the rhythmic chant of the twenty boys who had encircled him in the basement of Caxton Hall at the Illinois State Home for Boys. The room was large and low-ceilinged, dimly lit, smelling of piss and sweat. It was the room they called 'the Dungeon', and at some point, the name had simply been shifted to the school.

'Come to Jesus.'

'Are you with me, Bolden?' demanded Coyle, a determined, muscular kid of eighteen who'd lived at the Dungeon for six years. They called him 'the Reverend'.

It was midnight. They had come for him in the dormitory, wrapping a pillowcase around his head, binding his hands and dragging him downstairs to the basement.

'No,' said Bolden. 'I'm not.'

Coyle smiled sourly. 'Have it your way.'

He came at Bolden, knife held down low, blade turned up, circling him slowly. The vain, sure smile had faded from his sallow face. His eyes were steady. Black marbles, dead as a shark's.

Bolden threw his hands in front of him and bent low. He'd seen it was coming. He'd been at the school a month, and a month was long enough to learn the rules. The rules said that either you went to Coyle and asked to be part of his crew, one of his 'choirboys', or he came to you. Coyle was a bully, and nothing more, a big, strong kid, older than his years, who preyed on anyone who was smaller, fatter, weaker, or slower than he was. Bolden didn't like him. He wasn't going to be anyone's choirboy. And he knew that Coyle was scared of him. Coyle never waited a month.

The knife flashed and Bolden jerked backward. A spasm of fear gripped him. When it relaxed, he felt cold and emotionless. He'd known how to fight his entire life without ever being taught. He knew that he had to keep moving to draw Coyle in. You never stayed still. Never. He glanced behind him. The circle had tightened. It didn't matter that he was surrounded. Get out of here, and he still had nowhere to run.

Come to Jesus. The voices continued chanting. Coyle's paean to his righteous Catholic upbringing.

Suddenly, Coyle lunged forward, knife outstretched. Bolden jumped to the side and toward Coyle, turning at the waist, closing the gap between them, the blade slicing his T-shirt. The move caught Coyle off guard. For a moment, he was exposed, arm extended, foot forward, off balance. Bolden lifted his arm and drove his elbow in the larger boy's neck. At the same time, Coyle had twisted his head to look back at him. The blow landed with a sickening crunch. The elbow seemed to bury itself in the outstretched neck. To go down and down for ever. Coyle collapsed like a rag doll and lay motionless on the floor. He didn't get up. He didn't cry out. He lay still.

No one else in the room moved either. The chanting stopped. The circle of boys stood frozen.

Bolden kneeled down next to him. 'Terry?'

Coyle blinked, his mouth working, but no words came.

'Get a doctor,' said Bolden. 'Call Mr O'Hara.'

Still no one moved.

Coyle's depthless black eyes were filling with tears, imploring him to do something.

'You'll be okay,' Bolden said, knowing it was a lie, sensing that something terrible had happened. 'Just got the wind knocked out of you, that's all.'

Coyle's mouth moved. 'Can't breathe,' he managed in a pained whisper.

Bolden stood and forced his way out of the circle. He ran to the headmaster's cottage and summoned Mr O'Hara. When they returned, the other boys were gone. Coyle lay in the center of the floor. He was dead. The blow to the neck had fractured his second vertebra. He had suffocated to death.

'You killed him,' said O'Hara.

'No, he had a . . .' Bolden looked at Coyle, and then at the rip in his shirt where Coyle had cut him. He ran his hand over his belly and his fingers came away red with blood. His eyes searched the floor for the knife, but the others had taken it. 'A knife . . .' he tried to explain, but like Coyle, he could no longer talk.

Bolden blinked and the memory faded. A knife.

A gun. A man dead. Coyle. And now Sol Weiss. He was a murderer.

Checking the company directory, he pulled up Diana Chambers's e-mail. He wrote, 'Diana, please contact me as soon as possible. Who did this to you? Why? Tom.' It was a futile gesture, but one he had to make.

Bolden replaced the BlackBerry on his belt, and set off down the street. A stiff wind blew intermittently, the gusts driving the drizzle in horizontal sheets that stung his cheeks. He needed a hot bath, and fresh clothes. He weighed going home or to Jenny's apartment, but decided both were too risky. Any number of interested parties might be waiting for him: the police and Guilfoyle, to name two. He was no longer confident that one was independent of the other.

He lowered his head and turned up the collar of his jacket. If the temperature dropped another degree or two, the sleet would turn to snow. He hurried down the street, avoiding puddles and patches of ice. He tried not to think about Jenny.

First, there was the picture of Diana Chambers. If the photo was genuine – and he believed it was – someone had to have punched her in the face. It was no fairy kiss, either. It was a rock-solid blow. Something 'Iron Mike' Tyson might have thrown in his prime.

What did they offer you, Diana?

He'd always picture her as the chirpy Yalie who sang 'Boola Boola' to the corporate finance department after he'd suggested everyone do a few tequila slammers to liven up a company-sponsored Circle Line cruise around Manhattan. How had they convinced her to go to the police and incriminate him? Did persuasion have anything to do with it? Or was it coercion, plain and simple? He couldn't imagine that Diana was thrilled with her new makeup. An orbital fracture, according to Mickey Schiff.

An old woman approached him, her eyes skipping from his feet to his face, her mouth stretched in a pitying smile. He needed shoes. He needed a coat. A policeman would not smile. He would ask questions. Up the street, he spotted a men's store.

Bolden blew a long breath through his teeth. Someone at the firm was working with Guilfoyle. There was no other way to explain how they had gotten to Diana Chambers so quickly, or how they could have manufactured the flirtatious e-mails and planted them on the company's mainframe on such short notice. There was too much evidence in too little time. The more he thought about it, the more reckless their actions became.

Bolden tilted his head and looked into the sky. A fat snowflake landed on his nose and he wiped it away. The great reckoning, he was thinking. The scales of fortune tilting against him after a run of good luck. He wasn't surprised.

As a kid, he'd hardly been an angel, granted. But when he'd been given a chance, he'd grabbed it with both hands. He studied and scrimped and saved. He worked tirelessly. And when success finally arrived, he gave back. First out of duty, then from enjoyment. He'd done nothing to deserve this. He hadn't stolen a twenty out of his foster father's money clip, or beaten up the latest bully at his latest school. He hadn't lied about where he'd been the night before, or how it was that a picture of someone else's parents had gotten into his wallet.

He had done other things, though. Things that could not be easily forgotten. Things that *he* could not forget, no matter how he tried.

Hurrying his pace, he wondered if retribution had finally found him. If this was just one more disaster in a recurring line, or if it was the final act of abandonment that had begun when he was six, and had held him hostage ever since. Bolden laughed at himself. Bitterly and with disdain. Somewhere in his past, someone had loaded his mind full of Eastern ideas of karma. Of good energy and bad energy. Of *chi* and the balancing of the scales. It was all nonsense. The past. The future. There was only now.

Bolden never looked back.

Chapter 25

It was a run-down, smelly apartment. One bed-room, a living room, and a bath, the kind of dilapidated quarters she'd seen in the *Times* in its 'Neediest Cases' articles. Jennifer Dance sat in the center of the sagging single bed and crossed her legs. She had to pee, but she couldn't get herself to set foot in the bathroom. The door was open, revealing a peeling linoleum floor and some rotting wood beneath it. The toilet was circa 1930, right down to the chain flush and cracked wooden toilet seat. A plumber's helper sat on the floor next to it. The abrasive odor of bleach and ammonia drifted into the bedroom. Somehow it made her find the place even grungier.

Jenny could deal with mess and stink. The johns at school weren't a whole lot better. Just last week, some wise guy had set his business afloat on a raft of toilet paper, squirted an entire can of lighter fluid on it, and lit it. 'Just like crêpes suzette,' they'd caught him boasting in the hallway.

What bothered Jenny were the cockroaches, which were numerous and straight out of central casting. She craned her neck for a look and caught a shadow flickering beneath the flooring, and then another a few inches away.

Voices carried from the living room. Jenny tilted her head, trying to pick up a word or two. Who were these people? First, they spirited her out of school with the threat that she would never see Thomas again if she didn't come right then and there, and now they told her to shut up, sit tight, and do as she was told. She didn't know if she was being protected or held prisoner.

'Keep the curtains closed,' the woman had said, when Jenny arrived. 'Stay away from the window.'

Jenny wondered about the orders. They certainly weren't to keep her from learning where she was. She was in Brooklyn, the Williamsburg section. There was no secret about that. She'd been driven over in a clunky Volvo; her, the clean cut guy who'd taken her from school, and the driver, a curly-haired, unshaven man of fifty who had given her a very weird smile. No names. Never a hint as to their identity, or what they wanted with her. No, Jenny decided, the curtains weren't to keep her from looking out. They were to keep others from looking in.

The two men were in the other room right now with the woman. The woman was the boss. Jenny had no doubt about that either. She stormed around the room like a besieged general planning her retreat, and the others were sure to give her leeway. She was tall and thin, her face pinched, forever concentrating, the eyes locked on a different plane. She wore her black hair in a ponytail and dressed like a college student in jeans, a white oxford shirt that she kept untucked, and Converse tennis shoes. It was her drive that frightened Jenny. One look, and you shared her resolve, whatever it was.

Apart from the warning to stay away from the window, she hadn't said a word to Jenny. She had, however, given her a fierce once-over. One look up and down, the whole thing lasting maybe a second, but it was more invasive than a strip search.

A door slammed. A new set of footsteps pounded down the hall.

Jenny got up from the bed and pressed her ear to the door. She recognized the woman's voice. It was calm and urgent at the same time. 'They what?' she demanded. 'They're desperate.' Then, in a much softer voice altogether, which Jenny would have sworn belonged to someone else: 'Is he all right?'

Before Jenny could hear the answer, the door opened inward, forcing her back a step.

'Come on,' said the woman. 'We have to leave.'

'Where are we going? Is Thomas all right? Was it him you were talking about?' It was Jenny's turn to demand. She backed into the center of the room and stood with her arms crossed over her breasts. But if she was expecting a fight, all she got was a postponement to another day.

'Better hurry,' the woman said. 'Our presence has been noted.'

'Where are we going?' Jenny repeated.

'Someplace safe.'

'I want to go home. That's someplace safe.'

The woman shook her head. 'No, sweetheart. Not any more it isn't.'

But Jenny was no longer in a believing mood. The distrust and paranoia that surrounded these people had infected her. 'Is Thomas all right?'

'Bolden? He's fine for now.'

'That's it. For now? I've had enough of your half answers. Who are you? What do you want with me? Who's chasing Thomas?'

The woman rushed forward and grabbed Jenny's arm. 'I said, let's go,' she whispered, as her nails dug into Jenny's skin. 'That means now. We're friends. That's all you have to know.'

A different car was waiting at the kerb. Jenny slid into the back seat, along with the woman and the man who had taken her from school. The car pulled out before the door was shut. They'd driven a hundred yards before the driver yelled at everyone to get down. Two sedans approached, traveling at high speed. She could make out a pair of heads silhouetted in each. Jenny pressed her face into the woman's lap. A moment later, she felt their car buffet as the sedans raced past. 'Was that them?'

'Yes,' said the woman.

'Who are they?'

'I believe you met them last night.'

'How do you know . . .' Jenny didn't know how to finish her sentence. How did they know about last night? Or, how did they know it was the same people?

The woman laughed, and the laugh traveled round the car, pulling everyone in. 'I've had a little practice in this matter,' she said, afterwards.

The driver turned his head and looked at the woman. 'Jesus, Bobby, that was close.'

'Yes,' said Bobby Stillman. 'They're getting better.'

Chapter 26

'Do you have another card, sir?' asked the sales clerk.

'Excuse me?' Bolden stood at the counter, slipping his belt through the last loop of a new pair of blue jeans, and notching it around the waist. His soiled clothes had been folded and slipped into a bag for him to carry out. Besides the jeans, he wore a dark flannel shirt, a hip-length work jacket, and a pair of ankle-high Timberlands. Everything was new, down to his socks, underwear, and T-shirt.

'The card has been refused.'

'You're sure? It's probably a mistake. Can you run it again?'

'I've run it three times already,' said the clerk, a punk-come-lately with spiked hair, a bad complexion, and a dress shirt three sizes too big around the neck. 'I'm supposed to confiscate it, but I don't want any hassle. Here, take it back. Don't you have a Visa or Mastercard?'

Bolden handed over his Mastercard. There was no reason for his credit card to be turned down. He paid his bills on time and in full. He'd never been one to live beyond his means. When his colleagues talked matter-of-factly about their new Porsche Turbo, or their second home in Telluride, or the superiority of a seven-thousand-dollar made-to-order Kiton suit, he felt strangely out of place. He didn't think there was anything wrong with buying nice things, he just didn't know how to spend money like that. The Cartier watch he'd given to Jenny was the single most expensive item he'd ever bought.

'Declined,' said the clerk from the end of the counter. 'I'll have to contact the manager. You can talk to him about it if you want.'

'Forget it,' said Bolden. 'I'll just pay cash.' He thumbed his billfold. A fiver and a few ones looked up at him. He glanced at the pimply clerk with his oversized collar, and thought that it made perfect sense. They can stake out a team to kidnap you off a busy street in the middle of the city. They can fabricate e-mails. They can beat a woman's face to a pulp and convince her to tell the police that you did it. Of course, they can hijack your credit. 'Doesn't look like this is going to work. Let me go change out of this stuff.'

'Don't worry about it,' said the clerk, putting down the phone. 'Happens all the time. Just leave the clothes on the chair in the changing room.'

Bolden picked up the bag holding his dirty suit and cut through the pants section. He couldn't go back out on the street in his old clothes. They were filthy, and called attention to him from fifty feet away. He looked one night away from being a bum. The two changing rooms sat side by side down a corridor to his left. A few customers browsed here and there, but otherwise, the store was deserted. Bolden stopped and pretended to look into his bag, as if making sure everything was there. The emergency exit was dead ahead, past the shirts and shoes and the manager's office. In a mirror, he saw the clerk come out from behind the counter and make his way slowly toward him.

Just then, a bearded, heavyset man emerged from the office, a few feet away from Bolden. He held a clipboard in one hand and was talking into a cell phone with the other.

'Hey,' Bolden called to him. 'You the manager?'

'Hold on a sec,' the man said into the phone. Putting a smile on his face, he lumbered over. 'Yes sir, how can I help?'

Bolden nodded his head toward the clerk. 'Your cashier's got some mouth on him,' he said, angrily. 'You should have a word with him.'

'Jake? Really? I'm sorry to hear that. What exactly did he—'

'Here, take these.' Bolden pushed the bag of soiled clothes into his arms.

As the manager fumbled with the bag, Bolden walked past him.

'Hey!' the clerk shouted. 'That guy hasn't paid. Don't let him go.'

'But I got the clothes,' replied the manager, holding up the bag.

The path to the exit was clear. Bolden took off down the aisle.

The clerk ran after him. 'Hey, man. Get back here. He hasn't paid. Stop!'

Bolden hit the door at a run. It flew open, and rebounded against the wall with a loud crack. The alley was empty, a Dumpster to the right, piles of cut-down cardboard boxes to the left. Instead of running, he stopped short and pressed his back to the wall beside the door. The clerk emerged a moment later. Bolden grabbed him by the shoulders and flung him against the wall. 'Do not follow me,' he said. 'I'll be back. I will pay for this shit, okay?'

'Yeah, man, sure. Whatever you say.'

Bolden smiled grimly, then slugged him in the stomach. The clerk doubled over and fell to the ground. 'Sorry, man, but I can't trust you.'

*

There was a banking center a few blocks up. Bolden chose 'English' as the language he'd like to do business in, then entered his PIN: 6275. Jenny's birthday. When the ATM chirped, and the main menu appeared, he sagged with relief. He selected 'Cash', then keyed in a thousand dollars. A second later, the screen informed him that the amount requested was too high. He typed in five hundred instead.

Waiting, he stared at his new boots. You could trace a man's life by his shoes, he thought, remembering his PF Flyers, Keds, and Converse high-tops. As a teenager, he would have killed for a pair of Air-Jordans, but priced at seventy-five bucks, they were beyond reach. Beyond dreaming even. In college, his first cheque from work-study had gone to buy a pair of Bass Weejuns. Oxblood with tassels. Shift managers at Butler Hall were required to wear dress shoes. Sixty-six bucks so he could look nice shoveling tuna casserole and potatoes au gratin onto a plate. Every Sunday night, he'd spread the front page of the Sunday *Times* on the floor, gather his toothbrush, Kiwi polish, chamois, and rag, and spend an hour polishing them. Sixty-six bucks was sixty-six bucks. The shoes lasted him through three years of college. He still refused to pay more than two hundred dollars for a pair of shoes.

He stared at the screen, waiting for the pleasing whir and grind that signaled his money was being gathered. A new screen appeared informing him that the operation was not possible and that due to an account discrepancy, the bank was confiscating his card at that time. For any further questions, he could call . . .

Bolden stalked out of the cheerless office. The

chill air was like a slap in the face. He jogged to the
end of the block. At the corner, he opened his wallet
and recounted the bills inside. He had eleven dollars
to his name.

Chapter 27

'Who were they?' asked Jennifer Dance, as the old sedan bumped and rattled up Atlantic Avenue toward the Brooklyn Bridge.

'Old boyfriends,' said Bobby Stillman.

'Are they the reason you had me keep the curtains drawn?'

'Boy, she's full of questions, this one,' said the driver. 'Hey, lady, put a lid on it.'

'It's all right, Walter,' said Bobby Stillman. She twisted in her seat, bringing her intense gaze to bear. 'I'll tell you who they are,' she said. 'They're the enemy. They're Big Brother. Remember the Masons' "All-Seeing Eye"?'

Jenny nodded hesitantly.

'That's who they are. They watch. They spy. *Scientia est potentia*. "Knowledge is power." They report. They silence. They brainwash. But that's not enough for them. They have a vision. A higher calling. And for that calling, they're willing to kill.'

The woman was crazy. Big Brother and the Masons. *Scientia est dementia* was more like it, or whatever Latin gobbledygook she was quoting. Any second now she was going to start babbling about the aliens among us, and the miniature transmitters hidden in her molars. Jenny had a physical need to move away from her, but there was no place to go. 'How do you know them?' she asked.

'We go back a long way. I keep coming after them, and they keep trying to stop me.'

'Who's they?'

Bobby Stillman threw an arm over the seat, shooting her an uncertain glance as if she was deciding whether she was worth all the effort. 'The club,' she said. Her voice was calmer, sober even, gaining traction now that she was back on planet Earth. 'It's funny, isn't it? But that's what they call themselves. A club of patriots. Who are they? The big boys in Washington and New York with their hands on the levers of power. How do you think they found Thomas? They're inside.'

'Inside what?'

'Everything. Government. Business. Law. Education. Medicine.'

Jenny shook her head, uncomfortable with these vague accusations. She wanted names, faces, plans. She wanted something she could read about in the *New York Times*. 'Who's in the club?'

Bobby Stillman ran a hand over her hair. 'I don't know all of them, and believe me, darling, I wouldn't tell you if I did. Then you'd be number two on their hit parade with your boyfriend, right after yours truly. All you need to know is that they are a group of men, maybe even women—'

'A club . . .'

Stillman nodded. 'A club of very powerful, very connected individuals who want to keep their hands on the tiller steering this country of ours. They meet together. They talk. They plan. Yes, it's a club in the real sense of the word.'

'That does what?'

'Primarily, they interfere. They're not content to let the government work the way it's supposed to. They don't trust us, and by us, I mean the people –

you, me, and that guy over there selling Sabrett hot dogs – to make the decisions.'

'Do they fix elections?'

'Of course not,' Bobby Stillman flared. 'Aren't you listening? I said they're inside. They work with those in power. They convince them of the purity of their aims. They scare them into acting. Into usurping the people's voice . . . all in the name of democracy.'

Jenny sat back, her mind racing. She looked at her nails and began tearing at her thumb, a habit she'd gotten over at the age of fourteen. It was too much for her. Too big. Too ill-defined. Altogether too spooky. 'Where's Thomas?' she asked again.

'We're going to meet him now.'

'I don't believe you.'

'Don't you two have lunch planned? Twelve o'clock? At your regular place?'

Jenny bolted forward in her seat. 'How did you know?'

'We listen, too,' said Bobby Stillman. 'But we're not mind readers.'

Walter, the driver, turned his head and looked at Jenny. 'Where to, kid?'

Chapter 28

At ten-thirty, the main branch of the New York Public Library, known officially as the Humanities and Social Sciences Library, was mildly busy. A stream of regulars filed up and down the stairs with a workaday stiffness. Tourists meandered through the halls, identified by their hip packs and their agog expressions. Only the library personnel walked slower.

Built on the site of the old Croton Reservoir in 1911, the Beaux-Arts structure spanned two city blocks between Fortieth and Forty-second Streets on Fifth Avenue, and at the time of its construction, was the largest marble building ever erected. The main gallery was a heaven of white marble, its ceiling soaring a hundred feet above the floor. Imposing staircases framed by towering colonnades rose on either side of the great hall. Somewhere inside the place was a Gutenberg Bible, the first five folios of Shakespeare's plays, and a handwritten copy of Washington's Farewell Address, the most famous speech never given.

Hurrying across the third-floor rotunda, Bolden traversed the length of the main reading room and passed through an archway to the secondary reading room, where the library's computers were kept. He signed his name on the waiting list, and after fifteen minutes, was shown to a terminal with full Internet access. He slid his chair close to the desk, rummaging in his pocket for the drawing he had made in his apartment earlier that morning. The paper was wrinkled and damp, and he spent a moment flattening it with his palm. *I'm fighting a dragon with a paper sword,* he thought.

Accessing the search engine, he selected 'Image Search', then typed in 'musket'. A selection of postage-stamp-sized photos, or 'thumbnails', filled the screen. Half showed a slim long-barreled rifle that reminded Bolden of the gun Daniel Boone had used. There were also pictures of men dressed in Colonial military garb: Redcoats, Hessians, Bluecoats (better known as the Continental Army); a thumbnail of a poodle staring at the camera. (Was the dog named Musket?) And, a shot of three friends raising obscenely decorated beer steins. Sex was never more than a click away on the Internet.

The second page included a thumbnail of a miniature iron musket balanced on the tip of a man's index finger. Impressive, Bolden conceded, but irrelevant. Another photo of the drunken revelers. The caption called them the Dre Muskets, which he took as Dutch for 'Three Musketeers'.

Then he saw it. The third picture along the top row. The oddly shaped rifle butt differentiated the musket from the others he had seen. The butt was asymmetrical, shorter by six inches across the top than on the bottom. The caption identified it as a 'Kentucky Flintlock Rifle, ca. 1780'. He checked it against his drawing. It was the one. He clicked on the picture and was directed to a fuller description of the gun.

'The Kentucky flintlock rifle was a favorable alternative to the more popular British Brown Bess musket. Not only was the Kentucky flintlock considerably lighter at eight pounds, versus the Brown Bess's fourteen pounds, but the rifle's spiraled-groove barrel permitted accurate fire from up to 250 yards, far outdistancing the Brown Bess's (notoriously inaccurate) range of only eighty yards.'

The word 'minutemen' caught Bolden's eyes. He thought it sounded like the name of a secret group that might select a tattoo of a Revolutionary War-era weapon as their symbol. He typed in 'minutemen' and spent a few minutes clicking on the more relevant citations. He read brief histories of the Minutemen, Paul Revere, and William Dawes. He hadn't known that the Minutemen were a handpicked elite from the militia – only a quarter of the militia served as Minutemen – or that they had been in existence since 1645 to fight off all manner of foreign invasion and to protect the frontier against Indians. To his mind, Minutemen were the valiant bunch who fought off the British at Lexington and Concord in 1775.

Another citation interested him. 'Minutemen Ready to Battle Communist Threat.' The article discussed an ultra-right-wing group founded in Houston, Texas, in the 1960s to fight the Reds should they ever land on American soil. It was a kind of Rotarian paramilitary organization that offered marksmanship training to all its members. Bolden marked them as John Birchers with guns. Just the type that might evolve into an organization that could foul up his credit cards and plunder his banking records.

Bolden clasped his hands behind his head and rocked on the chair's back legs. Detective Franciscus believed that Wolf and Irish could be civilian contractors to the military. Bolden plugged in the names of the companies he had mentioned, one by one, and reviewed their websites. Executive Resources, Tidewater, and the Milner Group. All were actively looking for new employees. Job specifications were stated up front: all positions required the applicant to have spent at least five years of active duty in an army, navy, or Marine Corps unit, usually in one of the combat arms: infantry, artillery, or armor. Some went further, screening for applicants who'd served in an elite division: 82nd Airborne, 101st Airborne – the 'Screaming Eagles' – Army Rangers, Special Forces, Delta Force, SEALs, Air Force Rescue, or as a marine infantryman. The sites were noticeable most for their subdued, corporate layout. On none, however, did Bolden find a symbol of a Kentucky flintlock rifle.

After twenty minutes, he pushed his chair back and went to get a drink of water.

'Mr Guilfoyle. I have something you need to take a look at.'

Hoover waited until Guilfoyle was standing by his shoulder, then pointed to the wall map of Manhattan. The red pinlight that denoted Thomas Bolden's location was no longer bouncing from spot to spot, but was holding rock steady at the corner of Fortieth Street and Fifth Avenue. 'He's in the New York Public Library. The signal's strong, so he must be near an entrance, a window, or on the top floor.'

Guilfoyle stared at the solitary red light, weighing his options. 'How long has he been there?'

'About twenty minutes.'

'Nothing yet on where Bolden's supposed to meet his girlfriend?'

'Still processing.'

Guilfoyle pinched the fat gathering beneath his chin. 'Get me Wolf.'

'Kentucky flintlock rifle.'

Bolden plugged in the words and waited for

the posted results, hoping to find a decent picture to print out. Flipping through several pages, he noticed a photo that didn't belong in the group. Instead of a musket, there was a picture of four men smiling broadly, standing with their arms linked over their shoulders. The photograph was dated. The men were straight out of the fifties or early sixties, wearing crew cuts, white short-sleeved shirts, black ruler ties, and tortoiseshell glasses. They looked like poster boys for the 'fast-paced engineering lifestyle'. The Few. The Proud. The Geeks. What captured his attention was the large sign behind them that read, 'Scanlon Corporation. World Headquarters.' The silhouette of a Kentucky flintlock rifle sat beneath the company name. He brought his face closer to the screen. The silhouette was identical to the drawing he had made, down to the unique notched rifle butt, a distinct feature he'd never seen, or at least, never noticed before.

Bolden clicked on the picture and got a 'Forbidden. You do not have permission to access this site.' He returned to the photo and printed out a copy. The caption read, www.bfss.org/yearbook/ 1960/Billf.jpg, but Bolden didn't hold out much hope of tracking down 'Bill F', whoever he was. He tried typing in 'BFSS', but got nothing. Then he tried 'Scanlon Industries'. He was disappointed not to find a corporate website. There were, however, a few pages of articles.

The first mentioned Scanlon in passing as the winning bidder for a highway project in Houston, Texas, in 1949. A second provided more detail. Scanlon Corporation, it read, was founded in 1936, in Austin, Texas, as a civil engineering firm engaged primarily in road construction. The article went on to list a few of its projects and ended by saying that its newest endeavors involved working in concert with the United States Armed Forces.

The third article was more informative and came from the *Army Times*.

> . . . Scanlon Industries of Vienna, Virginia, has been awarded a $45,000,000 indefinite delivery/indefinite quantity contract by MACV (Military Assistance Command, Vietnam) to construct three airbases and landing facilities in the Republic of Vietnam. The airbases will be built at Da Nang, Bien Hoa, and Phu Cat.
>
> 'Scanlon has proven time and time again not only to be the low-cost bidder, but also a company in whom the American people can have the deepest trust,' said army spokesman Carl McIntire. 'Our boys in uniform deserve the best and Scanlon delivers.' Scanlon President Russell Kuykendahl added, 'We are proud to have been chosen by the Department of Defense and MACV as the sole contractor to construct and improve the United States Army and the United States Air Force's operational facilities in the Republic of Vietnam and hope our work will ensure that the country's tenure in Vietnam will be brief and successful.'

Bolden reread the article. Scanlon had struck it rich with that one. To be named sole contractor for building landing strips and airbases on the eve of the biggest overseas deployment in American history was a sweet piece of business. He thought it strange that the name didn't ring a bell. He added Kuykendahl's name to his short list, then in large block letters added: CIVILIAN/MILITARY CONTRACTORS.

Intrigued, Bolden began to check every link to Scanlon. A dozen mentioned Scanlon in the same sentence as government contracts. There were contracts to build generators, munitions storage areas, to bury electrical distribution lines, even something referred to as typhoon recovery at Andersen Air Force Base, Guam. The amounts were substantial. Twenty, fifty, one hundred million dollars.

The last few articles spoke of a change in the company's focus. Instead of construction, Scanlon had begun to receive contracts to assist in the training of the Colombian and Philippine armies. While no dollar amounts were listed, the articles went so far as to mention that forty-five 'trainers' were being sent to the countries in question for a period of no less than six months.

Finally, there was a notice dated June 16, 1979, stating that representatives of the Scanlon Corporation would be interviewing job candidates at the Fayetteville Holiday Inn. Bolden knew his military history well enough to recognize Fayetteville as the hometown of Fort Bragg, North Carolina. Scanlon was doing its recruiting at the home of the United States Special Forces.

As quickly as he had found it, the trail went cold.

There was no mention of the company anywhere after 1980. No word of bankruptcy, merger, LBO, nothing. Scanlon had fallen off the end of the earth. One thing was for certain: they didn't just curl up and die. A corporation of that size, with those kinds of government contacts, had to have been gobbled up by somebody. The field of candidates was necessarily limited to corporations in the defense, construction, and, possibly, oil-field services sector. Back in 1980, there were maybe thirty companies that could have purchased Scanlon. Fewer today.

Bolden shifted in his chair and slipped his BlackBerry off his belt. Skimming through his address book, he recognized the names of a dozen people who might be able to fill him in about Scanlon. He set the compact device on the desk. By now, every one of his clients had received a call from the firm informing them that Thomas Bolden no longer worked at Harrington Weiss. A quiet voice would add that if the client had heard rumors about Bolden beating up a certain female colleague, they would not be remiss to believe them. And yes, it was true that Sol Weiss had been killed while confronting Bolden with the evidence.

Thomas Bolden was persona non grata.

He stood and, after notifying the librarian that he would be back in a few minutes, walked to the rotunda, where he began placing calls. He thought of all the congratulatory e-mails he'd received that morning. There had to be someone who'd give him a hand. He started with Josh Lieberman, an M and A banker at Lehman.

'Hello, Josh, Tom Bolden.'

'Should I be talking to you?'

'Why not? I know what you might have heard, but none of it's true. Trust me.'

'You calling me from your BlackBerry?'

'Yes,' said Bolden. 'Listen, I need a—'

'Sorry, pal . . . no can do . . . but, hey, good luck.'

Bolden tried Barry O'Connor at Zeus Associates, another sponsor. 'Jesus Christ, Bolden, do you have any idea the shit you're trailing?' whispered O'Connor, breathlessly. Bolden might have climbed Everest or sequenced the human gene. 'My man, you are in a heap of it!'

'It's some kind of setup. I didn't touch the girl.'

'The girl? I haven't heard a thing about the girl. Word is you killed Sol Weiss.'

'Weiss? Of course not—'

'Get yourself a lawyer, buddy. I'm hearing bad things. Very bad things.'

'Hold on . . . I need a favor.'

'Tom, I'd love to but . . .' O'Connor's voice grew hushed. 'The phones, man, they're wired, you know that.'

'Real quick. Some info on a company . . .'

'I don't think this is the time to be thinking about business. Another call's coming in. Good luck, Tommy. Get that lawyer.'

As Bolden flipped through his phone directory, a name caught his eye. It came to him he'd been silly to concentrate on bankers in New York. Rumors spread like wildfire on the Street. It was better to look elsewhere for help. He dialed a number with a 202 area code that he knew by heart.

'De Valmont.' The voice answered lazily, with the hint of an English accent.

'Guy, it's Tom Bolden.'

'Hello, Tom,' said Guy de Valmont, senior partner at Jefferson. 'What gives? Everything all right on the Trendrite deal?'

Bolden sighed with relief. Finally, someone who hadn't heard the news. 'Everything's fine. I was wondering if you could help me with a query. I'm looking something up on a company named Scanlon Corporation. They were a defense contractor in the fifties and sixties, big into Vietnam. I can't find hide nor hair of them after 1980. I know that Jefferson's been active in that sector for a long time, and I was wondering if you might be able to track them down.'

'Say again? Scanlon? Doesn't ring a bell, but 1980's a lifetime ago. I'll be happy to have a look. Get you back at the office?'

'Call me on my cell.' He rattled off the number.

'Where are you? Reception's lousy.'

'I'm in . . .' Bolden hesitated before revealing his location. It would only be a matter of time until de Valmont learned about Sol Weiss's death. Bolden didn't want him phoning the NYPD saying he'd just talked to the alleged killer, who had admitted to being inside the New York Public Library. 'I'm at Grand Central,' he said.

'Give me a few minutes, say half an hour, and call back. But do me a favor and get a better connection than this.'

'You can't look now? It's an emergency.'

' 'Fraid not. J.J.'s been yelling for me. Bye-bye.'

Bolden hung up, then hurried back to the reading room. At his desk, he stared at the prompt on the computer screen. For the heck of it, he typed in 'Bobby Stillman'. There were lots of Robert Stillmans, but no Bobbys. Pushing back his chair, he walked to the periodicals desk. 'I need to do a search on a company,' he said, when the assistant came to serve him. 'Scanlon Corporation. I'd like to look in the *Wall Street Journal*, the *Army Times*, *Fortune*, and *Forbes*. How much will that run me?'

'How far back?'

'Nineteen seventy-five.'

'I'll need a minute to check that we have microfilm on all those. *Army Times* might be iffy.'

The periodicals desk was located at the near end of the room, in a three-sided pen that abutted the wall. The archway to the main reading room stood adjacent to it. As Bolden waited for the woman to calculate the cost of his request, he found himself looking at two men who had just entered the room. Clean-cut, dressed in blazers and slacks, they stood on either side of the door, finding their way.

'Sir?'

'Yes,' said Bolden, returning his attention to the woman.

'You'll be happy to know we have the *Army Times*. The total will be twelve seventy-five. Three dollars for each search, plus tax. For twenty dollars, we can run a LexisNexis search. It's much more comprehensive.'

Bolden counted out seven dollars from his wallet. 'I'll just take two searches: the *Times* and the *Wall Street Journal*.'

'I'll have your change in a moment.'

'Sure thing,' said Bolden distractedly. He was interested in the two men. Instead of walking to a free computer or proceeding to one of the reference desks, they remained rooted to the spot, their heads slowly scanning the cavernous room. Bolden shifted his gaze to the opposite archway, perhaps two hundred feet away. Two men, dressed similarly in casual business attire, had taken up position just inside the arch. They sported the same short haircuts, the same watchful attitude.

Bolden lowered his face. It couldn't be. There was no way anyone could have traced him to the library. He hadn't been followed. He hadn't checked, but he'd been sure he was alone when he left Jenny's school. He had no doubt that he'd been alone inside the clothing store. Impossible.

'Here you are sir. Sixty-six cents change.'

And then, he saw it. The man nearest him inclined his head toward his lapel and whispered a few words. Bolden tensed. His ears stopped up and he swallowed to clear them. *Move*, a voice commanded him. *Get out now. They've seen you.*

'Sir? Are you all right?'

Bolden bent over the counter. 'Can you show me to the bathroom?' he asked with a pained expression. He held his hands to his stomach and winced. 'I'm not well. I need to get there quickly.'

'Why, of course. It's just outside the main reading room, sir. Don't you worry.'

The librarian came to his side of the counter and took his arm. Together, they walked out of the computer room, brushing past the men positioned on either side of the passage. Out of the corner of his eye, he caught one of the men giving him the once-over.

Bolden shook free his arm and ran. He didn't look behind him. He had ten steps, no more. He dashed across the main reading room, up the wide center aisle, past table after table, his tread thundering on the parquet floor. Everywhere heads turned to him. Voices called, 'Quiet!' and 'Slow down!' But when he cocked an ear behind him, he heard footsteps behind him, gaining.

He sprinted out of the main reading room, continuing across the rotunda to the top of the marble stairs. At the far side of the great hall, one of the men from the second team consulted with another, then began to run toward him. Bolden attacked the staircase recklessly, taking three or four stairs at a time. If he stumbled, he'd risk a broken ankle at best, and more probably a broken neck. Making the turn on the second-floor landing, he caught sight of his pursuers. Two of the men rushed down the stairs behind him. The other team started down the far staircase.

Breathing hard, he reached the ground floor. He heard a shout and saw a man tumbling head over heels down the far staircase. His eyes darted to the main entrance. Five sets of double doors governed entry and exit to the library. If only he could get outside, he might have a chance. He checked over his shoulder. The two behind him were rounding the last flight. One had unbuttoned his jacket and

Bolden caught a glint of blue steel inside. He had to decide on a path. He slowed, hesitating when he could not afford to. He looked back at the main entrance. It couldn't be. The same beefy shoulder, the neck corded with steel. The fanatical glare.

Wolf saw him at the same moment, and immediately the man broke into a run, arms pumping like a sprinter.

Bolden ran in the opposite direction, toward the rear of the library and the warren of corridors that housed the administrative offices and scholars' reading rooms. He charged down one corridor, then made a sharp left down another. Doors on either side were stenciled with names and titles. A woman exited an office ahead of him, her head buried in her papers. Bolden crashed into her, sending her slamming into a wall. He stopped to help her up, then ducked into her office and shut the door. A young, bookish man sat at his PC, jaw agape, staring at him.

'Can you lock it?' Bolden demanded. When the man didn't answer, he yelled, 'Can you lock it?'

'Turn the dead bolt.'

Bolden slipped the dead bolt into place, then walked past the stunned man, into the adjoining office. A broad sash window gave onto the library's café and Bryant Park, a wide expanse of snow-covered grass extending the width of the block. Bolden grasped the window's handle and turned. It was stuck. There was pounding at the door. Wrapping his fingers around the handle, he turned it with all his might. The handle budged. With a yank, the window opened.

Behind him, the door burst in, exploding in a shriek of splintered wood. There came the sound of glass breaking and of objects toppling to the floor. The young man shouted in protest.

Bolden dropped to the ground ten feet below, landing on a dining table, slipping and crashing to the ground. Standing, he stumbled again, this time on an island of ice, then finally found his footing and ran into the park.

Wolf slipped his legs over the sill and jumped to the table. He landed poorly, his right knee bowing, and collapsed onto the ground.

Daring a look over his shoulder, Bolden saw him try to stand, then fall back to the ground. In seconds, the figure was a blur, and then he was impossible to see altogether.

Bolden did not stop until he'd left the park and reached Sixth Avenue. Even then, he walked briskly, keeping an eye behind him.

How? he asked himself. *How did they find me?*

Chapter 29

Ellington Fiske walked up the stairs leading to the United States Capitol. 'What's wrong here?' he asked the horde of men surrounding him.

'Mike's on the fritz,' said one.

'Something's gone south with the wiring,' said another.

'Where's my chief electrician?'

'On the dais,' someone else answered.

Fiske pushed his way through them, counting members of the Capitol Police, Park Police, a member of the Presidential Inaugural Committee, and a pair of full bird colonels attached to the Military District of Washington. He stopped when he reached the spot where the President would be sworn in and deliver the inaugural address.

Behind him, risers had been set on the stairs leading up to the Capitol esplanade. Rows of chairs, all of them numbered, were neatly in place. There was room for approximately one thousand invited guests. Each had to present a ticket and identification. That went for the chief justice of the Supreme Court on down to Senator McCoy's four-year-old niece.

'Who's looking for me?' A stout, unshaven man in blue overalls and a ratty parka presented himself. 'Mike Rizzo,' he said, holding up his credentials. 'You're here about the microphone?'

'That's correct,' said Fiske. 'If it's broken, why

don't you just replace it? Unscrew the damn thing and stick on a new one.'

'Doesn't work that way,' said Rizzo. 'The microphone's built into the podium. It's integrated into the body of the lectern itself. Actually, there are four directional mikes built into it, each the size of a postage stamp.' He shrugged to show he wasn't too impressed. 'The latest and greatest.'

Fiske ran a hand around the edges of the podium. It was impossible to even see the mike.

Jesus . . . for want of a nail . . .

The rain was falling harder now, fat little bombs that exploded on his cheeks. The forecast called for it to worsen during the night, and possibly turn to snow. He made a mental note to double-check with DC traffic authority and have all snowplow drivers on call. 'Will somebody please get the protective canopy in place?' he shouted.

Planning for the inauguration had begun in earnest twelve months earlier. Fiske had broken down the security work into nine operational areas: intelligence; explosives and hazardous materials; legal; emergency response; credentialing; site-specific; multi-agency communications, or MACC; transportation; and aviation. The problem of the podium fell into the site-specific committee's purview. 'Site-specific', as the name implied, was tasked with physically outfitting the Capitol for the event. That meant installing all seating, supervising placement and construction of the television tower, setting up an area for the press pool, and making sure all electrical fixtures functioned properly.

A dead mike when the President was swearing her Oath of Office was the *second* worst thing that could happen tomorrow morning.

Fiske circled the lectern. It was no different from the one the President used at any outdoor function.

A wood base led to a navy blue lectern with the presidential seal attached by magnets. It was manufactured in Virginia from Georgia maple, Chinese fiberboard, and Indian plastic. That was as close to American-made as anything came these days. He looked around him. Giant American flags hung from the walls of the Capitol. A blue carpet ran from the podium up the stairs. He was happy to note that it was still covered with plastic. Ballistic glass ran the perimeter of the balcony and on either side of the reviewing stand. His eye darted to the strategic spots on the Capitol roof where his snipers would take up position. Out of public sight behind them, batteries of 'Avenger' anti-aircraft guns had been installed. TelePrompTer reflectors stood to either side of the lectern. He had no doubt that they worked.

Fiske turned and looked out toward the Washington Monument. Twenty yards away, the skeleton of the TV tower rose, partially blocking his view of the Mall. The long promenade was a splotchy brown, the dormant grass patched with melting snow. The Mall was utterly vacant, except for pairs of policemen (some his own men) patrolling the fences set up to regulate the crowds. In twenty-four hours, rain or shine, over three hundred thousand people would crowd the area. Americans eager to witness the most solemn rite in their country's historical pageant. The swearing in of the forty-fourth President of the United States.

'Isn't there any way we can change out the mike?' Fiske asked Rizzo.

'Only one,' volunteered a new voice. It belonged to a young man, white, clean-cut, bland. 'Bill Donohue. Triton Aerospace. We built the podium. The only way to get around using that mike is to go into the repair panel and cut the wires. Then put an external unit on top.'

'An external unit?' asked Fiske.

'Yes sir, you know, a regular microphone. We can drill a hole and run the cable inside the podium and hook it up to the PR system.'

Fiske smiled and shook his head, as if this young pup Donohue were trying to pull a fast one on him. *An external mike.* A big black banana that would stick up in the middle of Senator McCoy's face as she spoke to 250 million Americans and billions of others around the world. Senator McCoy standing all of five feet four inches tall with heels. That was not a solution. Not unless Ellington Fiske wished for an immediate transfer to the Sierra Leone field office.

'Anything new from intel?' Fiske asked Larry Kennedy, his assistant.

Intelligence was charged with monitoring any leads from the CIA, FBI, DIA, or any credible law-enforcement agency pertaining to any and all possible threats. Anything from a concerted terrorist action to a lone gunman. For two hours tomorrow, the front steps of the Capitol would be the world's biggest bullseye. It would also be the world's hardest target.

'Negative,' said Kennedy.

'Mr Donohue,' barked Fiske.

'Yes sir.'

'Do you have another podium ready for us?'

'Yes, Mr Fiske. It's being prepped at the warehouse in Alexandria right now. Should be here at four o'clock. They're just applying the presidential seal.'

'Get it here by two.' Fiske stomped away from the podium. 'And be sure you test it first. I want to make sure the thing is working before we install it. Call me when it arrives.'

Fiske stared up at the sky. Policing three hundred thousand people in pouring rain would make things decidedly more difficult. If the podium was his only problem, he'd get away easy. A sudden burst of rain drenched his face. 'Where's the canopy?' he asked no one in particular. 'The first female President of the United States is going to be sworn in within twenty-four hours and she will not have a lousy hairdo. That woman is going to look good.'

Chapter 30

Whenever John Franciscus entered the shimmering, bustling, Plexiglas world of 1 Police Plaza, the headquarters of the New York City Police Department in downtown Manhattan, he whispered the same moldy adage to himself. 'Those that can, do. Those that can't, man a desk at One PP.' To his way of thinking, cops policed. Which meant they knocked heads and solved crimes. The suits down here . . . well, they were just that . . . *suits*. Men who viewed police work as a ladder to the exalted lofts of city power. Who ordered their day according to the clock, not according to the cases open on their desks. Who took no pride in the wearing of a blue uniform. He'd seen them squirming in their dress blues on St Patty's Day, yanking at their high collars, adjusting their watch caps, and generally looking three shades of embarrassed.

Franciscus felt his cheeks flush. It wasn't right, he cursed silently, keeping his eyes down so no one would think he was crying. It just wasn't right. But when the anger waned, he couldn't explain what it was, exactly, that wasn't right, or why it had bothered him so much.

Records had changed floors, but the lights were still too bright and the ceilings too low. A chubby Hispanic man with thinning hair and a push broom mustache sat behind the long chest-high counter, reading a magazine.

'Matty L.,' said Franciscus, as he passed through the door. 'Can't get rid of you either?'

'Gentleman Johnny Fran! What brings you to this fluorescent shithole?'

The two shook hands, and Franciscus found himself not wanting to let go. Lopes had occupied the desk next to him at Manhattan North for twenty years before catching a bullet in the spine during a botched arrest. A year in rehab and a Purple Shield medal awarded by the mayor himself in a ceremony at Gracie Mansion had landed him on this swiveling stool supervising Records. Behind his back, everyone called Lopes 'Sticky Fingers'. Word was he'd dropped his piece going in for the bust that fateful day.

'I'm checking up on a cold case,' said Franciscus. 'Goes way back. Nineteen eighty.'

'Nineteen eighty? That's the Ice Age.'

'Double homicide up in Albany. You may know it.'

'Got the victims' names?'

'Brendan O'Neill and Samuel Shepherd.'

'Sentinel Bombing,' said Lopes, not missing a beat. 'Who doesn't remember it? Whole state was in an uproar.'

Lopes was right about that. It had been an electrifying crime. At the time, though, Franciscus was out of state, interviewing a suspect in a multiple homicide, and hadn't caught the climax on live TV like twenty million other New Yorkers. Before coming downtown, he'd read a few articles about the case that had appeared in the *Times* and the local Albany *Times Union*. These were the facts, as reported.

At 11:36 P.M., July 26, 1980, a powerful bomb blew

up the headquarters of Sentinel Microsystems, a maker of computer chips and software in Albany. Bomb experts estimated that over two hundred pounds of TNT packed inside two Samsonite suitcases were placed next to the first-floor R and D laboratory and detonated by remote control. Police tracked the explosives to a theft the week earlier from a nearby construction site. Two witnesses were found who reported seeing a suspicious U-Haul rental truck circling Sentinel's headquarters the day before the explosion. A check of the local U-Haul agency led police to the residence of David Bernstein, a respected law professor, better known as Manu Q, self-styled revolutionary and spokesman for the radical Free Society.

As officers O'Neill and Shepherd approached the house to question Bernstein, gunfire erupted. O'Neill and Shepherd were shot and died at the scene. A SWAT team was called in, and when Bernstein refused to surrender, the house was stormed.

News of a fugitive suspect surfaced a few weeks afterwards, when a second set of fingerprints was discovered on the handgun used to kill O'Neill and Shepherd. The prints reportedly belonged to Bobby Stillman, a.k.a. Sunshine Awakening, a known member of the Free Society, and Bernstein's common-law wife. Her involvement in the bombing was corroborated by witnesses who reported seeing her near the construction site where the dynamite used in the bombing had been stolen.

But Franciscus wasn't interested in what the newspapers had to report. He wanted to learn what the homicide dicks had to say about the case. The good stuff never made it to the paper.

'Why you calling it a cold case?' asked Lopes. 'They nailed the guy who offed the cops. His name was Bernstein. Guy was bananas. Called himself Manu Q. I remember it like it was yesterday. Shot him like forty times. They posted his picture in the *Gazette*.'

Franciscus recalled the picture. The corpse had looked like a piece of Swiss cheese. Cop killers didn't deserve any better. 'There was a second suspect,' he said. 'A woman who got away.'

'I don't remember that. And she's still running?' Lopes's eyes narrowed in disgust. 'All this time and no one's nailed her? Shame on us. What's her name?'

'Bobby Stillman, but she's got more aliases than Joe Bananas.'

'Give me five minutes.' Lopes walked the length of the counter, tapping his fingers as he went. 'I'll pull the file. Original's in Albany, but we'll have an abstract.'

Franciscus sat down in the corner of the little waiting area they'd set up. A coffee table offered a few magazines. He skimmed through a month-old *Newsweek*, then checked what was on TV. A television in the corner was broadcasting *The View*. Five broads yakking about why they never got laid. The guys at the squad room watched it every day. Kinda made sense, Franciscus decided, giving himself over to the show. It wasn't exactly like cops wanted to sit around watching reruns of *NYPD Blue*. They had enough of that shit parked in front of them.

After a few minutes, he checked his watch, wondering what was taking so long. The watch was a gold-plated Bulova with a fake alligator strap, a gift to recognize thirty years on the job. The dial was embossed with the symbol of the New York City Police Department. He tapped the crystal with his thumb, as if to make sure the watch was keeping proper time. Once, he'd calculated that he'd spent over two thousand hours on stakeouts.

It seemed like only yesterday that he'd graduated from the academy and gone to his first posting with the tactical squad, busting up riots, demonstrations, sit-ins, and the like. It was 1969, and the world was going apeshit. Vietnam. Women's lib. Free sex. Everyone shouting, 'Turn on, tune in, and drop out.' The last thing anyone wanted to be was a monster in a blue uniform donning full riot gear, but Franciscus had signed on, and that's what he did. No questions. No complaints. He'd always thought it was an honor to serve.

For the second time in an hour, his cheeks flushed and the back of his neck heated up. He looked up at the television to gather himself, but Barbara Walters was so blurry that not even another face-lift could straighten her out. Franciscus looked away, pinching his nose between thumb and forefinger. Going all fuzzy twice in the same day. What the heck was the matter with him? He fished a hankie out of his pocket and blew his nose.

Just then, he heard a welter of voices raised in heated argument from the back of the storeroom. A minute later, Matty Lopes reappeared. 'I can't believe it,' he said. 'File's gone.'

Franciscus stood and walked to the counter. 'Someone check it out?'

'No, man. It's like "gone" gone. The whole thing has been ripped out of its folder. Like "stolen" gone. I called Albany. Same thing. Gone. Not even an update slip. Nothing. Just "gone".'

'Since when?'

'I got no idea. No one's got any idea. The thing's just gone.'

Franciscus thrust his hands in his pockets and caught Lopes giving him the once-over. 'You sure you telling me everything about this case?' Lopes asked.

'Cross my heart.' Franciscus was thinking that every case, both open and closed, belonged to someone and was registered as such on the central computer. 'Who was the catching detective?'

'You want, let's check.' Lopes unlatched a waist-high gate and waved him through. 'Come on back. I'm pissed, let me tell you. This is my house. Nobody takes my stuff without asking.'

Franciscus followed him past the rows of shelves stuffed to the ceiling with case files. One day, they would all be scanned and stored on the mainframe, but that day was still a way off. At the back of the room, there was a table with five desktop computers. Instructions for their use were taped to the wall. Lopes sat down and motioned for Franciscus to take the place next to him. Consulting a scrap of paper, he keyed in the case file number.

'Theodore Kovacs,' said Lopes, when the information had appeared. 'Died 1980. Three months after the bombing.'

'How old was he?'

'Thirty-one.'

'Young to have his gold shield. What was the cause?'

'Special circumstances.'

Franciscus traded glances with Lopes. 'Special circumstances' was department shorthand for suicide. In copspeak, Theodore Kovacs had eaten his gun. 'Jeez,' he muttered. 'Who was the backup?'

It was also a rule that two detectives had to sign off on a case.

'That's it. Just Kovacs.' Lopes pointed at the screen for Franciscus to take a look.

'Come on,' said Franciscus, sliding back his chair. 'Can't file without two names. You going to tell me that someone broke into the computer and stole that, too?'

For once, Matty Lopes didn't have an answer. Shrugging, he shot Franciscus an earnest look. 'Seems like this case ain't so cold after all.'

Chapter 31

Guy de Valmont walked down the corridor in the rolling gait that was his calling card. A casual stride, one hand in the pocket, the other ready to wave a hello, fire off one of his charming salutes, or brush the pesky forelock out of his eyes. He was a tall man, and thin, in his skivvies all bones and right angles. But the miracle of Braithwaite and Pendel of Savile Row, combined with his naturally broad (but bony) shoulders, gave him the haphazard and elegant carriage of an English gentleman. To de Valmont, there was no higher calling.

It was his fifty-third birthday and to celebrate, he'd allowed himself an early glass of bubbly. The zest of it was still fresh in his mouth, the mark of a good vintage. His birthday, along with the gala dinner that evening, and perhaps, too, the champagne, had put him in a rare, contemplative mood. He was not concerned with his age, so much as with the realization that he had spent twenty-five of those fifty-three years at Jefferson. Day in, day out, with four weeks of vacation a year . . . well, more like eight weeks lately. Still, twenty-five years doing the same damn thing. Lines of worry appeared on de Valmont's pale forehead. Where had they gone?

It seemed like yesterday that he and J.J. had founded the place. Jacklin, then in his forties, with his tenure as Secretary of Defense freshly behind him, and he, Guy de Valmont, the Wall Street Wunderkind, who'd thought up the harebrained scheme. Buy troubled companies with other people's money, turn them around, wring every last cent of cash out of them, then get rid of them, either via an IPO, or, preferably, an outright sale. On paper it looked easy, but twice in those first years, they'd almost gone bust, buying the wrong companies, using too much cash or too much leverage, and never enough common sense. That was before Jacklin got the inspiration that would make Jefferson great. The revolving door, he called it. The currency-thin barrier between Wall Street and Washington, DC. Oh, it had always been there, right back to Andrew Jackson's 'Kitchen Cabinet'. But until now, it had been something whispered about, something not quite kosher. Jefferson came along and practically institutionalized the thing.

De Valmont whistled softly, taking up 'It's a Long Way to Tipperary'. The occupants of the offices to his left and right read like a Rolodex of the high and mighty. Billy Baxter, budget director for Bush I. Loy Crandall, Air Force Chief of Staff. Arlene Watkins, Chief of the General Services Administration, the office that okayed all contracts between civilian corporations and the government. The list went on. Counsel to the President. Senate majority leader. President of the Urban League. Director of the International Red Cross. The only one missing was the head of the Boy Scouts of America.

They were all at Jefferson, making up for years of government penury, feathering their nests for retirement, or for their children's retirement, or their children's children's. Pay at Jefferson was generous. (He, himself, had become a billionaire long ago. In fact, he'd passed the five-billion marker somewhere around his fiftieth birthday.) And all Jacklin asked was that they make a few calls, pull a few strings, cash in a few favors. Swing a vote to increase funding for this or that project. Soften regulations to allow export of a new military technology. Amend a piece of legislation to include another state. If companies in Jefferson's portfolio benefited, all the better.

'J.J.?' he called, sauntering into Jacklin's palatial lair. Jacklin had insisted it be at least ten square feet larger than his office at the Pentagon. De Valmont spotted him, poring over some documents at his desk. He walked closer, realizing that Jacklin had turned his hearing aid down. All those missions in an A-6 had left him deafer than a bat. De Valmont stopped a foot behind his back.

'Bang!'

Jacklin jumped out of his socks. 'Damn it, Guy,' he said, his cheeks flushing red. 'You scared the crap out of me.'

De Valmont ignored the outburst. 'You'll never guess who I just spoke with. Tom Bolden from HW.'

Jacklin's face froze. 'The kid who shot Sol Weiss?'

'One and the same.'

'Whatever for?'

'He called. Asked me if I knew anything about Scanlon.'

'Scanlon! God, there's a name from the past.'

'And not one we'd particularly care to remember. He sounded upset.'

'I'd imagine so. What'd you tell him?'

'That I was busy and that I'd look into it and call him back.' De Valmont shrugged and studied his nails. He needed a manicure. He couldn't go to the dinner this evening looking like a Goth. 'What do you think he's found?'

*

'Sir!'

'Yes, Hoover. Still here.'

Hoover shook his head, startled. 'I thought you'd gone somewhere.'

'Standing right by your side.' Guilfoyle lowered himself to a knee. 'What do you have?'

'A restaurant at Sixteenth Street and Union Square West called the Coffee Shop. Bolden called the place twice the same day that Miss Dance visited the pharmacy. He used an ATM right around the corner at twelve-sixteen P.M. Oh, and they don't take credit cards.'

'The Coffee Shop,' said Guilfoyle. 'Good work.' He hurried to his desk overlooking the operations center and picked up his cellular phone. Unlike standard-issue models, this phone carried a sophisticated scrambling device rendering his transmissions a collage of squawks and beeps and indecipherable white noise to surveillance devices. The phone he called was equipped with a similar device, capable of unscrambling the transmission in real time.

'Sir,' answered a deep, unsatisfied voice.

'I have some good news.'

'I'll believe it when I hear it,' said Wolf.

'We've pinpointed where Bolden will be at noon. The Coffee Shop at Union Square.'

'You're sure?'

Guilfoyle peered over his desk at the lines of technicians busy at their consoles. Heads bowed, hands racing furiously over keyboards, they brought to mind the galley slaves of ancient Greece. Men enslaved by machines. 'Cerberus is,' he answered. 'I want you to take in a full field team.'

'How many men do we have in the vicinity?'

'Eight, not including you and Irish. They can form up on your location in twelve minutes.'

'Any shooters?'

Guilfoyle ran a mouse over the red pinlights indicating his men's locations on the wall-mounted map. In turn, the name of the operative and his field grade appeared in a box beneath it. 'Jensen,' he said. Malcolm Jensen. A former marine sniper. 'I want you to act as his spotter.'

'His spotter . . . but sir—'

'Jensen will need someone who knows what Bolden looks like. We can count on him being in some kind of disguise. You'll have to keep a sharp eye.' Wolf began to hesitate, but Guilfoyle cut him off. 'I can't have you in the middle of things. Bolden knows your face by now. We can't risk spooking him. That's final.'

'Yes sir.'

'I think Mr Bolden's given us enough of a run for our money. Don't you?'

Chapter 32

The BlackBerry, thought Bolden.

By law, every cell phone possessed a GPS chip – a chip that broadcast the phone's location to within a hundred feet. His pager number was published in HW's directory. That number, in turn, could be traced to a service provider – in his case, Verizon Wireless. But to pinpoint the signal – to actually get a read of the GPS coordinates, so many minutes and seconds longitude and latitude – required getting inside the phone company. Being able to tap into their transmission networks and track down a specific number.

Bolden clutched the device in his palm, pedestrians passing to either side of him, as if he were a stone in a stream. The phone was a homing beacon. He'd made it so easy for them. Hurrying to the nearest corner, he tossed the BlackBerry into a trash bin. The signal turned green. People flooded the crosswalk. Bolden stepped off the kerb, hesitated, then returned to the trash bin.

'Taxi!' he called, raising a hand in the air.

A moment later, a cab pulled over.

Bolden opened the door and stuck his head and shoulders inside. 'How much to Boston?'

'To Boston? No, no . . .' The Sikh cabby thought about it for a second. 'Five hundred dollars plus gas. Cash. No credit card.'

'Five hundred? You're sure?' As Bolden

pretended to consider the offer, he slipped the BlackBerry into the pouch behind the passenger seat.

The Sikh nodded vigorously. 'Ten hours' driving. Yes, I am sure.'

'Sorry, too steep. Thanks anyway.' Stepping back to the kerb, Bolden watched the cab disappear into traffic.

At Lexington and Fifty-first, he ran down the stairs of the subway, then hugged the wall and watched dozens of men and women file in after him. Five minutes passed. Satisfied he was no longer being followed, he jumped the turnstiles and descended the stairs to the south platform.

He was safe. No GPS signal to home in on, no office to stake out. While he had no doubt that Guilfoyle had been monitoring his home phone, he hadn't mentioned the name of the restaurant where he intended to meet Jenny. It was their inadvertent secret.

He boarded the express train, and ten minutes later, got off at Sixteenth Street.

Jenny slid into the booth, huddling against the wall. Keeping her eyes in front of her, she unwrapped the scarf from her neck and loosened the buttons on her overcoat. She'd tucked her hair into a black beret, and that she kept on.

They were here. Bobby Stillman had promised her that. Bobby didn't say how many of them there might be, if they were men or women, or how they could have known. Just that they were here. It was a fact you had to count on, Bobby had said. A tenet of faith. And if they weren't, you'd better pretend they were, because they sure as hell would be there the next time. Amen.

The Coffee Shop was boisterous and bustling.

Every table was taken, the aisles cluttered with waiters and waitresses shuttling back and forth between the dining room and kitchen, refilling coffee cups, ferrying trays piled high with meat loaf and burgers and grilled-cheese sandwiches. It was the kind of place that served lunch on thick porcelain plates and coffee in chipped mugs, and where the staff hollered to one another across the room.

They're here.

Just like *Poltergeist*. They're here but you can't see 'em. Jenny pushed her mug out for some coffee. After it was poured, she added two packets of sugar and warmed her hands on the porcelain. Turning her wrist, she saw that it was already 12:05. Tom was five minutes late. She started to look over her shoulder, then caught herself. *It's only five minutes. He'll be here any second. He got caught in the office.* There were always delays at the bank, last-minute corrections, meetings that went long. Except that Thomas was never late. For Thomas, 'on time' meant ten minutes early. He was a disaster as a boyfriend. He never learned that dates should arrive five minutes late, and that parties didn't really get going until an hour after they began. All of which meant he'd be a wonderful father.

She took a sip of coffee, letting her eyes flit around the restaurant. She looked at the two guys inhaling their hamburgers while insisting on talking at the same time. The older man engrossed in his crossword puzzle. The table of executives sipping iced tea and pretending to be enthralled by what the big boss had to say. And why not women? Shouldn't she be suspicious of them, too? Maybe it was the two blondes picking at their salads. Or the gaggle of college students strewn across the booth

like pieces of clothing. Or . . . Jenny dropped her
eyes to the pool of black liquid. It could be any of
them. Why not all of them? She stopped herself. It
was infectious. Bobby Stillman's paranoia had
gotten to her, too.

Where was Thomas?

Guilfoyle stared intently as the blue pinlight made
a stop-and-go circuit around the Upper East Side of
Manhattan. It was moving much too fast for
someone on foot. The pinlight circled a block, then
stopped for a few minutes. It zoomed ten blocks
uptown and then ten blocks back. Presently, it was
making a beeline across the Triborough Bridge. *An
airport fare*, Guilfoyle said to himself. It was the
cabby's lucky day.

'Hoover,' he called.

'Yessir.'

'Cancel tracking Bolden's BlackBerry signal.'

The pale, washed-out face turned to him in
concern. 'Did we get him?'

'Other way around, I'm afraid. Bolden's on
to us.'

Guilfoyle allowed himself a private laugh as he
watched the blue pinlight negotiate the wilds of
Queens, and finally disappear off the map. To his
eye, it was all the more proof that Bolden was
headed in the opposite direction. Downtown. To
Union Square.

The threat of snow and rapidly falling temperatures did nothing to discourage the lunchtime
crowd, Bolden decided as he made a circuit of
Union Square. The sidewalk was knotted with men
and women, their parkas, scarves, and berets a
rainbow against the woolen sky. He kept close to
the buildings, hugging the walls. Occasionally, he

cut into a doorway and lingered there a moment or two. He kept his eyes down, his chin and mouth buried in the folds of his jacket. But all the while he was looking.

A raft of students blocked the area immediately in front of an NYU dorm, petitioning for signatures against the newly reinstated draft. Across the street in the park, a horn quartet serenaded a gaggle of listeners with a Bach fugue. Farther along, a smaller ensemble had gathered in front of a boom box pounding out a reggae beat. Bolden could see nothing out of place. Everything was moving at its usual frenetic pace.

Leaving Union Square, he headed west two blocks, then turned south and circled back. He slowed by the entrance to the alley that led to the rear of the Coffee Shop, the restaurant where he'd planned to meet Jenny for lunch. His eyes traveled up and down the street, but again, he saw nothing out of the ordinary.

The back door was open. The low, steady rumble of conversation reached him, along with a pulse of warm air. He stepped inside. The heat wrapped itself around him like a blanket. The rest rooms were on the right, and past them, a coffee station. On the left, swinging doors led to the kitchen. He advanced a few steps and gazed across the dining room. Jenny was seated alone in a booth next to the window, huddled over a cup of coffee. She was dressed in jeans, an ivory Irish fisherman's sweater, and a camel-hair overcoat.

Bolden studied the noontime crowd, his eyes sliding from face to face. There was no one staring at Jenny.

No one except him.

It was safe.

*

She spotted him.

The blond-haired man seated alone at the table, next aisle over. This was the second time Jenny had glanced in his direction and found him staring back. He was one of them. Had to be. He was young. He looked strong, athletic. She observed that he was dressed in slacks and a blazer, like the two who had come after her last night. Bobby Stillman had been right. *They were here.* Jenny didn't know how it was possible, just that it was. He was proof. Sitting there fifteen feet away pretending not to look at her, but looking at her, all the same. She looked up again only to meet his eyes. He was handsome, she'd give him that much. They'd chosen their operatives well. *Operatives.* It was Bobby Stillman's word. Except this time, he didn't look away. He smiled. He was flirting. Oh, Lord, he even raised an eyebrow.

Jenny's gaze dropped to the table like a lead weight. She could cross him off the list of potential bad guys. With a microbiologist's zeal, she examined the rim of her coffee cup. She wasn't any good at this. Not the lying. The acting. The pretending. The simplest fib left her trembling with shame. She felt as if she were on stage, every set of eyes in the restaurant secretly examining her.

'How's your arm?'

Jenny started, not knowing whether she should look up and answer or just ignore Thomas altogether. She didn't recognize him in jeans and a dark work jacket. 'Ten stitches,' she said. 'How did you know?'

'Long story.'

'Don't tell me. We have to get out of here.' She slid a leg out of the booth, then froze. Her hand reached out to his cheek. 'My God,' she whispered.

'It's nothing,' he said.

'Nothing?'

'Actually, it's gunpowder. The good news is that the guy missed.' Bolden narrowed his eyes, confused. 'What's wrong? Why are you so worried about me?'

'They came to get me,' said Jenny. 'They told me you were in trouble, and that I might be in danger, too. They took me to this apartment in Brooklyn so I'd be safe. But then these other guys—'

'Who came for you? Who told you I was in trouble?'

'Bobby Stillman. She said you'd know who she was.'

'She?'

Jenny nodded. 'She's waiting for us. They're here. The ones who are after you. We have to go now. We have to get out of here.'

'Slow down, Jen.'

'No!' she whispered, her teeth on edge. She wished that for once he would just do as she asked without arguing. 'We have to go.'

But Thomas didn't move. 'It's all right,' he said, looking around the restaurant. 'I promise you. They don't know we're here. No one does. I don't know what anyone told you, but no one followed me here. It's impossible, okay? This is our place. No one else knows about it.'

'You're sure?'

'Yes. For once, I'm sure.'

Jenny could sense his worry beneath the confidence. His eyes looked tired. She leaned across the table and reached for his hand. 'What in the world is going on?'

Thomas spent a few minutes going over what he had been through during the past twelve hours. When he was finished, he said, 'I didn't know what to think when I stopped by school and you weren't there. At first I thought it was just because you were feeling lousy, but then . . .' He smiled, and she could feel his affection, his love. 'Tell me about her. Who is this Bobby Stillman?'

'So you don't know who she is?'

'Contrary to popular opinion, no.'

'She's scary. She's very intense. She has too much locked up inside her. She's like a hydrogen bomb, all this dark energy and fear, just ready to go off. She said it's "a club" that's after you. Or a "committee". I'm not exactly sure. They think you know something about them. They're scared. That's all I know, other than the fact that she's on the run, too.'

'You said she came for you at school?'

'Not her, but a friend of hers did. They said that if I ever wanted to see you again, I had to come with them. At first, I didn't believe them, but then there were those cars coming after them, and now, here you are with gunpowder on your cheek.' Jenny found a napkin and wiped her eyes. 'They're going to help you get out of this mess . . . they're going to help *us*. Please come with me now. We can't stay. She said they might figure out we're here. It's all so crazy. Mind readers and Big Brother and the All-Seeing Eye.'

'Did she say anything about Scanlon? Or, about a group calling themselves Minutemen?'

'No. Who are they?'

Bolden explained about the tattoo he'd seen on Wolf, and how he'd found a similar drawing related to the Scanlon Corporation, a 'civilian contractor' that had once built military bases for the army. How Scanlon had branched off into private security work that included providing military trainers for other nations' armed forces. 'The connection seemed too perfect to be a coincidence.'

'And who are the "Minutemen"?'

'Some group of right-wing crazies back in the sixties. All I know is that they're from Houston, too, where Scanlon started up, and that they used the same Kentucky flintlock rifle as a logo for their group.'

'I've never heard of them . . . outside the regular Minutemen. Paul Revere. Lexington and Concord. One if by land, and two if by sea. The Old North Church.'

Bolden looked away and she could see the disappointment in his eyes.

'I'm sorry,' said Jenny.

'It's all a wild goose chase.' He wrung his hands. 'Where did you say they took you?'

'Harlem. Hamilton Tower. Near Convent Avenue.'

'I know where it is. It's one block from Alexander Hamilton's old home. The Grange.'

'And so?'

'And so, I don't know . . . you're the one talking about Minutemen and flintlock rifles. Bobby Stillman said the club had been around for ever. Actually, she said, "since the beginning". Maybe it's been around since Hamilton was secretary of the treasury.'

'That's over two hundred years ago.'

'There are lots of clubs older than that. The Order of the Garter. The Society of the Cincinnati.' Jenny looked at her watch. 'Come on. We've been here too long. You can ask her yourself. She's waiting.'

She stood and led the way past the cashier, through the pack waiting to be seated. Thomas tapped her on the shoulder. 'Hey, Jen,' he said. 'You never got to tell me what you wanted to talk about.'

'You sure you want to know? It's not the best time.'

'Of course, I want to know.'

'All right then.' Turning, she took his hand. 'I'm—' Jenny felt her mouth go dry. Around the room, several men were standing from their tables and hurrying toward the cashier's desk. They were all of a kind: near her age, fit, neatly dressed. The Romeo who'd been giving her the eye was on his feet, too. She counted five men in all. *They're here.*

'Hurry up,' she said, yanking Thomas's hand. 'The club's here.'

'What do you mean?'

'They're here! The club. The committee. Whatever she called them. We've got to hurry. Please, Tommy. You've got to follow me.'

Jenny shoved open the door and ran onto the sidewalk. A line of customers three deep waiting for a table snaked down the block. Jenny pushed through the crowd and rushed to the kerb. 'There's supposed to be a car here for us,' she said, looking up and down the street.

Union Square West was off limits to through traffic. A lone Dodge Dart was parked against the far kerb, near the park. Farther up the block, she noticed a Lincoln Town Car, mount of choice for every limousine service in the city. She checked over her shoulder. The men were filing out of the restaurant, spreading out on the sidewalk behind them.

'Where's the car?' Bolden asked.

'I don't know,' Jenny said, tugging at her hands.

Bolden looked behind them. 'We can't stand here. We've got to—'

Just then, the Dodge Dart parked across the street exploded.

Chapter 33

Smoke billowed from the hood of the car. Tongues of flame curled from the engine block, the trunk, the passenger seat, lapping at the sky. The heat was tremendous. The line of customers waiting to get into the Coffee Shop had turned into an agitated throng. People stood, stunned and shaken. They held each other. They pointed. They ran. The daring approaching the burning car.

'There's someone inside,' a voice shouted.

'Get him out!' urged another. 'Hurry!'

The wall of heat was intense enough to erase even the most heroic notions.

Bolden guided Jenny away from the car. His ears were ringing from the blast, his eyes watering from the bales of smoke. He checked the area near the car for any wounded bystanders, but could find no torn and bloodied shirts, no blackened faces. If it had been a car bomb, there would be casualties, dead, wounded. If it had been a car bomb, he would have been a pile of smoking rags and a pair of empty shoes. He glanced around him. Hidden somewhere among the milling crowd were the men whom Jenny had spotted in the restaurant. The explosion had given him a few seconds.

'It's her,' she said, pointing. 'It's Bobby Stillman.'

A woman had emerged from the smoke, standing near the hood of the car, braving the fire. She was shouting, beckoning them to come. A tall, pale, pinched woman in her fifties.

Like a hydrogen bomb, all dark energy and fear, ready to go off.

The woman – Bobby Stillman – continued to motion for him to come. 'Thomas,' she was saying. He could read her lips. 'Hurry!'

But you have to know each other, Guilfoyle had insisted.

It took him another second to fault Guilfoyle on that count, too. He had never seen her before in his life.

Jenny started across the street, but Bolden held her back. He didn't want to go into a park, where he could be surrounded and overwhelmed. The crowd was his friend. Turmoil. Chaos. He had learned these things as a kid. He understood that it was Bobby Stillman who'd detonated this 'smoke bomb', and that it was a diversion to help him get away. And with that knowledge came the rest of it: that she had known about his kidnapping, and therefore knew Guilfoyle.

He looked at Bobby Stillman a moment longer, and made his decision.

'Come with me,' he said to Jenny.

'But . . .'

Tightening his grip on her hand, he began walking away, the walk turning to a jog.

They headed down the block to Fifteenth Street, dodging in and out of the masses converging on the burning car. The petitioners had abandoned their tables. The musicians clutched their horns to their chests as if they were cradling their children. Students poured out of the dormitory, rapt expressions testifying that real life beat books any day. Nearby, a siren began to wail.

Someone collided with Bolden. Jenny's fingers

slipped from his. He spun, relieved to find her at his back. 'We're almost out of here,' he said. 'Just around the corner.'

Jenny pushed the hair out of her face and nodded.

When Bolden turned back, he was met by a pair of determined brown eyes. A man his own age with straight blond hair stood in front of him blocking his path. He moved closer and Bolden couldn't mistake a rabid zeal. Something hard struck Bolden's ribs. He glanced down and saw that it was a pistol. 'Who the hell are you? What do you want with me?'

The man answered with a calm that belied his coiled tension. 'Time to stop interfering.'

The pistol pushed harder into Bolden's ribs and the muscles in the man's jaw flexed.

'No!' shouted Bolden.

And then the man's face slackened. His eyes wavered and rolled back into his head. All at once, he was collapsing at the knees. Another man caught him. He was tall, lean, mid-fifties, unshaven, a stubble of iron gray hair peeking out from a longshoreman's cap. His right hand clutched a fat leather sap. His bloodshot eyes passed from Bolden to Jenny. 'Go, sweetheart,' he said, in a rough voice. 'Get out of here. Situation's under control.'

Bolden skirted him and hurried down the sidewalk. 'You know him?' he asked over his shoulder.

'Harry,' she said. 'He's a friend.'

'That's good,' said Bolden. 'We need friends.'

At the south end of the street, a police car turned in and accelerated toward them, siren whooping on and off. A second police car followed it. Bolden looked over his shoulder. The scene reminded him of a newsreel from a sixties protest, people scattering, air clouded with tear gas, an atmosphere of rage and incomprehension. The two men were gone – the grim, blond-haired assailant and Harry, the worn-out jarhead who'd knocked him unconscious – both of them swallowed by the unruly crowd. And the others? He knew they were there, looking for him. He told himself that they were closer than he expected. They had to move. To escape. But where?

Two police cars drove past. The crowd opened up to allow them a clear path.

'What is it, Thomas?' Jenny asked, bumping into him.

He rocked a step forward. 'Noth—'

He heard the bullet strike Jenny. The impact was as distinct as a slap on the thigh. A red film sprayed from her shoulder. She lurched back a step, falling hard to the ground, striking her head on the concrete. Bolden dived to his left. A bullet ricocheted off the ground where he'd stood. He waited for the crack of a rifle, but none came. He looked around. The tide of pedestrians that had momentarily parted to allow the police cars to pass had engulfed them again. Rising to a knee, he searched the buildings opposite the square for some sign of where the shot had come from. He spotted movement in a third-floor window directly opposite him. A dark figure looming at an open window. A head cradled over a narrow object. Then it was gone.

Jenny was unconscious, her eyes closed, her breath coming in shallow gulps. A hole was cut in her camel-hair overcoat the size of a dime. Beneath it, he saw raw flesh. 'Hang on,' he pleaded.

Two policemen were rushing over. At the corner, a third police car had stopped. The doors flew open. Peaked caps rose and started toward them. Already a crowd was gathering, as one by one, passers-by figured out that someone had been shot.

Bolden leaned over and kissed Jenny on the forehead. He looked at her for a last moment, then rose and disappeared into the crowd. She would be all right, he said to himself. She would live.

Chapter 34

'Her name was Dance? You're sure of that?'
Franciscus asked, after the officer in charge had
explained what had happened as best he knew.
There were at least twenty uniforms securing the
area, and as many blue-and-whites parked up and
down the street. A crime scene had been set up,
yellow tape forming a perimeter that ran from the
burnt-out car down the block to where Franciscus
stood.

'Yeah. Jennifer Dance,' the officer replied, double-
checking his notepad. 'She's on the way to NYU
Emergency. Gunshot wound to the shoulder. Don't
know how bad it is.'

'She with anyone? A guy, maybe? Six feet. Dark
hair. Solid.'

'We got a report of someone running from the
scene, but no description.'

'She talking?'

'Not yet. All she said was that one second she
was standing there, the next she went down. I've
got two men heading over to the hospital to speak
with her. We're still interviewing witnesses. Why?
You got something I should know about?'

'Maybe. Can I get back to you?'

Franciscus patted the uniform on the shoulder
and headed up the street toward the car.

Wisps of smoke rose from the engine block like
steam from the subway grate. The hood was blown

up into the shape of an arc. Somehow, it was still attached. Flames had charred the chassis and melted the windshield. A few firefighters stood around the wreck, extinguishers in hand. Franciscus joined them, waving at his nose. 'What in the name of Jehovah is that smell?'

'Sulfur.'

'Sulfur? What is it, a stink bomb?'

One of the firefighters was bent forward, inspecting the bowels of the engine. 'Got it!' he shouted, emerging with a twisted piece of metal the size of a wine cork with frayed wires sprouting from it. 'Blasting cap,' he said, handing the misshapen chunk to the detective.

Franciscus inspected the blasting cap, turning it this way and that. 'Tell me this: why didn't the whole car explode?'

'No gas,' said the firefighter, whom Franciscus figured to be an arson specialist. 'There was only a gallon or so in the tank. Looks like they spread a little in the trunk and on the interior, but just enough to make a wicked fire. Not enough to go ka-boom. The whole thing was a very controlled job. Look at the hood. The force of the blast was directed up. Vertically. There was enough of a charge to make a loud bang, but not enough to blow this baby apart. This wasn't about killing anybody, it was about making a big friggin' noise and a heck of a lot of smoke.' He stuck his head back under the hood and pointed to the charred crust lining the engine wall. ' "Willy Pete". White phosphorus. It's what made the smoke. Same stuff we use in our smoke canisters. This ain't a stink bomb. No sir. What we got here, Detective, is a giant smoke bomb.'

Franciscus bent his head over the radiator. The vehicle identification number had been sanded down. He'd bet the license plates were stolen, too. He walked around the car. A Dodge Dart. What a pile. 'So, I take it that we're not talking Osama bin Laden?'

'More like Mr Wizard.'

Franciscus was leaving 1 PP, heading back uptown, when the radio had started going crazy with chatter. A car bomb in Union Square Park. A report of gunfire. One wounded. Possible fatalities. All available units to respond. It sounded like war had broken out. He threw the siren onto the dash, and in a few seconds, had the Crown Vic up to sixty. As he neared Twelfth Street, he caught a plume of black smoke curling into the air.

The day was turning out to be one big bouquet of roses.

After learning that the file on the Albany bombing was missing, he'd made a beeline for Central Booking to check on the status of the perp Bolden had brought in the night before. Busted teeth or no busted teeth, Franciscus intended on finding out from him why he'd wanted to assault Thomas Bolden, and why his buddies had such a hard-on for Bobby Stillman, a woman with a warrant for capital murder on her head who had dropped off the radar a quarter of a century earlier. To his surprise, the perp had given himself a name – Trey Parker – a social security number, and had, thereupon, been flushed out of the system. No arraignment. No bail. *Nada*. This, in flagrant contravention of New York State law calling for a mandatory one-year sentence for those convicted of illegally possessing a firearm. Worse, Franciscus couldn't find a soul who knew anything about it. The paperwork concerning his release had disappeared with Mr Parker himself.

It was at this point that Franciscus had decided to talk to Bolden personally, and give him a heads-up that Parker might be looking for him. There was something about Bolden that he liked. Maybe it was that tattoo: 'Never Rat on Friends.' Anybody else working with a tight-ass firm on Wall Street would have had the artwork removed long ago.

A call to Bolden's office had led to a conversation with Michael Schiff, HW's CEO, who was quick to inform him that Solomon Weiss had been killed that morning. The man had gone on to rant for ten minutes about Bolden being the killer and a lot of stuff that Franciscus still couldn't bring himself to believe.

A real bouquet of roses, he thought, as he walked into the Coffee Shop, looking for something to drink. The place had a juice bar over in one corner. A young Puerto Rican guy was sitting on a stool behind the counter, chewing on a section of sugar cane.

Franciscus took a seat on the sparkling ruby red barstool. 'What do you have that'll do an old fart some good?'

'You like wheatgrass?'

Franciscus made a face. He'd tried wheatgrass twice. The first and last times. You might as well eat lawn clippings. 'Got some coffee?'

Franciscus tried to pay, but the man wouldn't hear of it. In the end, he left a two-dollar tip on the counter.

'Excuse me, sir, but are you Detective Francioso?' A woman's head protruded inside the front door, like a turtle peeping out of its shell.

'Close enough,' he said.

The woman stepped inside, and looked around hesitantly. 'I have a movie. One of the boys said you might like to see it.'

'A movie? What kind of movie?' Franciscus twirled his stool to get a better look at her. She was fifty with short, red hair, a kindly face, and a few extra pounds around the middle.

'I'm in town visiting my daughter. She's a student at NYU. Journalism. We had a lovely day until this. We saw the Empire State Building—'

'Ma'am, you said you had a movie?'

'Oh, yes. I was outside in the park when everything happened. I was filming Sharon with some of her friends . . . musicians . . . they're very good . . . when that poor young lady was shot.'

'You mean you filmed her being shot?'

She nodded. 'I thought it was something the police might like to have. You might find something useful.'

Franciscus was on his feet in a heartbeat. 'That's very considerate of you. Do you think I might have a look?'

'Yes, of course.'

Franciscus guided the woman to a table in a quiet corner of the room. Helping him extend the two-inch-by-two-inch screen, she pressed the play button, then fiddled with a volume control. The picture appeared.

The images showed a young woman standing in the park listening to the horn quartet. The picture was steady. No zooming in and out. The lady knew how to make a home movie. The camera panned until the Coffee Shop was in view. The sky blue Dodge sat in the foreground. Her daughter walked into the frame, heading toward the restaurant. Next, he picked out Thomas Bolden and Jennifer Dance coming out of the restaurant and hurrying to the kerb. Despite the line of customers waiting to get into the restaurant and the general lunch-hour to and fro, Franciscus was also able to spot three men emerging from the restaurant behind them, and assuming a distinctly menacing stance.

At that point, a flame burst from the car's hood, followed by a tremendous cloud of smoke. (The noise was terrifying, even coming from a button-sized speaker.) The picture shook chaotically. When it came back into focus, it was pointed at the ground. Then, the woman trained the lens on the car. The area nearby was a mob scene. A new figure appeared in the foreground, standing half in, half out of the billowing smoke. The camera circled the car and stopped on a woman waving her arms. He hit the pause button and stared at the face, then hit 'play' again. The camera panned down the street. Bolden was speaking to a trim, blond-haired man. Their interaction was obscured by the constant passage of pedestrians in front of the camera.

A scream punctuated the soundtrack, and the camera whipped back and forth, finally zooming in on Thomas Bolden cradling Jennifer Dance on the sidewalk. The blond-haired guy was gone. The video ended.

'Lady, you're a regular Robert Capa,' said Franciscus. 'I can't thank you enough for coming forward.'

'I thought it was the right thing to do.'

'I'm afraid we'll need your tape. Tell you what . . . I'll have a copy made for you. If you'd give me your address, we'll ship it to you as soon as possible.'

Franciscus watched the woman leave, then polished off his coffee. He walked outside and stood in the spot where Jennifer Dance was shot, trying to figure out where exactly the bullet that hit her might have come from. He spotted an open window across the way. He called an officer over and instructed him to go into the building and check for signs of forced entry, shell casings, or any other evidence.

Watching the officer hustle across the square, Franciscus replayed the film in his mind, comparing one of the faces he had seen to that printed in a newspaper article some twenty-five years ago. The two were not entirely dissimilar. The hair was a different color, the face leaner now, sharper, perhaps altered by a surgeon's knife. But the eyes were the same. That part you couldn't change.

Franciscus's impression was that the woman in the movie was Bobby Stillman.

Go figure.

Ole Matty Lopes was right. This case wasn't cold any more.

Chapter 35

James Jacklin, chairman of Jefferson Partners, adjusted his chair and slid the microphone closer to him. 'Can you hear me, Senator?'

'Loud and clear, Mr Jacklin,' said the Honorable Hugh Fitzgerald, senior senator from the state of Vermont and chairman of the Senate Appropriations Committee. 'You are one man who never hesitates to make himself heard.'

'I'll take that as a compliment.'

'You may take it any way you like. Now then . . .' Fitzgerald cleared his throat, and the reverberation seemed to rattle through every nook, cranny, and crevice of his 350-pound body. 'Mr Jacklin has come to testify on behalf of the Emergency War Powers Appropriations Bill before this committee. He's here to convince us why it's so urgent for the taxpayers to hand over six point two billion dollars to the Pentagon to refill our pre-positioned stockpiles.'

Since the Cold War, it had become accepted doctrine to pre-position massive amounts of arms and weaponry (everything from combat boots to M1 Abrams tanks) at strategic points around the globe for rapid transshipment to a combat zone, the theory being that it was quicker, cheaper, and just plain easier to move a fifty-ton battle tank from Diego Garcia in the Indian Ocean to Iraq than from Fort Hood, Texas. 'Pre-pos', as the pre-positioned stockpiles were called, allowed the armed forces to field combat-ready troops in days, not weeks. Currently, the armed forces maintained pre-pos in Guam, Diego Garcia, and Romania, as well as floating platforms in the Pacific, the Mediterranean, and the Indian Ocean. Pre-pos were considered a linchpin of the United States' ability to project power overseas.

'That's right, Senator,' said Jacklin. 'As a former pilot and combat veteran, and as a consultant to the Government Accounting Office, I feel it's my duty to speak on behalf of the fine men and women in the armed forces who find themselves in hostile territory with insufficient supplies.'

'We appreciate and share your heartfelt sincerity,' said Hugh Fitzgerald.

'Then you'll know why it is that I was so shocked to learn from the GAO's report that our pre-pos are nearly depleted. Our country is in a state of unprecedented danger. Our troops overseas are operating at the breaking point.'

'Now, now, I do think you're exaggerating. The report says that only two-thirds of our pre-pos are *understocked*, and it doesn't say anything about a breaking point.'

Fitzgerald slipped on a pair of bifocals and gave his attention to the papers lying before him. Behind the half-moon lenses, his blue eyes were hard and depthless as marbles. Ruptured capillaries shot through his sagging cheeks. He was dressed in his winter uniform: a black three-piece suit with a fob watch tucked into his vest like some relic from the nineteenth century. Black wool in winter, ivory linen in summer. He'd been wearing the same damn suits since he came down to the Capital thirty-five years earlier and Lieutenant James J. Jacklin USN, freshly returned from Vietnam with a DFC pinned to his tunic, was a junior puke doing his two-year rotation as a White House fellow.

Fitzgerald went on, 'Frankly, I'm hard-pressed to see how a war involving less than ten percent of our active-duty troops can strain anyone to the "breaking point". I'm tempted to suggest we take this as a lesson to be more careful before we intervene.'

'Senator, I'm not here to debate policy, but to speak about the facts stated in this eye-opening report,' said Jacklin. It was not his job to like or dislike any sitting member of Congress, he reminded himself. Just to use them. 'We have over ten thousand pieces of rolling stock on the ground in the Middle East. Tanks, personnel carriers, jeeps and the like. Almost all of it came from our pre-pos, not to mention ammunition, MREs, and most important, spare parts for these items.'

'And you propose that I recommend passage of this bill so that we can buy new ones?'

'Yes, I do.'

'Can't we wait until hostilities have ceased, ship them back to the pre-pos, and use them again?'

Jacklin shook his head emphatically. 'The desert is a harsh environment. Tanks break down and have to be fixed. We're so short of engines and trans-missions that we're being forced to cannibalize our existing combat-ready machinery. I remind you those tanks may be over there for another five years. Less than ten percent of them will be worth bringing back.'

'So we need new ones?'

'Yes sir.'

'New tanks, new personnel carriers, new Bradleys?'

'Yes sir.'

'To refill our pre-pos.'

'That's right.'

'All so we can go traipsing off to war at the drop of a hat again? I won't have it!'

'So that we can protect ourselves!' retorted Jacklin.

'I didn't see any Iraqi planes over Pearl Harbor, Mr Jacklin. I caution you to differentiate between empire-building and protecting the republic.'

But they're the same thing, Jacklin replied silently. You couldn't just sit back and wait till a snake bit you in the ass. They did that once, and it was called World War II. The only way to make the world safe was to spread democracy. You had to knock out the tyrants and despots, and let everyone have a chance at getting their own piece of the pie. It wasn't empire-building. It was economics. An empty stomach breeds discontent, and these days discontent had one target: America. Get rid of the discontent, and not only did you get rid of the anger, but you also opened up a new market.

'Senator, we're simply talking about bringing our armed forces to a basic state of combat readiness. Not about gearing up for war.'

Fitzgerald theatrically removed a paper from his colleague's folder and began reading it. 'Eight hundred and seventy-nine million dollars for combat helmets, boots, and silk underwear. One hundred and thirty-two million dollars for bolt-on armor. Two billion dollars for new equipment. Correct me if I'm wrong, but don't we actually have all the equipment this bill is asking for, right here in the United States?'

'Most of it, yes. But it's too expensive to transport overseas.'

'Will it cost six point two billion dollars?' Fitzgerald shook his head, and smiled his unctuous smile. 'Lordy me, what's going to happen when somebody decides to fight back?'

Jacklin knew better than to respond. He concentrated on his posture. His back was killing him, that damned piece of Gook shrapnel exacting its revenge thirty years after the fact. If he'd known the hearing would drone on so long, he'd have brought his Princeton chair. He blinked and kept his eyes focused straight ahead. An old warhorse, bent but not broken.

'Now then, Mr Jacklin, there is one item in this bill I wanted to discuss personally with you. I see here in the bill a request for seven hundred Hawkeye Air Defense vehicles. The Hawkeyes are manufactured by Triton Aerospace Company of Huntington Beach, California, which your very own Jefferson Partners saw fit to purchase a few years back.'

'Seven hundred is the initial order,' responded Jacklin.

'But the Avenger – the system it is to replace – is only ten years old, itself. I see here the Avenger shoots eight Stinger ground-to-air missiles. Can be reloaded in six minutes, and possesses a mighty machine gun. Doesn't break down very often. Easy to use. And very effective. I like this Avenger more and more. Can you remind me why we need to replace one of the few weapons systems that actually does what the manufacturer promises?'

'It's not a question of replacing the Avenger at this stage,' Jacklin explained. 'But of augmenting our air defense capabilities. The country's recent hostilities have required us to move over seventy percent of the Avengers into the battle zone.'

'Forgive me if I've missed the news of the enemy air force's latest sorties. I thought it's those roadside bombs that are doing our boys in.'

'The Avenger is outdated, outmoded, and obsolete,' Jacklin continued. 'The Hawkeye shoots sixteen Stinger Two missiles – a newer and much more accurate weapon. It can be reloaded in only four minutes and possesses a heavier, American-made side armament. The Avenger's machine gun is manufactured in Belgium.'

'And I thought that the Belgians only made lace,' said Fitzgerald. A laugh rippled through the gallery and Jacklin forced himself to go with it. Americans hated a poor sport. 'The Avenger can shoot Stinger Twos, too, can it not?' Fitzgerald asked.

'Yes, it can.'

'Now refresh my memory. We've seen each other so many times over the years. But, did you not sit before me in that very chair some ten years ago and swear to me that the Avenger would last a minimum of twenty-five years?'

'I think we're all astonished at the tremendous advances made in technology these past years.'

'I'll take that as a yes.'

'The army views the Hawkeye as a priority.'

'Speaking of the army, I'd like to ask you if the name Lamar King means something to you?'

'General King is a counselor working on Jefferson's behalf.'

'A counselor?' said Fitzgerald, with ceremony. 'Is that what the rest of us mortals call an "employee"?'

'He is employed by Jefferson.'

'And wasn't it General King who placed the army's original order for five hundred Avengers all those years ago?'

Jacklin nodded. 'It was through our work together that I came to know and respect General King. In fact, General King is consulting on the Hawkeye program. All of us at Jefferson are proud of his association with our organization.'

Fitzgerald stretched his neck and directed his view to the highly decorated military officer sitting directly behind Jacklin. 'General Hartung, I see by the three stars on your shoulders that you're due to retire soon. May I ask if you have any intention of joining your predecessor, General King, in working for Jefferson at that time?' Fitzgerald was quick to wave away the question. 'You do not have to answer that, sir.

'I do not doubt that the Hawkeye is marginally superior,' Fitzgerald went on. 'Or that our armed forces deserve the very best we have to offer. I also have no doubt that we can put the two hundred and seventy million dollars earmarked for the Hawkeye program to better use.'

Jacklin stared hard at Fitzgerald. The fact was that Triton Aerospace desperately needed the contract. Its communications division was lagging. Its consumer electronics area was all but dead. The company was in the shithouse. Without the army's purchase of the Hawkeye, no other allied nation would come aboard. Australia, Indonesia, Poland – they all wanted what the United States Army had. Scrap the army's order, and he'd have to cancel the entire Hawkeye program. He might as well shutter the company. Jefferson's investment in Triton would be a write-off. Five hundred million dollars down the drain. An embarrassing and costly defeat at the very worst moment.

'It's our duty to be prepared for any eventuality, Senator,' he said. 'Two hundred and seventy million dollars is a small price to keep our fighting men and women out of harm's way.'

'May I ask how many other companies Jefferson holds in its portfolio that will benefit from the swift passage of the Emergency War Powers Appropriations Bill?'

'Senator, I find your suggestions unseemly.'

'Not as much as I. Thank you, Mr Jacklin, you are excused.'

Chapter 36

The moment the hearing recessed Jacklin got to his feet and signaled Hugh Fitzgerald that he'd like a minute of his time. The senator from Vermont lumbered to the stairs at the end of the dais and extended a hand for Jacklin to help him down.

'Well, well, J.J., to what do I owe this honor? A personal word with an honest-to-god billionaire. Should I swoon or just ask for an autograph?'

'Cut the crap, Hugh,' Jacklin said, managing to keep his smile in place and even sound the slightest bit respectful. 'What's all this resistance to the pre-pos?'

'Do you mean to the pre-pos or to the Hawkeye?'

'Both! We did a damn good job building and delivering the Avenger and we'll do a better job with the Hawkeye. Give it a chance. Cut the initial order to six hundred units and I'll knock ten percent off the unit cost and throw in some free spare parts.'

'Horse-trading, are we?' Fitzgerald picked up a scuffed briefcase and began a laborious walk toward the exit. 'J.J., my old friend, this is just one program we don't need. The Avenger's got a good ten years left in it. Longer with upgrades. Look at the F-Fourteen. We're still using that warplane after thirty-five years. Signing this emergency funding bill is like handing a drunk a loaded gun.'

'President McCoy's about as likely to take us to war as you are. Be serious.'

'Things change. That's the one thing that I've learned. Put a pacifist in the White House and before a month's gone, they're just as likely as . . . as . . . well, as *you*, to have us at war. I won't have the blood of any more American boys on my hands.'

'For Godsakes, stop your moralizing. I'll say this for you. You're a cool customer, Hugh. It takes a stiff spine to turn down the army these days.'

'Nonsense. Just a sharp pen.'

Jacklin roared, clapping the man on the back. 'Can I buy you a drink?' he asked, almost sincerely. 'It's nearly one. Bar opens at noon on the Hill, doesn't it?'

' 'Fraid not, J.J. No offense. Just doctor's orders.'

'Time you looked after yourself a little better. You been here how long now? Thirty years?'

'Coming up on thirty-six. Sometimes I feel like the only way I'm ever going to leave is if they carry me out of here feet first.'

Jacklin moved closer to Fitzgerald, letting their shoulders brush. 'There are other ways for a man of your accomplishment to end his career.'

Fitzgerald stopped and drew himself up to his full height of six feet four inches tall, effectively dwarfing the smaller man. 'Is that an offer to join General Lamar King as one of your *counselors*?'

'We pay a helluva lot better than the taxpayer. Salary's good, but equity's the real kick in the pants. Turn around a company like Triton, find the right buyer . . .' Jacklin raised an eyebrow, saying nothing and everything.

Fitzgerald continued down the passage. 'I'm flattered, but you can't teach an old dog new tricks.'

'Nothing new to teach,' said Jacklin. 'You already know how to use that pen. Just a question of finding one with black ink instead of red. Tell me you'll think about it. You'll find lots of your old friends over at our place.'

'More than I'd care to admit, I imagine. A regular revolving door, we're made to understand.'

'Ah, Fitz, don't be so damned hard on yourself.'

Reaching the door, the two shook hands. Jacklin covered Fitzgerald's with his own and stepped closer to the bigger man, so the two were chest to chest. 'Tell you what. We're having a little dinner party this evening for a few of our better clients. Eight o'clock at my place, White Rose Ridge. Frances Tavistock has agreed to speak to us.'

Hugh Fitzgerald's face dropped. 'Don't tell me, she's signed on, too?'

Jacklin raised his eyebrows. The announcement that the former British prime minister had joined Jefferson Partners as a 'counselor at large' was to crown the evening's festivities. 'You'll be in good company, Hugh. It's a regular pantheon these days. Time the nation paid you back. God knows . . . we owe you.'

Fitzgerald appeared to savor the words. 'Eight o'clock?'

Chapter 37

'You again?' the doctor said.

Jenny lifted her head from the gurney. 'Hello, Dr Gupta.'

The young Indian yanked the curtain closed and consulted the chart log. 'I told you I did good work, but this is going a bit far.'

'What are you still doing here?'

'Me? I'm an intern. I live here morning, noon, and night. You're lucky. I just had a nap. Very slim chance of malpractice. But you never know.' Gingerly, he pulled back the bandage covering her shoulder. 'Let's have a look, shall we?'

'I was shot,' said Jenny.

'So I see. I imagine they've already told you that you were incredibly lucky.'

Jenny nodded. She'd come to in the ambulance, where an emergency medical technician had treated and bandaged the wound en route to the hospital. The bullet had struck the corner of her shoulder and passed through her upper arm, carving a shallow trench out of her skin. There was surprisingly little blood, and she decided it looked worse than it felt. 'More stitches?'

'Nothing to stitch. We'll let it heal naturally. If it looks too nasty afterwards, then we'll send you to my older brother. He is a plastic surgeon. Good hands run in the family.' He picked up her arm and spread her fingers across his palm.

'Move your fingers one at a time. Make a fist. Lift.'

Jenny did each exercise in turn.

'You're getting good at this,' Gupta said.

'A real pro.' It was only when Jenny lifted her arm that she felt anything different. A sudden stiffness as if she'd been lifting weights strenuously, followed by a white-hot pinprick that made her wince.

Nonetheless, Gupta appeared pleased. 'No nerve damage. The bullet didn't touch anything but flesh.' Laying her arm by her side, he stepped to the counter and began preparing an antiseptic rinse. 'How's the pain?'

'Right now, it just aches.'

'I'll give you something to take care of it.'

'Will it make me sleepy?'

'A little.'

'Then I don't want it.'

Dr Gupta looked over his shoulder. 'Why is that?'

'I just . . . just don't,' she stammered. 'I need to be with it. I can't afford to be woozy or drowsy.'

'Are you planning on operating some heavy machinery this afternoon? Forklift? Backhoe?'

'No,' she said, all too seriously.

Gupta put down the gauze bandages he was folding. 'Jennifer, I am going to rinse out the wound with saline solution, apply a topical anesthetic, and then, my dear, I am going to have to cut away a little of your skin. We call it debridement. Bullets are famous for carrying all sorts of nasty bacteria. We can't leave any of that behind, or we're risking infection. I'm going to give you some Vicodin. You'll feel a little woozy, but nothing more. At most, you'll want to take a nap, which given everything you've been through today, is a good thing.'

'No,' Jenny said more forcefully. She sat up too quickly, and the blood rushed to her head. Gasping for breath, she lowered herself to the table. 'I mean, thank you, but no thank you. I don't want any of that stuff. I'm not staying.'

Dr Gupta folded his arms over his chest, narrowing his eyes. 'I can't demand an explanation, but I'd appreciate one. It isn't a coincidence that you're here twice in one day, is it?'

Jenny regarded the doctor, with his deep brown eyes and sympathetic smile. She sighed. 'No, it isn't. To put it in a nutshell, the men who shot at me are the same ones who slashed open my arm last night. They kidnapped my boyfriend, and when he managed to get away, they tried to kill him. Except that they missed, and hit me. Only we're not so sure whether they really did miss.'

She'd expected a skeptical smile, but Gupta's expression was dead serious. 'Are you saying that these men might have followed you to the hospital?' he asked.

'Exactly.'

'And that they might wish to harm you while you convalesce?'

'You got it.'

Gupta left the examining room without a word. He returned two minutes later. 'I had a talk with security. All inquiries about you will be turned down, unless you care to give me a list of people you'd like to speak with. The admitting nurse has been informed. Any parties asking about you will be directed to security or to me.'

'Thank you,' said Jenny.

'Don't thank me. It's purely selfish. If they miss you next time, they might hit me.' Smiling, he took off his lab coat, and folded up his shirtsleeves to the mid-forearm. Reaching toward the counter, he picked up a bottle of saline and began to rinse the wound. 'How many weeks are you, anyway?'

Jenny turned her head away. 'Almost eight.'

'Are you still feeling poorly?'

'Miserable. But just in the mornings. By noon, it's all gone.'

'Boy or girl? Any preference?'

'Just healthy,' she said, though she was sure she had a baby boy inside her. She placed a hand on her stomach. She could feel him there. Not kicking or moving. He was still much too small for that. But she could feel him growing. In the mornings, his demands on her system left her sapped and nauseated. The nights were a different story. Every evening at six on the dot, she experienced a rush of well-being she could only term euphoric. And she kept feeling good until she went to sleep.

'Does he know?' asked Dr Gupta.

'Tom? I wanted to tell him this morning, but then . . . events got in the way.'

'I'm sure he will be thrilled.'

'I'm sure, too . . . kind of.'

Gupta applied a film of topical anesthetic. Jenny felt it tingle and her shoulder grow numb. Gupta picked up a pair of forceps and began to peel away the top layers of the wound. 'The good news,' he said, 'is that this is nothing compared to childbirth.'

'One or two slices?' the counterman asked again.

Bolden glanced at the menu board above the ovens. A plain slice went for $2.25. A slice of pepperoni cost $2.75. 'One. Make it a pepperoni. And a Dr Pepper. To go.'

'Next!'

Bolden slid down the counter. The shop was warm and fuggy, the smell of baked tomato, garlic, and hot cheese wafting in the air. Despite the inviting aroma, he had no appetite. A jackhammer was working overtime inside his skull. Grit from the explosion had lodged in his eyes, making them sore and watery. The cashier rang up his total. He paid and took a place against the wall, waiting for the pizza to come out of the oven. On top of the soft-drink cooler, a television broadcast the midday news.

'News Four has obtained disturbing videotape showing the shooting of Solomon H. Weiss,' the anchorwoman announced.

Bolden's eyes shot back to the TV.

The anchor went on, 'Weiss, chairman and cofounder of the prestigious investment bank Harrington Weiss, was shot dead this morning in an apparent employment dispute with a longtime executive. We caution audiences that the tape is graphic and has not been edited for broadcast.'

Bolden watched the events of that morning unspool as recorded by a camera planted in the frame above the door. The tape lasted ten seconds and showed Bolden struggling with the security guard, the gun going off, and Sol Weiss falling to the floor. There was one difference, however, between the events of that morning and the scene broadcast on television. The security guard was wearing Bolden's head and vice versa. To all the world, it appeared that Thomas Bolden had shot Sol Weiss.

The anchorwoman reiterated his views a few seconds later.

'The suspect, Thomas Bolden, aged thirty-two, is at large and considered to be armed and dangerous. If any viewer has information about Bolden's whereabouts, they are asked to call the number below.'

Bolden's photograph filled the screen. It was his

most recent passport photo and he wondered how in the world they had dug it up. He didn't stare at the camera, so much as glower at it. It had been taken after an all-nighter at an attorney's office correcting the proofs of an offering memo. He was pale with dark rings under his eyes. He looked menacing. He looked like a killer.

'Here you go, sir.' The pizza chef handed Bolden his bag.

The cashier, who had been watching the segment along with Bolden, turned toward him, then looked at the television again. Meanwhile, the TV station was replaying the images of Thomas Bolden, killer, shooting Sol Weiss.

'That's you,' the cashier said, in a flat voice.

'No,' said Bolden. 'Just looks like me.' He turned to leave the pizzeria.

'That's you,' she said again. 'That's him,' she announced to her customers, this time louder, as if she'd just looked at her lottery ticket and realized she'd hit the jackpot. 'Oh my God, that's him!'

Dr Gupta returned to the examining room, fifteen minutes later. 'I am happy to report that the waiting room is free of all bad guys. No one carrying machine guns, machetes, or hand grenades has been seen.'

'And elephant rifles?'

'I'll have to go back and check. Actually, I do have some good news. Your brother, Daniel, is here. The police brought him in. He's quite concerned.'

Jenny felt the ground shift beneath her. 'My brother lives in Kansas City.'

'Tall fellow. Blond hair. A handsome chap. I just had a word with him in the hallway. I didn't know you had a history with dangerous firearms. He told me all about how you shot him in the cheek with a

BB gun. I can't say I see the resemblance, but I'm sure he'll take good care of you.'

'Danny's five nine, and weighs two hundred and fifty pounds. He's bald and can't jog from the porch to the mailbox.'

'No, but . . .' Gupta looked over his shoulder, then back at her again, confused.

'Where is he?' she asked, standing from the table. She wasn't sure what frightened her more – that there was someone in the hospital trying to get to her, or that he knew that she'd plugged Danny with a Daisy Repeater . . . only it had been in the butt.

'At the nurses' station talking to Dr Rosen, chief of the ER. I said I'd bring you out in a moment.'

'A shirt. I need a shirt.' Jenny stood bare-chested, the bandage taped to her shoulder.

'But you can't leave. I need to get you some medicine . . . a prescription . . . you need to sign the charges.'

'The man outside tried to kill me and my boyfriend,' said Jenny. 'Give me your shirt.'

'What? But . . .'

She threw out a hand. 'Give it to me now! And your jacket.'

'But he's with the police . . . they want to talk to you, too. I'm sure it's all right.' Reluctantly, Gupta removed his lab jacket and unbuttoned his shirt. 'Here you are.'

'Stethoscope?'

'They're expensive,' Gupta protested, but he handed his to her, all the same.

Jenny threw on the shirt, and the jacket on top of it. 'Do you have a rubber band?'

'Yes, I think so.' Gupta rummaged in a drawer. 'Just one?'

'One will do.' Jenny tied her hair in a knot and put it up. She looked at herself in the mirror. Close up, she wouldn't fool anyone, but from down the hall she'd look like just another doc. 'Do you know a back way out of here?'

'I've been living inside this tomb since July fifth of last year. I know ways out of here even the architect didn't imagine.' Gupta caught himself, indecision wrinkling his face. 'But really...'

Jenny walked to the door. 'Which way out? Not by a front door or the ambulance port. A side exit. Someplace no one uses.'

Gupta looked around nervously, mumbling to himself. 'Yes, all right then. I know the place. Go down the hall to the vending machines, then turn right. Take the stairs to the second floor. There's a walkway that connects this building to the one next door, where the pediatric ward is located. Once you're there, continue to the far side of the building and take the elevator to the parking garage. There's a food court there. And stairs up to the street. That's the best I can do.'

Jenny looked at the doctor, thin and naked to the waist. 'Thank you,' she said. 'I hope we don't see each other for a really long time.'

'Good luck.'

Jenny opened the door and turned down the hallway, away from the nurses' station. She saw him out of the corner of her eye. Just for a split second, but it was enough. The white-blond hair. The wind-kissed complexion. She knew him in an instant. The man who'd stolen her watch last night. Thomas had said his name was 'Irish'.

She hurried down the hall without a look behind her.

Chapter 38

Bill Donohue rushed across the floor of Triton Aerospace's Alexandria-based warehouse. 'Is the replacement for the President's podium ready yet?' he asked the VP consumer sales.

'We're getting ready to load it onto the truck.'

'Check the wiring. The Secret Service is pretty steamed.'

'Everything's up and running. Waterproof and airtight.'

'Where is it? I promised Fiske that I'd have the podium on the Hill by two.' Donohue checked his watch. It was already 2:40. Traffic had been bumper-to-bumper getting out of downtown. With the snow starting to come, it would only be worse getting back. He was on the verge of Excedrin headache number nine.

'Follow me. You can give us a hand.'

Donohue walked toward the loading dock. Forklifts noisily motored up and down the floor, carrying pallets stacked with electronics gear. Men called to one another from atop thirty-foot-high columns of packing boxes. All the while, speakers belted out Lee Greenwood's 'God Bless the USA'. The Alexandria warehouse handled shipments and repairs for all of Triton Aerospace's nonmilitary products. These included shortwave radios, police band receivers, and communications systems, public address systems, and spare parts.

Like many Triton executives, Donohue had joined the firm straight out of the service. A graduate of the Naval Academy, he'd done an eight-year hitch driving S-3 Vikings, workhorses whose mission it was to track Soviet submarines. With the Russians pretty much out of the sub business, the need for his specialty was low and falling. Donohue had been offered a promotion and a billet in recruiting if he would stay. He'd tolerated the military's long hours and low pay because he loved flying. If he had to take a desk job – and this particular billet was located in Detroit, Michigan – he wanted to earn a little coin. He'd resigned his commission and joined Triton. As a newlywed with his first child due in six months, it was time to start putting some money in the bank.

'Here she is,' said the VP, a guy named Merchie Rivers. Rivers walked and talked like a hard-charging ground-pounder who'd forgotten he'd taken off his green beret five years earlier.

Donohue watched a pair of workers wheel the pressure-wrapped podium toward them. 'Looks bigger.'

'It's the newest model. If we're going to have a billion people watching, the boss wants to have the best up there. It's two inches wider across the base. Weighs thirty pounds more.'

'Why the increase?' asked Donohue. As a pilot, he'd been trained to question every extra pound his aircraft took aboard.

'The thing's got enough bulletproof armor to stop an RPG. Kevlar ain't light.'

'Good. There's no such thing as being too safe on this one.'

'Amen,' said Rivers.

The workers lifted the podium into the payload of a delivery van and strapped it in place.

Donohue slammed the rear doors closed. 'Just make sure it has the presidential seal on it.'

'Not to worry, buddy,' said Rivers, shaking his hand as if it were a rag. 'This one was custom made for President McCoy.'

Chapter 39

Godforsaken machines.

Guilfoyle sat at the head of the conference table inside the Quiet Room, surrounded by four of the firm's top information analysts. Scattered across the table was Thomas Bolden's credit history, his medical records, school transcripts, credit-card bills, gas, electricity, and phone bills, banking and brokerage statements, a list of magazine subscriptions, travel records including his preferred seat assignment, driving record, insurance policies, tax returns, and voting record.

All of it had been fed into Cerberus, and Cerberus had spat out a predictive model of Thomas Bolden's daily activities. The forty-page report, bound neatly and set on the table in front of Guilfoyle, was titled 'Core Personality Profile'. It told Guilfoyle where Bolden liked to eat, how much he spent each year on clothing, in what month of the year he tended to have a physical, what kind of car he was likely to drive, his 'must-watch' TV, and not incidentally, how he would vote. But it could not tell him where Thomas Bolden would be in an hour.

'We can ascertain, sir, that Bolden has a point-four probability of eating at one of three restaurants downtown,' one of the men was saying. 'Also, that he has a point-one probability of going shopping after work and that he has a point-ninety-seven probability of visiting the Boys' Club in Harlem tonight. I caution that the results maintain a bias of plus or minus two standard deviations. Regardless, I'd suggest stationing men at all three restaurants, as well as the Boys' Club.'

'The man is on the run,' said Guilfoyle. 'He is not behaving according to his regular daily patterns. He went shopping, but it was at ten A.M. in a store he'd never visited before. I can promise you that he will not be visiting the Boys' Club tonight. If for no other reason than he knows that we'll have a dozen men surrounding it.'

'If I might interject, sir,' said Hoover, a flaxen-haired giant with skin as fluorescent as the damnable lighting. 'The acute psychological profile Cerberus provided shows that Bolden is aggressive, proactive, and that he tends to cope well with physical stress . . .'

'Tell me something I don't know,' Guilfoyle said, his calm fraying by the minute. 'The man is a cipher, as far as I'm concerned. He's supposed to be an investment banker, yet he acts like a seasoned operative. Where does Cerberus tell me anything about that?'

'It's his childhood, sir,' said Hoover. 'Clearly, we don't have a complete picture. If only we could input some relevant data pertaining to . . .'

Guilfoyle raised a hand, indicating that Hoover should contain himself. Hoover had spent too long with the machines. His answers always began with 'If only . . .' *If only* we could improve this. *If only* we could get more of that. Like the mother of a mischievous child, he had become an apologist for the system's shortcomings.

A picture window ran along one side of the Quiet Room, giving a clear view of the communications center. Guilfoyle slipped on a pair of glasses and directed his attention to the wall. Projected onto the screen was what was called a link map. A bright blue ball with the initials 'TB' glowed at its center. Phone numbers belonging to his home, office, cell phone, and BlackBerry ran beneath it. Emanating from the ball, like rays from the sun, was a cluster of lines each leading to its own ball, some small, some large. Those balls, too, had initials, and below them tightly scripted phone numbers. Many of the balls were interconnected, lines running between them. The whole thing looked like a giant Tinkertoy.

Each ball represented a person with whom Bolden maintained contact. The larger balls represented those whom, according to his phone records, he spoke with most frequently. They included his girlfriend, Jennifer Dance (at last report, undergoing treatment at NYU Hospital), several co-workers at Harrington Weiss, the Harlem Boys' Club, and a dozen colleagues at other banks and private equity firms. The smaller balls included less frequently contacted co-workers, other colleagues, and a half dozen restaurants. In all there were approximately fifty balls in orbit around Bolden's sun.

Guilfoyle had programmed Cerberus to monitor all the phone lines indicated on the link map on a real-time basis. Automatically, Cerberus would compare the parties speaking with a voiceprint of Thomas Bolden taken that morning. Guilfoyle didn't have enough manpower to stake out all of Bolden's acquaintances. With the link map, it didn't matter. Should Bolden phone any of these numbers, Guilfoyle could listen in. More important, he could get a fix on Bolden's location.

The problem was that Bolden was a sharp operator. He had learned firsthand that his phone had been bugged and that using a cell phone meant risking capture. The link map was therefore a waste of time.

Guilfoyle rubbed his eyes. Over a hundred monitors running floor to ceiling occupied another corner of the room. The monitors drew a live feed from exterior surveillance cameras around midtown and lower Manhattan. The pictures switched rapidly from location to location. Software analyzed the faces of all pedestrians captured by the cameras and compared them to a composite of three photographs of Thomas Bolden. Simultaneously, it analyzed the gaits of the subjects, and using a sophisticated algorithm, compared them to a model established from the video of Bolden striding down the corridor at Harrington Weiss earlier that morning. It wasn't the walk it was analyzing as much as the exact distance between his ankle and knee, knee and hip, and ankle and hip. The three ratios were added together to yield a composite number that was as unique for every man, woman, and child, as their fingerprints.

That was the good news.

The bad news was that snow, rain, or any kind of moisture in the atmosphere degraded the picture enough to render the software program ineffective.

For all the money the Organization had poured into Cerberus, for all the millions of man-hours the brightest brains in the nation – in the world, dammit – had spent developing the software to run it, Cerberus was still a machine. It could gather. It could hunt. But it could not intuit. It could not guess.

Guilfoyle removed his glasses and set them delicately on the table. The discipline that had governed his entire life fell round him like a cloak, smothering his irritation, dampening his anger. Still, it was only by the utmost self-control that he did not shout. Only Hoover noticed the tic pulling at the corner of his mouth.

Machines.

Wolf Ramirez sat quietly in a dark corner of his hotel room, drawing the blade of his Ka-Bar knife across the sharpening stone. A clusterfuck was what it was, he thought, as he reversed direction and drew the blade toward him. Too many people running in too many directions trying to get the simplest thing done. Well, what did they expect? You didn't send a pack of hounds to do a wolf's work.

Wolf's eyes lifted to the cell phone he had set on the table in front of him.

After a moment, he concentrated on the knife again. To hone the blade as sharp as he liked, he needed to work on it for a solid hour. Only then would it be truly razor sharp. Sharp enough to slip into the skin as easily as a needle and cleanly separate the dermis from the sheath of fat below it. Only then could he lift the six layers of tissue off a man as neatly as if he were filleting a trout. Straight, unfrayed lines. That's what he liked. Precision.

Wolf didn't like to leave a man messy. When he was finished with the bad guys, he wanted their souvenir of their time with him to be a work of art, geometric in its precision. The pain would soon pass. But the scars would be with them for ever. Wolf was proud of his skills.

He stared at the phone.

This time it rang.

He smiled. Sooner or later Guilfoyle always came back to him.

'Yeah?' he said.

'Can you find him?'

'Maybe. But you have to level with me.'

'What do you need?'

'Just one thing. Tell me what you don't want him to discover.'

Chapter 40

Bolden walked past the entrance to Harrington Weiss's world headquarters. Tall glass windows allowed him an unobstructed view inside. At one-thirty, the lobby was moderately busy, a thin, but steady, stream of people flowing in and out of the building. By now, Weiss's body had been removed, the office cordoned off, and hopefully cleaned, witnesses interviewed, and reports taken. Other than the usual building security, he didn't see a single police officer.

Like a messenger who'd overshot his address, Bolden turned right back around and walked inside. A white marble floor, high ceilings, and stout granite piers gave the lobby the look and feel of a train station. He presented himself to the reception desk.

'Ray's Pizza. Delivery for Althea Jackson. HW. Forty-second floor.' He plopped the brown paper bag holding the pizza and soft drink on the counter, and slipped a business card he'd taken from Ray's along next to it.

'Let me make that call,' said the security guard. 'Althea on forty-two?'

Bolden nodded, and looked around.

Less than ten feet away, a dozen uniformed police officers stood huddled around two plain-clothes officers, listening intently to their instructions. He kept his face turned away from them.

After seeing his picture on TV, he'd spent the last of his money on a cheap baseball cap and some even cheaper sunglasses. He had no doubt that Althea was in the office. Any normal place of business you'd get the day off after seeing a man's brains blown out. The whole firm might be expected to shut down, if for no other reason than to show respect for the boss, a founder no less. But investment banks were anything but normal. No nine-to-fivers need apply. Currencies did not halt trading when a country defaulted on its loans. Deals didn't fall out of bed if a principal dropped dead. The march of finance was unsympathetic and unstoppable.

Bolden was point man on the Trendrite deal. He might be MIA, but the deal had a momentum of its own. He was certain that Jake Flannagan, his immediate boss, had taken up the reins, as he had on a past occasion when a senior partner had suffered a heart attack and been put out of commission for a week. Jake would be all over Althea to supply him with the proper paperwork, phone numbers, and generally to bring him up to speed.

'I don't care if you didn't order pizza,' the security man was bellowing into the phone. 'Someone ordered it. Now, come and get it, or I'll eat it myself. Smells good, hear what I'm saying?' He lowered the phone and looked at Bolden. 'What kind?'

'Pepperoni.'

The guard repeated the words. 'Darned right you'll be right down.' He hung up. 'She's coming.'

Bolden threw an elbow onto the counter. On one of the napkins, he'd written Althea a note. It read, 'Don't believe a thing you hear or SEE. I need a favor. Do a LexisNexis search on Scanlon Corporation and Russell Kuykendahl. 1945 – present. Meet me in front of the kiosk at the southwest corner of the WTC subway station in an hour. I need $$$!!! Believe in me, for Bobby's sake.' He signed it 'Tom.'

As much as he wanted to leave the bag and the pizza inside with the security guard, he had to stay to get paid and collect his tip.

Behind the counter, a ten-inch television was tuned to the news. The station was showing the footage of Sol Weiss's shooting over and over, with short breaks to discuss it with their analyst du jour. A few guards gathered, watching with something between enchantment and horror. Someone tapped on Bolden's shoulder. 'Hey.'

Bolden turned and looked at the policeman.

'Got any extra slices? Outside on your bike or something?'

Bolden shook his head. 'No, Officer. I'm sorry. You want to place an order, here's the number.' He handed the business card to the cop.

The policeman pulled Althea's bag toward him and opened it. 'Smells good,' he said, rooting around inside the bag. 'Sure she don't want to split it?'

'Ask her. I'm just the delivery guy.'

'Jesus!' shouted the cop. 'It's him. It's the fuckin' doer.' He had just gotten sight of the television. 'Guys, check this out. Got the doer cold.'

Another cop ambled over. When he figured out just what he was watching, he whistled and yelled for his buddy to get his ass over there. Pretty soon all the police officers were crowded in a horseshoe around Bolden watching the television. One after another, they offered their opinions about the crime.

'Guess he didn't get the bonus he expected,' said one.

'Naw, he wanted that corner office.'

'Hey, boss, here's what you can do with that evaluation form.'

The laughs grew louder with every comment, the policemen pressing him against the reception desk. The tape ended, and was replaced by a full-screen photograph of the suspect. Trapped, Bolden stared at himself. He kept his face down. He didn't look around him. At any moment, he expected one of the officers to nudge him in the shoulder and say, 'Hey, pal, isn't that you?'

Glancing to his side, he caught Althea doing her power walk, barreling across the lobby. He couldn't risk her reaction when she recognized him. Any attention could prove disastrous. 'Excuse me, Officer,' he said, grabbing the bag and trying to shoulder his way through the policemen. It was like wading through concrete. The cops stood firm, their eyes locked on the television, waiting for the promised replay.

And then it was too late.

Althea placed her elbows on the far side of the desk. 'Who placed this order?' she asked the security guard. 'Wasn't me. I didn't order any pizza.'

'Ask him,' said the guard, a finger pointed at Bolden.

'I said, who placed the order? I most certainly did—' Althea's words dropped as cleanly as if they'd been chopped off by the guillotine. 'Oh yeah,' she added. 'That's me, all right.'

Fighting clear of the swarm of policemen, Bolden handed her the bag holding the slice of pizza and soft drink. 'That'll be four-fifty. Plus a dollar delivery charge. Five-fifty total, ma'am. Something in there from the manager.'

Althea opened the bag and cocked her head to

get a look inside. Slipping in a finger, she freed the napkin and read the note. One of the cops had good radar. Sensing something wasn't kosher, he walked over and looked at both of them. 'Everything all right, here?'

'Just fine, Officer,' said Althea, closing the paper bag. 'Boy messed up my order, that's all. Sometimes I'm surprised they can even find the building.' She fished inside her purse for her wallet and handed Bolden a twenty. 'Got change?'

Bolden looked at the bill. He'd spent his last dime on the hat and sunglasses. He reached for his wallet, anyway, aware of the policeman's intent gaze. 'Just for a ten,' he said, lying. 'Slow day.'

'No sweat,' said the cop, reaching into his hip pocket and pulling out a gambler's wad. He ripped off two tens from the middle of the stack and traded them for Althea's twenty. 'And you,' he said, yanking down Bolden's sunglasses with a finger and shooting him a do-not-fuck-with-me look in the eye. 'Pay closer attention next time. Don't go screwin' up the lady's order.'

Not caring to wait for a response, he sauntered back to the others.

Althea handed Bolden a ten.

'Jenny's hurt,' he whispered. 'She's being treated at a hospital somewhere in lower Manhattan. I can't explain, but I need you to check on her.'

Althea nodded her head, but said nothing.

Bolden raised his eyes expectantly.

'Get my list?' He was referring to the list he'd asked Althea to compile of all companies that his clients had bought and sold over the past ten years. It was the only place he might find a clue to who might have been involved with a military contractor. Althea frowned. 'It slipped my mind.'

'I really need it. And your phone.'

Althea dug into her purse and handed him her cell phone. 'Don't be calling Australia,' she whispered. 'I'm on a budget.'

'One hour,' said Bolden. 'Get my list!'

Before he could thank her, she had turned and begun her march back to the elevator. Nobody needed to teach Althea Jackson how to act in front of the police.

Chapter 41

Detective John Franciscus drove slowly down the street, checking the addresses of the clapboard colonial homes. A light snow fell, adding a fresh layer to lawns already covered with six inches of the stuff. Icicles hung from bare branches that swayed in the wind. It was going to get worse before it got better. The forecast called for the brunt of the storm to hit the New York metropolitan area sometime that evening. Anywhere from six inches to two feet was expected. He turned up the heater a notch.

The hamlet of Chappaqua belonged formally to the city of New Castle. Though an NYPD detective had jurisdiction throughout the state, it was common courtesy to alert the local shop that he was paying a visit. Even so, Franciscus hadn't phoned ahead. Crime folders like Bobby Stillman's didn't go missing without a reason. Men due to be arraigned did not commonly walk out of jail leaving no trace behind them. Other eyes were watching. It was best to be invisible for a while.

He pulled the car to the kerb and killed the ignition, listening to the engine tick and the wind scuff the windshield. A look in the rearview to make sure his teeth were clean. A check of his necktie. A breath strip, and he was ready to go.

Franciscus climbed out of his car, checking for any ice on the pavement. Sixtieth birthdays and broken hips went together like beer and pretzels. Next house over, a man about his age was getting a snowblower out of his garden shed. Seeing Franciscus, he waved and shook his head disconsolately, as if he'd had enough snow for this winter. The image of the red-faced man struggling with his snowblower stayed with him. In a year, that would be him. Then what? What would a Wednesday afternoon hold in store for him?

Done clearing the snow, he'd go inside and take a shower. He'd come downstairs smelling of baby powder and aftershave, pour himself a seven and seven, and grab a bowl of Japanese rice crackers for some nibbles, before settling into the La-Z-Boy for a long, slow night in front of the tube. He'd end up watching reruns of *I Dream of Jeannie* and *Bewitched*. At some point, he'd fall asleep in his chair, only to wake up half out of it, dazed and bleary-eyed, wondering how in the hell he'd gotten there in the first place. Not in the chair, but how he'd gotten to be sixty-three, retired, with a gold watch, a pension, and a zipper running down his breastbone that promised him twenty more years of the same.

Franciscus rang the doorbell. An attractive brunette in her mid-forties opened the door a moment later. 'Detective Franciscus?'

She was a knockout, tall and willowy with hair cut short, nicely styled. Kovacs had been thirty-one when he'd called it quits. Franciscus had assumed his wife to be the same age. Put the word 'widow' in front of a woman's name and she became sixty, frumpy, and about as comely as a sack of potatoes. He returned the smile. 'Mrs Kovacs?'

'Please come in.'

'Call me John,' he said, stepping past her, into the cool of the foyer. 'I appreciate you seeing me on such short notice. I hope I'm not interrupting.'

'Not at all. When you mentioned my husband, I was glad to make the time. Please, call me Katie. Why don't we sit in the den?'

Katie Kovacs led the way across the foyer, past an open kitchen and down the hall. Franciscus couldn't help but notice that the place was tricked out with all the latest gadgets and gizmos. There was granite in the kitchen, a stainless-steel fridge, and a PC in the work nook. Immediately, he began working out what kind of money she had to be making to live in this kind of style. It was a professional hazard. A salary of eighty-five grand a year left you with a sizable chip on your shoulder.

'Here's Theo,' she said, pointing to a framed photo, hanging in the center of the wall.

So that was Kovacs, thought Franciscus. The picture showed a young policeman in his blues, his peaked cap worn soberly. Trusting eyes, toothy grin, chipmunk cheeks. Franciscus pegged him as the cheery, indomitable type. The guy who took KP three nights running and didn't complain. He didn't look like a cop who'd end things by eating his gun. But then, no one started out that way.

They continued down the hall. Katie Kovacs pointed out her office. A sleek desk ran along two sides of the room, dominated by three large flat-screen monitors on which a blizzard of red, green, and white symbols flashed like Christmas lights. Documents were stacked in several piles. A few stray papers littered the floor. She smiled apologetically. 'I clean up every evening.'

Franciscus observed Kovacs's business attire. She was dressed in navy slacks and a starched white blouse. 'I hope I'm not keeping you from an appointment.'

'No, no,' she said. 'I work out of the house. I like to dress to keep me in the right frame of mind.

Otherwise, I'd be snacking all day and watching TV.'

'I doubt that,' said Franciscus, as they continued down the hall. 'May I ask what you do?'

'I'm a municipal finance specialist. I help cities around the state raise money. Just small issues: anything under a hundred million dollars.'

'Sounds exciting,' said Franciscus, meaning, *it looks like you're making some dough.*

Kovacs chuckled. 'It's not.'

They sat on a long white couch in the den, under the watchful gaze of a forty-two-inch plasma screen. She had set out a tray with a coffeepot, cups, and saucers, and a few cans of soda. He accepted a cup of coffee and took a sip. He noticed that she didn't serve herself anything. She sat across from him, perched on the edge of her chair. Her smile had disappeared.

'As I said on the phone, something's come up that concerns your husband,' Franciscus began. 'One of the suspects wanted in the bombing of Sentinel Microsystems and the murder of Officers O'Neill and Shepherd has popped up on our radar. We're calling her Bobby Stillman, but she went by a different name back then.'

'Sunshine Awakening, if I'm not mistaken.'

'Yes. So you recall the details of the case.'

'Intimately.'

'I'm sorry.' Franciscus knew that many survivors viewed suicide as murder by unseen forces.

'It wasn't suicide,' she said, as if to underscore his thoughts. 'Theo wasn't the type. He was just thirty-one. He was still bubbling about making detective. I've read all the psychobabble the department gives the grieving widow about how a policeman takes a job home with him. That wasn't my husband.'

Franciscus sat with his hands steepled, his thumbs opening and closing to emphasize a point. 'Why exactly do you believe the case was responsible for your husband's death?'

Katie Kovacs considered the question. Suddenly, her eyes narrowed. 'Did you find her?' she asked. 'The other one, the woman who got away – Bobby Stillman? Is that why you're here?'

'Not exactly. She's peripherally involved in another case I'm working. When I was checking her record, I noticed a few discrepancies with the paperwork on the case.'

'Just a few?' she asked sarcastically.

'You're not surprised?'

'My husband didn't kill himself, Detective. He was murdered.' She let the words sink in, then stood. 'Will you excuse me, Detective Franciscus?' She took a step toward the door, then stopped. 'I'm sorry, but after everything I'm not comfortable calling policemen by their Christian names.'

Franciscus stood as she left the room.

Katie Kovacs returned a minute later carrying a cardboard moving box. Setting it down on the coffee table, she took a seat next to him. She pried off the lid and began sorting through folders, newspaper clippings, and police files. 'Here we are.' Kovacs handed Franciscus an article from the front page of the Albany *Times Union* dated July 29, 1980. 'Read it,' she said.

'Sure.' The article detailed the storming of a house on Rockcliff Lane by the Albany Special Weapons and Tactics unit after a two-day siege, and the death of its tenant and sole occupant, David Bernstein, a former New York University law professor. Bernstein, a self-styled underground revolutionary, who went by the moniker Manu Q, was suspected of carrying out the bombing of

Sentinel Microsystems, and later, to have shot to death the two Albany police officers sent to question him.

'Done?' she asked.

Franciscus nodded, and she handed him another photograph. It was an eight-by-ten of the notorious crime-scene photo that had made the rounds all those years ago. It showed Bernstein, or 'Manu Q', naked to the waist, lying in a twisted pose on a wooden floor. Bullet holes dotted his torso. Too many to count. He handed the picture back. 'I've seen it.'

'Now take a look at these.' Katie Kovacs extended several black-and-white photographs, all showing spent bullets misshapen by impact. 'Three eleven-millimeter slugs. All of them were fired from the same pistol. The Fanning automatic that was found in David Bernstein's hand. The first two bullets were those that killed Officers Shepherd and O'Neill. The last one was dug out of Bernstein's brain.'

Franciscus studied the pictures. They were standard ballistics shots, the slug placed in scale by a ruler. All three had similar markings. 'Are you saying that Bernstein shot the policemen then turned the gun on himself?'

'Not exactly. The coroner estimated that the bullet that killed Bernstein was fired from a distance of ten feet. It's what drove Theo crazy. Not *crazy* crazy, so that he'd commit suicide, but regular crazy. How could David Bernstein shoot himself in the forehead from ten feet away? And, if he was already dead, why did the SWAT guys shoot him so many times afterwards?'

'The article mentioned an exchange of gunfire.'

'The theory was that it was Bobby Stillman – Sunshine Awakening, the newspapers called her –

firing at the police. But Bernstein's pistol was fired only three times. It had eight bullets remaining in the clip.'

'And Bobby Stillman was never caught,' added Franciscus.

'They claimed that she escaped from a house surrounded by a SWAT team.' Katie Kovacs laughed disgustedly. 'Not likely. Which brings me back to my original questions. How does a man shoot himself in the head from ten feet away? And if he's already dead, why shoot him so many times?'

'Good question. Did your husband follow it up?'

'Theo was the original bull terrier. Once he got hold of something, he wouldn't let go.'

'What did he find?'

'There was a second set of prints on the gun. A few of them were very clear. It was enough to convince him that David Bernstein was murdered before the SWAT team stormed the house. He told me he'd run the prints and gotten a man's name.'

'He was sure it was a man?' asked Franciscus.

'I can't say for certain, but I assume so. Otherwise he would have said something. Were you expecting it to be Bobby Stillman?'

'Maybe,' said Franciscus. 'It would have made sense. And he never told you who the prints belonged to?'

'No,' she said, her shoulders collapsing. 'Theo didn't bring it up, and I never asked. I was nineteen. It was 1980. I was into Bruce Springsteen and *Dallas*.'

'You don't have to apologize.' Franciscus patted her arm. 'You couldn't have known what would happen.' Leaning forward, he rummaged inside the box. 'What actions did the department take?' He was thinking of the file with the pages torn out of it at 1 Police Plaza. Of the detective who had erased his name from the case record.

'None. The chief refused to move on it. Bernstein was dead. They had the murder weapon. It was a good collar. There were already enough questions about why the police had failed to nail Bobby Stillman. He didn't want any more about who really killed Bernstein.' Kovacs swiveled on the couch so she could look Franciscus more directly in the eye. 'What upset Theo was that even his partner wanted him to let it go.'

'I assume they'd discussed the second set of prints.'

'Of course. Theo thought the world of him. Everyone did. He was the department's shining star. The mind reader. They called him Carnac, just like the guy on the Johnny Carson show. "Carnac the Magnificent". Theo never did a thing without clearing it with him.'

'Carnac the Magnificent', who had erased his name from the case's master file at 1 Police Plaza. Franciscus slid forward on the cushions. 'Any reason why his partner wouldn't want to look into the matter?'

Franciscus had one answer. The partner knew who the prints belonged to, and knew better than to get involved.

'Theo never said a word, but it upset him terribly. He did as he was told and let the case go. He was ambitious. He wanted to be chief. He said that in the long run everything would balance out. He'd win more than he'd lose. Two months later, he was murdered. You know the funny thing? A few days before, he'd traded his Smith and Wesson for a Fanning eleven-millimeter.'

'His partner had one, too, didn't he?'

Katie Kovacs snapped her head in his direction.

'How did you know?' When Franciscus didn't answer, she looked away, her eyes focused on some faraway place. 'He had eyes that looked right into you, right down into your soul.'

'What was his name?'

'Francois. He was a French Canadian originally. He left the force after Theo's death. He told me he'd had enough of police work. I don't know what's become of him.'

'Detective Francois?'

'No, that was his first name.' She took a breath. 'Francois Guilfoyle.'

Franciscus must have twitched or moved somehow, because Katie Kovacs asked him if he knew the name. He said no, he'd never heard of him, but he'd look him up. She packed up the box and returned the lid. 'If you'd like, you can take the box. Maybe you'll find something useful.'

'Thank you. I'll get it back to you soon.'

'Take your time. I've spent twenty-five years asking the chief to take a second look, but it hasn't done me any good.' She stood and together they walked toward the door. 'I'm sorry if I didn't answer your questions.'

'As a matter of fact, ma'am, you've answered them all.'

Chapter 42

It was a bit overwhelming, thought Senator Megan McCoy as she walked down the upper hall on the second floor of the White House. Every room had a name, and a history. The Map Room had been used as a situation room for special briefings by FDR during WWII. The East Room had served as a pen for the alligator that the Marquis de Lafayette, then a general, had given John Quincy Adams. *An alligator*. That made McCoy feel better about her own menagerie of three cats, a parakeet, and a hundred-year-old tortoise named Willy, reputed to have belonged to President William McKinley. She stared down the brightly lit corridor. Tomorrow night, and for the next four years – eight, if she did her job well – she would be sleeping under this roof.

'At last, we come to the Lincoln Bedroom,' said Gordon Ramser, the President of the United States. 'I'm sure you know by now that Lincoln never slept there.'

'It used to be an office, didn't it?' McCoy asked.

'During the war, Abe used it as his private office. He kept maps on the wall instead of these portraits.'

McCoy stepped inside the bedroom. A massive bed, nine feet by six, took up one side of the room. The furniture looked like Lincoln himself could have used it, chintz sofas, chiffon armchairs, heavy mahogany dressers. A recent President had turned an overnight stay in the Lincoln Bedroom into the ultimate 'thank-you' to his top political donors, corporate bigwigs, and those special few who counted the President as a personal friend. Ramser had raised the bar higher. It was said the cost for a night in the Lincoln Bedroom was five hundred thousand dollars, payable in discreet sums to the PAC of his choice. It was also said that no stay was complete without having sex there. It beat the 'Mile High Club' by a longshot.

Not that she would have a chance to find out. At fifty-five, Megan McCoy was twice married, twice divorced, and regretfully without children. While her election had infinitely boosted her dating prospects, the chance of actually sleeping with a man had gone down the toilet. McCoy was from the old school. She could only sleep with a man she loved. Nobody was in the batter's box at the moment – or on deck for that matter – and she feared that her schedule as commander in chief would not permit for the candlelight dinners and moonlight promenades necessary.

Ramser pointed across the room. 'The rocking chair by the window is identical to the one Mr Lincoln was sitting in at Ford's Theatre the night he was assassinated. A lot of people feel his presence here. A few of the staff refuse to go in. So does my dog, Tootsie. She never barks except when she passes the door. You cannot get that animal to cross the threshold.'

'Are you saying you believe in ghosts?' McCoy asked, with a smile.

'Oh yes,' said Ramser, more earnestly than she would have liked. 'You can't hold this office without feeling quite a few pairs of eyes on you. I don't know if I'd use the word "ghost" exactly. Maybe "spirit" is better. The "spirit of the past".

The office of the President is a living thing. You don't invest it, so much as it invests you.'

Ramser walked past the bed and through a narrow doorway. 'In here is the Lincoln Sitting Room. It's a nice place to get away from things for a minute or two. I come here when I need to be alone. You don't get many opportunities for solitude when you're in this office.'

'I get plenty every night when I go to sleep. The benefits of being single.'

Ramser smiled. 'No one said it's a cakewalk getting here. We all take our lumps.'

McCoy's marital status had been a prime target for her opponents' mudslinging. As had her looks. With a tendency to carry an extra twenty or thirty pounds, McCoy did not fit any definition, past or present, of a beauty. She wore her hair short and liked its natural gray color. She favored loose-fitting black pantsuits because they didn't make her look like the *Hindenburg*, and she couldn't stand contact lenses because they made her eyes itch like crazy. Her campaign manager was an African-American woman and her press secretary was a gay male from Greenwich Village. In the eyes of the attack dogs, that made her a fat, four-eyed bull dyke who wanted to pack the cabinet with queers, niggers, and people of un-Christian orientation. The salve of victory was only beginning to soothe her feelings.

'Like to take a seat?' Ramser asked.

'Certainly.' McCoy knew this was not really a request. She'd noted Ramser's anxiety since they'd begun the tour an hour earlier. 'My feet are killing me,' she said. 'I feel like I haven't rested since February.'

Ramser took a chair opposite her. For a few moments, neither spoke. Rain drummed against the roof. An occasional gust rattled the windows. A joist in the wall moaned. Behind the fresh paint and the Stinger missiles, it was easy to forget that the White House was over two hundred years old. At length, he said, 'I understand Ed Logsdon had a chat with you a few days ago.'

'The chief justice and I had an engaging conversation.'

'I know that we don't have much common ground, Senator, but as holder of this office these past eight years, I'd like to ask you – *urge you*, in fact – to reconsider his request.'

'Secret clubs and backroom discussions are not my style, Mr President.'

'Gordon, please. It's time I get used to that again.'

'Gordon,' she said, dutifully. 'I ran on the slogan, "The Voice of the People." The vox populi. I don't think my voters would be too enamored with me if they learned I was sneaking around smoke-filled rooms and making decisions without their approval.'

'I felt the same way. The office carries with it a tremendous responsibility. It's because of that responsibility that I served on the Committee. You see, the President's responsibility goes beyond the trust placed in us by the voters, to the very idea of America, itself.'

'And you think everyday citizens are incapable of sharing those ideas?'

'Yes and no. People's needs are by nature selfish. Remember what Mark Twain said about never trusting a man who didn't vote with his pocketbook? The average voter is motivated by his well-being and the well-being of his family. Are you better or worse off than four years ago?'

'And what's wrong with that?'

'Why nothing. I'm the same way myself. But the President can't make decisions that will affect this country for a hundred years on what might please or piss off the voter for the next six months.'

'Coming from a man who needs a poll to tell him whether to wear a blue or a gray suit, that means something.'

Ramser ignored the jibe. 'Your responsibility is to the country first, the people second.'

'I thought they were the same thing.'

'Not always. There are times when the President alone has to decide what's the best course of action. Without congressional bickering. Without the polls that I admit I relied too heavily on. See if you don't! When he has to act quickly and unambiguously. And secretly. That power is also implicit in the trust given us.'

'Are you saying that the people expect us to lie to them?'

'Essentially, yes. They expect their commander in chief to make decisions in the country's interest. Hard decisions that they might not agree with in the short term.'

'And that's what this Committee is for?'

'Yes. And it has been since it was founded in 1793.'

'Chief Justice Logsdon told me about your role in the Jay Treaty.'

'Keep it quiet or we'll have to rewrite the history books,' said Ramser, sotto voce.

McCoy did not share his smile. 'There's more?'

'Much.'

'Such as?'

'It wouldn't be right of me to say until you join us. I will say, however, that I don't disagree with a single action the Committee has taken.'

'I always thought that you looked like a man who slept well at night.'

'Jefferson, Lincoln, JFK . . . every sitting President

THE PATRIOTS' CLUB 295

has been one of us. It would be an honor to count you as a member. There are some issues that require your attention.'

'I'm sure they'll be covered in my PDB.'

'Probably not.'

McCoy leaned forward. 'I don't share your pessimism about the American people. I've always found that if you give it to them straight, take off the sugar coating, they're more than capable of making the right decision. Your problem, Gordon, is that you never trusted them to begin with. Maybe we never have. Somehow we've convinced ourselves that the people – our husbands, and brothers, and best friends – need to be hoodwinked into thinking things are better than they are or worse than they are. Bigger and Scarier and More Threatening. I have a different opinion. I think the people have had enough of the bullshit and just want to see things the way they really are.'

'That kind of talk worked in the campaign, Meg. Unfortunately, this is the real world. Believe me, people don't want to see things how they truly are. They are much too frightening.'

'We'll see about that.'

Ramser bowed his head and sighed. When he looked up, his complexion had paled. He looked like an old man. 'I take it that's your final answer.'

'No, Gordon, it's not. Here's my final answer. The day and age when a group of fat cats and powerbrokers can operate behind the scenes to make things happen is over. I'm not going to join the Committee because the Committee will be no more. After I swear the oath tomorrow, I'm going to make it my first priority to root out every one of you secretive bastards.'

'How will you do that?'

'I have some friends at the *Post* who will be very

interested in what you've told me. It will make Watergate pale in comparison.'

'The press?'

Senator McCoy nodded. 'I think this is something that's right up Charles Connolly's alley.'

Ramser nodded. 'Oh, you're right about that, Meg. I'm sure Charles Connolly would find your story very interesting, indeed.' For a long second, he stared into her eyes. 'I am sorry, Meg.'

Senator McCoy felt a profound shiver rustle her spine. The emotion in his voice disturbed her. The President of the United States sounded as if he were offering his condolences.

Chapter 43

'Professor Walsh?'

A bearded, shaggy-haired man in a black cable-knit sweater and tortoiseshell glasses glanced up from his desk. 'We're officially closed,' he called gruffly. 'Office hours are Monday and Friday from ten to eleven. They're posted on the window and on your syllabus, if you haven't had a chance to take a look at it.'

'Professor Walsh, it's Jennifer Dance. Senior seminar . . . the Historical Society.'

Behind the pebble lenses, watery blue eyes stirred. 'Jennifer? Jennifer Dance? That you?'

Jenny stepped tentatively into the office. 'Hello, Professor. Sorry to disturb you. I wouldn't be here if it weren't important.'

Walsh stood and gestured for her to enter. 'Nonsense. Come in, come in. I thought you were another one of my geniuses carping about their grades. The kids these days . . . either it's an "A" or you're jeopardizing their future. Ingrates is what they are.' Turning to the side, he slipped past a bookcase filled to overflowing. He was broad-shouldered and burly, more a mountain man than a tenured professor of American history and the president of the New York Historical Society. 'Still giving tours of the city?'

Jenny closed the door behind her. 'Not for a while. Actually, I'm teaching. High-risk teens at the Kraft School.'

'Teaching? Bully for you. Remember my motto: "Those that can, teach . . . and the hell with the rest of 'em." My God, look at you. It's been too long.'

Walsh spread his arms and Jenny accepted the hug. 'Eight years.'

'Ssshhh,' he said, putting a finger to his lips. 'That makes me sixty. Don't tell a soul. The cult of youth. It's everywhere. New department chair is forty. *Forty.* Can you imagine? I was still growing my sideburns at forty.'

Jenny smiled. As a student, she'd spent considerable time in this office. After taking four classes with Professor Harrison Walsh, she'd served as his teaching assistant senior year while he supervised her thesis. Professors fell into three categories. Those you hated, those you tolerated, and those you worshipped. Walsh counted among the last. He was loud, long-winded, and wildly passionate about his subject. God help you if you hadn't done your reading. It was either a one-way ticket out of the class, or an hour of sheer hell in the hot seat.

'Take a seat, kiddo,' said Walsh. 'You look pale. Coffee? Hot chocolate? Something stronger?'

'I'm fine,' said Jenny. 'Just a little cold.'

She glanced out the window. Walsh's office overlooked the main quad, Low Library, and the statue of Alma Mater, which every Columbia University student knows means 'nourishing mother'. The sky had fused into a pearl-gray dome that pressed lower and lower, crushing the city beneath it. A light snow danced in the air, whipped about by contrary winds, never seeming to fall to the ground.

Harrison Walsh clapped his hands together. 'So what brings you back to school on a day like this?'

'A question, actually. Something about the past.'

'Last I checked this was still the history department. You've come to the right place.'

Jenny set her purse on her lap, trying to keep from wincing as she settled into the chair. 'It's about a club,' she began. 'An old club. I mean, very old. Dating from the beginning of the country. Something like the Masons, but different, more secretive even, made up of government officials, big wheels in industry, important people. They might call themselves the Committee, or something like that.'

'And what does "the Committee" do when they're not practicing their secret handshakes?'

Jenny recalled Bobby Stillman's words. 'They spy, they listen, they interfere. They help the government get things done without the people's consent.'

'Not them again,' Walsh complained.

Jenny sat forward. 'You mean you know who they are?'

'Sure, but I'm afraid you've come to the wrong room. You need Conspiracy 101: Introduction to Fruitcakes. Jenny, you're talking about everyone from the Trilateral Commission to the fellows at Bohemian Grove, with a spice of the Council on Foreign Relations thrown in. They all fit the bill. The invisible hand that rocks the cradle.'

'This isn't a conspiracy, Professor,' said Jenny, soberly. 'It's a real group of men who are trying to shape government policy for their own ends.'

'And this club is still around?'

'Definitely.'

Walsh narrowed his eyes. After a moment, he picked up a paperweight made from an old World War I shell casing, and tossed it back and forth from hand to hand. 'Okay, then,' he said, finally. 'The first thing that comes to mind is a group led by

Vincent Astor that called themselves the Room. They helped out Wild Bill Donovan during the thirties when he was setting up the Office of Strategic Services. Strictly volunteers. Businessmen, mostly rich New Yorkers, who'd meet on Astor's yacht upon returning from their world travels and trade gossip while getting silly on bourbon. Sound like who you have in mind?'

'No. These guys are concerned about what's going on in the country. With affecting the course the nation takes. They kill people who don't agree with them.'

'Not good guys.'

'No,' said Jenny, stonily. 'Not good guys.'

Walsh put the shell casing down and plonked his elbows onto the desk. 'Come on, Jenny, is this for real?'

Jenny nodded, but added nothing. She didn't want to go into it any further. At the moment, she was feeling very shaky.

Walsh studied her closely. 'Are you in any kind of trouble?'

'No,' she said. 'Of course not. Just curious.'

'You're sure?'

Jenny forced a smile. 'Can I take you up on that coffee now?'

'Sure thing.' Walsh stood up and moved to a cluttered sideboard. Finding a Styrofoam cup, he poured some coffee from a warming pot.

Jenny took a sip. 'I see you haven't upgraded.'

'Good old Maxwell House. Starbucks will have to make do without me.' He sat back and let her drink in peace. After a minute, he wrinkled his brow, and said, 'What else can you tell me about this "real club"?'

Jenny searched her mind for anything else Bobby Stillman might have said. 'One more thing,' she said. 'One of their phrases was *Scientia est potentia*.'

' "Knowledge is power." Good motto for a bunch of spies.' He banged his palm on the table, and said, 'Can't help you, Jen. This one goes right over my head. Me, I'm a twentieth-century man. T. R. to the present. Not my area, I'm afraid.'

'It was a longshot. I'm sorry to have taken your—'

'Not mine,' Walsh went on. 'But Ken Gladden might be able to give you a hand. He's our resident Founding Fathers freak. You might even find him in his office if you hurry.'

Chapter 44

The daily exodus was in full swing, the ninety minutes of madness when New York's working masses trudged from office to subway, train, and ferry, and headed home. The slope from Broadway to Vesey Street was packed with commuters as tightly as sardines in a can. Everyone leaving early to beat the storm.

'Just keep walking,' said Bolden, as he drew up alongside Althea Jackson. 'Keep looking straight ahead. I can hear you just fine.'

'Why, Tom, what in the . . .'

'Eyes to the front!'

'What is this, the army?' Althea demanded.

Bolden checked over his shoulder. He had shadowed Althea for several blocks. If he hadn't known her so well, her clothing, her hairstyle, the way she walked carrying her feed bag of a purse and listing ten degrees to port, he would have lost her five times over. If she was being followed, he couldn't tell.

'Did you find her?' he asked.

'She's at NYU Hospital. "Currently being treated," is what they said.'

'Being treated? What does that mean? How is she? Is she in surgery? What condition is she in?'

' "Currently being treated." That's all they said. I asked them all those questions and didn't get a single answer.'

Bolden swallowed his worry and frustration. 'Did you speak with the doctor?'

'I didn't speak with anyone except the operator.'

'Come on, you could have said you were family.'

'I tried, Thomas, but that was as far as I got.'

'Okay. Take it easy.'

They walked a few more steps, bumping against a group waiting for a signal to turn. Pedestrians pushed into them, forcing them to step forward. Bolden felt caged. He had to resist the instinct to turn around and check the faces behind him. The light turned. After a few seconds, the pressure lessened. Lodged in the human thicket, the two crossed the street.

'I'm scared,' said Althea. 'There are men all over your office. They took out your computer, boxed your files.'

'Police?'

'Lord, no. Police left at two. Right after I saw you. They had manners. These ones?' Althea shook her head with distaste.

'Who are they?' Bolden asked. 'Guys from the firm? Tech support? Maintenance?'

'I've never seen any of them. I tried to watch over them, make sure they didn't take anything personal, but they kicked me out. Put down the blinds. They're saying you shot him. They're calling you a murderer. I said you most certainly did not. I told everyone who'd listen that I saw what happened and that it was some kind of accident. No one believes me. Everyone keeps telling me to watch that tape on the television.'

'That's something, isn't it?'

'Thomas . . . you didn't shoot him, did you?'

'You were there. You saw what happened.'

'I know. I thought that it was the guard who fired, but since I've seen that tape on the television . . .' She shook her head, as if mystified.

Bolden swallowed his frustration. Such was the power of images. Althea had witnessed Weiss's murder with her own eyes. Even so, she was no longer sure what she'd seen. 'No, Althea, I did not shoot Sol Weiss. I loved Sol. Everybody loved Sol. It was the guard who shot him.'

But in his topsy-turvy world, he was beginning to wonder about that, too.

'And you didn't go hitting little Diana Chambers?'

'No, Althea, I didn't.'

'Then why are they—'

'I don't know,' said Bolden, too forcefully. 'I'm trying to figure it out.'

He considered telling Althea to take her son, Bobby, and leave town for a few days. God knows he was endangering her by asking for her help. He decided against issuing any kind of warning. The safest thing for her would be to show up for work the next day, and the day after that. He gave her a month before they found a justifiable reason to fire her. Probably after the Trendrite deal closed.

'What did you get on Scanlon?' he asked.

Althea frowned. 'Not much. A few mentions in the late seventies about some military work. Training troops and the like. Scanlon Corporation was bought out by Defense Associates in 1980. No price given. It was a private transaction.'

'Defense Associates. Never heard of them. Did you run a search on them, too?'

'Defense Associates went bankrupt nine months after they bought Scanlon. That's all I was able to find out.'

'Did you dig up the bankruptcy filing?'

'The what?'

'The bankruptcy filing.'

'Oh, you mean the one that lists Mickey Schiff as a company director?'

Bolden darted a glance at Althea. 'Schiff? He was still in the marines in eighty.'

'No, child. According to the filing, Lieutenant Colonel Michael T. Schiff, *retired*, was a director of Defense Associates when it went belly-up. That other man you wanted to know about, Russell Kuy . . . I'm not even going to try to pronounce *that* name . . . well, he was its president.'

Bolden digested the information. He wouldn't exactly call it good news, but it was a start. The question was what had happened to Scanlon in the interim? If Defense Associates had gone belly-up, why were there civilian military contractors with the Scanlon logo tattooed on their breastbone chasing him all over Manhattan?

'Small world, isn't it?' she said.

'You mean about Schiff working for Defense Associates? I guess so.'

'No, I mean about Mr Jacklin working for them, too.'

'Excuse me? Do you mean James Jacklin?' If Bolden's thoughts had been elsewhere, the mention of Jefferson's chairman and founder brought him back to the here and now.

'I never knew Mickey Schiff had worked with Mr Jacklin. At least, I know why you had me looking at Scanlon. You being in charge of Jefferson Partners for the firm and all.'

'I'm sorry, Althea. It's been a tough day. I'm not following you.'

'James Jacklin was chairman of Defense Associates. Thomas, you okay? You're even whiter than usual.'

In 1980, James Jacklin had just finished his four-year tour of duty as Secretary of Defense. Bolden hadn't known that he'd left a failed business venture behind him. He suspected few others did, either.

'I'm fine, Althea. I hadn't been expecting to hear about Jacklin, that's all.'

'I did a search on him, too. Got too many articles to print. I just brought the ones about Scanlon and Defense Associates.' She paused. 'One other thing. You know who got left holding most of the worthless debt? We did. Harrington Weiss. HW was listed as Defense Associates' largest creditor.'

'How much?'

'Fifty-three million.'

Bolden whistled long and low.

The crowd slowed and grew more frenetic, as they approached the entry to the PATH terminal at the WTC. Through the tall mesh fence, dump trucks, cranes, earthmovers, and backhoes dotted the escarpment. From where Bolden stood, they looked like Tonka toys. As usual, Ground Zero provoked a complicated and transient mix of emotions. One moment, he felt angry, the next forlorn, and the next ornery and begging for a fight. Mostly, though, the memory of all that once had been – the ghost of the towers – left him feeling a little less human.

'You still interested in that list of companies your clients bought and sold?'

'Scanlon anywhere there?'

'No, sir.'

'Might as well take a look at it,' said Bolden. 'I don't want you to think you did all that hard work for nothing.'

Althea slowed and took hold of his arm. 'Thomas, you're not coming back, are you?'

Bolden put his hand on top of hers. 'I'd say my days at HW are pretty much finished.'

'What about me?'

'Just stay. Do your job. When I get out of this, I'll look you up. We're a team.'

'I got my Bobby.'

'He's a good boy.'

'Yes, he is. He deserves better.'

They walked a hundred yards without speaking.

'See that trash bin?' Bolden said, lifting his head and indicating a square container a few yards ahead. 'Drop the papers in there. I'll be along a minute later to pick them up. Go home and don't tell anyone you've seen or heard from me.'

'Okay, boss.' Althea extended a hand down low. 'I've got something else for you. Made a pit stop on the way.' Bolden grasped her hand and felt the crisply folded bills. He looked at her and she returned his gaze. 'Be careful, child,' she said. 'I don't know what I'll tell my Bobby if something happens to you.'

'I'll do my best.'

'You do better than that. You're saying they changed that man's face on the videotape and put yours in his place. Those people are rewriting the past. Better watch out or they'll rewrite you and me.'

Chapter 45

'I'm sorry I couldn't be of more help. Feel free to give me a call though, any time. Really.'

'Thanks anyway.' Jenny closed the door of Professor Mahmoud Basrani's office, walked down the hall, and collapsed onto the nearest chair. In the space of an hour, she'd visited two professors of American history, an associate professor of government, and a lecturer in sociology. Their reactions had run the spectrum from bewildered to bemused, but in the end, their responses were identical. None had the scantest notion what she was talking about. The search was over before it had even begun. Walsh had been right. It was time to sign up for Conspiracy 101.

Jenny felt tears welling up. She'd hardly begun to look for the club and already she felt defeated. *But it's real*, she'd wanted to scream. *They shot me. Do you want to see? How much more real can it get than that?*

A wave of fatigue swept over her and she wanted to go to sleep. Her shoulder was killing her, she was eight weeks' pregnant, and she had absolutely nowhere to go, and no one she could turn to without risking dragging them into this mess as well. Worst of all, the father of her child, and the man she truly loved, was running for his life, and she couldn't do a thing to help him. She slumped further into the seat, trying to find a spark, something that would light a fire inside her.

'You're Jennifer?'

Jenny looked up to find a thin, red-haired girl hardly out of her teens bent over her. A nod was all she could manage.

'I'm Peg Kirk. Professor Walsh's T.A. Harry told me that you'd visited him a little earlier. We talked about what you'd asked him.'

'About my "club"?' Jenny said, only half-facetiously. 'I know it sounds stupid. I just thought that someone around here might be able to shed some light on it.'

'No,' said Peg, earnestly. 'It's not stupid at all.'

Jenny looked at the slight girl, her plain face illuminated by a wide, believing smile and blue eyes that shone with enthusiasm. She was dressed in beat-up jeans and a baggy sweatshirt. *A student*, she thought. *A believer. God help me, I was like that once, too.* 'Thanks, but I know when I'm beat.'

Peg dropped into the next seat. 'Don't let them get you down. They're all a bunch of fuddy-duddies. They only know what they read. None of them go in for alternative history.'

'Alternative history?'

'You know . . . what might have been. Or as we prefer to say, "what really was," and has been papered over, hushed up, or just plain covered up since.'

'And you do?'

Peg shrugged. 'Actually, I'm not sure yet. But between you and me, it's the only area that's still out there for the examining. Everything else has been written to death. The Founding Fathers, the Civil War, Manifest Destiny. You can forget the twentieth century. It's all been done. I've got to read between the lines and ask, "What if?" '

'Have I got a story for you,' said Jenny, shaking her head.

'Not for me,' said Peg. 'For Simon. He's who you're looking for. *Scientia est potentia*. He'll love that.'

'Simon? Is he a friend of yours?'

'Simon Bonny? God no. Not a friend. I, like, worship him. He's a teacher. Head of the department at the University of Glasgow. He's a searcher. He looks in dark corners for the truth.'

Cue the *X Files* theme, thought Jenny. Next stop: the Bermuda Triangle. 'Glasgow,' she said, smiling ruefully. 'Well, that's a help at least.'

'No, silly,' Peg protested. 'He's not in Glasgow now. He's here at Columbia. Professor Bonny's teaching the freshman survey class this semester. He's exactly who you need to speak with.'

'And he knows about the club . . . this Professor Bonny?'

Peg bunched her shoulders. 'If anyone does, it's him. And you know what else?' She motioned Jenny close. 'He knows who really killed JFK.'

The Old Scotland pub was dark and woody with the smell of day-old beer hanging in the air and plenty of corners she wouldn't dare set foot in. Simon Bonny stood at the rail of the bar, a pint of beer in front of him, an unlit cigarette resting in the ashtray. 'You're Jenny?'

'Professor Bonny?' Jenny extended a hand. 'Thanks for seeing me at such short notice.'

'Not to worry,' said Bonny. 'As you can see, the waiting room's not exactly crowded.'

He was a tall string bean, dressed in blue jeans, a wrinkled button-down, and a tweed jacket. He was pale and anxious with slits for eyes, a fidgeting mouth, and a bobbing Adam's apple. Scotland's answer to Ichabod Crane. 'Your call whetted my appetite. A club of influential gentlemen founded two hundred years ago. Governing without the consent of the people. *Scientia est potentia.* "Knowledge is power." Fascinating, indeed.'

For once, some excitement. Jenny found his interest refreshing. 'Really? Does it ring a bell?'

'Maybe,' said Bonny, stuffily. 'First, let me tell you that I gave Harry Walsh a jingle. Had to check your bona fides. Hope you don't mind. He said you seemed a little rattled. He was rather worried about you. Any reason for that?'

'No, no.' Jenny lowered her head and laughed, as if upset with herself. 'I've just been doing some reading. Professor Walsh . . . uh, Harry . . . was my adviser when I was a student here. I thought he might be able to help me out.'

'Decent chap, but he never read a source he didn't believe. Takes everything as given. That's the problem, you know. History's written by the victors. If you want to really know what's going on you have to study the losers . . . how they might have construed things . . . search for any nuggets that give you their side of the story.'

'And that's what you do?'

'I, madam, am the patron saint of losers,' said Simon Bonny proudly, punctuating his declaration with a long draught of beer. 'Anyway, where were we? *Scientia est potentia.* That's the key.' He sniffed and rubbed a hand over his mouth. 'Talleyrand,' he said.

'What?'

'Not "what". "*Who*". Charles Maurice de Talleyrand-Périgord. Just Talleyrand. Foreign minister to Napoleon. Cheat. Scoundrel. Visionary. Patriot. Interesting bloke.'

'What about him?'

'Good friend of Alexander Hamilton's, actually. They palled around together in 1794. He'd come to

Philadelphia to get away from Robespierre and "the Terror". A minor event called the French Revolution.'

Oh no, thought Jenny. *A pedant without a leash.* 'And this has what to do with the club exactly?'

'Wait, darling. You see, Hamilton and Talleyrand were best buddies. They were both realists, interested in the effective exercise of power. Sneaky little shits, really. But smart, dear. Really fucking smart. Napoleon called Talleyrand "shit in a silk stocking", while Thomas Jefferson called Hamilton "an evil colossus who must be stopped at the first instance". When Talleyrand returned to France, the two kept up a correspondence. It's all in my book. *Shadow Monarch: Hamilton from 1790–1800.'*

'I apologize, Professor, but I missed it. My reading's more toward Jane Austen these days.'

'Whose isn't?' Bonny dismissed her apology with a good-natured laugh, surprising her. 'Be out in paperback next year in the spring. I'm sure you won't miss it a second time.'

Jenny knew he was trying to be funny, but she could barely bring herself to smile, let alone laugh. Her shoulder throbbed with a vengeance, and she was very much regretting her decision to turn down any pain medication.

'Back to these letters,' said Bonny, coming closer so that his narrow green eyes held hers. 'You see, Hamilton is very explicit about going to private – read "secret" – meetings in the Long Room at the Fraunces Tavern in New York, and the City Tavern in Philadelphia. All the big guns were there: George Washington, John Jay, Robert Morris, and later, Monroe, Madison, Gallatin, and Pendleton.'

'I don't know a Pendleton.'

'Nathaniel Pendleton. Friend of Hamilton's.

Lawyer and judge. Served as Hamilton's second at the duel of the century. Hamilton v. Burr.'

'Got it.'

'The meetings took place at the stroke of midnight. First, a prayer was spoken, always Washington's favorite that he had invoked at Valley Forge. No drinking was permitted. No cursing. No tobacco. The meetings were gravely serious and often lasted until morning. Afterwards, Washington would lead everyone to a dawn service at St Paul's Chapel, just as he'd led the members of his cabinet there after his first inauguration.'

'What did they discuss?'

'Hamilton never said exactly – he was too wily a fox for that – but I have my suspicions. He hinted to Talleyrand that the meetings were to come up with ways to help General Washington, then President, circumvent the legislature, or, as was equally the case, to more quickly put into effect what they would vote for six months hence.'

Jenny wasn't buying it. 'This is the same Hamilton who helped write the Constitution and the Federalist Papers? He created Congress. Why in the world would he want to rob it of its power?'

'Made a mistake, didn't he?' Bonny took a breath and looked around the pub, searching every corner as if needing to find a place to begin. 'It's 1793. Everywhere Hamilton looked, he saw the country falling apart. Too many parochial interests. Every man for himself. The farmers in Pennsylvania wanted one thing, the bankers in New York something else altogether. Hamilton favored a large country. In fact, he was one of the first who saw all lands west to the Pacific as being America's natural boundary. But the republic was hamstrung. Paralyzed by conflicting interests. All for want of a strong executive able to act decisively without the belabored approval of Congress. "Your people, sir, are a beast," he wrote in a letter, once. He didn't refute the idea that every man should have a vote, but he wanted something done to lessen the House and Senate's ability to restrict the "Chief Magistrate" from acting as he saw fit. Jefferson called him a monocrat. Half monarchist, half democrat.'

'But Hamilton didn't really want a king. He hated the monarchy.'

'To an extent, that's true. But his words argue the opposite. "All communities divide themselves into the few and the many," he said to Talleyrand. "The first are rich and well-born, then the mass of the people. The people are turbulent and changing. They seldom judge or determine right. Give therefore to the first class a distinct permanent share in the government. They will check the unsteadiness of the second." The "permanent share" he envisioned was the presidency. In his opinion, four years was too short a term. He preferred ten years. If not a monarch, then, a monarch in all but name.'

'But what did they do ... Washington and Hamilton and all of them? You said you had your suspicions.'

'They killed someone, didn't they?'

Jenny reacted skeptically. 'Are you sure they didn't just sit around the table and talk?'

'Oh, there was plenty of talk. No doubt about that. But remember who we're dealing with. These gents were soldiers used to spilling blood. Not an armchair general in the lot. Hamilton had two horses shot out from under him at the Battle of Monmouth, rode the third until it collapsed from exhaustion. Washington took his charger up and down the lines exposing himself to hellacious fire too many times to count. These were men on speaking terms with death.'

'Who was it?'

'A rogue. An upstart. Someone threatening the very life of the republic. Therefore an enemy. Do you remember the Jay Treaty?'

'Vaguely. Some kind of agreement that kept us out of war with Britain.'

'Precisely. Without the treaty, war was inevitable . . . and if war, the breakup of the states. At the time, you Yanks were much too weak to take on Britain again. You would have had your bottoms soundly thwacked. The country couldn't have survived it. There would have been a division along the same lines as the Civil War. North versus South. Hamilton knew it. The Jay Treaty's the most important piece of paper no one knows about.'

'Do you have a name?'

'Mr X. That's my secret. Subject of my next book.'

Jenny shook her head, doubtfully, then winced at a sudden stab of pain.

'What's the matter with your shoulder?' Bonny asked.

'Nothing.'

'You're coddling it,' said Bonny, reaching a hand toward her.

Jenny flinched, a reflex. 'Watch it!'

'What is it, then?' Bonny asked again.

'I was shot.'

Bonny sighed, rolling his eyes at the ceiling. He took a swig of beer, then said, 'I'm not kidding, Miss Dance. Really . . .'

'Someone took a shot at me three hours ago with a high-powered rifle. The doctor said he thought it was a thirty-aught-six. Actually, the bullet only grazed me, but it hurts like . . .'

'You're serious?' he said, setting the glass on the counter.

'Yes, I'm serious.'

'Gracious me!' exclaimed Simon Bonny. Suddenly, he was blinking uncontrollably, his lower lip moving as if he were talking to himself. Then he shuddered, and both the blinking and the lip thing stopped. 'What in the name of Jehovah are you doing here, then?'

'Trying to find out who it was before they take another one. I don't figure them as the types to miss twice.' Jenny pointed to his glass. 'Mind if I have a sip?'

'Christ, have a whole one. Better yet, have a scotch. On me.'

'I can't. I'm expecting.'

'My, but they're coming fast and furious today.' Bonny put the cigarette in his mouth, took a faux drag, then replaced it in the ashtray. 'Go on, then.'

'How much do you want to know?'

Bonny very carefully looked over either shoulder, then drew near Jenny. 'I know who sent the anthrax to the Senate building,' he whispered, with a nod to show he meant it. 'Try me.'

Chapter 46

Jenny set her purse on the bar and climbed onto a stool. 'It began last night,' she said. 'Two men mugged me and my boyfriend downtown, near Wall Street.'

'Been quite a day,' said Simon Bonny.

Jenny nodded and went on to recount the events of the past fifteen hours. She left nothing out – not Thomas being questioned by Guilfoyle about Crown and Bobby Stillman, her abduction from school that morning, and being grazed by an assassin's bullet in Union Square Park – right up to the point where a man impersonating her brother had tried to bypass hospital security. 'I don't think he wanted to bring me a get-well card.'

'Indeed,' said Simon Bonny. 'Yes, then . . . you're in some trouble, aren't you?'

'If you'd like to leave now, I understand. I don't want to involve you in something you don't—'

'No, no. Can't leave. You're the real thing, aren't you? A victim with a capital *V*. So, *Scientia est potentia*. This Stillman woman told you that was their motto, did she? That's the key, you know. It's what Hamilton said, too. One of his favorites. But why, Jennifer? Why all this cloak-and-dagger stuff? Why are they after your boyfriend? What does he do?'

'He's an investment banker. He works at Harrington Weiss handling the big private equity firms like Atlantic, Whitestone, and Jefferson. He pals around with billionaires, flies on private jets to Aspen, tries to convince them to buy a company and let HW do the deal.'

'Ever screw any of 'em over?'

'Thomas? Never. He's the last honest man. He says the whole thing is a mistake.'

Bonny pursed his lips and shook his head, letting her know it was no mistake. 'Any of the firms associated with the government? Tied in with the CIA, maybe?'

'God no. They're strictly private sector. Major profit motive. Scotch Nat's the greediest man on the planet, Tom says. And the best businessman.'

'*Scotch Nat?*'

'James Jacklin, the chairman of Jefferson Partners. It's his nickname.'

'I know who he is. Former secretary of defense. Stalwart of capitalism. But back up a second. What name did you say he goes by?'

' "Scotch Nat," ' said Jenny. 'It's what his friends call him. Not Thomas, of course, but you know . . . his buddies. I guess Jacklin's Scottish or something. Does it mean something to you?'

Bonny was blinking madly again. ' "Scotch Nat" was Pendleton's nickname,' he said, his voice jumping half an octave. 'Nathaniel Pendleton, Hamilton's bosom buddy. An original member of the club.'

'Must be a coincidence,' said Jenny, though she didn't quite believe it herself.

'You ever heard that nickname before?' Bonny demanded.

'No,' she admitted. 'But come on, we're talking two hundred years ago. More even. They're not still around.'

'Why not? In the eight years that Hamilton wrote

to Talleyrand, they'd already begun to rotate their members. Washington left, then died. John Adams took his place. Gallatin, the Swiss-born Treasury secretary, was recruited. Why shouldn't they still be around? Masons have a thousand years under their belt. Two hundred's just the beginning.'

'But you said Washington was involved? He was the President.'

'According to Hamilton, he came to every one of their meetings. Jefferson, too. After that we have to guess, don't we? But that was the whole point of the club. To help the President get things accomplished when Congress was too pigheaded to act. And they shot you, poor child. Goodness, this changes things.'

'I don't believe it. It's too far back.'

'Your friend, Stillman, said it herself. A club. Actually, they called themselves a committee, but who cares? The scale. There's the key.'

'What do you mean?'

'Just look at the scale of the operation that's been mounted to track down and eliminate you and your boyfriend. And make no mistake, they want to kill you. It's the country at stake. Oh, yes, scale, darling. Think of the manpower, the surveillance work, the tapping into phone networks, using your GPS signals to track you. Government has to be involved. Christ, they went all-out, didn't they?'

'That's jumping to conclusions.' Talk of the government frightened her. It all sounded so crazy, so far-fetched. 'You can't hang all of that on a nickname. Maybe there are dozens of "Scotch Nats".'

'Take it from me, lady, there aren't. I'm a bloody Scot, myself. Just forgot to wear the kilt, didn't I?' Bonny crossed his arms and began pacing back and forth, talking half to himself, half to Jenny. 'I knew it. I knew they were still around. I've seen their tracks, but no one believed me. Everyone said, "Bonny, you're a loon." "Bonny's round the bend." But no . . .'

'You've been keeping track of them?'

'You joking? Their tracks are all over the country's history. Who do you think bombed the battleship *Maine* in Havana Harbor?'

'It was an explosion in the coal room,' Jenny said. 'Spontaneous combustion or something. I just saw an article in *National Geographic* about it.'

'An explosion in the coal room?' Bonny shook his head, as if he pitied her. 'Spontaneous combustion? That's Greek for saying they have no bloody idea what happened. Someone put a bomb under that ship, and it propelled the US of A straight into the fray of the imperialist age. Not six months later, Teddy Roosevelt was charging up Kettle Hill. In a few years, Hawaii, Panama, and the Philippines were all US territories. Cuba and Haiti might as well have been. It was the country's birth as a world power. A regular coming-out party.'

Jenny shook her head. But her skeptical smile was all Bonny needed to goad him further.

'And the *Lusitania*?' he said. 'Who do you think got on the blower and tipped off the Hun that the boat was loaded to the gills with explosives?'

'A U-boat sunk it. Lots of ships were going down. It was the middle of World War One. Unrestricted submarine warfare and all that.'

'Ah, the young and naïve,' said Bonny. His eyes hardened. 'May the seventh, nineteen hundred and fifteen. Despite repeated warnings of U-boats in the area, Captain Charles Turner takes his boat directly into waters where three boats were sunk in the past weeks. Not only that, the man actually slows the boat down and guides her close to the Irish shore, where everyone knew U-boats loved to lie in wait.

Did Captain Turner zig and zag like any God-fearing man with nearly two thousand souls on board? Did he? No. Captain Turner keeps her straight as she goes. Fog, he said, was the reason. *Fog? So what?* What was he watching out for? A bloody iceberg? It was May, and a warm May at that. One torpedo took the *Lusitania* down, a four stacker, in eighteen minutes. Four smoke stacks! A behemoth she was! One lousy German torpedo with a twenty-pound charge. Come on, dear. It was a setup from the git-go. One thousand one hundred and ninety-five souls went to the Lord that night. Captain Turner was not among them. No, he saved himself, didn't he? Eighteen months later, the doughboys are shouting "Yee-ya-yip, over the top!" Alvin York, Dan Dailey, and the rest of the Yanks are taking Belleau Wood. Come on, you don't think those things just happened, do you? You can't, really? Not after today. There are forces at work. And not necessarily dark forces, either. Some might say they're rather enlightened.'

'Even the *Lusitania's* almost a hundred years ago.'

'Nineteen sixty-four. Gulf of Tonkin. You don't really think the North Vietnamese were stupid enough to have one of their PT boats fire on an American destroyer, do you?'

'Simon, that's all a bunch of conspiracy gibberish.'

'Really? Well, before you go knocking my conspiracy theories, I suggest you take a look in the mirror. You, darling, are a conspiracy theory waiting to happen.'

'Me?'

Bonny nodded gravely. 'Tomorrow or the next day, someone will walk up to you, put a gun in your back, and pull the trigger. Good-bye, Jenny. Good-bye, baby. The police will say robbery. Or just a random murder. All will agree it's a tragedy. Case closed. Mention the club and see the look you get.'

'But . . . but . . .' Jenny felt stranded, violently alone. She reached over and drank the rest of Bonny's beer. 'Jesus,' she said, her breath leaving her.

'Somewhere there's a record of it all,' said Simon Bonny, whispering now, his eyes gone buggy, his chin bobbing in seven directions at once. 'Hamilton was specific about keeping the minutes so that posterity would know of his contributions. The Founding Fathers were such vain twits. All of them so concerned about how history would look back on them. All of 'em scribbling away in their diaries and letters and newspaper articles. Each one trying to outgun the other. Old Scotch Nat knows. He kept the minutes. He had to. Only one of them not in the government's service. Apparently, they held quite a lot of meetings at his house, too. He lived on Wall Street, next to his best friend, Mr Hamilton.' He stopped and fixed Jenny with a frightened, quizzical stare. 'You're not carrying one now, are you? A phone?'

'Yes, but it belongs to my doctor. I took it by accident when I left the hospital.'

Bonny took his wallet and began ripping out bills and throwing them on the bar. 'Ten? That enough . . . oh bloody hell, give 'em a twenty.' He scooped his cap off the stool and grabbed his overcoat and scarf. 'Get rid of it . . . might as well have a homing beacon planted on your head.'

'But they don't know I have it.'

'How can you be so sure? They knew about you shooting your brother with a BB gun. I don't even want to imagine how they found out that little nugget of information. Someone's been on the phone with Daddy, haven't they? Scale, my dear.

Scale. Look around you. It's the biggest government in the whole damned world!'

'But . . .'

'But nothing!'

With a final anguished sigh, Simon Bonny stormed out the door.

Chapter 47

Dr Satyen Gupta picked up the phone at the nurses' station. 'Yes?'

'This is Detective John Franciscus out of the three-four uptown. Shield M one eight six eight. I understand you're the physician who attended to Jennifer Dance.'

'I treated her for a gunshot wound. It was a graze that required disinfection and debridement. Nothing too serious.'

'Everything went well?'

'Just fine,' Gupta confirmed.

'Do you have her close by? I need to ask her some questions about the shooting.'

Gupta stood at the nurses' station in the ER, the phone held to his ear. 'Miss Dance left the hospital a few hours ago.'

'Did you sign her out?'

'No. She left on her own. There was a man claiming to be her brother asking to visit her. She felt he meant to harm her. She insisted on leaving immediately.'

'And this man was there . . . *at the hospital*?'

'Yes, he was. After she left, I confronted him.'

'What did the man say?'

'Nothing. He turned right around and left. Did you want to get in touch with her, Detective?'

'Yes, I would.'

'I gave her my jacket to help her avoid the man's

attention. My cell phone was in the pocket. I hope
she discovered it there.' Gupta read off his number.
'You might try reaching her. A woman in her
condition shouldn't be out in this weather fearing
for her life.'

'I thought you said the gunshot wound wasn't
serious?'

'I'm not talking about the gunshot. Miss Dance
is eight weeks' pregnant. That kind of stress is more
than enough to cause even the strongest woman to
miscarry.'

A long silence ensued. Thomas Bolden stared at
the phone, his throat scratchy from imitating the
detective's gravelly voice. It was his last shot. He'd
tried to get through to Jenny a dozen times, but the
switchboard had been prohibited from giving out
information.

'Detective, are you still there?'

'Yes,' said Bolden. 'I'm still here. Thanks for the
information.'

Clad in his boxer shorts and socks, Bolden stood in
the back room of the Ming Fung Laundry Company
in Chinatown, Althea's cell phone to his ear.
'Answer the call, Jenny. Pick it up. Let me know
where you are.'

After four rings, Dr Gupta's recorded message
began. 'Hello, you have reached . . .'

Bolden hung up, exhaling through his teeth.
Around him, several men and women guided giant
canvas baskets filled with dirty clothing across the
floor to industrial washing machines, arranged
shirts on ironing boards, and transferred them to
tall piles to be packed and moved up front.

As a freshman at Princeton, Bolden had looked
on the Ming Fung Laundry as his own Barneys.
Every few months he'd take a train into the city to

sort through their left-behinds, finding Ralph Lauren shirts in perfect condition for five dollars, and dress flannels for ten. These days, shirts ran ten bucks, and pants went for twenty. The blue blazer he'd chosen had set him back fifty. If there was anyplace he might hide, it was Chinatown. A world within a world.

Eight weeks' pregnant.

Why hadn't she told him? He sighed, angry with himself. She had wanted to at lunch, but he'd been so busy going on about his own problems that he hadn't given her half a chance to get to it. But, why not before? Why not after dinner last night? Or when they'd been lying in bed Sunday morning? Or any time after she'd found out? What had he done to make her so reluctant to tell him? He knew the answer. He'd been himself. The emotionally remote, self-centered financial genius in all his blazing glory. She'd hinted at it last night, and what had he said? He'd called her a body snatcher. *Good going, jerk!* Bolden sat down and ran a hand over his forehead. A father. He was going to be a father.

Slowly, a smile lit up his face. Of all the things to learn on this day . . . he was going to be a father. It was wonderful. It was beyond wonderful. Eight weeks' pregnant. The baby would be born in September. He shook his head. A father. He hadn't expected to be so happy at the news. He hadn't expected to feel like this . . . to feel liberated. Yes, that was it. *Liberated.* It was as if someone had turned on the lights ahead of him and for the first time, he could see all the way down the tunnel. A father.

And then his joy dimmed.

Eight weeks' pregnant. And they shot her. They aimed a rifle at her and gunned her down as if she were no better than an animal. A rage such as he had never known filled Bolden, causing him to tremble and grow red in the face. He would not let it stand.

Bolden sorted through the folder Althea had given him. It was all there, in black and white. Scanlon Corporation had belonged to Defense Associates, a company that named Mickey Schiff as a director, and James Jacklin, its chairman. When Defense Associates went bust, Schiff moved over to Harrington Weiss. Jacklin spun the dice again, starting up Jefferson Partners with Guy de Valmont, at that point a young partner at HW. Was it a trade? Schiff to HW. De Valmont to Jefferson. Some kind of payout to make up for the fifty million and change HW had had to write off when Defense Associates shut down? Common sense would dictate that Sol Weiss never put another dime in one of Jacklin's ventures. But twenty years down the road, the ties between Jefferson and HW were tighter than ever. HW had invested in all of Jefferson's funds and the investments had paid off richly. Returns of eighty percent, a hundred, higher even, were not uncommon. Until lately . . .

The private equity industry was growing crowded. 'Overfished', was a term people used. The same five or six behemoths trawling the same waters for the same deals. When a company came up for sale, all six would make bids. An auction ensued. One or two might drop out, but the rest would eagerly join the bidding, upping the ante one hundred million dollars, two hundred million, a billion at a time. With each uptick, the return on the investment declined. It was simple math. Profit equaled the price you received for selling the company minus the price paid to purchase it.

And here was the problem: HW invested in all of its clients' funds, as did most of the larger pension funds, college endowments, and investment banks. It was a way of diversifying, of keeping risk within acceptable measures. The result was that HW was, in effect, bidding against itself. When Jefferson bid against Atlantic, they were using HW's money. When Atlantic counterbid, they were using HW's money, too. It was like playing against yourself at a poker table.

The problem was that HW couldn't just invest with Jefferson. Atlantic (and the other sponsors) might take that as a compelling reason to stop sending business HW's way. Fees, not investment income, were HW's bread and butter.

After analyzing the declining returns HW was earning on its investments with the larger sponsors, Bolden had written a memo to Sol Weiss suggesting the firm stop putting its own money into these megafunds, and instead seek out smaller, more aggressive funds that concentrated on buying companies valued at less than a billion dollars. The potential return was markedly higher, as was the risk. But at least they weren't bidding against themselves.

Jefferson Partners, in particular, was showing lagging returns.

Jefferson. It kept coming back to them.

Bolden shuffled through the list Althea had compiled detailing all companies Bolden's core clients had bought and sold during the past twenty years. Over and over again, his eyes returned to the column under Jefferson's name. TruSign. Purchased in 1994. Sold in 1999. National Bank Data. Purchased in 1991. Sold in 1995. Williams Satellite. Purchased in 1997. Sold in 2004. Triton Aersopace. Purchased in 2001. Still held. The list went on.

TruSign was one of the primary operators of the

Internet backbone, handling something like twenty billion Web addresses and e-mails each day. They also managed the largest telecom signaling network in the world – a network that enabled cellular roaming, text messaging, caller ID – as well as handling more than forty percent of all e-commerce transactions in North America and Europe.

National Bank Data handled check-clearing services for over sixty percent of the nation's banks.

Bell National Holding was a prime supplier of phone service for the Mid-Atlantic region.

All these companies gave Jefferson unfettered access to e-mail transmissions and the Web, banking and credit records, phone and satellite communications, insurance and medical records, and much more. Taken together, they provided a network that could eavesdrop on anyone who owned a cell phone or maintained a bank account, used credit cards or visited an ATM, held medical insurance or regularly traveled. In short, they could spy on every American between Sag Harbor and San Diego.

And now, Trendrite. A deal Bolden had brought to their doorstep. Trendrite was the capper, the consumer loan processing company that promised its customers a 360-degree view of every American consumer.

And Scanlon? It had disappeared but it hadn't died. There at the bottom of Althea's list was a company purchased by Jefferson in their very first fund in 1981. SI Corporation. Alexandria, Virginia. To this date the company had not been sold.

Scanlon was Jefferson's private army. Muscle on demand.

Bolden tried to call Jenny once more. When he received the same message, he hung up. He dialed information and asked for Prell Associates. The operator connected him.

'I need Marty Kravitz,' he said when the switchboard answered. 'Tell him it's Jake Flannagan from HW. And say it's an emergency. No, check that. Say it's a fuckin' emergency.'

'Excuse me, sir?' asked an offended voice, heavy on the starch.

'You heard me. Verbatim, if you please.' Jake Flannagan, Bolden's boss at HW, had the foulest mouth on the Street. In the trade, he was known as a screamer. He had three sons that he brought into the office once in a while. Quiet, handsome kids who never showed up without a blazer. The joke was he called them Fuckin' A, Fuckin' B, and Fuckin' C.

'One moment, sir. I'll put you through.'

Bolden moved to the back of the laundry and stepped inside a bathroom. Where he was going, he needed a suit. He closed the door as Marty Kravitz came on the line.

'Jesus, Jake,' said Kravitz. 'You're scaring the hell out my secretary.'

'Tough shit,' said Bolden, laying on Flannagan's Southie brogue. 'Probably needs a little excitement in her life anyway. Make those nipples stand at attention.'

'And here I was thinking you'd mellowed with age,' said Kravitz, formerly a special-agent-in-charge of the FBI's New York field office.

'I ain't a fuckin' bottle of wine.'

'How you holding up down there?'

'So you heard? What a disaster. Sol's dead.'

'The entire Street's in shock. The boss extends the firm's condolences. Allen tried to call Mickey, but he was with the police.' Then Kravitz's voice found another tone altogether, quiet, plummy, confiding. 'What in God's name is going on over there? News is saying it was an employment dispute. I saw the tape. I don't buy it for a second.

Looked like you guys were getting set to arrest the guy. Bolden, was it? What'd he do, then? Insider trading? Fiddle with the books? Screw the secretaries? What?'

'Between you and me?'

'You have the firm's word. Of course, I'll have to tell Allen.'

'No problem there.'

'Allen' was Allen Prell, and Prell Associates, the firm that bore not only his name, but also his imprimatur of ruthless efficiency and airtight secrecy, was the world's foremost private investigative agency. Investment banks had come to use the firm so much that it had gotten the nickname Wall Street's Private Eye. Harrington Weiss hired Prell to investigate corporate targets, assist with due diligence, and conduct background searches on prospective hires. But the firm's expertise went beyond the world of high finance.

Prell was a government in trouble's partner of choice to help track down stolen assets. It had helped Mrs Aquino locate the billions pilfered by Mr and Mrs Marcos. It had dug up a lesser sum spirited away by 'Baby Doc' Duvalier. And, more recently, it had assisted Lady Liberty in her search for the four billion dollars said to be stashed in Libya, and elsewhere, by Saddam Hussein. The company's ranks were filled with former policemen, army officers, and intelligence professionals. Men and women who moved comfortably in the shadows, and who knew that the letter of the law depended on which language it was written in. They were very expensive, very professional, and very effective. The joke went that if you wanted to find the guy who worked for Prell, just look for the man with dirt under his fingernails. No one dug deeper.

Bolden considered what to tell and what to leave out. He decided to tell the truth. 'Mickey Schiff went to Sol this morning with a story about Tom Bolden assaulting a gal at the firm,' he said. 'You know Tom?'

'Peripherally. Resident do-gooder, isn't he?'

'That's him. Anyway, I guess he asked her to blow him last night at some dinner party, and when she said no, he belted her one. You've heard it before, right?'

'Too many times,' said Kravitz. 'It's always the ones with the smiles you've got to look out for. Check for the halo, I say. That's the guilty man every time.'

'According to Mickey, the girl's attorneys called this morning to read him the riot act and threatened to sue the firm for every last shekel if Bolden wasn't turned over to the police pronto.'

'I'd have thought they'd sue anyway,' said Kravitz.

'Ditto. From what I heard, Tommy denied ever touching the girl. Security tried to arrest him and he went ballistic. I talked to a couple people who saw the whole thing and they swore the shooting was an accident.'

'Why didn't he stick around? Sounds to me he's a better shot than you give him credit for.'

Bolden bit back a four-letter response. 'If you find him you can ask him yourself.'

'Is that an assignment?'

'No. I think the police can cover it.'

'Where's the girl?' asked Kravitz. 'I'd like to talk to her first.'

'It's a question we need to answer. Her name is Diana Chambers. Sound familiar?'

'No, but we do all of HW's background checks. I'm sure she's on file. What firm's representing her?'

'Mickey didn't say. Just showed us some nasty pictures of her face. It's part of what raised our concerns. Listen, Marty, this is a rush job. We want to put out a name tomorrow about who'll be succeeding Sol. We love Mickey, but we've got to give him the once-over, like everyone else. Don't be surprised if you get a call asking about me. Everything's up in the air.' Bolden hung the possibility of Flannagan's taking over the firm out there like a slow one right down the middle.

'We're always here for you, Jake,' said Kravitz, donning his salesman's polyester jacket.

'One more thing . . .'

'Shoot.'

'Bolden. I need to see his file, too.'

'Yeah, let me take a look . . . well, well, how 'bout that . . . you're going to like this. Thomas F. Bolden. We performed a new check on him last week. Guess who asked for it?'

Bolden didn't have to. Kravitz was quick to answer his own question. 'Mickey Schiff.'

'Looks like he was ahead of the game. I want everything you can get me on Schiff and Bolden by six tonight.'

'No problem,' said Kravitz. 'I'll be happy to deliver it myself. I think I know quite a few ways Prell can be helpful to you in this matter. We very much enjoy working with chief executives.'

'The firm keeps a suite at the Peninsula on Fifty-fifth. The board's asked me to make it an off-site. Six o'clock okay by you?'

'Six o'clock.'

Bolden hung up. Jake Flannagan never said good-bye.

Chapter 48

The reference room on the fourth floor of the Hall of Records was strictly government-issue from the cracked linoleum floor to the yellowing 'No Smoking' signs that pre-dated the surgeon general's warning about the danger of cigarettes. A fleet of upright wooden card catalogues stood on the left side of the room. To the right, two dozen microfilm readers were arranged in neat rows like desks in a classroom. Only two were occupied. Behind them, receding into an infinite fluorescent glare, ran row after row of floor-to-ceiling bookshelves, packed to overflowing with ledgers, registers, and the dense memorabilia that testified to patient and meticulous recording of the births, deaths, marriages, and divorces over the three-hundred-year history of New York City.

Jenny crossed the room, her footsteps echoing. On this snowy Wednesday, the room had the eerie, deserted feel of a museum after hours. 'Hello,' she called, approaching the service counter and seeing no one.

'One second.'

A lone clerk sat at his desk in the bullpen behind the counter. He was a drab, chubby man with sleepy black eyes and frizzy black hair that surrounded his head like a swarm of flies. A copy of the *New York Post* sat open in front of him. Peering over the counter, Jenny saw that it was turned to 'Page Six'.

The gossip column. Jenny waited patiently, her public-works smile pasted in place. Finally, he closed the paper and dragged himself out of his chair. 'Yeah?'

'I'm trying to help a friend trace his family tree,' said Jenny.

'That right?' The clerk not only looked the professional cynic, but sounded it. 'Got a name?'

'James J. Jacklin.'

'And you're trying to find what? Grandfather? Great-grandfather?'

'As far back as I can go.'

'Date of birth, please?'

'Excuse me?'

'Give me Mr Jacklin's date of birth and we'll get this train a-movin'.' He moved his hands like an old steam train and made the appropriate chugging noises.

'I'm not sure. I thought you might be able to look him up on the Net. He's kind of famous.'

The man shook his head sharply. Clearly, it was a frequently asked question and he had the response down cold. 'No Internet access for private use.'

'Do you know where I might get on the Net around here?'

'Public library. The office. Your home. The usual.'

'It's kind of an emergency. I don't have time to go home.'

The clerk shrugged. Not his problem.

Jenny leaned closer. 'It's for the James J. Jacklin who used to be the Secretary of Defense.'

'The billionaire?'

Jenny checked over her shoulder before answering, as if concerned that others might hear her speak. 'He's my uncle.'

'*Your uncle?*'

'Yes.'

'So, it's kind of your family tree, too.'

'I suppose so,' Jenny agreed, feeling like she was finally getting through to this jerk.

'Then you won't mind paying the twenty-dollar fee.'

'What twenty-dollar—' Jenny asked sharply, stopping herself before it was too late. 'No,' she said, with exaggerated goodwill. 'I wouldn't mind at all.' She fished in her purse and handed over a twenty.

The clerk snapped it cleanly out of her palm, then turned and disappeared into the maze of aisles. He came back after a minute. 'Jacklin was born on September 3, 1938. Your birth indexes for all boroughs years 1898–1940 are going to be in cabinet four. Just to the left of the entrance. Start there. The birth certificate will give his parents' names. If Mr Jacklin was born in New York, you should be able to find them. Our records are indexed back to 1847. Prior to that date, you'll have to check the irregulars.'

'The irregulars?' Jenny asked.

'Mostly handwritten census data. Some old address books, hospital records, stuff like that. That'll take time. A long time. *A very long time.* You'll never get that far back tonight.'

Jenny looked around the room. Only one of the microfilm readers was in use now. She spotted a few ghostly figures flitting among the stacks. The place was as quiet as the graves she was investigating. 'What about you?'

'What about me?' the clerk asked.

'Do you think you can give me a hand?'

'If I helped you, I'd hardly be able to do my work.'

Jenny eyed the open newspaper. 'You look busy.'

'I'm swamped.'

'I'd consider it a favor.'

'A favor?' The clerk chuckled, as if he hadn't heard that word in a long time.

Jenny handed over another twenty.

'Maybe I can get away from pressing affairs for a few minutes.' The clerk put a hand on the counter and bounded over it. Jenny thought he'd probably been waiting a long time to use that trick. He extended his hand. 'Stanley Hotchkiss. Welcome to my world.'

They found James Jacklin without a problem. Born at Lenox Hill Hospital at 7:35 A.M. on September 3, 1938, to Harold and Eve Jacklin. 'What do you know about the father?'

'Not much,' said Jenny. 'I think he was from New York. He was a big shot during the Second World War.'

'Back to the Web.' Hotchkiss disappeared behind the counter. He returned a few minutes later. 'Born 1901. Congressman from the Third District of New York. Assistant Secretary of War. Served on House Un-American Activities Committee, as an aide to the un-American Joseph McCarthy. Harold Jacklin was a regular Nazi.'

Hotchkiss kneeled and pulled out the bottom drawer of the same cabinet number four. Finding the proper microfilm, he quickly had it up and on the screen of the nearest reader. 'Let's see here: 1901. Nope. Not here. You sure he's a native New Yorker?'

'His family was a member of the Four Hundred along with the Morgans, the Astors, and the Vanderbilts. They were as New York as New York gets.'

'A regular Knickerbocker, eh? Let's check out up through 1905.'

Ten minutes and several runs to the microfilm cabinet later, they were no better off.

'Don't worry,' said Hotchkiss. 'We're just warming up.'

Jenny took a seat at the machine next to him. 'Where else might we find records on him?'

Hotchkiss considered the question. 'Police census of 1915,' he said after a minute.

'Well?' Jenny asked, smiling now with excitement, rather than duty.

Hotchkiss stood rooted to the spot.

'Come on. Let's find it,' she said. 'I thought we were just warming up.'

'Sorry, lady, meter's run out.'

Jenny handed over her last twenty. 'This is it,' she said, keeping hold of the bill as Hotchkiss tried to wrest it from her. 'This takes me to the end of the line.'

Hotchkiss snatched the bill. 'Deal.'

Bolting to his feet, he marched off like a man on a mission, disappearing into the stacks. He returned carrying a pile of moth-eaten leather ledgers. 'Here we go,' he said, plopping them down on a table nearby. 'These here are the census books. Remember, back in 1915, they didn't have computers or database software. Everything was done by hand. Census takers brought their forms back to this building, and a clerk just like me entered the information into the census book.'

Jenny nodded, wondering what Hotchkiss was preparing her for.

'Which brings us to our problem,' Hotchkiss went on. 'The census was taken by district. The residents weren't listed alphabetically, but geographically. The census taker walked up Pearl Street, and started with the first house on the left, then the next and the next. When he was finished, he crossed the street and went down the other side.'

'Are you trying to tell me the census is listed by street address?'

Hotchkiss nodded. 'Yes, ma'am, I am. By the way, I don't believe you told me your name.'

'Pendleton,' she said. 'Jenny Pendleton.'

Jenny opened the top book. Each page was divided into several columns. Street farthest on the left, followed by name, occupation, sex, age, and citizenship status. 'Return of Inhabitants' was written across the top of the page in swirling Edwardian script. 'We'll be here all night.'

'Not necessarily,' said Hotchkiss. 'We know where Harold Jacklin lived when his son was born. If we're in luck, his father lived at the same address.'

With Hotchkiss's help, Jenny found the ledger containing the names of those people who had lived on Park Avenue in 1915. The list ran to three pages. There, at 55 Park Avenue, the address listed as Harold Jacklin's residence on his son, James's, birth certificate, was written a different name in neat but faded script. Edmund Pendleton Jacklin, born April 19, 1845, occupation noted as banker, definitely an American citizen. And below it, that of his wife, Eunice, and their children: Harold, fourteen, Edmund Jr, twelve, and Catherine, eight.

'Pendleton . . . that you?' asked Hotchkiss.

Jenny nodded.

'Eighteen forty-five,' said Hotchkiss, chewing on his lip. 'Now things get interesting.'

'I don't like the sound of that.'

Stanley Hotchkiss shot her an offended look. 'I never renege on a deal. Besides, you've got me caught up in this stuff, too. Okay, 1845. It was the Dark Ages back then when it came to record keeping. They didn't have regular hospitals. We can't check there. Everybody was born at home.'

'What about birth certificates? We know when Edmund Jacklin was born.'

'No go. The city's index of birth certificates only goes back as far as 1847. We just missed the boat.'

'Are there other censuses?'

'There's the jury census that was conducted in 1816, 1819, and 1821, but that won't help. We know they couldn't be in the same house at 55 Park Avenue, because no one was living that far up Park back then. New York only had about thirty thousand inhabitants.' Hotchkiss tilted his head and stared into the blinding maw of the fluorescent lights. 'Newspapers,' he said. 'If your family was as hotsie-totsie as you say, there would have been a birth announcement.'

'What was the paper back then?'

'There were a dozen of them, but our best bet would be the *New York American*. Besides, it's the only one we have on file.'

More microfilms were dredged up. Hotchkiss scrolled to the days following April 19, 1845. 'I don't see a thing,' he said. 'We better move upstairs.'

Jenny stood, anxious to get wherever they needed to go quickly.

'No,' protested Hotchkiss. 'I mean upstairs like going to Washington. The federal census. The government conducted a census every ten years. We'll try 1850. Don't get your hopes up. It's a crapshoot whether the information we need was ever transferred from their papers to the database. The upside is that it's alphabetized.'

Hotchkiss led the way behind the counter and pulled up a chair for Jenny to join him at the computer terminal. Hotchkiss logged on to ancestors.com, accessed the federal census of 1850, New York State, Manhattan, then entered the name of Edmund Jacklin. There were two of them, but only one was five years old. Edmund P. Jacklin, son of Josiah Jacklin, age thirty-two, Rose Pendleton, age twenty. Address: 24 Wall Street.

'Do you have city directories here?' asked Jenny. City directories were the phone books of the age, listing the names, addresses and occupations of the city, likewise by street.

Hotchkiss looked surprised that she knew about them. 'Sure thing. What year do you need?'

'Seventeen ninety-six.'

'Don't you want to look at the year he was born? Eighteen eighteen?'

'No,' said Jenny. 'Humor me.'

'I've got the originals. You want to see one?'

'Whatever's quickest,' said Jenny.

A woman called out Hotchkiss's name and shouted something about his finishing up whatever he was doing, and getting the place ready to close up. Hotchkiss didn't answer. Instead, he went off to retrieve an original city directory. He returned with Annum 1796. The leather-bound volume was in brittle condition, and barely half an inch thick. 'You do the honors,' he said.

Jenny handled the book with due care. She turned each page gingerly, noting the paper's thickness and quality, the gold leafing on the edge. Quickly, she found Wall Street. There, living at number 24, was Nathaniel Pendleton, alias Scotch Nat.

And living next door, at number 25, was Alexander Hamilton, his best friend.

Thick as thieves, Simon Bonny had said.

Jenny lowered her eyes. It was real. Bobby Stillman's club was real.

Chapter 49

It was five o'clock. Time for the 'Follies'. James 'Scotch Nat' Jacklin hurried across his office and turned on the television. Each day at 5:00 P.M., the Pentagon broadcast the announcement of contracts to be awarded by the Air Force, Army, and the Navy live over a closed-circuit feed. Around the office, the broadcast had been dubbed the Five O'Clock Follies. As so many companies in Jefferson's portfolio depended on government contracts, Jacklin liked to watch when he could. This afternoon, however, viewing was compulsory. No fewer than four of his companies were set to learn the decision on contracts totaling a billion dollars. For two of them, the decision was critical. Winning the bid would ensure a profitable future. Losing it would force them to close their doors and shut down operations. Jefferson would have to write down the value of the investments to zero.

'Cigars, gents?' Jacklin asked, holding out a box of his favorite Cohibas. 'These things always bring me good luck. Come on, don't be shy. You, too, LaWanda.'

Seated with him were several of his closest counselors. Lamar King, former Army four-star and deputy chief of staff. Hank Baker, who'd chaired the SEC for ten years. And LaWanda Makepeace, his newest hire and the cement behind the Trendrite deal. The men accepted a cigar. Mrs Makepeace politely declined.

The Pentagon spokesman stepped behind the dais. 'Good afternoon, ladies and gentlemen,' he said. 'We have quite a few contracts to go over this evening, so I'll get started right away . . .'

'Thank goodness,' muttered Jacklin to himself. He sat forward, hands on his desk, cigar clamped firmly in his mouth. He was too caught up to light it.

'We'll begin with the Air Force,' said the spokesman, a Navy commander. 'Lockheed Martin Aeronautics is being awarded a $77,490,000 contract modification for US Air Force economic order quantity funding . . .'

'We don't have to worry about this one,' said Jacklin, to one and all. 'Airplanes are a nasty business. No margins whatsoever.'

Glancing out the window, his eye landed on the dome of the US Capitol building, far across the Potomac. He thought about Senator Hugh Fitzgerald and the $6.2-billion appropriations bill. He thought about the effect the new contracts would have on his companies. Like manna from the heavens.

The appropriations hearings should be well over by now, and Fitzgerald at home in his beautifully decorated Georgetown townhouse, knocking back some of that single-barrel Tennessee bourbon he liked so much. Thirty years in the Capital had polished the former Vermont college professor's tastes. Along with his bourbon, old Hugh enjoyed handmade suits, a chauffeur-driven car, and a full-time Guatemalan maid, with whom, Jacklin had discovered, he was carrying on a torrid affair. (The pictures were revolting.) Keeping up that lifestyle while providing for his family back in Burlington wasn't easy on a senator's salary of $158,100. Jacklin had done some checking into his finances. He had not found any secret contributions from lobbyists, no shadowy honorariums for speeches he never gave, no numbered accounts in Zürich. Fitzgerald was clean. He was, however, up to his eyeballs in debt. Jacklin returned his gaze to the television.

'And now we'll turn to the Navy,' said the Pentagon spokesman.

'This is us,' said Jacklin.

'Hoo-yah,' added General Lamar King.

'A $275,000,000 firm-fixed-price contract for the US Navy's Missiles and Fire Control Command Systems is being awarded to . . .'

Jacklin scooted to the edge of his seat. 'Dynamic Systems Control,' he whispered, fists balled and held to his chest. 'Lord, let us have that one.'

'. . . Everett Electrical Systems of Redondo Beach, California.'

Jacklin banged his hand on the table. 'There's three more to come,' he said. 'Never say die!'

The spokesman went on: 'A $443,500,000 indefinite delivery/indefinite quantity contract to provide seven MPN-14K radar approach control systems, installation, flight check . . .'

'Triton Aerospace . . .'

'Leading Edge Industries, Radar Division, Van Nuys, California.'

'Horseshit!' shouted Jacklin, out of his seat now, brushing past the model of the battleship *Maine*, pacing the office. He hit the call button on his desk. 'Juan,' he said into the speakerphone. 'Get me a double scotch. Lamar, what'll you have?'

'Bourbon.'

'A sherry,' said Hank Baker.

'Sherry, my ass,' protested Jacklin. 'Have a man's drink!'

'Make it a bourbon then,' Baker said, uncertainly. 'Um . . . Wild Turkey.'

LaWanda Makepeace started to say Coke, but caught the blistering look thrown in her direction by Jacklin. 'Give me a Tom Collins, honey. If we're starting this early, I might as well do it right.'

'Two more,' said Jacklin, waving his cigar at the television. 'They can't shut us out altogether.'

Five minutes later, it was done. The final two contracts had been awarded to companies that did not belong to Jefferson's portfolio.

There was a knock at the door. Juan, the Filipino mess steward, entered the room. 'Good afternoon, sir.'

'Just put the drinks down, Juan. We can serve ourselves.'

Juan set his sterling-silver serving tray on the coffee table. With ceremony, he laid a napkin and then placed a crystal highball glass filled with ice and single-malt Scotch on it.

'I said we can serve ourselves, you little brown monkey,' shouted Jacklin.

'Yessir,' said Juan, an uncomfortable smile on his face.

'You blind as well as deaf? Light this fuckin' cigar!'

Juan produced a Zippo lighter. 'Very good, sir.'

Jacklin knocked back half his tumbler and rubbed his temples. Losing contracts was getting to be an all-too-familiar experience. He was going to have one helluva job figuring out how to spin this shitty news to his guests tonight. There was only one way to salvage the party. Fitzgerald. He'd have to get Senator Hugh Fitzgerald to say he was recommending passage of the appropriations bill.

Jacklin strode back to his desk. He might need those pictures sooner than he thought.

Chapter 50

Franciscus nudged the door to Vicki Vasquez's office open with his foot and leaned his head inside. 'You still here, Vick?' he called, struggling for a better hold on the moving box full of Theo Kovacs's files.

'Still here,' came a voice from the filing cabinets.

'It's me. I need a favor.'

'Coming.' Vicki Vasquez bustled in from the back room. Her jacket was buttoned. Her dark hair neatly combed. Franciscus noted that every PC in the office had been turned off; every desk immaculate. It was clear that she was in the closing phase of a well-executed campaign to get out of the office at quitting time. As she approached, she slipped her lipstick back into her purse. 'Hey, Johnny, what you got there?' she asked.

'Somebody else's junk,' he said.

'Need a hand?'

'No, thanks, I've got it.' Franciscus set the box down on the corner of the nearest desk. 'I need a favor, Vick. Shouldn't take long.'

Vicki Vasquez planted her hands on her hips. 'I've got tickets to the theater. A date, even.'

'It'll just take a minute.'

'A minute?' She checked her watch and took a tentative step toward the door. 'Can't it wait until tomorrow? You need me here at seven, I'll be here at seven. Say the word. Just not tonight.'

Franciscus smiled apologetically. 'I need an address on a retired cop out of Albany. Find out where they're sending his pension.'

'A pension?' she asked.

Franciscus nodded. 'A pension. That's it. Then you're free to go.'

'Does it have anything to do with the fugitive you turned up earlier? Bobby Stillman?'

'It does. I'm counting three homicides hanging on what you find out.'

At once, Vicki put down her purse and took a seat at the nearest terminal. 'What's the name?' she asked, as she powered up the computer.

'Guilfoyle, Detective Francois J. Retired in 1980.' Guilfoyle might take his name off a case file, but Franciscus was willing to wager he wouldn't skip out on his pension. It was congenitally impossible for a cop to turn down a government pay cheque.

Vicki glanced over her shoulder at him. 'It'll take a few minutes. I've got to call downtown and put in an expedited request. Might be a little late in the day.'

'I'll keep my fingers crossed.' He hefted the moving box. 'You gonna make your play?'

'We'll see.'

'I owe you,' said Franciscus. With over fifty thousand employees, the New York City Police Department was like an army. Only two of nine employees actually wore uniforms and carried a gun. The other seven ran the bureaucracy that supported them in the field. At the door, he turned around. 'Hey, Vick?'

'Yeah?'

'He a nice guy?'

'All right.'

'Got a name?'

'Same one his mother gave him.'

'So . . . you like him?'

Vicki Vasquez put her hands on her hips and sighed in exasperation. 'Go away and let me work.'

Franciscus carted the moving box across the hall and set it on his desk. The squad room was empty, which was the natural state of things. Detectives earned their living on the street, not watching *The View*. A sheaf of papers stuck out from beneath the box. The top form was titled, 'Disability Claim for . . .' The lieutenant had stuck a note on top with the name and number of a cardiologist. Franciscus slipped the papers out from beneath the box and shoved them into his desk drawer. Craning his neck, he scoped out the hall. The lieutenant's office was dark. He checked the clock. Five-oh-five. It wasn't the first time Franciscus was late with paperwork.

Standing, he began excavating the mess that was Theo Kovacs's files. After a few minutes, a ten-inch stack of paper teetered on his desk, most of it made up of articles about the bombing of Sentinel Microsystems, the shooting of the two police officers, and the siege that followed. Franciscus concentrated on the latter, in particular the sections detailing the shooting of Professor David Bernstein, a.k.a. Manu Q, and the escape of his common-law wife, Bobby Stillman, a.k.a. Sunshine Awakening.

He was quick to find some major discrepancies in the outline of events. There were shots fired from the house. There were not. Police spotted several suspects inside the house. Police believed Manu Q to be alone. He had acted alone shooting the two police officers. He had acted with the help of an accomplice. The newspapers, however, were unanimous in stating that a second set of prints found on his pistol belonged to Bobby Stillman. Theo Kovacs had thought differently. If you believed his wife, it had cost him his life.

Franciscus spotted a brown folder that had the look of a case file at the bottom of the box. Prying it loose, he opened the cover and skimmed its contents for the fingerprint sheets. Bernstein's prints were there, but he couldn't find any others. Neither Bobby Stillman's, as the various and sundry newspapers had reported, or those belonging to the third party Theo Kovacs claimed to have discovered himself.

The police report made clear that at no time had the assailant, David Bernstein, fired at the SWAT team surrounding his house. Similarly, at no time had the police observed a second party in the house with him.

As Franciscus sorted through the stack of interviews and statements, he thought of Thomas Bolden. Half the city was looking for him in connection with the shooting of Sol Weiss. Headquarters had blast-faxed a copy of his picture to every precinct with the order that it be copied and handed out to all patrolmen. But, Franciscus wasn't buying it all. First off, the tape was fuzzy. It looked very much like an accident. Second, there was the matter of the perp with the broken jaw who'd been released from One PP. And third was this business of blast-faxing Bolden's picture all over hell's half acre. For a second-degree-murder beef? Come on! The whole thing reeked of politicking, or worse. Mostly, John Franciscus wanted to know why a retired detective named Francois Guilfoyle wanted to question Bolden about Bobby Stillman, a woman who'd been a fugitive for a quarter of a century.

Grabbing a block of paper, he wrote down the facts as he saw them.

Roberta Stillman and David Bernstein had bombed Sentinel Microsystems. That part was a given. When officers were sent to arrest Bernstein, they were shot and killed. Bernstein barricaded himself in his home and when police stormed it forty-eight hours later, he was killed by SWAT fire. Later, Theo Kovacs discovered that Bernstein had not died from the SWAT team's fire, after all, but from a single gunshot wound to the head fired from eight or ten feet. And that the bullet had come from the same gun that killed Officers O'Neill and Shepherd, in theory Bernstein's pistol.

Theo Kovacs discovered a second set of prints on the gun – ostensibly of the murderer – but his partner, Detective Francois Guilfoyle, discouraged him from following up on the lead. Kovacs went ahead anyway. Before he could share his discovery, he killed himself.

Twenty-five years go by, and the same Guilfoyle is chasing down Thomas Bolden, and asking him what he knows about Bobby Stillman and something called Crown.

Franciscus tossed his pencil onto the desk. Something was missing here, and he knew what it was. It was the set of fingerprints that Kovacs had found on the gun.

He put aside the case file and sifted through the remaining papers. There was a class shot from Kovacs's days at the academy. Some snaps of the guys at work. Franciscus examined them, trying to pick out Guilfoyle. Eyes that looked into your soul, Kovacs's wife had claimed. A mind reader. Carnac. Franciscus settled on a creepy-looking guy with milk white skin and dark drooping eyes.

He put aside the picture and picked up Kovacs's badge. It was his patrolman's shield pinned to the cardboard backing that you wore under your shirt. The kid must have been one helluva cop. He had about six meritorious medals running above the badge. Definitely a comer. One of the pins came loose and he put down the badge. There was a trick that every cop knew to holding the medals in place. You needed to pin 'em through your shirt to the tiny rubber stoppers found on crack vials. Worked every time. He picked up the badge to fix it, and it separated from the cardboard backstop altogether. 'Crap,' he murmured, as the two pieces fell apart.

'John, I've got something for you!'

Franciscus tossed the badge onto the table and hustled into Vicki's office. 'What is it?'

'Guilfoyle's address and phone,' she said, holding out a piece of notepaper. 'Were you expecting an extra ticket to the show?'

'Not tonight,' he said, holding her eyes. 'Now, get out of here. You've still got time to make it. But if the bum gets out of line, you give me a call.'

'Yes, Dad,' she said. She wasn't taking her eyes away either.

With a sigh, Franciscus sat down at his desk. A name. An address. Francois Guilfoyle, 3303 Chain Bridge Road, Vienna, Virginia. Big deal. Guy wasn't even hiding. He was happy to collect his pension every month and go about his business. Unexpectedly, Franciscus felt a lump form in his throat, a big rough-edged lump that felt like a chunk of coal. He read the name. Guilfoyle. He didn't know the man. He'd never met him, wasn't even sure what he looked like, but he hated him all the same. He'd screwed his partner. Franciscus didn't have any proof, but he knew it was true, just like Katie Kovacs knew it. Theo Kovacs had come to him with a set of prints that did not belong on David Bernstein's gun, prints that had no business whatsoever being there, and what did Guilfoyle do? He told him to forget about it. Case closed. Move on.

Franciscus frowned. That was not kosher.

When you were young and starting out on the force, you and your partner weren't a team. You were a unit. Indivisible. One had a hunch, a lead, a whatever, and you both followed it. One of you was in trouble, the other pitched in. That didn't just go for work. It also went for your personal lives. Advice, money, a pat on the back, you lent it. You didn't tell him to go to hell. You didn't . . . Franciscus couldn't bring himself to say 'kill him'. That was going too far. You didn't pin murder on anyone until you had proof. That wasn't kosher either.

Franciscus replaced all of Kovacs's files into the moving box. He put the articles in first, then the police file. Finally, there was only the badge. He looked at it lying on his desk. The goddamn badge. He picked it up and weighed it in his hand. Thirty years on, it still meant something to him.

He reached down to pick up the rectangular piece of cardboard backing and put the two back together. A corner of it had peeled away. A sharp-edged transparency protruded. He brought it closer to his eyes. 'What the—' he muttered.

Opening his drawer, he found a set of tweezers and slipped the square free. The clear plastic was a little bigger than a stamp and folded into quarters. Unfolding it, he raised it to the light. The transparency showed a photograph of two perfect fingerprints. Handwriting at the bottom attested to the fact that the prints were dusted and lifted from the barrel of David Bernstein's .11-millimeter Fanning automatic on July 29, 1980.

Chapter 51

The fire door opened and a young African-American woman showed her face. 'You Mr Thomas?'

'Yes.' Bolden hugged the wall next to the employee entrance of the Peninsula Hotel. A slim cornice one story up deflected the snow from his head and onto the toes of his shoes. In his dark overcoat, blue blazer, and flannel trousers, he could be the night manager waiting for his shift to begin, or a boyfriend wondering why his girl was always late.

'I'm Catherine. Come with me.' Without waiting for his acknowledgment, she turned and led the way inside.

Bolden followed at her heel. She was dressed in hotelier's garb – black blazer, gray skirt cut below the knees, and a pressed white blouse. She walked quickly, never checking to see if he was keeping up. At the staff elevator, she pressed the call button and assumed her professional hostess's stance. Hands folded at the waist. Head slightly bowed. But her eyes were anything but welcoming.

'I've put you in four twenty-one. It's a junior suite,' she said, as the elevator arrived and the two stepped inside. 'Darius says to call if you need something else. *Anything*. He made me say it like that.'

Her name was Catherine Fell, and her official

title was assistant front-office manager. Bolden had met her once over lunch at Schrafft's. As a favor to her brother, Darius, he'd used the company's pull to help Catherine get a job at the hotel. Darius Fell was his one great failure at the Boys' Club, and not incidentally, the man who'd beaten him in a scant twenty moves at last weekend's chess tournament. Chess, however, was one of Darius's secondary endeavors. What captured the lion's share of his formidable mental powers was crime. Drugs, guns, numbers: Harlem's holy trinity. Darius Fell was a major player in the Macoutes street gang, the American offshoot of the feared Haitian secret police, the Tonton Macoutes. *Un homme d'importance*, according to the gang's bloody hierarchy.

When they arrived at the room, she handed him a key. 'You're registered as Mr Flannagan.'

'Thanks,' said Bolden, attempting a smile. 'Don't worry. I won't take anything from the mini-bar.'

But Catherine Fell was immune. Her brother was bad news, and so were his friends. 'Be out by nine P.M. Housekeeping performs a second room check. I don't want them to ask any questions.'

The suite was as opulent as you had every right to expect for twelve hundred dollars a night. There wasn't a square inch that wasn't decorated, laden, or stuffed with elegant accoutrements. The quilted king-size bed, the claw-footed desk, the Egyptian divan, and chiffon curtains: all were done in warm golden tones of vast wealth.

Bolden grabbed an orange from the fruit basket and sat on the bed. He picked up the phone, then set it back in its cradle. He could not risk making a call that might be traced. Still, he couldn't drive her from his mind. He turned on the TV. All three networks were showing the video of him shooting Sol Weiss. He closed his eyes, wanting to doze, but sleep wouldn't come. He imagined Jenny asleep in his arms, her face the color of alabaster. *Wake up*, he wanted to tell her. *We'll start the day over. This never happened*. But she didn't move.

A sharp knock at the door startled him. He stood immediately. He had dozed, after all. The bedside clock read 6:05. 'Yeah,' he called. 'Coming. Who is it?'

'Martin Kravitz,' came the muted reply. 'Prell.'

Bolden paused by the couch where he had laid his overcoat. From a side pocket, he withdrew a slim leather sap, about six inches long. Its length was deceptive. Swing it and the spring inside extended the sap to fourteen inches, lending the lead weight at its tip a deadly force. One blow could lay open a man's scalp to the skull.

He peered through the peephole. Marty Kravitz stood in the hall, briefcase in hand. Bolden studied him for a few seconds, checking for a tip-off that he'd alerted the police or brought a second. Pressing his cheek to either side of the hole, he trained his eye down the corridor. Miles of golden carpeting stared back.

He opened the door. Turning swiftly, he made as if to return to the sitting room, showing Kravitz his back. 'Come on in,' he said.

'How goes it, Jake?' asked Kravitz. 'Not bad digs. If you've got to keep a safe house, this will do nicely.'

Bolden waited for the two-tone thud of the door closing properly. He let Kravitz catch up, then spun quickly and slugged the investigator in the stomach. Breath hissed out of him like a punctured tire. 'I'm not Jake,' he said, shoving him against the wall, bracing a forearm under the man's chin, raising it high so that he could look him in the eye. 'Recognize me?'

Kravitz nodded, his eyes bulging. 'Bolden.'

'Nice to meet you, too. Listen up. I'll tell you this once, and only once: I didn't kill Sol Weiss. The tape you saw was altered by . . . well, all you need to know is that it was altered. Got me so far?'

'Yeah,' croaked Kravitz.

'The way I see things, you have two choices: come in, have a seat, and tell me what you've learned about Mickey Schiff, or struggle. If you put up a fight, I promise it'll go badly for you.'

Kravitz raised a hand in surrender. 'Okay,' he gasped. 'Just relax. It's all good. All good.'

Bolden released his pressure and stepped back. Kravitz stumbled down the hall and collapsed on a divan. In his late forties, he was short with sloped shoulders and a runner's wiry physique. His hair was curly and black. He had a long, bony nose and a weak chin, but his brown eyes were formidable. After a moment, he gathered his breath. 'You're in some deep kimchee, my friend.'

'You can say that again.'

Kravitz held his stomach, grimacing. 'Here I was thinking I was doing scut work for HW's next CEO. Oh well.'

Bolden sat down on the edge of the bed. 'What did you find?'

'First, you tell me something. What makes you so interested in Schiff?'

'I have my reasons. Take my advice: you don't want to know them. Let's just say that Schiff's a dirtbag.'

'If you're trying to prey on my conscience, you can forget it. I checked it at the door when I started at Prell. We're not in the good-fairy business.'

'I'm getting sick and tired of people telling me

they don't care what's right and wrong,' said Bolden. 'You want to know what my reasons are. Okay. Here's one of them: last night some men kidnapped me off the street and decided to ask me some very interesting questions while I was standing on the girder of a high-rise seventy stories above the ground. I had no idea what they were talking about, but it didn't matter. They weren't in the good-fairy business either. One of them had a tattoo on his chest that I'm pretty sure identifies him as working for Scanlon Corporation. I did some checking and found that Mickey Schiff worked for a company that bought Scanlon twenty years ago. That good enough for you?'

'Marginal. I'd have added that he was standing right next to you when Sol Weiss got shot. I saw the tape, by the way. I take it you believe Schiff was involved with your dismissal from the firm. The coincidences are piling up, I'll grant you that. Looks like you took out the wrong man.'

'I didn't shoot Sol.'

'So you told me.' Kravitz sat back, crossing one leg over another. 'At least I know why you filed a police report for felonious assault at the Thirty-fourth precinct last night.'

The two men looked at each other. 'Someone's trying to kill me,' Bolden said, finally.

'That's a good reason,' said Kravitz. He nodded to the entry-way. 'My briefcase. There's some material you may find interesting.'

'Does this mean you're going to let me know what you found on Schiff?'

'May I?'

Bolden stood and retrieved the briefcase, setting it down between them. Kravitz opened it, and methodically withdrew one folder after the next, setting each on the table beside him. 'All right then, first things first,' he said. 'Diana Chambers.' He picked up a folder and opened the cover. 'No record of her at any hospital. She isn't at home either. Or, if she is, she's not answering her phone or door. Easy ruse: send over takeout. There's been no police report filed, either. Not in the five boroughs, at least, and you said the crime took place in Manhattan.'

'Downtown.'

'Yeah. Anyway, not a peep about big bad Bolden beating her to a pulp. No record at all of someone by her name pressing charges against you.'

'But Mickey Schiff said she'd filed a complaint. He had detectives waiting to take me to the station.'

'He was lying,' said Kravitz, matter-of-factly. 'We had better luck with Schiff. Didn't know he was a marine.'

'Yeah, Mickey's our own Chesty Puller,' said Bolden.

'I'd watch invoking the name of a legend to describe Mr Schiff.' Kravitz settled a folder on his lap. 'Lieutenant Colonel Schiff served in supply. A procurement officer. Outstanding record. Numerous medals, commendations. All in all, a fine career. After leaving the military, he joined the firm of Defense Associates.'

Bolden nodded, feeling a gear lock into place.

'Schiff lasted at said company for all of nine months, then jumped ship to HW.'

'Defense Associates went bankrupt,' said Bolden.

'Nothing fishy there. Just a few lousy investments. Paid too much for Fanning Firearms and couldn't turn it around despite Mr Schiff's best efforts. That's that.'

'What happened next?'

Suddenly, Kravitz went mute. One by one, he slipped the folders back into his briefcase.

THE PATRIOTS' CLUB   359

'We're not done here,' said Bolden.

'Speak for yourself.' Kravitz buckled his briefcase and stood. 'The way I see it, Tom, you've taken advantage of me enough as it is.'

Bolden remained seated. 'Did you expect me to stop you? Go ahead, if you want. But I'll leave it to you to explain to Allen Prell that you used the firm's resources on behalf of a suspected murderer without doing any double-checking. You said it yourself. You thought you were helping the next CEO of HW. Guess you screwed up. Right now, your ass is on the line as much as mine. You help me, and you're helping yourself. If I get caught, sooner or later it's going to come out that we met. I don't think Prell likes to be caught in bed with a murderer any more than HW.' Bolden shrugged. 'Your call.'

Kravitz walked past Bolden to the door. 'Good luck, Tom.' He opened it and stepped outside.

Bolden let him go. He wasn't about to beg. What was the point? Kravitz had confirmed what he knew. Schiff had been involved with Defense Associates. He opened a bottle of water and drank greedily from it.

The knock on the door startled him. He looked through the peephole, then opened the door. 'You're back?'

Martin Kravitz swept past him into the bedroom. 'I'm not quite the cynical bastard you think I am. If you'd killed Sol Weiss, you'd never have allowed me to leave. Therefore, I'm left with the conclusion that you are innocent, and that someone at your firm is helping to frame you. Given the information I discovered this afternoon about Mickey Schiff, I believe I can help you get out of this mess.'

Bolden nodded. 'Glad to hear it. Have a seat.'

Kravitz sat down, and once again, unpacked his briefcase. He sighed, slapping his hands on his knees. 'And so . . . Lieutenant Colonel Schiff's last project as a procurement officer was overseeing bidding to equip the Marine Corps with a new generation of sidearm. Following his recommendation, the Marine Corps signed a seventy-million-dollar contract with Fanning Firearms for the purchase of nine-millimeter automatic pistols.'

'Interesting.'

'Not as interesting as Mr Schiff's purchase of a $1.2-million home in McClean, Virginia, a few months after his retirement from the military. This was 1984, I remind you, when a million-dollar home bought you something more than a tract house with marble flooring and a toilet that washes your butt. The place was located next door to the Kennedy estate, Hickory Hill.'

'Sounds like a good neighborhood.'

'Schiff's maximum pay grade was "0–10". With nineteen years in, Lieutenant Colonel Schiff earned a maximum of fifty-two hundred dollars a month.'

'Did he have a trust?' asked Bolden, playing the devil's advocate. 'Did his parents leave him any money?'

'No to both questions. The highest balance his account at the credit union ever saw was twenty-two thousand. Respectable, but hardly sufficient to make a three-hundred-twenty-thousand-dollar down payment on the home.'

'Three hundred-twenty thousand? That's not bad for a career military officer.' Bolden looked squarely at Kravitz. 'You're saying that Schiff steered the contract to Defense Associates and got the house and a job as his reward.'

'I'm saying no such thing. I have no proof of any wrongdoing, Tom. What I offer you is conjecture based on the information I was able to gather. But,' he added, a moment later, 'a reasonable man might make that assumption.'

Kravitz paused and took a breath. When he next spoke, his voice was softer, pitched high with a tangible fear. 'Are you currently doing any business with Jefferson Partners?'

'Yes, I'm assisting them in the purchase of a consumer data company. Trendrite. Heard of it?'

'Oh yes, most definitely.' Kravitz dropped his eyes to the floor. 'Earlier you mentioned Scanlon Corporation. Back in the late seventies, Scanlon was split into two divisions. One concentrated on surveillance software systems, and interestingly, using that software to gather information from consumers. I believe it's called data mining now. They started a company called Sentinel Microsystems in Albany, New York.'

'I've never heard of it.'

'Oh, you wouldn't have. Before your time. What you should know is that the company changed its name a few years back. Now they call themselves Trendrite.'

'You said they split into two divisions?'

'The other is their training side. Contractors. Officially, they've ceased to exist, but unofficially...' Kravitz shrugged.

Before Bolden could question him further, he delved into his briefcase and came out with a buff envelope. 'I almost forgot. You asked for the background check we performed on you. Here it is. Interesting about your name. Do you know of any reason why your mother changed it?'

Bolden said he didn't.

Kravitz packed up his briefcase, rose, and patted him on the shoulder. 'You're messing with the big boys on this one. Watch out.'

'No,' said Bolden, as Kravitz walked to the door. 'They're messing with me. If you talk to them any time soon, give 'em the same message.'

Chapter 52

In the spacious parlor of his Georgetown townhome, Senator Hugh Fitzgerald kicked his stockinged feet onto an ottoman and succumbed to the pleasures of his worn and comfortable leather chair.

'Ahh,' he sighed loud enough to rattle the windows. 'Marta, a glass of Tennessee's finest, *por favor*. And *generoso. Muy generoso.*'

From the start, it had been a taxing day. A prayer breakfast with his conservative counterparts across the aisle at seven – yes, even Democrats like Fitzgerald believed in God – was followed by the usual office business, the meeting and greeting of visiting dignitaries from his home state. Today, that meant pumping hands with the head of the Vermont Dairy Promotion Council and saying hello to this year's National Spelling Bee champion, an impressive young man who hailed from Rutland. Then came the dreadful appropriations hearings that had drawn on and on.

Six point two billion dollars to refill the military's pre-positioning depots, or pre-pos, as they were called so affectionately. It boggled the mind that the armed forces could require so much money. Six point two billion . . . and that just to return the country to fighting fettle. It was a minimum. Not in any way earmarked to expand manpower, or to gear up for imminent conflict. Six point two billion dollars to bring the water back to the level mark and ensure that the United States of America could respond with adequate force to two regional conflicts. Six point two billion dollars to buy boots and bullets and uniforms and MREs. Not a dollar of it to commission a new tank, buy a new airplane, or build a new boat.

The terrible irony was that while America had the finest equipment and the best-trained troops, she did not have enough money to finance their use in battle. Waging modern war was prohibitively expensive, even for the wealthiest nation on the face of the globe. One year prosecuting a half-assed war against a pitiable opponent had cost the country over two hundred billion dollars. And for what?

As chair of the appropriations committee, Hugh Fitzgerald was party to the nasty details the public could never see. Like the fact that a crack division of the army had run out of food for two days – not a biscuit or tin of peaches to eat. Another had gone short of water, preventing it from joining in an attack. His favorite tidbit belonged to the marines. An entire battalion had actually run out of bullets during a prolonged engagement in the Sunni Triangle. *Bullets*. The little devils cost fifty cents a piece, and the fightingest men on God's green earth had run out of them. Even those dirty little Arab bastards had bullets. They had 'em by the truckload.

'Here you are, Senator.' Marta padded into the room and handed him the evening's cocktail.

'*Gracias*,' he said. 'Yes, yes, *muy generoso*. You're too good to me.' He took a generous sip and set down the glass. 'Come, Marta, sit next to me. An old man requires some attention after a long day.'

Marta squeezed onto the arm of the leather chair. She was a svelte woman, barely a hundred pounds. Her black hair was pulled into a ponytail, and she smiled at him with dark, mournful eyes. Slipping a hand behind his neck, she began massaging his shoulder.

'That's better,' he said. 'Very good, indeed.'

Fitzgerald closed his eyes and let Marta's hands do their work. It was hard to believe such a slight woman could be so strong. Her fingers were like steel. He sighed as her kneading broke his tension into little pieces and banished it to another place. He decided he needed more of this and fewer battles on the Hill.

Six point two billion dollars. He couldn't get the figure out of his mind.

He might be able to push off the bill this session, but it would be back the next, and then with another billion or two tacked on for inflation. Part of him thought this the best course. Delay. The fox couldn't raid the henhouse if he didn't have any teeth. On the other hand, there was the security of the country's men and women to think of.

Fitzgerald considered Jacklin's offer of a post at Jefferson Partners. There were worse places to end a career, he conceded, even if he did despise the vain, cocksure man. Politics, however, had for ever ruined his ability to hold a grudge. There was no such thing as friendship on the Hill, or its opposite. There was only pragmatism. He imagined himself strutting the halls of the investment bank, welcoming clients to his large, well-appointed office. A view of the Potomac would be mandatory. There would be prestige and power and money by the boatload. He didn't have to look far to see what a partner at Jefferson earned. Jacklin and his ilk were billionaires to a man. *Billionaires*. He'd seen a few of the homes and the cars purchased by men who'd made their name on the Hill, then gone and sold it to Jefferson.

Fitzgerald had grown up on a dairy farm in the thirties and forties. Having money meant buying a new set of clothes for Christmas and putting three meals on the table each day. If they were lucky enough to make a trip to the coast each summer, they were considered rich. His father never made more than two thousand dollars a year his entire life.

A billionaire. If Jacklin cared so deeply about the troops' well-being, he should throw a few hundred million of his own into the kitty. Not that he'd notice it gone.

The strong, supple fingers continued their work, kneading away the tensions of the day, clearing his mind. Fitzgerald weighed his alternatives. Another run for office. Six more years working the corridors of power. Six more years of horse-trading ... and with it, the promise of expiring under the Chesapeake sun. It was too much for a Green Mountain boy to take.

Of course, he could return home to his wife, take up a teaching post at the university, and earn even less than he did now. He snorted loud enough to make Marta jump. 'Excuse me, dear,' he said, opening his eyes and gazing at the kind, loving woman next to him. And Marta?

Reaching out a hand, he patted her leg. She grasped it, and slid it toward her thigh.

'Lord, no!' exclaimed Fitzgerald, guiding his hand back to a safer area. 'The very thought exhausts me. I've got a party to go to this evening. Any hanky-panky, and I'll be out till the morning.'

Marta smiled. She was hot-blooded, was what

she was. He brought her close and kissed her on the cheek. He could not leave his Marta.

Six point two billion dollars.

These days, it wasn't that much money, was it?

Later, he told himself. He would decide later.

Chapter 53

Franciscus hurried down the hall into the booking room. A beige, waist-high machine that resembled a copier stood in the corner. It was a LiveScan machine – officially labeled the TouchPrint 3500. It had been three years since he'd rolled a suspect's fingers over a messy inkpad and struggled to get ten decent prints onto a booking sheet. To make matters worse, not to mention waste infinitely more time, the suspect's prints had to be taken twice more as he advanced into the bowels of the criminal-justice system. Once for the state police in Albany, and again for the Department of Justice in DC. These days, all you did was press the suspect's fingers one at a time onto a card-sized scanner, check on the pop-up monitor that the print was properly recorded, and – bingo! – it was transferred automatically to Central Booking downtown, Albany, and DC. All at the touch of a button.

Franciscus flipped open the peripheral scanner and laid the transparency onto the bed. A piece of paper set on top was necessary to ensure a good read. The LiveScan machine hummed as it digitized the prints and copied them into its memory. Franciscus keyed in instructions to send them to the NCIC, the National Crime Information Center in Clarksburg, West Virginia, as well as the FBI's Criminal Justice Information Services Division. The collected databases would check the prints against any on file. The list ran to federal employees, current and past military personnel, aliens who had registered to live in the United States, and the department of motor vehicles in forty-eight states.

Franciscus left the room, closing the door behind him. It would take an hour or so for the system to come up with any matches. If, and when, LiveScan found one, it would notify his PC. As he advanced down the hall, he spotted Mike Melendez's head popping out of the squad room.

'Hey, John!'

'Short Mike. What's doin'?' Franciscus could see that Melendez was worked up about something.

'I should be asking you. Chief's on the phone.'

'Whose chief is that? You mean "the Loot"?'

'The friggin' chief. Esposito. On line one.'

'Impossible. It's after five.' But Franciscus made sure he hustled to his desk.

'The Chief' was Chief of Police Charlie Esposito, 'Chargin' Charlie' to his friends, 'Charlie Suck' to others, but to all the highest-ranking uniformed cop in the city. Only the commissioner and his deputy stood above him, and they were appointees. Franciscus and Esposito had processed through the same class at the academy back when their peckers still stood straight up. But where Franciscus had gone to work for love of the job, Esposito had always had his eye on the brass ring. He'd never made a single decision without asking himself first how it was going to advance his career. Officially, they were still friends.

'Detective John Franciscus,' he said, unable to keep himself from standing a little straighter.

'John, this is Chief Esposito. I understand you've been looking into some old police business?'

'Like what?'

'The Shepherd and O'Neill murders up in Albany.'

Franciscus didn't answer. He was dumbstruck. Part of him had somehow come to the conclusion that Esposito was calling to give him grief about his failure to hand in his medical papers. But as that illusion rapidly dissolved, he was all the more confused. How in God's name had Esposito gotten wind of Franciscus's informal investigation? And even then, what was his motive for calling?

'And so?'

'That case is closed.'

'Really? From what I see, there's a suspect that's been on the run for the better part of twenty-five years.'

'That matter's been adjudicated,' said Esposito.

'Excuse me, sir, but I beg to differ.'

There was a pause. An unhealthy sigh that said it all. 'I want you to drop it, John.'

Franciscus took a breath. He should have seen that coming as soon as Esposito had announced himself as 'Chief'. 'Charlie,' he said, turning his back to the squad room and speaking in a quieter voice, man-to-man, no bullshit. 'Look, Charlie, it's a long story, but it's got something to do with the crazy business that went down in Union Square today. I had a guy in here last night name of Tom Bolden . . .'

'Bolden? That's the Weiss murderer. We have an APB out on him. Feds are getting into the game, too. It's not your beef. Leave it to Manhattan South.'

'No, no, listen to me, Charlie. You know the girl who was shot? Her name's Jennifer Dance. Bolden was right next to her when it happened. She's his girlfriend. You getting this, Charlie? Someone wanted to take out Bolden and they missed.'

'I'm not following where the Albany murder ties into this, and frankly, I don't care to know. You've done enough snooping around. Bolden belongs to Manhattan South. Don't concern yourself with him.'

'Charlie, this is me you're talking to.'

'You heard me, John. Do yourself a favor.'

'Do me a favor or you a favor? Come on, Charlie, who's leaning on you?'

'John, I've been made to understand that you're not a well man. Officially, you're operating in violation of duty regulations. I know that no one values those rules more than you. I'm officially taking you off active duty. As of now, consider yourself on paid leave.'

'This is my turf, Charlie. I've been keeping the peace here for over thirty years. Something happens on my turf, it's my business to clear it up.'

'Bill McBride's on his way up now. He wants to have a little talk with you.'

'About what?' asked Franciscus, copping an attitude.

'About me taking your badge and your gun for good. Then you can pay for your bypass yourself! Or you can drop dead!'

'Who's leaning on you, Charlie?' Franciscus's heart was rattling like a southbound train, and somewhere along the line, he'd lost his breath. *Sonofabitch*, he kept whispering to himself. He had to sit down.

'John.' Esposito's voice had lost its bluster. It was the man speaking, not the uniform. 'Listen to me. This is one beef you want no part of.'

Franciscus hadn't heard that voice since Esposito's son had been nabbed in a heroin bust uptown and Chargin' Charlie had called Franciscus to ask that his boy walk on the charge.

'Why are you sending McBride? Is he gonna knock my teeth out if I don't cooperate?'

'When Bill gets there, I want you to give him what you got from the Kovacs woman.'

'The who?'

'You know who. We know what you've been up to, John.'

Franciscus hung up the phone. His chest felt like it was in a nutcracker. He extended his left arm and curled his fingers into a fist, expecting a sharp, debilitating spasm to seize the left side of his body. He exhaled sharply and his breath came back to him. The pressure lifted from his chest. He glanced at the ceiling and chuckled. He was turning into a real drama queen.

He felt Melendez tap him on the shoulder. 'Johnny, you okay? What's going on?'

'Get me a glass of water, would you?' asked Franciscus.

'Sure thing. Right away.'

'Thanks.' Franciscus leaned over his desk and put his face in his hands. It didn't pay to get himself worked up like that. Melendez arrived and handed him the glass. Franciscus took a sip, feeling better.

He checked his incoming e-mails for a notification about Theo Kovacs's prints. There was nothing yet. He picked up the phone and dialed a number at 1 PP. 'Yeah?' an unfamiliar voice answered.

'I'm lookin' for Matty Lopes.'

'Not here. Who's callin'?'

'John Franciscus.'

The voice dropped a register. 'Don't you learn?'

'Excuse me?'

'Word to the wise, Johnny. Be careful. You know what we do to nosy people? We cut off their noses.'

'Who is this? You one of Guilfoyle's buddies? What game are you playing, anyway?'

'One that's bigger than you.'

'Bigger than me? I'm a cop. One guy. I'm nothing. This is the law we're talking about. Shooting people. Killing them. No one's bigger than that.'

'The law? I'll let you in on a secret, Detective. We are the law.'

Franciscus slammed the phone in its cradle. 'Says you,' he cursed to himself.

Outside in the hall, Franciscus could hear Bill McBride's booming voice, yukking it up with Short Mike and Lars Thorwald. He ducked into the booking room. Plugging his pass code into the LiveScan, he brought up the last search and checked for any results. He heard McBride asking after him. 'Where's Gentleman Johnny?' as if his visit were purely a social one. 'Anyone seen the old dog?' Thankfully, he didn't hear Melendez offer up any answers. Everyone knew McBride as the bag man from downtown. He was well hated across the five boroughs.

The LiveScan's status screen was blank. As of yet, no matches were forthcoming from any of the databases. Franciscus was out of luck. Esposito could have his badge, but he'd be damned if he handed over Katie Kovacs's papers.

He put his hand on the door, figuring out where to stash Theo Kovacs's moving box. Opening the door a crack, he peered into the hall. McBride's broad back was to him and he appeared in no hurry to leave.

Just then, the LiveScan bleeped. Franciscus hurried to the screen. The system had found a match in the Federal Identification Database. That meant the print belonged to a government employee, or someone with past military service. He highlighted the database and clicked the mouse. A moment later, the name of the man whose fingerprints were on David Bernstein's Fanning .11-millimeter pistol appeared on the screen, along with a social security number, a home address, and the notice that the individual had no outstanding warrants in his name. Suddenly, Franciscus didn't give a crap about the moving box.

'Oh, Christ,' he muttered. Charlie Esposito was getting leaned on all right. Leaned on from the top.

Chapter 54

'What is "Crown"?' shouted Bobby Stillman.

'I have no idea,' said the man they had captured in Union Square for what she thought was the fortieth time.

'Of course, you know,' she insisted, then slapped his face, her sharp fingernails leaving angry furrows on his cheek.

He sat kneeling in the center of the hard terrazzo floor, wrists and ankles bound, an executioner's hood pulled tight over his head, and a broom handle laid across the backs of his knees. Prime US beef buffed up, brainwashed, and trained to kill by the finest minds in the military, then spat out onto the streets to ply his trade for the highest bidder.

'You work for Scanlon,' she said, walking a circle around him, spitting her words at him like bullets. 'Or is that musket on your breastbone just to attract the girls? Scanlon hires out exclusively to Jefferson. Why were you in New York?'

'We go where we're ordered.'

'And your orders were to kill Tom Bolden?'

'No ma'am. Please, may I stand up?'

He'd been sitting in this position for thirty minutes. The weight of his buttocks and upper body pressed the broom handle into the crook of his calves, cutting off all circulation to his extremities. By now, the balls of his feet and his toes felt as if thousands of razor-sharp needles were stabbing him again and again. Soon the pain would advance to his ankles, his calves. She'd forced the experience on herself. It was unbearable. She had screamed in less than half the time.

'No,' she answered. 'You may not. What brought you to Union Square?'

'We were supposed to find Bolden.'

'You were supposed to kill him, weren't you!'

'No.'

'Your shooter missed. He wounded an innocent woman. Tell me something I don't know. What is "Crown"?'

The man tried to lift himself off his knees, but Bobby Stillman pushed him back down. He moaned, but refused to answer. When his moans became shouts, and then screams, she lifted her foot and pushed him onto his side. 'Five minutes,' she said. 'Then we start over.'

Bobby Stillman walked outside the cottage and gazed into the falling snow. She was tired. Not just fatigued from the events of the day, the last week, but bone tired. She'd been on the run for twenty-five years. She was fifty-eight years old and her belief in her cause was fading.

A gust brought a flurry of snowflakes onto the porch. At least five inches had already fallen, clogging the mountain roads that led to her cabin in the Catskills. In an hour, two at most, the roads would be impassable. They would be stranded. She breathed deeply, and listened to the silence. The man's shouts remained with her. It was necessary, she told herself.

She remembered a night long ago. The hot, humid air was electric with the chirping of crickets and the rattle of cicadas. And then the tremendous blast as the bomb that she and David had so carefully put together exploded outside the R & D lab of Sentinel Microsystems. It had been her first step; the moment when she decided to vote with her feet. To act. To rebel. No, she corrected herself. To exercise her rights as a defender of the Constitution.

Twenty-five years . . . a lifetime ago.

She had arrived in Washington, DC, in the summer of 1971, a young, ambitious woman eager to make her mark. A graduate of NYU law school, editor of the law review, a vocal opponent of the Vietnam War, she burned with a desire to serve. She had never viewed the law as a license to earn money, but as a call to duty, and her duty was to ensure that the rights granted by the Constitution to individual and government alike were scrupulously enforced. When she accepted a job as a staff attorney on the House Subcommittee on Intelligence her friends were shocked. To cries that she had jumped the fence and joined the establishment, she said, nonsense. The choice was a natural one. There was no better place to exercise her calling than Capitol Hill. 'Make law, not war,' was her activist's motto.

The vice chairman of the subcommittee was a maverick second-term congressman from New York named James Jacklin. Jacklin was a decorated veteran, a winner of the Navy Cross, as close to a real-life 'hero' as she'd ever met, if that's what you could call a man who dropped napalm on women and children from the safety of a supersonic steel tube zipping high above their heads. She came to work prepared for battle, a red-haired rebel in a miniskirt with a maxim for every occasion and attitude to spare. Her job on the committee was to advise on the legality of actions proposed by the intelligence community. Even then she was a watchdog.

Instead, the two hit it off immediately. Jacklin was not the hawk she had expected. He, too, was against the war, and never afraid to express his opinions. For her every lick of fire, he contributed a chunk of brimstone. Together they exposed the secret war on Cambodia. They argued against the CIA propping up General Augusto Pinochet, the corrupt Chilean strongman. They called for an end to the firebombing of Hanoi. If her rulings were not always adopted, he urged her to keep fighting. To speak up. Jacklin anointed her the committee's conscience.

The words were praise, indeed. He had served. He had lost a brother in the war. He knew firsthand the cost of conflict. He said that the price paid for a government's foreign involvement was measured not only in lives, but also in loss of influence, and a ceding of moral authority. It was this last that America could least afford. America of all nations. America must be a beacon of democracy, a bastion of freedom. America was the only country in the world not formed on the basis of common geography, but on a common ideology. America must remain a symbol.

And she loved Jacklin for it. For daring to speak out. For putting his ideas more eloquently than she ever could. For showing her that America's values were not a question of politics, but of common sense.

Until the night she discovered him secretly copying her briefs and leaking them to his friends in Langley.

James Jacklin was a spy. A mole, in the vernacular that was just beginning to make itself known. And his mission was to infiltrate her and the 'team' he said she represented. 'The left.' His job was to gain her trust. To influence her rulings. To report the enemy's actions in advance. He succeeded brilliantly.

Bobby Stillman's initiation into the radical fringe was immediate.

She resigned her position on the Hill. She left Washington for New York. And she took a job with the organization that was the bane of all lawmakers regardless of age, color, creed, or party affiliation: the American Civil Liberties Union. She filed briefs. She argued cases. She wrote articles to halt the incursion of the government into the private sphere. Yet, her passivity sickened her.

From the sidelines, she watched as Jacklin rose to the position of Secretary of Defense and quietly rebuilt the nation's military. She listened to his promises of a peacetime force and a need to look inward and knew he was lying. Every day that passed, she promised herself that she would act. Her anger grew in proportion to her frustration. After four years, she had her opportunity.

Jacklin had left the Pentagon and started Defense Associates, an investment firm that specialized in restructuring businesses active in the defense sector. When she saw that he had bought Sentinel Microsystems she knew she had found her chance.

Sentinel Microsystems, which produced the most sophisticated listening devices known to man. Parabolic surveillance dishes capable of picking up conversations a half mile away. Miniature bugs that could listen through walls. The Reds didn't have a chance. He had talked about the technology lovingly back when they had shared a bed. The thought that he would turn it against the people was the final straw.

Then came Albany.

*

A cry echoed from inside the dilapidated cottage. Reluctantly, Bobby Stillman walked back inside. Her colleagues had returned the Scanlon operative to his kneeling position. *Look at him*, she told herself. *He's the enemy*.

She was no longer sure.

Sometime in the last hour, she had come to believe that she was as guilty as he.

'What is "Crown"?'

Chapter 55

Bolden stared at the pair of diamond-crusted ruby earrings. Twenty-seven thousand nine hundred dollars from Bulgari. The next display held watches. Ten thousand dollars for some rubber and stainless steel.

Through the jewelry store's windows, he enjoyed an unobstructed view across the lobby of the Time Warner Center. Smoked-glass doors guarded the entry to 1 Central Park, the address given the luxury residences occupying the fiftieth through seventy-fifth floors. He had been waiting ten minutes. In that time, a lavender-haired matron and her two shih tzus, a once-famous movie star, and a harried, instantly recognizable rock musician had scurried past the guards to disappear behind the smoked-glass doors.

A welter of bubbling voices drew his attention. Parading through the building's main entrance at Columbus Circle was a tight-knit group of six or seven men and women. Several carried briefcases, one a round cardboard tube commonly used to transport building plans. All were dressed in black outfits. But it was the strange, geometric eyeglasses that gave them away. Architects, thought Bolden.

He watched them closely, waiting for them to veer to the left or right, toward the pavilion of retail shops flanking the entrance. The group steered a course toward the smoked-glass doors. Leaving his position by the jewelry store, Bolden strolled briskly across the lobby. A young woman trailing the pack caught his eye. 'Just move in?' he asked, catching up to her.

'Me? Oh, I don't live here,' the woman responded.

'But you should,' he said. 'The views are marvelous. On a clear day . . . well, you know how the song goes.'

Ahead, the leader of the group waved to a guard who had already swung the door open and was ushering them in.

'The top floors are a must,' Bolden prattled on. 'Cost a fortune, but the way I see it, if you're going to break the bank, why not go all the way. What's this, a birthday party? Someone get a raise?'

He was the bullshit artist he'd always despised, throwing one line of garbage after the next. To his horror, he saw that it was working. Not only was this serious, reserved-looking woman giving him the time of day, she seemed flattered by the attention.

'A celebration,' she said. 'We just won a commission. Champagne at the boss's place.'

'Congratulations, then. I'm sure you did all the work.'

The woman smiled self-consciously. 'Only a little.'

'You're lying. I can tell. Your cheeks are turning red. You did it all.' Bolden never removed his gaze from the woman. Out of the corner of his eye, he could see the guards giving every member of the group the once-over, doing a head count as they passed. It was then that the woman stumbled. Her heel caught on the carpet and she turned an ankle. As Bolden put out a hand to steady her, he bumped into the security guard holding the door. The woman cried out briefly, caught herself, and laughed. The entire group stopped as one, and turned to check that she was all right. The boss, an older man with a long iron-gray ponytail, insisted on escorting her to the elevator. The group ambled down the hallway, their voices merry.

Left alone, Bolden turned and smiled at the guard. He was waiting for the hand to fall on his shoulder and ask him who he was, and just what in the name of God did he think he was doing trying to fake his way into the apartment building. Instead, he received a gracious 'Excuse me, sir,' followed by 'Have a nice evening.'

And then it was over. He was through the doors, strolling across the muted-gray and polished-silver lobby, past the oriental antiquities and faux Bayeux tapestry.

He caught up to the group and they all filed into the same elevator. The architects got off at fifty-five. Bolden waited until the last had gone, then pushed seventy-seven. The penthouse. Gossip around the office was that it had gone for a cool twelve million.

'On a clear day,' he whistled, for the security camera and for himself. Reaching into his overcoat, he pulled out his baseball cap. A few calls had established that Schiff was at home, waiting to be picked up by Barry, his chauffeur, and driven out to Teterboro Airport to fly down to DC for Jefferson's Ten Billion Dollar Dinner.

The elevator opened and he stepped into a cool beige corridor. Beige carpeting, beige paneling, dim lights. A door on either side of the corridor led to the penthouse apartments. Schiff's he knew faced east, toward the park. Bolden rang the bell. He stood with his shoulder to the door, his head cocked to obscure his face. He waited, hearing nothing from inside the apartment. Just then, he heard a buzzer. The latch turned automatically. A voice issued from an invisible speaker. 'That you, Barry?'

'Yes sir.'

Bolden pushed open the door.

Mickey Schiff rounded the corner of the entryway. He looked tanned and dapper, dressed in evening attire. Bolden rushed forward, took him by his collar, and slammed him into the wall.

'Get out of here,' said Schiff. 'I already called security.'

'If you called security, you wouldn't have let me in.'

Bolden pushed Schiff in front of him, guiding him into the living room. The condominium was decorated in a bachelor's style, with sleek, arty furniture that didn't look particularly inviting, the living room dominated by a sixty-inch plasma screen and a very large Picasso from his Blue Period. A bachelor worth a couple of hundred million dollars, that is.

'Sit,' said Bolden, pointing to the couch.

Reluctantly, Schiff lowered himself onto a cushion.

'You going to the Jefferson dinner?'

'Isn't everybody?'

Bolden sat down on a matching couch across the coffee table. 'First thing you have to realize is that you're screwed.'

'How's that?' Schiff asked, brushing dust from his tux.

'Let me lay it out, just so we're clear, *Lieutenant Colonel Schiff*. I'll keep it simple. Your last act as a marine supply officer was to steer a seventy-million-dollar contract to Fanning Firearms, a company owned by Defense Associates, an LBO fund James Jacklin set up in 1979, right after he left the Pentagon. In exchange for handing Defense Associates the contract, he paid you over a million dollars. Three hundred and twenty thousand went for the down payment of the house in Virginia. The rest, he wired to your new account at Harrington Weiss. In addition, you received a cushy job at Defense Associates and a starting salary of five hundred thousand dollars. Even today that's a lot for a guy with no banking experience. Back then it was a fortune.'

'I did no such thing,' spat Schiff. 'That's a shameless lie.'

'Numbers never lie.' Bolden removed a sheaf of papers he'd stuffed into the rear of his waistband and threw it onto the coffee table. 'It was the first thing you taught us in our training class. Anyway, you'll find all the details there.'

Schiff examined the papers. 'Where did you get these . . .' he began, then dropped the papers on the couch. 'That was twenty-five years ago. The statute of limitations has run out.'

'Who's talking about pressing charges? I'm going straight to the *Wall Street Journal* with this. I can't think of a reporter that wouldn't kill for this scoop. Hell, Mickey . . . it's not an article. It's a book. Besides,' added Bolden, 'integrity's mandatory for running a Wall Street firm. The statute of limitations never runs out on that.'

'You want to believe that, go ahead.'

'You know something? I do want to believe that.'

Schiff considered the information, his eyes darting from the papers lying on the coffee table to Bolden and back again. He ran a hand across his mouth, alternately frowning and pursing his lips. 'Okay, okay,' he said, finally. 'What do you want?'

'What do you think? Your help.'

'And then?'

'I'll tear up the papers.'

'Your word?'

'I can't destroy the records, but I'll give you my word that I won't turn you in. But you don't get HW. I won't do that to Sol.'

'Sol? Is he the saint now?' Schiff looked away, and for a moment, Bolden was sure he was about to cry. But if anything his eyes were steadier, his expression set in stone. 'Shoot.'

'You weren't the first person Jacklin bribed to get a contract, and you certainly weren't the last. It's his modus operandi. Five'll get you ten that half of Jefferson's counselors are on the take. All I'm asking is for you to help me take a look.'

'And for that you'll forget everything you know about my involvement with Defense Associates?'

'Not quite. You're going to the police and telling them that I didn't kill Sol. You're going to say that as a witness you are willing to swear that I wasn't holding the gun when it went off. You're also going to write a memo informing everyone at the firm that I didn't touch Diana Chambers.'

'Anything else?' asked Schiff.

'There is one more thing,' said Bolden, leaning forward, arms resting on his knees.

'What's that?'

'I want you to tell me about "the committee" or "the club".'

'What club is that?'

'The club that gives you your marching orders. The people who told you to act dumb when you saw the doctored tape of me shooting Sol Weiss on television. The people who ordered you to beat up Diana Chambers, and to plant those fictitious e-mails on the company server. I know Jacklin's involved, but I think there are others, too. It's too big.' Bolden stood and circled the coffee table, eyes locked on Schiff. 'Help me out, Mickey. It's got to have a name.'

'I really don't know what you're talking about.'

'You're out of luck then.' Abruptly, Bolden scooped up the documents and walked toward the door.

Schiff let him get five steps before shouting, 'Sit down, Tom! Come back. You got me by the balls, okay?'

Bolden remained standing.

'Look, you're a good kid,' Schiff went on. 'I'm sorry you've gotten mixed up in this, but there are some things you have to know. The world is not always run according to the rules.'

'Is that supposed to surprise me? So do you agree or not?'

'Yeah, sure. Have a look at the accounts. But I'm not saying a thing about Jacklin. You want to expose me? Go ahead. Call the *Journal*. Call the *Times*. Do what you got to do. But that's as far as I go.'

'As far as you go?'

'Yeah.' Schiff tugged at his cuff, and spent a moment adjusting it so that exactly one inch of white cotton was showing.

Bolden crossed the distance between them in four steps. He grabbed a handful of Schiff's hair and yanked his head back. 'They shot my girlfriend. Do you understand that? She's pregnant. I asked you who are they, Mickey?'

Schiff arched his back, and batted at Bolden's hand. But beneath the pain, he was looking at him sadly, as if for all his own problems, he didn't envy Bolden one bit. 'All you have to know is that they exist.'

Bolden let go of Schiff's hair. 'Get up,' he said. He was disgusted with Schiff and disgusted with himself for having to make a deal with the devil.

'You can drive me down to the office in your Maybach. I'm curious to see if it smells like the shit covering your hands.'

'I need my keys and my wallet.' Schiff gestured haltingly toward his bedroom.

'Help yourself,' said Bolden, keeping a half step behind him.

They'd covered half of the corridor when Bolden heard a noise coming from the door to his right. A muffled cry. He stopped. 'What was that?' He put his ear to the door. 'Who's in there?'

Schiff looked at him, then bolted for the door of his bedroom.

Bolden hesitated, then ran after him. Ahead, the door slammed shut. Bolden rammed a shoulder into it, feeling it budge. The lock flew home. Bolden backed up a step and kicked at the door handle. Two blows splintered the doorjamb. The third sent the door buckling on its hinges.

Schiff stood next to his bed, a phone cradled under his ear, pulling an imposing nickel-plated automatic from the drawer of his night table. He was desperately trying to chamber a round. Bolden stalked across the room. Schiff dropped the pistol and picked up a ten-inch jade statue. Lunging, he brought the statue down on Bolden's shoulder. Bolden ducked, but the blow staggered him. Schiff raised the statue again. Bolden grabbed his wrist and wrenched it. The statue fell to the carpet. Still grasping Schiff's arm, Bolden freed the phone and slammed it into the carriage.

'Who's in that room?'

Schiff didn't answer.

'Who's in that—'

Schiff's knee caught him in the stomach. Bolden doubled over. A blow to his back forced him to the ground. Schiff ran from the bedroom. The pistol lay a few feet away. Rising to his knees, Bolden picked it up, and followed, stumbling, fighting for his breath.

Schiff paced at the far side of his living room, his back to the window. A lone figure floating on clouds. He had a phone to his ear.

'Put it down,' said Bolden.

Schiff stared defiantly at him. 'Hello,' he said. 'This is—'

Bolden raised the gun. The trigger had a feather's weight. The window behind Schiff shattered, but did not break. Schiff fell to a knee, clutching the phone. 'Hello,' he said. 'Mr—'

Bolden clubbed Schiff on the neck with the butt of the pistol. Schiff fell to the carpet. Bolden hung up the phone and returned to the room where he'd heard the muffled voice. The door was unlocked. Diana Chambers lay on the bed. A stack of melted ice packs sat on the night table, alongside several containers of painkillers. Her eye was puffy, the bruise a deep purple. 'I heard shouting,' she said, pulling herself up.

'It was just Mickey.'

'Is he all right?' Even drugged up, she sounded like she really cared. 'You didn't shoot him, too?'

'What's it to you?'

The look she gave him said it all. She was in on it, too. Mickey's office squeeze looking to do her share for the cause. What was a black eye, after all, compared to the daily bruising she took just trying to crash through the glass ceiling?

'What did he promise you?' Bolden asked. 'A raise? A promotion? A ring?'

Diana slumped back on the bed, her eyes fixed to the ceiling.

Bolden came closer. 'Why is Mickey doing this? Did he tell you?'

Diana Chambers glared at him, then turned her head away. Bolden took her by the jaw and returned her face toward his. 'You're being very rude, Diana. We haven't finished our conversation. Tell me something. What is "Crown"? Did Mickey mention that? Did he ever talk about a woman named Bobby Stillman?'

'No,' said Diana, after a moment. 'Never.'

'Then why is he trying to destroy me? What did he tell you to make you agree to let him hit you? You're a smart woman. There had to have been a reason.'

'I don't know.'

'You don't know or you won't tell?'

'I don't know,' she repeated.

'Bullshit!' Bolden slammed a hand on her pillow, just missing the injured eye. 'Tell me!'

'It's for them. His friends.'

'What friends?' Bolden leaned over her, his face inches from hers. 'You will tell me, Diana. I promise you that. You'll tell me, or I'll go get that gun and shoot you like I shot Mickey.'

'You didn't?'

Gently, he pressed the tip of his index finger to the center of her forehead. 'Right there,' he whispered. 'One shot. You won't feel a thing. It sure as hell won't hurt as much as that black eye he gave you. Or did someone else do the honors? A guy named Wolf? Tall, bad attitude, built like a block of cement?'

Diana shook her head, anguish stiffening her body.

'Go take a look,' said Bolden.

She started to get up from the bed, then fell back again. She stared at Bolden, then slapped him across the face. He grabbed her hands and locked them to her sides. 'Who are his friends?' he asked, shaking her. 'Names! I want names!'

'No!'

'Tell me, dammit.' Bolden fought to keep her on the bed. She was possessed of a fear, a hatred, that he could not comprehend. Finally, she calmed, but her face remained a mask of revulsion.

'The club,' she said. 'In Washington. They make things happen. Big things. The power behind the throne . . . you know how it goes.'

'I don't actually,' said Bolden. 'What are their names?'

'Mickey's Mr Morris. I don't know the others, except that he calls them Mr Washington, and Mr Hamilton . . .' She looked away. 'It's for the country, that's all I needed to know. Mickey told me it was my chance to serve. After all, he'd put in his twenty years in uniform. Why shouldn't I take a couple of bruises for Uncle Sam?'

'And it was fine by you if they knocked me off in the process.'

'You're dangerous. You're trying to harm the club. You and Bobby Stillman. She's been after them for years. She's crazy, you know, just in case you think you're really doing something good. You're both crazy. You'll never win, you know. They'll stop you.'

'Maybe they will. Maybe they won't. We'll see. One thing's for sure, though: you lose.'

Bolden found duct tape in the pantry and socks in Schiff's dresser. Returning to the guest room, he taped her ankles together. When she cried out, he stuffed a pair of silk dress socks into her mouth and taped that, too. Finally, he taped her wrists together and dragged her into the bathroom. He locked the door before pulling it closed.

It took him five more minutes to give Schiff the same treatment.

Somewhere in the house a phone rang. *Security*,

he thought. Then he recognized the ring as belonging to a cell phone. He looked around and identified the noise as coming from the kitchen. He found the compact phone, next to Schiff's wallet and keys. 'Yes.'

'Mr Morris. We'll be meeting in the Long Room following the dinner this evening. Twelve o'clock. I trust you're coming despite the weather.'

'Yes,' said Bolden. 'I'll be there.'

Chapter 56

John Franciscus pulled his police cruiser to the kerb in the center of the 'No Parking Zone' fronting the Delta Shuttle Terminal at LaGuardia Airport. Grabbing his 'Police Business' card off the passenger seat, he slid it onto the dashboard and climbed out of the car. He left the keys in the ignition and the doors unlocked. Let someone else move the car. He had a plane to catch.

The terminal was busy. Commuters rushed to gates, many of them hurriedly buying coffee and newspapers on the way. Those just arriving made a beeline to baggage claim. Everyone had someplace to go, and from the look of it, they were all late. New York City, he thought. It was a place you couldn't wait to get to, and couldn't wait to leave.

Franciscus showed his badge to the security supervisor, who guided him around the metal detectors. He jogged up the incline to the ticketing area. The line of passengers waiting for a boarding card stretched to fifty feet. He walked directly to the counter.

'Police business,' he said, laying out his badge and identification for inspection. 'I need to be on the seven-thirty flight to DC.'

'Yes, um, let me check.'

'It's urgent, ma'am.'

'Of course, Detective. That will be two hundred dollars.'

Franciscus paid by credit card. Without further ado, she issued him a boarding pass.

He did not see the fit, dark-haired man who had followed him to the desk and demanded a seat on the same flight to the nation's capital.

The black BMW 760LI slowed at the corner of Forty-sixth and Broadway. A window rolled down. 'Hey . . . get in.'

Bolden opened the door and slid into the back seat. The car accelerated into traffic. A young African-American male sat behind the driver. He was dressed in a navy business suit that Bolden knew was the work of Alan Flusser. He wore a high white collar and an oversized pink Italian necktie – or a 'cravate', as Bolden had been told it was called on more than one occasion. His shoes looked like they'd never touched the pavement. Only the sparkling diamond watch gave any indication that he might not work in the same office as Tom Bolden.

Darius Fell kept his eyes straight ahead, his face a mask of indignation. 'Mr T.,' he said, after a moment. 'Howzit?'

'Not real good.'

'Respect,' he said. 'Now you know I'm right. Can't trust no one. Never.'

'I didn't come to argue.'

'You lookin' all business. Saw you on the TV. You look like a Russian or something, one of them guys from Little Odessa, know what I'm sayin'? You one scary motherfucker.'

'The tape's a fake,' said Bolden.

Darius Fell laughed and for the first time turned to look at Bolden. He extended an open hand. 'Ain't it always?'

The two shook hands. 'White Man's Handshake', Fell called it. Nothing fancy. No changing grips, snapping of fingers, or pointing at the other guy. In the four years he'd known Darius, Bolden often felt that the only thing he'd taught him was the meaning of a formal handshake and where to buy a decent suit.

'My sister help you out?'

'She did. Tell her thanks again. I owe you.'

'Nah. You just keep doing what you doing. We even, then.'

Video screens mounted in the back of the headrests played a pornographic movie. Tucked in a custom holster near the driver's left leg was an Uzi submachine gun. Fell did nothing to camouflage the rise under his left arm.

'Tell your partners, we're going downtown,' said Bolden.

'Where to?'

'Wall Street.'

The concourse of the executive parking lot beneath the Harrington Weiss building was reserved for senior partners and visiting big shots. Located on the first underground level, it was not so much a parking lot as a very large automobile showroom. At any time, one could expect to find a selection of late-model Porsches, Ferraris, BMWs, and Mercedes. Tonight, however, the parking lot was deserted. HW's senior partners had flown the coop by seven-thirty. At least half were en route to Washington, to attend Jacklin's 'Ten Billion Dollar Dinner'. A lone car remained. Sol Weiss's ten-year-old Mercedes.

The BMW slowed. Bolden jumped out.

'Chill for three minutes, then get movin',' said Darius Fell.

Bolden nodded and slammed the door.

*

His name was Caleb Short and he was the officer in charge of security for 55 Wall Street. Short sat at a console of video monitors, a paper bag on the desk holding his evening's dinner and snack. His wife had prepared a liverwurst sandwich, peanut butter and celery sticks, carrots, and a tin of organic apple sauce. He had stuck in the Clark bar himself. He couldn't make a twelve-hour shift without a little candy. A man had his limits.

'You believe what went down here?' Short asked his shift partner, Lemon Wilkie, a scrappy kid from Bensonhurst who liked to wear his sidearm low on his hip.

'Some bad shit,' said Wilkie. 'Just goes to show, you never really can tell about some people.'

'You know him? Bolden?'

'Seen him around. He's a suit. You?'

'Yeah. He works late. Real friendly. Wouldn't figure him to be the type.'

'Yeah,' laughed Wilkie, into his hand. 'What do you know?'

Short sat up, wanting to tear into him, then thought the better of it. Short knew plenty ... certainly more than a twenty-two-year-old Army reservist like Lemon Wilkie. Short had put in his twenty as an MP with the Army's 10th Mountain Division and got out a master sergeant. Three chevrons on top. Three rockers on the bottom. In the five years since he'd gotten out, he'd put on a solid fifty pounds. Being a little overweight didn't mean he wasn't on top of his game.

Short checked the bank of monitors. There were twenty in all. The four positioned directly in front of him were permanent feeds from the lobby, the garage, and the forty-third floor, where Harrington Weiss's top executives worked. The others rotated among the cameras on the different floors. He looked at a few, then took out his sandwich. In three years on the job, the most exciting thing that had happened on his watch was one of HW's partners having a heart attack while waiting for an elevator to take him to his radio car. Short had spotted him on one of the monitors, lying there wriggling around like a landed fish. His call to 911 had saved the man's life. Every year the man invited Caleb Short and his wife to his home for Thanksgiving dinner and slipped him an envelope with a even grand inside it, along with a bottle of French wine.

'You want first rotation or me?' he asked Lemon.

Each night, Short and Wilkie were required to make a minimum of six tours through the building, meaning a stop at each floor to have a look around. A tour took a little more than an hour.

'Sure, I'll go,' said Wilkie.

A skeleton staff was on duty. Besides the two Somalis working the reception desk, there was just Short and Wilkie.

Caleb Short handed him the keys, but Lemon Wilkie wasn't looking his way.

'Ah, shit,' said Wilkie. 'Check out camera three.'

Short looked at the monitor providing a wide-angle view of the lobby. Three African-American males were approaching the reception desk. It appeared that two of them were brandishing pistols and the third an Uzi. 'Holy shit,' he muttered.

'You want it . . . or me?' asked Wilkie.

Regulations called for one man to remain in the security control room.

'I'll take it,' said Short.

'Yes sir.'

Short glanced at Wilkie. That was more like it.

It was then that he heard the shots go off like a string of firecrackers. Holes appeared in the floor and the ceiling. The security room was situated directly above the reception desk. Short stared at the monitor. The three men were spraying the lobby with bullets. 'Come on, Wilkie. Get your piece out. We're going down there together.'

'I'm calling the cops. I ain't going anywhere.'

Caleb Short shook his head. 'The hell you aren't. This is our building and we don't let no one mess it up.'

Wilkie stood and fumbled with his pistol. His face had gone whiter than a ghost.

The two men were out the door a few seconds later.

Neither saw Thomas Bolden emerge from the elevator on the forty-third floor.

Recessed lights burned dimly, casting shadows on the reception desk, lengthening hallways, and in between, leaving pools of darkness. Bolden walked briskly, keeping an ear open for any activity. He had five minutes, ten at the most. Darius Fell promised to keep his buddies lighting up the place until NYPD showed up and not a minute longer. From somewhere distant came the whirring of an incoming fax. He turned the corner, passing Sol Weiss's office.

Weiss, the self-made striver, the genial, charismatic leader, the staunch defender of the firm as a partnership. How many times had he turned down offers to sell the company, to boost the firm's capital through an initial public offering, or to merge with one of the titans of the Street? He'd said it was to guard the firm's entrepreneurial culture, to stay a specialist in chosen fields. Mostly, though, he liked to say that HW was a family company. His family. Bolden had never looked past the explanations. Was it that strange for at least one man to be satisfied with what he'd built himself?

In fact, Sol Weiss had had other reasons for keeping the firm private.

Bolden continued past the private dining room and the executive boardroom. The door to Mickey Schiff's office was locked. Bolden tried three keys before he found the right one. He opened the door and slipped inside. It wasn't an office so much as the living room of an Italian palazzo. The room stretched seventy feet and was decorated in a sumptuous style the diametric opposite of Schiff's home. There was a section for guests, another for the lord of the manor to roam, and a formal work area at the far side. Somewhere hidden among the floor-to-ceiling bookshelves was a secret door to his private bathroom. Schiff had brought Bolden up on a Saturday a year ago and given him the nickel tour. It was the standard 'this all could be yours someday' speech. Show the galley slaves what they're working toward. Gold-plated faucets, Hockney prints, and an office the size of Rhode Island. That was the carrot. They didn't have to worry about the stick. HW chose their employees carefully. The single overarching trait was a monstrous fear of failure. The employees provided their own sticks.

Bolden moved to Schiff's desk and took a place in the low-backed captain's chair. An identification card was required to gain access to Nightingale, the firm's proprietary banking software. The card governed one's clearance within the system, dictating what areas of the bank he had a right to explore. Schiff saw it all. Bolden slid the card through the scanner located on top of the keyboard. The screen powered up. After a few false starts, he accessed the portfolio management rubric. A prompt appeared asking him to enter the customer's name or account number. He tried to remember who had most recently joined HW.

He typed in the name 'LaWanda Makepeace'.

Six months earlier, LaWanda Makepeace had served as commissioner of the FCC when the regulatory body had inexplicably altered a holding rule allowing one of Jefferson's telecom companies to market its service beyond its home state. Two months later, she'd left the FCC to join Jefferson Partners. It seemed a reasonable place to start.

Three account numbers appeared on the screen. Two of the numbers belonged to standard brokerage accounts. He opened each in turn. Both held a variety of blue-chip stocks, municipal bonds, and cash in the form of money-market shares. Their combined total teetered on the cusp of a million dollars. All in all, a reasonable portfolio for a fifty-year-old government professional who had counted her pennies.

The third account was labeled Omega Associates.

Bolden opened it. There at the bottom of the page, in the all-important box listing the total account value, stood the number thirty-four, followed by six zeros. Thirty-four million dollars. Definitely not what one would expect for a woman who had spent her professional working life toiling in the government's stables, not even for cleaning all of them out. Bolden blew a stream of air through his teeth. Thirty-four million dollars. It wasn't a bribe. It was a dynasty.

A look at the account's history showed that the cash had been deposited in two tranches. The first, six months earlier, and the second sixty days ago, corresponding to the time the FCC had ruled in favor of Jefferson.

Bolden recalled Marty Kravitz's line about

conjecture, and something a reasonable man could assume. Screw conjecture. It was time to dig up some proof.

By shading, then double-clicking on the deposit transaction, he was able to trace the routing of the thirty-four million dollars. The money had been wired in from a numbered account at the private bank of Milbank and Mason, domiciled in Nassau, the Bahamas. Finding the bank's SWIFT number, the international identity code given to each licensed bank, he asked the software to locate and exhibit all transactions involving the bank and HW's clients.

A list appeared, running to several screens. Two million here. Ten million there. There wasn't an incoming wire from Milbank and Mason for less than seven figures. The sum added up to a fortune, but it was peanuts to a firm that year in, year out, earned its investors a staggering twenty-six percent rate of return. The names were equally staggering. Senators. Commissioners. Generals. Ambassadors. Movers and shakers, all. The men and women whose hands operated the levers of power. He counted no less than seven who currently worked for Jefferson Partners. All of them were here. All were clients of Harrington Weiss.

And then, Bolden stumbled across his divining key. The transaction that tied it all together. Not an incoming wire, but an outgoing payment to said bank of Milbank and Mason, Nassau, the Bahamas. The sum: twenty-five million dollars. The recipient: a numbered account, but as was the custom, the account holder's name was indicated for HW's internal records. Guy de Valmont, vice chair of Jefferson Partners.

Bolden double-checked the account number. It was the same used to pay LaWanda Makepeace and several others.

The trail was complete.

There was a last name, too. Solomon H. Weiss. The amount: fifty million dollars. No doubt a payment to ensure the long-lived partnership. A little pocket money to keep prying eyes at bay.

Bolden sent the information to the printer. He was done with conjecture. He had his proof. The printer began to spit out pages. He checked one. Bribery wasn't the right word, he thought. More apt was robbery. But robbing what? Integrity. Faith. Accountability. Tammany Hall had nothing on Jefferson. Jefferson had hijacked the government and stuffed it in its back pocket.

When the printer had finished, Bolden logged off the computer and left the office.

He shut the door and looked down the hall.

'Bang,' said a voice, from behind him. 'You're dead.'

Bolden froze.

Wolf stood three feet away, holding a silenced pistol. 'Don't even think about it,' he said.

Chapter 57

'Wolf's got him,' said Guilfoyle, striding up to James Jacklin outside his office.

'Well, hallelujah. I thought I'd never see the day. Where'd they nab him?'

Guilfoyle took Jacklin to one side. 'In Mickey Schiff's office.'

'What the hell was he doing there?'

'Looking into the financial affairs of some of our counselors.'

'He's one resourceful individual. I'll give him that much.'

'Does it surprise you?' Guilfoyle monitored Jacklin's expression. As ever, it was impossible to read anything in the man's features except scorn and a general frustration that the world didn't run quite the way he'd like it to.

The office was quiet for a Wednesday evening. The entire staff had received invitations to the dinner. Most of the executives were either at Jacklin's home or on their way. A few stragglers hurried up and down the hallways, throwing on their dinner jackets, spending a last moment adjusting their ties.

'Have you talked to Schiff?' asked Jacklin.

'Voice mail. But I plan on speaking with him as soon as he arrives. Bolden had these documents with him.'

Jacklin accepted the sheaf of papers that had been

faxed to DC for Guilfoyle's inspection. 'Busy bee, isn't he? Most people would have done the smart thing and run for the hills.' He thumbed through the copies, frowning when he came across the LexisNexis reports listing Schiff as a director of Defense Associates.'These reports were printed this afternoon. Who does he have on the inside?'

'His secretary helped him. Her name is Althea Jackson. We can assume she's conversant with the material.'

'Married?'

'Single. One boy. Twelve years old.'

'Dammit,' said Jacklin. He shook his head and sighed. 'See that the boy's well taken care of. Set up a scholarship or something. Remind me to give St Paul's a call. I know the rector. They're good about taking needy cases.'

Guilfoyle nodded. 'I spoke with Marty Kravitz. He swore that Bolden impersonated one of HW's senior executives when ordering the reports. Apparently, Bolden strong-armed him into handing over the information. I think we can count on Kravitz keeping his mouth shut. If Prell tattled every time they found something incriminating, they wouldn't have any customers left.'

'All right then, get Bolden down here. I want to talk to him face-to-face.'

'He's on his way.' Guilfoyle stepped closer to Jacklin. 'Got a minute?'

'I've got the limo waiting downstairs. I can give you a lift.'

'It won't take long.' Guilfoyle took Jacklin by the arm and guided him into the confines of his office. 'There's something you need to know. Something about Albany.'

Jacklin folded his arms, giving Guilfoyle his undivided attention. 'What about Albany?'

'A detective in New York ran latents of your thumb and index finger through the NCIC's database and got a match.'

'Where the hell did he get copies of my fingerprints?'

'I don't know, but we have to assume the worst.'

'And that is?'

'The prints came from the gun used to kill David Bernstein.'

'How is that possible? I thought the matter was cleared up a long time ago.'

'I never found the prints. It bothered me at the time, but without Kovacs there wasn't a reason to be concerned. The problem was localized and contained. Twenty-five years, J. J. Really, I'm as shocked as you.'

'That I very much doubt,' said Jacklin. When he spoke next his voice was quiet as a rattlesnake's whisper. 'It was our bargain. You cleaned up that mess in exchange for a cozy job with Jefferson. I had thought it a fair one at the time. I'm no longer so sure.' Jacklin stepped toward the model of the battleship *Maine*. 'Who ran the prints?' he asked.

'Detective John Franciscus. He's the same one who questioned Bolden last night.'

'What makes him so damned curious?'

'Just a good cop, I guess. We've tracked him to a flight to DC.'

'He's coming here? Wonderful. Maybe we should leave an invitation to the gala at the airport for him.'

'Hold on, J. J. I'm as upset about this as you.'

'You?' Jacklin shook a finger at him. 'You cold-blooded bastard. You haven't got a feeling inside you. What do you know about being upset?'

Guilfoyle felt part of him lock up. He knew as much about emotions as anyone. He knew how destructive they were. How they controlled you.

How once you gave in to them, you were powerless. He said, 'We had a man at LaGuardia keeping an eye out for Bolden. He was able to get on board the plane with Franciscus.'

'What are you waiting for then?' asked Jacklin.

'He's a police officer.'

'So? It didn't stop you before. Those fingerprints can put both of us away.'

'First, they need a witness to place you at the scene.'

'They have one,' Jacklin flared. 'Bobby Stillman. Those fingerprints are her ticket to freedom.'

Chapter 58

The Scanlon operative lay on his side panting.

'Not bad,' said Bobby Stillman. 'I didn't expect money to buy that kind of loyalty.' She dropped to a knee and put a hand under the man's shoulder. 'Get up.'

When he didn't move, she yanked him to his feet. His face was red from where she'd slapped him, but other than that he was no worse for wear. Still, she couldn't help but notice that her friends were eyeing her differently.

She was a mean bitch. Count on it.

'So, you really don't know what Crown is?' she asked.

The man shook his head.

'Then you won't mind if I try one last way of finding out?' Bobby Stillman pulled a carpet layer's X-Acto knife out of her pocket. She paid the blade out slowly. *Click. Click. Click.* Millimeter by millimeter the steel snout emerged, until the razor-sharp triangle had grown to the size of a thumbnail. She laid the blade against his cheek.

A calm had come over her. After all the yelling, cajoling, browbeating, and finally striking her mute captive, she had made a dangerous peace with herself. All along she'd wondered how far she would go; what she would do if, ultimately, he refused to talk.

She stared into the man's eyes. She was sure she

saw his willful self staring back. Never for a moment had she believed that he didn't know. J. J. had always said that it was important to trust your men, to give them the truth, and let them come to grips with it. And so, she decided that there weren't any rules. Screw the Geneva Convention and the Marquess of Queensberry. This wasn't a war or a boxing match. She'd been living outside the bounds of the civilized world for so long that she was surprised she hadn't come to the conclusion earlier. God knows, Jacklin had. He was always willing to subordinate everything to the result. The end was all. The means meant nothing.

Bobby Stillman placed her lips next to the man's ear. 'You will tell me,' she said.

For the first time, she read fear in his eyes, as if he had finally taken a test of her mettle.

J. J. would be proud of me, she thought, and the idea made her terribly sad.

It had been a hot day. A hot day after many other hot days. Everyone's nerves were shot. People had worn through their good cheer. It was only July, but summer had gone on for a week too long already. Bobby came home to finish packing. She carried a grocery bag full of things they couldn't find when they left. Skippy peanut butter, granola bars, and a new pair of Superman pajamas for Jacky Jo. The flight for Buenos Aires left at eleven out of JFK. They would disappear for a year, longer if it suited them. She found David speaking with Jacklin in the front hall.

'What are you doing here?'

'Didn't you think I'd keep an eye on you?' Jacklin asked, smiling scornfully. 'Once that building went up, I knew who was responsible.'

'They have it on tape,' said David Bernstein. 'A surveillance camera got it all.'

Jacklin took a step toward Bobby. 'Don't make it hard on yourself, sweetheart. Police are on the way now. You can give them your excuses.'

An alarm bell sounded in her mind. *This isn't right*, she thought. *Why is J. J. waiting for the police to come?*

'What are we standing around for?' she said to David, grabbing his hand. 'Let's go. Now. Let's get out of here.'

She turned for the stairs. Two of Jacklin's goons waited at the upper landing. Broad shoulders, short haircuts, closed faces. She knew the type.

'I'm sorry, Bobby,' said Jacklin, flashing their airline tickets in his fist. 'I came to settle this misunderstanding once and for all.'

'Misunderstanding? I thought it was a felony.'

'Call it whatever you like.'

'There's nothing to settle,' said Bobby. 'You're a fascist. You want to spy on everyone to make sure no one's doing anything you don't like. You think you're Big Brother, even if your feet can't touch the kitchen floor. Just because you're out of the government doesn't mean you're not still in cahoots with them.' She spun to face the men on the stairs. 'Who are these gorillas? Tweedledee and Tweedledum? Why'd you bring them? Can't handle things by yourself? I thought you were a hero.' She went on goading him, her anger at the boiling point, her temper shot. 'J. J., you always were just a clown in a cowboy suit, trying to be the man your mother wanted you to be.'

'That's enough, Bobby.'

It was then that she saw the pistol in his hand.

'We just bought the company,' he said, giving it a waggle. 'Fanning Firearms. Figured I ought to get something out of it.'

'Oh, Christ, J. J., this is too much. A gun? Did you think we were going to fight back? Two lawyers? The Constitution's gunslingers? That there's Bernstein the Kid, fastest Jew in the West. And I'm . . .' She stopped midsentence and turned to her lover. 'Would you look at him, David?'

'Be quiet, Bobby,' said David Bernstein in a sober voice.

He knew. Bobby Stillman chided herself, twenty-five years later. He'd grown up the son of a police officer. He knew the cardinal rule about guns. You never drew one unless you were going to use it. And she, for her part, had done everything humanly possible to make sure his premonition came true.

'Oh, put it down, J. J.,' she went on. 'The police are coming. Good!' She thrust her wrists in front of her, as if welcoming the cuffs. 'Let them arrest us. The courts will be the forum we need to shine a bright fucking light on your crappy little company. You really expect everyone to believe that those devices Sentinel's making will only be used by the military? Overseas? I bet the FBI has a big order in already. Who else? Customs? Treasury? DEA? Everyone on the block will want one. They'll be installing them in every phone switching center within a year. All courtesy of James Jacklin and Sentinel Microsystems.'

'As usual, Bobby, you're a little too smart for your own good,' said Jacklin.

He gave her a last supremely pissed-off look, then turned and fired a bullet into David Bernstein's head. He collapsed to the floor without so much as a grunt. She would never forget how his knees buckled, his entire body going limp, as if someone had unplugged him from the wall and all the current had instantly gone out of him. And then

THE PATRIOTS' CLUB   411

lying there, he did a terrible thing. He kicked. One leg bucked the air. One heel of one leather shoe clomped onto the wooden floor. And then he was still.

Jacklin walked over to look at him. 'No one is going to testify in any court about Sentinel, sweetheart,' he said. 'National security.'

Bobby froze. Then she began to shake her head. Tears came. She didn't want to cry but she was overwhelmed. 'You monster,' she sobbed. 'You killed him. But you called the police? They're coming.'

'I surely hope so.'

Just then, a police car pulled to the kerb in front of the house. Two officers climbed out, slipping their batons into their belts. A scream rose in her throat. She ran to the window. One of Jacklin's men stopped her, sweeping her in his arms and clamping a hand over her mouth. The doorbell rang a minute later.

Jacklin opened the door. Before either could see David Bernstein, he shot them. Once through the heart, so close that the cloth of their shirts briefly caught fire.

He pointed the gun at her. 'Go outside,' he said.

Shaking, she stepped over the bodies onto the wraparound porch. He stood with the gun aimed at her for a minute. Neither moved.

'And Jacky Jo?' she said.

And so, Jacklin had created the myth of Bobby Stillman, cop killer. He had made her a permanent fugitive. It was a brilliant move. It robbed her of everything. Her freedom. Her credibility. And her son.

Bobby stepped back from the man. With one hand, she yanked his boxer shorts to the floor. She allowed him a moment to savor his vulnerability. Just a second or two to feel the wind blow.

She took a firm hold of his penis.

'What is Crown?' she asked, placing the carpet layer's knife under his manhood. She flicked the blade upward, drawing blood. 'Last chance.'

'DC . . . Senator McCoy,' he said, in dry gulps.

'More.'

'A sanction.'

'When?'

'The inauguration . . . *tomorrow*.'

Chapter 59

Delta flight 1967, New York LaGuardia to Washington Reagan National Airport, touched down at 8:33 P.M., thirty minutes behind schedule. Detective First Grade John Franciscus was the second passenger off the plane, held up only by a purple-haired matron in a wheelchair. Checking the overhead signs, he found his way to the car-rental desk. He had two or three friends on the DC Metro force he might have asked to pick him up, even a couple of Maryland state troopers. They were all good guys, but he didn't want to bring anyone else in on this. It wasn't the time to figure out who was his friend and who wasn't. A flash of the badge got him the last four-wheel drive. Keys in hand, he walked to the sidewalk to wait for the shuttle bus to take him to his car. If anything, the snow was falling heavier here than in New York. It came down in great fat feathers, an ocean of goosedown suspended in the air. The bus arrived. Beneath the harsh sodium lights, he caught his reflection in its window. Grey, he looked, and grey he felt.

At some point on the flight down, someplace between Trenton and Gettysburg, Franciscus had decided to go ahead and have the procedure. Twenty years with a zipper on his chest was better than twenty years without one. He'd even come up with the harebrained notion of moving out to LA, wrangling himself an adviser's job on one of the cop shows. They needed someone to straighten them out. He, personally, was sick of the crime-scene stuff. He wanted to see things done the old-fashioned way. His way. Bracing a guy at two in the morning in the stairway of the Jackson Projects until he gave up the doer. Or traipsing up to Albany on a hunch and coming back with a set of fingerprints that tied a man to a murder twenty-five years after the fact. Maybe he'd even ask Vicki Vasquez to come with him. He'd done crazier things.

Franciscus lifted his eyes and stared into the sky. It boiled down to this: even if he got the collar, his time was up. You didn't spit in the chief's face and live to talk about it. Esposito was a vindictive son of a bitch. He wouldn't forget. Franciscus would make sure the city paid for his procedure. His buddies in the union would back him. The lieutenant was right. Thirty-four years on the job was a career. Who said sixty-one wasn't a good time to start over?

He climbed aboard the bus, the flood of warm air more comfortable than he would have liked to admit. He'd had an argument once with his wife about what was worse, heat or cold. He said heat. With cold, you could always put on another layer of clothes. There was only so far you could go to keep cool, and not get arrested. He was beginning to think he was wrong.

The bus groaned to a halt. The driver looked over her shoulder. 'Here you are, young man,' she said. 'No bags?'

'Just me.'

'Stay warm,' she said.

As Franciscus trooped down the stairs and climbed into his rental car, he couldn't decide what was worse: her depressing sincerity or the look of concern in her eye.

He closed the door and cranked the heat to the max. The car had an automatic navigation system and he spent a minute programming in Francois Guilfoyle's address. Just in case, he opened the glove compartment and retrieved a map of DC and Virginia. 'Chain Bridge Road,' he murmured to himself, flipping through the index.

A shadow passed close to the car.

Franciscus looked up, but saw nothing.

He returned his attention to the map.

Just then, the passenger-side front and rear doors opened and two men climbed into the car. The one nearest him shoved an automatic into his gut. 'Try anything and you're dead,' he said, leaning across his chest and clearing Franciscus's pistol. 'Start the engine and drive.'

'Senator Marvin, good evening, sir. Great to have you with us.' Dapper in his dinner jacket and cummerbund, a dab of pomade to groom his hair, James Jacklin stood inside the entry to his home, greeting his guests. Every man got a thunderclap of a handshake, every woman a peck on the cheek and a heartfelt compliment. If people remarked that he was happier than they remembered, warm even, they would be correct. After a day and a night of stress and uncertainty, things were headed back his way. Not only did they have Bolden in custody, but Guilfoyle had nabbed the detective from New York as well. He only needed one more to make it a hat trick, but he was too old a dog to ask for more. He'd been chasing that rabbit for twenty-five years with no luck. All he really wanted to hear was a 'yes' that Hugh Fitzgerald, senator from Vermont, would vote in favor of the appropriations bill and the night would be a doozy.

'General Walker, it's a pleasure, sir,' said Jacklin,

with a hand to his shoulder. 'Any word from Fitzgerald about the pre-pos? The nation is in a dire state.'

'Let's keep our fingers crossed,' said Walker.

'Director Von Arx, glad to see you,' said Jacklin to the director of the FBI. And in a whisper he added, 'I thank you, Mr Hamilton. We have the young man in custody as I speak. All's well that ends well. Let's have a drink together afterwards.'

'Make it a double,' said Von Arx.

There was a break in the line of guests. Jacklin stepped outside to survey the cars and limousines clogging the long, curving driveway. Even the weather couldn't keep people away. He checked the sky. The clouds were as dense as a bowl of cotton, the snow falling steadily. The broad front lawn sprawled before him as white as a wedding cake.

'Well, well, the billionaire himself.' Senator Hugh Fitzgerald lumbered up the stairs. In his greatcoat and black tie he looked like a coachman from the nineteenth century. A very large coachman. He wore a blood red carnation in his lapel. 'I thought you'd have a butler answering the door.'

'Now, Hugh, I've been waiting here just for you,' said Jacklin, seizing his forearm as they shook hands, and drawing him near. A gesture reserved for the closest of friends. 'You're on my short list. I don't suppose you've done any thinking . . .'

'But I have, J. J. In fact, I've done nothing but think.'

'And?'

'Ah . . .' Fitzgerald offered a pat on the shoulder and an Irishman's wink. 'I didn't say I'd decided.'

Jacklin joined him in convivial laughter, as he turned to the next guest. 'Ah, Secretary Luttwak . . .'

But under his breath, he swore.

*

The line of parked cars ran up and down both sides
of the narrow two-lane road for as far as she could
see. Jenny pulled the rental behind the last one and
killed the engine. The wipers skidded to a halt. In
the seconds before snow dusted the windscreen,
and the world was whited out, she saw a man in a
red windbreaker running up the hill, then another
running down it. A car pulled in behind her, the
lights illuminating the interior. For a moment, she
caught her own eyes in the rearview mirror. The
pupils were pinpricks. Her mouth appeared drawn;
her complexion waxlike. She forced herself to take
a breath. To calm herself, she applied a fresh coat of
lipstick and ran the eyeliner a second time beneath
her eyes. *I can't do this*, she said to her reflection. *I'm
a teacher, not a spy.* Her hand rested on her stomach.
She thought of the new life growing inside her. *A
spy.* She remembered that Mata Hari had died in
front of a firing squad. It was better than a bullet in
the back, or not seeing it at all.

'Excuse me,' she called, opening the door.

The parking attendant was a young man, his
thick black hair crowned with snow. 'Ma'am?'

'Do you have an umbrella?'

'Bring your car to the top of the driveway. I'll be
happy to park it for you.'

'I might need to make a quick getaway.'

He came nearer and got a look at Jennifer. His
frown dissolved into a welcoming smile. 'Wait right
here. I'll be back.'

He disappeared into the falling snow, a pair of
legs running at full tilt. It took him five minutes to
return, long enough for Jenny to erase any ideas
about a quick getaway. He offered Jenny the
umbrella and his arm. She accepted both. She didn't
like the idea of slipping in her high heels. Shoulder

to shoulder, they marched up the street, then crossed it and continued up a long, curling drive.

The house was Mount Vernon's ugly stepsister, bigger, bolder, and more garish in every way. To shield guests from the elements, a temporary porte cochère had been erected in front of the entry. A car drove by on their left, braking once it passed under the awning. Jenny paid careful attention as each couple presented their invitation to a very large doorman before being admitted. Elsewhere, she noted men in dark overcoats standing like sentries near the garage and at either end of the house.

'Why so much security?' she asked, as they began the long walk up the hill.

'The President is due here at ten. He's going to eat some dessert and say a few words. The Secret Service owns this place.'

Jenny felt her throat catch. 'Damn,' she said. 'I forgot my invitation.'

'Is it in the car? I can run back and get it for you.'

'No. At home, I'm afraid. Can you run to Georgetown? Things look pretty tight up there.'

The valet caught Jenny's disappointed look. 'Come with me,' he went on. 'I'll slide you in the kitchen entrance. I don't think you qualify as a threat.'

'You never know,' she said, squeezing his arm.

A host of parking attendants stood inside the garage, helping themselves from a table laden with roast beef sandwiches, chicken legs, soft drinks, and hot coffee. Two Secret Service agents stood among them, talking. Jenny smiled as she walked past. She even waved, thinking a tall blonde with all-American good looks couldn't possibly raise any alarm bells.

A moment later, the two agents were standing in front of her. Both had four inches on her, necks the size of fire hydrants, and a discreet wire trailing from their ears.

'Your invitation, ma'am?' asked one.

Jenny answered earnestly. 'I forgot it at home. I know it was stupid. I even told this young man, here, and he was nice enough to help me get in.'

'I'm sorry, but we can't permit you onto the premises.'

'I know,' said Jenny. 'It's just that I'm here on behalf of my boss and I'm sure he'll be upset if I don't show up. The Ten Billion Dollar Dinner. You can imagine, it's a big deal.'

'Your name, ma'am?'

'Pendleton,' she said 'Jennifer Pendleton.'

The lead agent brought his mouth toward his lapel. 'Dallas one, this is Dallas four. Requesting a guest check. Jennifer Pendleton.' He turned his attention back to Jenny. 'This will take a moment. In the meantime, I'll need to see your driver's license.'

'Oh, yeah, sure.' Jenny opened her purse, fiddling with her Kleenex and lipstick and eyeliner and chewing gum. The last thing she wanted to show the Secret Service was a driver's license giving her real name. Not being on the guest list was one thing. Lying about it, another.

Presently, three more Secret Service agents arrived, forming a semicircle around her. The man who'd asked for her license addressed a short, barrel-chested agent whom she assumed to be his superior. 'Unwarranted entry,' he said. 'The lady doesn't have an invitation. Not on the guest list, either.'

The agent in charge took her by the arm. 'Do you have a driver's license? Or any form of government-issued identification?'

Jenny shook her head. 'No, I'm sorry. I seem to have left it at home, too.'

'With your invitation?'

'Yes.'

Nods all around. She sensed a definite increase in the tension level. *This is where they unbutton their jackets and tuck their coats behind their revolvers*, she thought.

'If you don't mind, I'd like you to come with me,' said the barrel-chested agent. Another motion toward the lapel. 'Mary, we have a Code Alpha. Meet me in the garage.'

Ten seconds passed. A trim, olive-skinned woman dressed in the same navy business attire as the male agents emerged from the house and bustled across the garage.

'This is Mary Ansenelli,' said the agent in charge. 'She's going to escort you inside. We're going to ask if it's all right if we frisk you. You have a right to say no, in which case, you will be arrested and taken to the local police station.'

'Arrested? I'm a guest of Mr Jacklin and Jefferson. I'm sorry if they made a mistake and my name isn't on the list. I work for Harrington Weiss. I couldn't care less if you frisk me. You can do it here, for all I care. I just want to go to the party, preferably before dessert is served.'

'I understand, you're upset, ma'am. If you'll just cooperate, I'm sure we can work things out.'

'Cooperate? What else do I have to do? I parked where I was supposed to. I came at the right time. I didn't know strip poker was on the agenda.'

The female agent grasped her arm firmly. 'If you'd come with me, please.'

Jenny shook it off. 'No, I won't!'

'Gary, shoot me some cuffs.'

'You will not put handcuffs on me. I am a guest at this event. Not some two-bit party crasher!'

The agent in charge took hold of her arms and

tugged them behind her back. 'Please keep still. We just need a little cooperation.'

'Let me go!' shouted Jenny, struggling. 'Get Mr Jacklin. I'm his guest!'

Handcuffs clamped her wrists. Someone spun her around, while the female agent led her toward the front of the garage. An agitated voice called for a car. Another was radioing ahead, advising someone to expect an incoming prisoner. A hand in her back pushed her forward. Jenny marched past the parking valets and the table laden with coffee and sandwiches. She glanced over her shoulder. The door to the kitchen was getting farther and farther away. 'Be careful,' she said, angrily. 'I'm pregnant.'

A sedan drew up a few feet away. A short, curly-haired man with vicious pockmarks stepped out and took Jenny's arm. 'Watch your head,' he said, opening the rear door and placing his hand on her head and forcing her into the car.

'Is there a problem, Agent Reilly?'

Jenny turned and stared into James Jacklin's stern face.

'This woman was trying to gain entry to your party, sir,' said the agent in charge. 'She doesn't have an invitation and her name's not on the guest list.'

Jenny looked between the two men. Catching Jacklin's eye, she smiled with heartfelt relief. 'Mr Jacklin, it's me . . . Jenny Pendleton. You probably don't remember me, but I work at Harrington Weiss in New York. I'm in the structured finance group under Jake Flannagan.'

'Of course, I know Jake. I'm sorry he couldn't make it.' Jacklin looked from one agent to another. 'Gentlemen, I think it's all right if you remove the handcuffs from this poor woman.'

Reilly, the agent in charge, unlocked the cuffs.

Jenny put a hand to her chest, sighing. 'Thank God. Someone who doesn't take me for a criminal. Jake'll kill me for being late, but . . .'

Jacklin waved away the Secret Service agents. 'I think we can take it from here. Miss Pendleton's with one of Jefferson's most important clients. I'll be happy to vouch for her.' He extended a hand and Jenny took it. 'Right this way, m'dear. I'll be happy to show you around. First though, let me get you a drink. I insist. Cold outside, isn't it?'

Jenny nodded, the smile frozen in place. Strangely, she couldn't say a word.

Chapter 60

The jet was an older Gulfstream III. A ten-seater with cracked leather seats, faux burled-wood paneling, and not quite the ceiling height of newer models. Bolden sat in the center of the cabin, his hands and ankles bound by plastic restraints that cut deep into his skin. Wolf sat at the tail of the cabin, screwing and unscrewing the silencer onto the muzzle of his pistol. 'Low-velocity shells,' he'd informed Bolden when they'd boarded. 'Just enough powder to put a hole in you, but not enough to carve one in the fuselage.'

It was not Bolden's first trip on a private jet. Nor his second, nor even his tenth. The business of buying and selling billion-dollar corporations was conducted at a fever pitch. Time was money. No one could afford to waste hours stuck in ticket queues, clearing security, or being at the whim of a late-arriving aircraft. In the course of six years as an adviser to many of the nation's largest companies, he'd logged no less than fifty flights aboard corporate aircraft.

In comparison to the others, this flight ranked near the bottom. 'Spartan' would be a good word to describe it. He did not enjoy the usual amenities. There was no Diet Coke, ginseng tea, or Red Bull to revive his flagging spirits; no chilled Dom to celebrate a successful closing; no homemade biscuits and jam; no Concord grapes and Brie; no tortilla chips and guacamole to nosh on. No warm towels. And certainly no onboard aesthetician to inquire whether he'd prefer a manicure or a ten-minute 'power' massage.

Bolden reflected that it was odd how much a man's life could change in twenty-four hours. Last night, he was the cock of the walk. Man of the Year. A high-ranking executive with a boundless future. It had changed in another, more important, way. He was the father of a child growing in the womb of the woman he loved. He stared out the window, seeing Jenny's face in the darkness.

The plane banked to the left, dropping out of the clouds above Georgetown University. They came in low over the Potomac, the Kennedy Center nipping at their wing. The plane shuddered as the landing gear came down. They flew at monument level, looking through the Lincoln Memorial down the Reflecting Pool, the Washington Monument half obscured by mist and snow.

It would be, he thought, his final landing.

'Are you sure we've met?' asked Jacklin. 'I don't know that I could have forgotten someone so lovely.'

Jennifer Pendleton nodded eagerly. 'Actually, once . . . but it was a while ago. I can't thank you enough for coming to my rescue. I was actually starting to feel a little afraid.'

'Not to worry, m'dear. It would have worked itself out.'

The two were standing in the main salon, surrounded by a swirl of men and women in tuxedos and evening finery. Jenny laid a hand on Jacklin's arm and Jacklin couldn't help but step closer to her. She was damned cute. 'You say you're a Pendleton?'

'As a matter of fact, we share a great-great-grandfather. Edmund Greene Pendleton. Our side of the family moved to Ohio. We were farmers, not politicians.'

'Where would this country be without farmers? George Washington raised some tobacco in his day, if I'm not mistaken.'

'Tell me, Mr Jacklin . . .'

'J. J., dammit, you're making me feel old.'

'Tell me, J. J.,' she went on, pointing to the oil portraits that adorned the wall. 'Are any of these Pendletons?'

'Jacklins mostly.' He patted her hand. 'I'll be happy to give you a tour.' He led her around the room, offering brief biographies of his ancestors. Harold Jacklin, his father, the distinguished congressman. Edmund Jacklin, before him, a railroad man and banker. *She is a charming girl*, he thought. Not at all like the cold fish that strutted up and down Wall Street. When he'd finished talking about the paintings, he was happy to find her hand still on his arm.

'You know, J. J.,' said the woman, 'I've always believed that the Pendletons are America's forgotten family. Nathaniel Pendleton is hardly mentioned in the history books, yet he was a close friend of Alexander Hamilton and George Washington. It's time to give our family its due.'

'I couldn't agree more. You know I'm a bit of a history nut, myself. Tradition runs in our blood. A respect for the past. I'm the fifth generation Jacklin to serve his country. I'm a Navy man. Old Nat Pendleton was a colonel in the cavalry.'

'South Carolina, wasn't it?'

'Now you're talking. I see you know something of the family.'

'Actually, I'm a history nut, too. I used to give

walking tours of old New York. We'd start at the Fraunces Tavern, then walk up to St Paul's.'

'The Fraunces Tavern? So you're familiar with the Long Room?'

Jennifer Pendleton nodded. 'Where General Washington said farewell to his officers. I believe it was December 4, 1783.'

Jacklin looked at the girl in a new light. She was sharp as a tack. He'd have to give Mickey Schiff a call and see if she might take Bolden's place. He'd be more than happy to steer a little extra business in HW's direction, if it meant making a few overnight company visits with this golden-haired damsel. He checked his watch. 'Would you like to see it right now?'

'*The Long Room?* New York's a bit of a trip.'

Jacklin pulled her closer and whispered in her ear. 'Who's talking about going to New York? Come with me, but we've got to hurry. Dinner's due to be served. Picked out the menu myself. Are you partial to truffles?'

Jacklin led the young woman upstairs. When he came to the door, he stopped. 'This took me twenty years to get just right. Every detail is just as it was that night in 1783.'

The woman sported an expectant smile. *Well, I'll be damned*, he thought. *She really is a history nut. Just like me.*

Jacklin pushed open the door and turned on the light. He walked around the table and pointed out the display case holding Lincoln's Bible and Hamilton's hair. Her rapt attention reminded him of his own ardor for the subject. 'Nat Pendleton used to meet with General Washington and that fox Hamilton in this very room. It was more a club for them than a tavern.'

'A club. Really?' Jenny's heart beat faster. It was

real. Just as Bobby Stillman had said. Just as Simon Bonny had promised.

'Yes. A place where they could repair in private, smoke a cigar, have a few tankards of ale. But Washington was a serious fellow. He came here to do business. See to the affairs of the country.' Jacklin ran a hand over a large burled-wood humidor set atop a matching burled-wood stand. 'See this?'

'It's beautiful,' she said.

'Handmade to match General Washington's own. Not a replica. A twin.' Opening the humidor, he selected a Romeo y Julieta that would go nicely with the port being served with dessert. He remembered that these days women smoked the damn things, too. He didn't want to be taken for her granddad. 'Care for one . . . Jenny, is it?'

'Oh no, I believe that cigars are best left for the man of the house.'

Jacklin nodded appreciatively. She was talking his language. He walked the length of the table. 'Yes sir,' he said. 'More important decisions were made in this room than I'd care to guess.'

'I'm getting goosebumps,' said Jenny.

'There, there. Let me warm you up.' Jacklin rubbed her arms. 'You're shaking.'

'I should have brought a shawl.'

'Nonsense.' Jacklin slipped his arm around her, letting his hand drift lower and caress her bottom. Christ, but she was built. He felt himself stir. There might just be time for a kiss.

'And you said that General Washington had meetings here?' she asked. 'Even when he was President?'

'Oh yes. There were some things he couldn't talk about in Philadelphia. Too many spies. You have no idea—' A bell sounded from downstairs. Jacklin looked toward the door. 'There's dinner.' He allowed his hand to linger and noticed the woman didn't seem to mind. Well, well, the night might turn out a little more exciting than he'd planned. 'What table are you at, m'dear?'

'I left my invitation at home. I don't remember what it might have said.'

'You're welcome to join Leona and me, if you like.'

'No, really, I don't mean to intrude. I've already taken up enough of your time.'

Jacklin switched off the lights and closed the door. 'Consider it done,' he said, feeling the glow of an impending conquest. 'We're family after all. We have to stick together.'

Chapter 61

It was Jacklin's house. Franciscus knew it without being told. He could see it through the glade of pines as they drove up an unpaved road adjacent to the property. A classic Colonial with fluted white columns, forest-green shutters and a portico you could drive a hansom cab through. Some party, too. The place was lit up like Tavern on the Green. Mercedes, BMWs, more than a few Rolls lined the driveway. Not a Ford in the lot. The car pitched and rumbled over loose rock and gravel, and came to an abrupt halt. Several men emerged from the woods and formed a cordon around his door. At their signal, he was spirited out of the car and marched to a stable house three hundred yards down a manicured stone trail. A lone guard was posted outside. As they approached, he spoke some words into his lapel mike and opened the door. Franciscus walked inside, along with the two men who had driven him down from Reagan Airport.

They passed a line of empty stalls and led him to a tack room with saddles draped on wooden rods and horse blankets stacked in one corner. The room was small, fifteen feet by fifteen, with a poured concrete floor, an antique bench, and a hurricane lamp hanging from the ceiling. He sat down on the bench and rubbed his hands together. It was frigid and damp inside. He had on an overcoat and his suit, but the walk had raised a sweat. Before long, he was shivering.

Franciscus didn't have much experience being a captive, and the truth was that it scared the shit out of him. He'd seen David Bernstein's body, looked at the slug that had killed him. He knew that the men who held him were capable of murder. Mostly, he was scared because he knew what they wanted, and he had decided that he wasn't going to give it to them.

The door opened and a sallow hunched man about his age walked in. His tux identified him as a member of the ruling classes. His eyes came to rest on Franciscus. Dark. Depthless. Eyes that looked into your soul.

'Hello, Carnac,' said Franciscus.

'It's been a while since I've heard that. I don't like it, by the way.' Guilfoyle motioned for the other men to leave. When they were outside, he took up position by the door. 'Where did you find the fingerprints?' he asked.

'They were in Kovacs's things,' said Franciscus, agreeably.

'Really? I thought I'd given all of his belongings a good going over. Where exactly?'

'Does it matter? I looked through his papers and I found them.'

'I trust you have them with you.'

Franciscus looked at him as if he were nuts. 'You used to be a cop. Ever carry evidence around with you?'

'Did you leave them in New York? We've had a look through your desk and inside your home. Any place we might have missed? Just so you know, we erased the file from LiveScan's memory. You've got the only existing copy of Mr Jacklin's prints. That's to your advantage.'

Franciscus shrugged. 'Actually, I gave them to Bill McBride.'

'I wouldn't trust McBride with my laundry ticket. Really now, Detective, we must have the fingerprints.'

'I'm sorry to disappoint you, but I really don't have 'em with me.'

'Mind if we search you?'

'Be my guest,' said Franciscus, raising his arms to either side and turning a circle. 'But the lottery ticket's mine. I've got a good feeling about it.'

'Take off your jacket and trousers.'

'It's not going to help you.'

'Just do it,' said Guilfoyle.

Franciscus handed Guilfoyle his jacket and trousers, and watched as he went through them, turning out the pockets, patting the lapels, feeling the seams. Guilfoyle was doing all the work, but it was Franciscus who felt the energy seeping out of him. A few times, he'd fought off nausea spells, noticed his vision getting fuzzy at the periphery. Guilfoyle picked his wallet up from a milking stool and looked through it. He took out the money, then the credit cards, then the scraps of this and that that Franciscus had at one time or another deemed important enough to hold onto. Finished, Guilfoyle replaced the wallet on the stool, beside his credit cards, his badge, and his police ID. 'I need the fingerprints, Detective. Now.'

'That I can imagine,' said Franciscus. 'Those prints were all over the gun that killed Officers Shepherd and O'Neill, and David Bernstein.'

Guilfoyle ran a hand over his chin. Suddenly, he turned his attention back to the stool where Franciscus had set his wallet and his badge.

Knocking both aside, he snatched up Franciscus's ID holder, flipped it open, and wedged his thumb behind the photograph. He sighed, then dropped the case on the floor.

'Detective Franciscus . . . you know what you've stumbled into. Mr Jacklin's an important man. I confess that I have an interest in those prints, too. There's no reason we can't release you if you simply hand them over. We live in a world of evidence, not hearsay. I know your kind. You don't go tilting at windmills. You're like me. A realist. Give me those prints and you're a free man. I'll have one of my associates give you a ride to the airport. You have my word.'

Franciscus stared at him with disgust. 'Too bad you left the force. You're very persuasive. Very smooth.'

'The prints, Detective. You may either give them to me, or tell me where they can be found.'

Franciscus shook his head. 'I don't make deals with scumbags. You killed Theo Kovacs. Maybe you had a hand in taking care of Shepherd and O'Neill, too. You tried to knock off Bolden and ended up shooting his girlfriend instead. You made a mess on my turf, and I'm going to see to you that you do some time for it.'

That was it. Franciscus had spoken his piece. He'd expected it to resonate more. But in the cold, barren stable, his words ended up sounding flat and powerless. Standing there barefoot, barechested, and shivering, he felt stupid. Worse, he felt defeated.

'I've got a dinner to go to,' said Guilfoyle, after he'd summoned his security men back into the shack. 'Boys, do your best to make the detective a little more talkative.'

*

Dinner was served inside a large tent erected on the tennis court. White trellises laced with live bougainvillea decorated the walls. A parquet wood floor had been laid. Tall space heaters stood rooted like trees between the tables. A stage rose at the far side of the tent. The orchestra played an upbeat number with verve and brio.

The first course had been cleared. Jacklin wandered between tables, making the rounds. He spotted Guy de Valmont at the bar and went to speak with him.

'Well, J. J., are you happy?' asked de Valmont. 'Full house despite the lousy weather. I'd say it's a home run.'

Jacklin surveyed his assembled guests. 'Never seen 'em so relaxed. Remind me to have all our fundraisers at my home.'

'They're all here. Every last one of them showed up.' De Valmont looked around the room, calling the names as he saw them. 'The boys from Armonk, Jerry Gilbert from Grosse Pointe, the Brahmins from Harvard Endowment . . .'

'Even that shrew from Calpers made it,' whispered Jacklin. 'You know it's a hot ticket if the liberals from California start showing up.'

'I've already got a commitment for another two hundred million from GM,' de Valmont reported. 'It's going to be a good night.'

Jacklin beamed. 'The President's agreed to introduce Frances Tavistock. That should net us another half a billion.'

'Have you made it official with President Ramser about coming aboard?'

'Decorum, Guy. Decorum. It'll look a little nicer if he waits a year, does the lecture circuit. Remember, it doesn't do to hurry.' Jacklin clapped an arm around de Valmont and squeezed his shoulders. The defeats of that afternoon were as fleeting as smoke from a distant fire. 'Ten billion. We're almost there.'

The music faded as Jenny made her way upstairs. A Secret Service agent stood next to the banister at the top of the stairs. The President was due any minute. Jenny motioned toward the ladies' room. A nod of the head granted her free passage.

The hall was narrow and brightly lit, a runner of sky-blue carpeting over a wood plank floor. Jenny passed the bathroom and opened the door next to it. The Long Room was dark, shadows from the rustling branches flitting across the floor. She closed the door behind her and waited a moment. Ghosts. She could feel them hiding in the corners, watching. There was Lincoln's Bible and Hamilton's hair and a splinter from Washington's coffin. The relics of saints.

They met at midnight. A prayer was said first . . .

Jenny turned on the overhead light. The similarity to the real Long Room was eerie. But why copy it? she asked herself as she crept across the floor. Was it a history buff's nostalgia fix? Or was there another reason? Besides the table that ran down the center of the room, the furniture consisted of a low dresser, a desk, and a glass-fronted armoire. She opened every drawer, tried every cabinet. She found nothing.

They kept a record, Simon Bonny had said. *They were all so worried about how posterity would treat them.*

The door to the adjoining room was locked. The keyhole was fitted for a church key, one too large to fit into someone's pocket. James Jacklin had been faithful in his reproduction of that, too. Jenny ran her hand along the doorframe, then looked inside the top drawer of the cabinet standing nearby. The key lay inside. The lock turned readily, a single tumbler. Authentic to the last detail. She freed the key and the door glided open, beckoning her inside.

Books.

Floor-to-ceiling bookshelves lined three walls, a sash window overlooking the Jacklin estate's front lawn occupying the fourth. She closed the door and turned on an antique reading lamp with a green-glass shade. Books filled every inch of every shelf. Old books bound in leather, gold-leaf titles worn and all but impossible to read. She ran her hand over the leather spines. The room smelled musty and dank, as if a window hadn't been opened in years. She looked behind her. In the dim light, the books seemed to close in on her, intent on imprisoning her along with the past. She pulled out one volume: Francis Parkman's *France and England in North America*. Next to it, she found a first edition of Ulysses S. Grant's autobiography. The flyleaf was autographed by the author with a note: 'To Edmund Jacklin, citizen patriot, with esteem for your years of service.' Jenny returned the book to its place, feeling the floor reverberate in time to the orchestra's tune. She checked her watch. She'd been absent six minutes. Pressing her ear to the door, she listened for any sounds in the hallway. All was silent.

Where to start? Jenny stood in the center of the library and turned a circle. There were hundred of books, if not thousands. All were bound like the classics offered on the back page of the Sunday book section. None looked remotely like a personal journal.

Then she saw it: a shelf spaced more widely than the others, enclosed by glass doors. The lock securing the doors was all too modern. She adjusted the reading lamp so the light shone through the milky glass. Inside rested several large, coffee-brown ledgers stacked one on the other, similar in size and style to the census ledgers she had consulted at the Hall of Records.

Jenny hiked up her dress and wrapped her right hand in the thick muslin cloth. Stepping close to the bookshelf, she thrust her fist through the glass, shattering it. The noise was muted, a few wayward shards tinkling onto the floor. She turned her head toward the door, waiting, praying no one would come. Reaching inside, she freed first one volume, then another. Six remained. She carried the two volumes to the chair and sat down. With care, she opened the cover of one. The pages were brittle and yellow with age. Tea stains darkened the paper. *The records*. She was sure she had found them.

The first page was blank.

The second as well.

Jenny's heart beat faster.

On the third page were photographs. Four wallet-sized black-and-white prints affixed to the page by corner holders. The pictures were wrinkled with age. In each, a smiling blond child dressed in a sailor's suit held a sailboat to his chest. The writing beneath each picture was hard to read in the dim light. Lifting the scrapbook closer, she read, 'J.J. 1935.'

She turned the page and found more pictures. Jacklin with his mother and father. With the housekeeper. With his sister. Closing the cover, she rose and checked the other books inside the glass cabinet. The Jacklin family photo albums and nothing else.

Frustrated and anxious, she put the books back, then returned to the Long Room. She swept her eyes from one wall to the other, but saw no place where you could hide any books. She'd already checked the cabinets. She was growing frantic. They had met here. *The club*. She was sure of it. Jacklin's smug tone had all but confirmed it. The horny old lech. Jenny shuddered, thinking of his hand kneading her bottom. What did he think she was made of? Cookie dough?

She thought back to her visit to the Hall of Records. The directory of New York City published in 1796 had been in remarkably good condition. Why? Because it had been stored in a cool place, away from sunlight. She poked her head back into the library. The bookshelves were exposed to direct sunlight at least half the day. The heat was roaring, the air dry as tinder. In the summer, it would be the air conditioning's turn. No one would store precious journals there.

A cool place shielded from sunlight.

A constant temperature of sixty-five degrees.

Just the right degree of humidity.

Her eyes fell on the humidor. It was built as part of the burled-wood cabinet, but after looking at it a moment, she saw that the cabinet had no doors. She crossed the room and flipped open the top. The rich, muscular scent of tobacco assailed her. Kneeling, she looked more closely at the cabinet, running her hands along the front and sides. A faint crack was visible at the right rear corner. Jenny slipped her fingernail into it and tried to pry it open, but the damn thing didn't give. She stood and closed the humidor's lid. Placing a hand halfway down either side, she lifted.

The humidor opened like a music box.

She peered inside.

A leather journal peered back. It was no larger than the standard hardcover novel. She picked it up, and noticed there was another under it, and another beneath that. The books were in impeccable condition. With care, she opened the cover. There, written in immaculate looping script, were the words:

The Patriots' Club
June 1, 1843–July 31, 1878
Minutes

Chapter 62

'J. J. . . . a word?'

'Yes, what is it?' replied Jacklin. 'Has the President arrived?'

'Not yet,' replied Guilfoyle, crouching at his side. 'He's due in eight minutes. His motorcade just crossed Key Bridge.'

Jacklin smiled obligingly at his guests. Dinner had been served. The dance floor was packed to bursting. The plates had been cleared; a *digestif* offered. He raised the snifter of Armagnac to his mouth and took a sip. 'What is it, then?'

'Bolden's woman is in DC.'

'I thought she was laid up in the hospital.'

'Hoover just contacted me from the operations center. Cerberus spat out some credit-card activity indicating she purchased a ticket on the US Airways shuttle and rented a car at Reagan National Airport.'

'Why are you telling me this now? Cerberus is a real-time program. It should have given us the information hours ago.'

'The boys in the op center thought she was in the hospital, too. No one inputted her vitals until a couple of hours ago.'

Jacklin checked his temper. He had half a mind to cuff this unfeeling robot right then and there. 'And you think she's headed here?'

'She also purchased evening wear from a boutique on Madison Avenue.'

Jacklin excused himself from the table and led Guilfoyle outside. A freshening breeze snapped at their cheeks. 'Look at that,' he said, scanning the leaden sky. 'We're going to have one hell of an inauguration.'

Guilfoyle looked up at the sky, but said nothing.

'And the cop?' Jacklin asked. 'You getting what you need?'

'In time.'

Jacklin turned suddenly and grabbed Guilfoyle by the lapels. 'We don't have time. Can't you get that through your head? I ask for results and you bring me more problems. For all your supposed intuition, you've shown all the foresight of a chimpanzee. First you screw up with Bolden, then you can't make this cop give us what we need. Now you're telling me that Bolden's girlfriend might be trying to mess things up. Thank God, it's just a woman.' He released the lapels, breathing through his teeth. 'What does she look like, anyway?'

'No picture, yet. She's thirty, tall and blond with wavy hair down to her shoulders. Reasonably attractive.'

'What's her name?'

'Dance. Jennifer Dance.'

Jacklin leaned closer. '*Jennifer?*'

This was the rough stuff. The stuff that happened when you got too close to the cartels, or hounded the Mob a little too much. This was the stuff you read about and shook your head, and when you went to sleep that night, you prayed it would never happen to you. When they beat you up before they start asking questions, when they hit you so hard that suddenly, you can't remember the last five minutes, or where you are even, you know it's the rough stuff. And you know how it's going to end.

'I'm a cop,' Franciscus said, through his broken teeth, though it sounded like 'Thime a thop.' 'I don't take evidence with me.'

'Did you leave it in New York?'

Franciscus tried to lift his head, but his neck seemed locked in a downward position. They had taken their time beating him. They'd started on his face, then worked down to his gut, going methodically step by step, like the local train stopping at every station. He was fairly certain that his cheekbone was fractured. He could still feel the punch that had done that. Contractors, he had told Bolden. The best his government could train.

Someone hit him again in the face, directly on the busted cheek. He heard the impact from afar, the bone shattering like a china plate. His eyes remained open, but he saw nothing, just sparks from a flare exploding in the center of his brain. He passed out for a minute or two. He had no idea how long, really, except that the same goons were still there when he came to. Both had removed their jackets. Their shoulder holsters cradled nine-millimeter pistols.

Lying on the concrete floor, he saw his thumb a few inches away. He willed it to budge, and a second later, it did, jittering as if juiced with a thousand volts. The sound of his breathing filled his ear. It was a thin, wheezing rasp, and he thought, *Christ, whoever sounds like that is gonna check out pronto*.

It was then that he decided, no. He wasn't done yet. He wasn't going to allow these two gorillas to finish him off. He would not let them kill him here and now, not without a fight. The drums of his rebellion pounded faintly, but unmistakably. War drums. A few hundred yards down the path, a hundred men and women were drinking and dancing the night away. Reach them and he was safe. He would flash his badge. He would give his name. He'd get the collar, one way or the other. Jacklin would be his.

Franciscus summoned his resolve. He needed to act quickly, while he had enough strength to make it to the main house. He lay as still as a rock, holding his breath. One of his interrogators knew right away something was wrong. You were supposed to jerk when you got hit, not just lie there. He came closer, looking at Franciscus as if he were a landed croc that might have some bite left in him.

'I think our man's checked out. He's blue.'

The other man laughed skeptically. 'Has he stopped sweating? That's when you'll know if he's dead.'

'I think it's his heart.'

'Let me have a look.' The man dropped to a knee and bent over Franciscus. First he put a hand on his wrist. Then he looked at his associate, and the look was enough to get the man down on the floor of the tack room, too. 'I can't find a pulse. See if you can feel anything.'

'He's cold. Fuckin' Guilfoyle. I told him it was stupid to beat up on a senior. My dad's a cop, too. I don't want this on my conscience.'

'Shh. I'm still listening.'

'And?'

'Nothing.'

'Go get him. The guy's turning bluer than a fish.'

Jennifer Dance was reading the minutes of the Patriots' Club.

December 6, 1854

Present: Franklin Pierce. Henry Ward Beecher. Frederick Douglass. Horace Greeley. Thomas Hart Benton.

'. . . the Committee votes in favor of a grant of $25,000 to assist Mr Beecher in the purchase of Sharps rifles for overland shipment to Kansas in support of the abolitionist/antislavery movement.'

The guns were later named Beecher's Bibles by the Northern press, and they turned the state of Kansas into a battleground that was nicknamed Bloody Kansas.

Sept. 8, 1859

Present: James Buchanan. William Seward. Horace Greeley. Ralph Waldo Emerson. Henry Ward Beecher.

'. . . all ammunition to be provided to Mr John Brown and sons in support of his proposed raiding of the arsenal at Harpers Ferry . . .'

John Brown's raid on Harpers Ferry failed, but his subsequent conviction for treason against the commonwealth of Virginia and his execution by hanging hastened the advent of the Civil War.

April 1, 1864

Present: Abraham Lincoln. William Seward. U. S. Grant. Salmon P. Chase. Horace Greeley. Cornelius Vanderbilt.

'. . . the Committee votes against General Lee's petition asking for a truce between the Union and the Confederacy, the Confederacy accepting the Emancipation Proclamation with all territorial issues reverting to status quo ante bellum.'

A truce? Jenny had never heard of a failed truce between the states. Abraham Lincoln had pressed the war until the South had surrendered, exhausted, depleted, and without any chance of further victory on the battlefield.

Jenny opened the second ledger, dated 1878–

1904. She thumbed the pages until she came to the date of January 31, 1898.

Present: William McKinley. Alfred Thayer Mahan. Elihu Root. J. P. Morgan. John Rockefeller. J. J. Astor. Thomas B. Reed. Frederick Jackson Turner.

'We can no longer overlook the pressing requirement for our nation to acquire global colonies. At the least, a string of coaling stations across the Pacific necessary for the expanding fleet . . . it is imperative that we check the British colossus as a world power.'

Her eyes skipped down the page.

'. . . an incident required to galvanize the American people in support of war . . . suitable targets: Cuba, Haiti, the Philippines . . . all lands where a democratic presence would be viewed as a liberator and widely welcomed by local populace . . . Mr Root proposed scuttling of USS Maine, *second-class battleship cruising in Cuban waters.'*

Voices carried into the room from the corridor. Jenny flipped the pages forward, faster and faster yet. She was searching for one more name, a last indication that against whatever argument she might muster, it was all true.

March 13, 1915. Present: Woodrow Wilson, Colonel A. E. House, General J. J. Pershing, Theodore Roosevelt, J. P. Morgan, Vincent Astor.

'. . . a means to enter European conflict is now of primary importance . . . unrestricted submarine warfare an assault on civility of conflict . . . the Cunard liner Lusitania *will depart New York on May 1. The War Department is shipping two thousand tons of ammunition for the allied war effort. Items are not on manifest . . . an irresistible target for German navy . . .'*

The door burst open.

Jacklin stood framed by the light. Two of his bodyguards waited behind him. She recognized them from the night before. Wolf and Irish. Jacklin walked slowly across the room and plucked the journal from her hands.

'Miss Dance . . . is it?'

Chapter 63

'Take off the restraints,' said James Jacklin, entering the guesthouse and laying eyes on Bolden. 'Jesus Christ. The man's a banker, not a convict.' The tall, grim-faced man hurried toward him, occasionally admonishing Wolf to get the job done faster. 'That better, Tom?'

Bolden rubbed his wrists. 'Yes,' he said. 'Thank you.'

'Well now,' said Jacklin, sizing him up. 'What can I get you? Beer? Scotch? Name your poison.'

'I could use a glass of water.'

Jacklin fired off a command for some water, and a little something to eat, but for all the talk about the restraints being some kind of mistake, he made sure to keep his bodyguard nearby. 'Jesus Christ, Tom, would you care to tell me how we got so far down the wrong road? As I recall, we even made you an offer a few months back.'

'You tell me. I think it might have started last night when Wolf, here, and Irish kidnapped me.'

'A regrettable mistake,' said Jacklin, lowering his head as if the whole thing plain embarrassed him. 'I do apologize. Mr Guilfoyle handles that side of things.'

'Mr Guilfoyle knows damn well that I had no knowledge of Crown or Bobby Stillman.'

A figure stirred in the corner of the room. Guilfoyle rose from a club chair. 'Maybe I can clear up the misunderstanding,' he said, hands tucked in his pockets, as close to a pleasant expression on his face as Bolden had seen. 'Tom, as you know, Jefferson holds in its portfolio a good many companies active in the information technology sector – companies engaged in the manufacture of both computer hardware and software, much of it with applications in the defense sector. Suffice it to say that our systems pinpointed no fewer than four indicators that you posed a threat to Jefferson.'

Trendrite. National Bank Data. Triton Aerospace. Bolden knew the companies to which Guilfoyle referred. 'I guess you've got a long way toward perfecting the code on that one. Tell me if I'm wrong, but wasn't that software designed to heighten national security? What's Jefferson doing messing with it?'

Guilfoyle answered matter-of-factly. 'There are corporate applications we'd be foolish not to take advantage of. One of them indicated that you'd been in contact with Bobby Stillman.'

'I've never spoken with any Bobby Stillman in my life,' said Bolden.

Guilfoyle persisted. 'How do you explain the calls placed from your home in New York to Ms Stillman's temporary residence in New Jersey?'

'There's nothing to explain. I don't know the man. I never made the calls.'

'The man?' Jacklin shook his head. 'Bobby Stillman's a woman as I'm sure you know. Records don't lie. You phoned her on the nights of January tenth, eleventh, and twelfth.'

'That would be difficult considering I was in Milwaukee the tenth and eleventh, and Denver the day after. Or didn't your software tell you that? And who are you to tell me that records don't lie? It was easy enough for you to hack into my bank's mainframe and destroy my credit. At least, I know now how you got into HW's system. Mickey Schiff helped you.'

'A necessity,' said Guilfoyle.

'It's a breach of privacy.'

Jacklin laughed bitterly. 'Exactly what Bobby would say.'

'*Bobby*? So you're friends?'

'Hardly,' said Jacklin.

'Who is she?' Bolden demanded. 'Why are you so hell-bent on killing me because you think I've been in contact with her?'

'A thorn in my side is what she is. We're still working to determine your status.' Jacklin exhaled loudly, raising his hands in a gesture of pacification. 'Look, Tom,' he said, agreeably. 'The world is a dangerous place. We're simply doing our job to protect the country.'

'It sounds to me like you're protecting your interests.'

'Take it easy.'

'No thanks.'

'Listen to me for a minute and you might find you'll learn something.'

Bolden decided that there was nothing to gain from defiance. He sat. 'I'm all ears.'

Jacklin sighed and took the chair across from him. 'Some of the companies Mr Guilfoyle referred to were involved in the government's efforts to build a terrorist surveillance system. The technology is sophisticated, cutting-edge stuff that involved being granted access to a lot of sensitive private data. When the public got wind of it, they grew nervous. No one likes the idea of the government having that kind of access. The potential for abuse is too high. They demanded the

Department of Defense put an end to it. But technology is a Pandora's box. Once it's opened, there's no denying what's inside. There's no going back. Either we capture that technology, control it, and fashion it to our purposes, or someone else will. Someone unfriendly to the cause. When things became touchy, some of my old friends at DOD asked if we might step in. Put the company in one of our funds. Let the Feds monitor progress from afar. Does that surprise you?'

'No,' Bolden admitted. Part of him even thought it was a good idea. Naturally, there were times when the government needed to work on projects out of the public domain. 'But you couldn't resist, could you?' he asked. 'The first thing you did was harness the little we knew and put it to your own use. That's how you ended up pinning everything on the wrong guy. I do have one question.'

'Shoot,' said Jacklin.

'If you're so damned tight with the government, why do you have to bribe every other retiring senator or to offer them jobs?'

' "Bribe"? Is that what you call it? We like to think of it as a pre-employment incentive.' Jacklin dismissed their difference with a wave of the hand. 'That's an operational issue. We make investments in individuals to assist our investments in companies. It's in our clients' best interests, and I admit, our own. Tom . . . you're a smart man. You've seen some things you shouldn't have. You've been subjected to some unpleasant things. We're here to put all that behind us. You've received my apology. Can we start there?'

'And Jenny? Did you apologize to her for shooting her? She's pregnant. Did you know that? Or would it even figure into your calculations?'

Jacklin's right eye twitched, but he kept the same

conciliatory expression, the freeze-dried grin firmly in place. 'As I said, I am sorry. I must, however, ask if you've showed the records of the financial transfers we've made to certain executives at our company and to certain officials on the Hill to anyone else? Have you made any copies? Have you e-mailed them to a friend?'

'Ask Wolf. He was there.'

'Wolf isn't sure.'

'And if I have?'

Jacklin looked to Guilfoyle, then back at Bolden. 'Tom, let me be blunt. We want you to join Jefferson. Like I said, you're a smart young man. You work like the dickens. You've got a tremendous record of accomplishment. The way I see it, we're over the awkward part. You've seen some of the dirty laundry. Is it really that big? Of course not. Not in the greater scheme of things. Let's work that to your advantage. I can use a personal assistant. I'm not going to be around that much longer. Ten years, if my liver holds out. I want you to work with me. At my side. Name your price. I can't offer you a partnership yet. But in three or four years? The sky's the limit for someone of your abilities. The boys at Scanlon couldn't believe how you put one over on them. We'll start you at a million even. You can count on double that for a bonus. Not bad for a young man who's still a little wet behind the ears. Bring Jenny to DC. She's a history buff, she'll love it. We'll set both of you up in a cozy little townhouse in Georgetown. Get you involved with the Boys' Club down in this neck of the woods. We need a man with some fire in his blood. Christ knows, I need someone to rouse my butt out of the sack on some of the cold mornings. What do you say, Tom?' Jacklin extended his hand. 'The world's yours for the asking.'

Bolden looked at the outstretched hand. Money. Position. Privilege. He smiled tiredly. It was a lie, of course. Jacklin had no intention of keeping such a bargain. Bolden sincerely wondered what he'd done to be taken for such a greedy fool, or if Jacklin just assumed everyone in his profession must share such values.

He raised his gaze and stared into Jacklin's brown eyes. 'I don't think my mother would like it very much.'

The triumphant expression melted from Jacklin's face like a late snow. 'Do you know what you're saying?'

'I have an idea.'

Jacklin looked to Guilfoyle, who shrugged, then back at Bolden. His face was harder now, the eyes set, the mouth turned down. 'Did you give the information to anyone else?'

Bolden shrugged. 'Maybe.'

'That's not good enough.'

'It'll have to be.'

Jacklin turned to Guilfoyle. 'Is he telling the truth?'

'I don't know.'

'What do you mean, you don't know?' Jacklin snapped.

Guilfoyle remained staring at Bolden. 'I'm sorry, J. J., but I don't know.'

'Bring her in, then.'

Bolden rose from the chair, starting for the door. Firm hands gripped him from behind, forcing him onto the seat. The door opened. Jenny walked in, accompanied by Irish. 'Tom . . .'

'Jenny!' Bolden reached out for her, but Irish held her back. She was alive, and unhurt. 'You're all right.'

She nodded, and he could see she was hiding something from him.

'I'll ask you again, Tom,' said Jacklin. 'Did you make any copies of the financial information? If you think I have any qualms about hurting Miss Dance, think again.' He crossed the short distance to Jennifer and backhanded her across the face, his ring opening a cut on her cheek.

'Stop!' yelled Bolden, struggling to get free. 'The answer is no. I didn't make any copies. I didn't send any of the information I found on Mickey Schiff's computer to anyone. I didn't have time. Wolf took the only copies I had.'

Jacklin offered a last look as he left the room. 'My guess is you're lying. We'll have to leave it to Wolf to find out if I'm right.'

Chapter 64

The tip of the knife came to rest a millimeter above Bolden's bare chest. It was a Ka-Bar, with white athletic tape wrapped around the handle. One side of the blade was serrated, the other sharpened like nothing Bolden had ever seen. Hands bound behind his back, feet tied to the legs of the chair, it was impossible to move.

'Why are you doing this?' he asked. 'You know I didn't send any papers. You were watching me the entire time.'

Wolf sniffed the air, giving the question his full consideration. 'Easy really: to settle the score. Make sure you go to the Lord with a sign that you crossed the Wolf's path. It's important to mark the bad guys.'

'Kill 'em all. Let God sort 'em out. Is that it?'

'Oh, I'm not going to kill you. Not yet.' He stuffed a cotton handkerchief into Bolden's mouth and pulled a piece of tape across his lips. 'Some of the guys liked to beat up the Muj. Knock 'em around until their brains were mushy, then start asking 'em questions. Others liked to work on fingers or toes. Crush their knuckles, whatever. Not me. I like the skin. Most people know what to expect when you snap their fingers or stuff bamboo under their fingernails. No one knows what it's like to have your skin peeled off your body, strip by strip. That's their fuckin' nightmare, man. It's medieval. I think it's the fear as much as the pain that makes them talk.'

The point of the knife pressed into Bolden's chest, an inch to the right of his nipple. A bead of blood bubbled around it. The knife cut deeper, Wolf drawing the blade in a straight line toward Bolden's belly. When he reached his waist, he cut horizontally an inch, then twisted the blade and brought it back up.

Until now, the pain had been extreme, but bearable. Bolden stared into Wolf's eyes and darkness stared back. The abyss.

'To those about to rock,' said Wolf. 'We salute you.'

Spearing the strip of outlined flesh, Wolf yanked the blade up.

Bolden screamed.

Jacklin spotted Hugh Fitzgerald deep in conversation with Frances Tavistock.

'I see you two have met,' he said, pulling up a chair and joining them at their table.

The former British prime minister was an elegant older woman, with coiffed graying hair, a stern countenance, and a patrician manner that would have done Queen Victoria proud. 'Senator Fitzgerald's been telling me about his time up at Oxford. Did you know we were both at Balliol? What a marvelous coincidence.'

'Yes, I had to admit to Frances that she wasn't all bad, considering she's a Tory.'

'Oh, Hugh,' she said, slapping his leg. 'Tony's practically come out of the closet himself.'

'Does that mean you're coming to our side of the table?' Jacklin asked.

'I do think we've made some progress educating the senator about the true nature of the world,' said

Tavistock. 'Bad, bad, bad. Isn't that so? It really is "us against them". One can never possess enough of an advantage.'

'Simple common sense,' said Jacklin. 'But it's the soldiers I'm worried about. Our boys don't deserve to die just because one society has an inferiority complex toward America. I'm sorry, but that's just the way I feel about it.'

'All right, you two,' said Hugh Fitzgerald. 'That's enough. You win. J. J., you'll have my recommendation for the appropriations bill tomorrow. Frances has convinced me that six billion dollars isn't too much to pay to ensure that our boys are as safe as they can be.'

'Hear! Hear!' said Frances Tavistock, grasping Fitzgerald's hand and giving it a squeeze. 'Doesn't it feel good to do what's right?'

'Offer still stands if you're retiring,' said Jacklin. 'We've an office with your name on it.'

'Oh, do sign up with Jefferson, Hugh. It would be lovely. I've got to have someone to join me for roast beef and Yorkshire pudding on my visits.'

But Fitzgerald would only go so far in one night. 'I'll think about it, J. J. Give me some time.'

Jacklin stood. 'Take all the time you need.'

The orchestra struck up 'Witchcraft'. Fitzgerald extended a hand toward Mrs Tavistock. 'Care to dance?'

'Once we had a real tough Muj,' said Wolf. 'He was as mean as a rabid dog. Six foot seven. Towered over me. These crazy blue eyes. We are talking wild. He was a warlord, had about two hundred savages under his control. And make no mistake, they were savages. I respect all religions, Islam, Buddha, what have you . . . but these guys . . . they came from another world, man. I mean, they weren't even human. I found this guy easy enough. We brought him back to the base at Bagram to do a debrief. To tell you the truth, I was scared of him. I thought this sonuvabitch was going to outlast me. He was walking around on a busted knee. How much does that hurt?' Wolf shook his head in amazement. 'Know how long it took before he spilled the beans? Ten minutes. Didn't even get to finish the star I was cutting into him, my little reminder of his time with Uncle Sam. Now you, you're still going strong. Tough little turd, aren't you?'

Wolf pulled the gag out of Bolden's mouth, then poked the tip of the blade into his chest. 'One more time, Tommy. Did you make any copies of Mr Jacklin's files?'

'Didn't have time,' whispered Bolden. 'You were there.' His mouth was dry, his lips crusted with spittle. He couldn't look at himself. It would be worse if he saw what Wolf had done to him. His breath came in short bursts, the slightest expansion of his ribs plunging a serrated spear into the farthest recesses of his belly. Fire. He was on fire.

'Liar,' said Wolf. 'I know you did. Just tell me where you sent them.'

'No time. You saw. No time.'

'Wrong answer,' said Wolf.

Beneath the flickering light, the knife flashed.

When he was finished, Wolf threw Bolden into the room with Jenny. 'Looks like he was telling the truth. Take care of your man. He's a tough one.'

Jenny stared at Bolden's chest, at the orthodox crucifix carved into his flesh, and stifled a scream. 'My God, what have you done to him?'

'Marked him for the Lord.'

Bolden staggered and fell into her arms.

Chapter 65

The old ship's clock struck midnight. Around the table, all heads bowed in prayer.

'. . . and so we thank you, Lord. Amen,' intoned Gordon Ramser, President of the United States. He looked up. 'We all have a busy day tomorrow. Let's keep this meeting as brief as possible. I'm sorry to report that my discussion with Senator McCoy did not produce the desired results.'

'Would've taken that bet at ten to one,' said James Jacklin.

'A shame,' said Ramser. 'She would have been a solid addition.'

'No shame at all.' Jacklin despised this maudlin hypocrisy. Either you stood with them or against them. All the moralizing in the world didn't change what the men in this room had to do, or what those actions branded them. 'We'd be looking at eight years of playing it safe,' he went on. 'Kissing our allies' asses and saying mea culpas for having the guts to do what was right, instead of what was expedient. Mrs McCoy's first trip would be to France, and she'd follow that up with a ride up the Rhine with her lips firmly planted on the German chancellor's ass, all in the name of re-establishing our reputation as a team player. Alliances breed indecision. There's not one thing to be gained from playing kissy-face with old Europe. Hell, they want nothing better than to see us fall on our ass, anyway.

McCoy's standoffishness is the best thing we could have asked for, besides getting our own man put into the White House. Any plans we had for Iran and Syria would have been scotched then and there. The whole Middle East would sink back into that pit of fundamentalist quicksand. Everything we've done would have gone for naught. I don't even want to think what she'd do to defense spending.'

'Defense spending?' asked John Von Arx, director of the FBI. 'Is that what this is all about? We're talking about taking the life of the next President of the United States. Jesus Christ, J. J., sometimes I think you confuse what's good for the country with what's good for your company.'

'What do you mean by that?' snorted Jacklin.

'It means I don't like you asking me to call out my boys to solve your own problems. I'm talking about Tom Bolden and what transpired this morning in Manhattan.'

'Bolden was a threat that needed to be neutralized.'

'I heard it was an error.'

'Who told you that?'

'I do run the FBI. I have a few sources.' Von Arx addressed the other members seated at the table. 'Some of my guys looked at that tape of Sol Weiss being shot. They say it was faked. Top-quality work, but their computers spotted it in a jiff. It would never hold up in court.'

'It was a judgment call,' said Jacklin. 'He was a threat to Crown. We needed to get him off the street.'

'Where is he now?' asked Von Arx.

'He's been contained. You don't have to worry about it any longer.'

Gordon Ramser clasped his hands on the table and directed a long, hard gaze at Jacklin. 'The rumors about Jefferson are getting out of hand,' he said. 'Your "revolving door" is becoming a popular topic for the press corps. All this talk about "access capitalism" has to stop. Are we clear on that, J. J.?'

'That's right, boys,' said Jacklin. 'I only bribe 'em when you tell me to.'

'The feeling is that you're gorging yourself at the public trough,' said Chief Justice Logsdon.

'Bullroar!' exclaimed Jacklin.

'A word to the wise, J. J.,' cautioned Ramser. 'Don't confuse the Committee's policies and your company's.'

Jacklin shook his head in disgust and disbelief. 'Don't talk to me about keeping public and private separate. Old Pierpont Morgan helped get us into the Great War and his company practically underwrote the whole thing. The history of this country is nothing but the government helping out the private sector, and vice versa. One hand washing the other. Hamilton knew it when he started the club with Nat Pendleton. Economics must dictate the country's policies.'

'You like to mention Hamilton so much,' said Charles Connolly, also known as Rufus King. 'He made it a point never to take a profit from policies he had a say in. He repeatedly turned down territories in Ohio and the Missouri Valley that would have made him immensely rich.'

'He also got us started down this rocky road by getting rid of that scoundrel who was threatening the Jay Treaty. Don't go moralizing to me about Hamilton. He was no saint. The man was a skirt chaser of the first degree. "The man had an overabundance of secretions no number of whores could satisfy." I believe I got that quote from your book, Charlie.' Jacklin pushed his chair back and stood up. 'I've read those minutes, too. Go tell it to

John Rockefeller and Standard Oil and Commodore Vanderbilt and his railroads. They all sat in my chair before me. Go tell it to Averell Harriman and his cronies. They all got rich from decisions that were made right here. The business of America is business. A wiser man than me already said it.'

'Those were different times,' said Gordon Ramser. 'Far less transparent. We can't afford to attract any undue scrutiny.'

Jacklin rested a hand on the back of his chair. 'What are you all driving at?'

'Just watch what you're doing,' said Ramser, forcefully. 'We can't risk your actions discrediting our motives. The good of the nation comes first. Remember that.'

'I'll be sure to tell it to Hugh Fitzgerald. He's decided to give us his vote. The appropriations bill will pass. Our pre-pos should be restocked within six months. We can continue with our plans to bring some light to that godforsaken desert.'

'Congratulations,' said Ramser. A few of the others joined in, but Jacklin thought their voices hollow, insincere. He noted the veiled stares, the averted faces. They'd been talking behind his back again. He knew the reasons why. He was too direct. Too brash for them. He was the only one who had the gumption to tell it like it is. Not one of these two-faced bastards dared look him in the eye. They'd been shoveling bullshit for so long, they'd grown to like the smell.

Jacklin cleared his throat. 'I believe we were talking about Senator McCoy. It's got to be done up close. I have something our British subsidiary developed for MI Six . . .'

'Excuse me, J. J., but I don't believe we've taken a final vote on the matter,' said Chief Justice Logsdon.

'A vote? We decided last night. Gordon gave it a

last shot and she turned him down. Our hands are tied. The President has always been a member. If she can't take the hint, then she's making her own bed. God knows, we're better off without her.'

'No!' said Charles Connolly, and the word echoed around the room.

'No what?' asked Jacklin.

'We can't do it. She's the President. The people elected her. It isn't right.'

Jacklin walked the length of the table. 'Since when do we care what the people say? This committee was created to temper the people's will. To stop them from running this country into the ground.'

'It was not created to kill the President,' Connolly retorted.

'Sounds like you're afraid you'll lose your special pass at the White House. Did McCoy already promise to pull back the curtains and give you an insider's view of how she saves us from the "new Vietnam"? Is that it, Charlie? No grist for the new book?'

'Don't you see?' Connolly continued. 'Any authority we claim comes from the President's presence. Without him ... or her ... we're not patriots, we're renegades.' He shot a corrosive look at Jacklin. 'Just a bunch of businessmen looking to enrich ourselves at the country's expense.'

'That's nonsense!' said Jacklin.

'Is it? The people expect the President to do what's necessary. They realize that there are times when he can't consult them, maybe even, when he shouldn't. It's their implicit trust in him that gives us our legitimacy. Hamilton would never have started the club without Washington.'

'Screw him,' said Jacklin. 'He's been dead two hundred years.'

'But his ideas are still alive,' shouted Connolly right back.

'The club's grown bigger than one person,' said Jacklin. 'I don't care if it's the President or not. We have responsibilities to the nation. We have a history. You ask me, the country practically belongs to us. We bribed that Frog Talleyrand to make the Louisiana Purchase happen. We convinced old Dupont to help underwrite the loan that paid for it. Whose idea was it to blackmail the Tsar so he'd sell us Alaska for three cents an acre? We've helped facilitate every major acquisition of territory in this country's history. You say we need the President. I say we are the President. This is the White House, right here!'

'Shut up, J. J.,' said Chief Justice Logsdon. 'You've gone too far.'

'No such place,' said Jacklin, dismissing the comment with a nasty wave.

'And you others?' asked Ramser. 'Have you changed your mind?'

For a few moments, no one in the room spoke. Only the ticking of John Paul Jones's ship's clock filled the room. Jacklin paced back and forth, like a beleaguered ship's captain. 'Come on, Von Arx,' he said, putting a hand on the FBI director's shoulder. 'You know what's right.'

Von Arx nodded reluctantly. 'I'm sorry, J. J., but I have to agree with Charlie,' he said. 'It's tampering. We've got to give McCoy a chance to come to us. Her time in office will make a convert out of her.'

'Me, too,' said Logsdon. 'Give the woman time.'

'And you?' Jacklin said, facing President Gordon Ramser.

'It doesn't matter what I say. That's three votes against. A unanimous vote is required for measures of this kind.'

'Screw the bylaws. What do you think we should do?'

Ramser rose from his chair and walked over to Jacklin. 'J. J.,' he said. 'I think we may have gotten ahead of ourselves on this one. There's no hurry now that Fitzgerald's given us his vote. The military needs at least six months before they can make any move. The joint chiefs are busy revising their battle plan. Let's all take a breath and calm down. Like the chief justice says, "Give the woman time." ' He laughed richly to paper over the discord. 'She has no idea what she's in for.'

Jacklin forced a smile to his face, joining the others in laughter. But inside him, his gut clenched and his nerves hummed with near unbearable tension. Gordon Ramser was right. She had no idea.

Chapter 66

They walked outside, descending a short flight of stairs, then starting down a gravel path flanked by neatly trimmed hedges. The path led into a patch of woods, and within a minute, the woods became a forest, menacing and primeval, a thick canopy overhead allowing only a smattering of snowflakes to fall to the ground. The dark was utter and complete.

'Keep walking,' said Wolf.

Bolden picked up his feet and shuffled forward. He wore a loose shirt unbuttoned to the waist and a stained Mackinaw jacket someone had thrown over his shoulders. His chest was raw, fiery, his horribly scored flesh tightening as the wound congealed. The brush of the cold air, the prick of the snow against his skin, brought tears to his eyes.

He glanced behind him. A third bodyguard had joined Wolf and Irish. Somewhere ahead and off to the left, he caught a pair of red lights flash, then go dark. Brake lights, he guessed. The others had seen it, too. Their lack of concern extinguished his hope. The lights belonged to his hearse.

Alone, he and Jenny had spent a few minutes together. They'd sat hand in hand taking turns sharing what they had learned. About Jefferson bribing so many government officials. About Jacklin and the Patriots' Club. Mostly, though, they talked about the baby.

Jenny told him, 'I'm sure it's a boy,' and Bolden suggested 'Jack' as a name. It was a name he'd always liked. He suggested they raise him in Costa Rica, or maybe Fiji. Somewhere warm and far away from the United States. After some prodding, he agreed to Connecticut or northern New Jersey. A house on the water in Greenwich sounded inviting. Jack could learn to sail. Tom would learn first, so he could teach him. They wanted him in public schools. Jenny thought piano would be nice. Bolden said basketball was a must.

And Bolden . . . what would he do? He was done with investment banking. That much was certain. He didn't know what he might be good at. He had some money saved, so he wouldn't have to do anything for a couple of years. Jenny would stay home with Jack. Her job showed her the effects not having a mother had on someone . . . just look at Tom. They'd laughed at that. Pretty soon, Jack would have a sister, and that would be all. She wanted to travel as a family, and four was a good, round number.

Dreams.

Bolden looked around him. Trees crowded in on the path. His universe shrank to a narrow tunnel with neither beginning nor end. He grabbed Jenny's hand. 'I love you,' he said.

'I love you, too.'

'For ever.'

For a moment, Bolden thought about running. But where? They were hemmed in on all sides. He couldn't see ten feet in front of him. He'd be lucky to get a step before they cut him down. It didn't matter. His ruined chest prevented him from running at all.

They came to a small clearing, a circular expanse that might have welcomed a bonfire.

'Hold up, hoss,' said Wolf. 'On your knees.'

Bolden stopped. Jenny looked at him and he nodded. They knelt together. The ground was icy, littered with twigs and small rocks. His heart was beating very fast. A gun was racked close to his ear. Something cold and hard touched the nape of his neck.

He reached out for Jenny's hand and prayed.

Bobby Stillman cut through the woods with a stealth born of experience. For twenty-five years she'd been ducking out of back doors, vaulting over fences and, in general, acting like a fugitive half her age. In all that time, she'd never used her skills to save someone else. Harry followed a step behind, Walter pulling up the rear. The forces of liberty and justice, she'd named them.

It was no miracle that they'd found Thomas. They'd forced their captive to contact headquarters and report that he'd been kidnapped by Bobby Stillman, but had managed to escape. Headquarters had informed him that Bolden was being transported to Jacklin's estate. It was technology that allowed Bobby Stillman to track the Scanlon operatives nearby. If Harry was their brawn, then Walter was their brains. He'd simply built a receiver to track the signals emitted by the chips implanted in the Scanlon operatives.

The footsteps ahead of them had stopped.

Bobby drew to a halt. 'Harry?' she whispered.

A hulking shadow came near. 'We've got to split up,' he said. 'Go around them. Walk softly. Heel to toe.'

In the dark, Bobby could make out a clump of figures. One, two . . . she wasn't sure how many. She waited a moment to let Harry get into position, then began to inch through the undergrowth. Twigs scratched her cheek. A branch blocked her way. With infinite patience, she pushed it aside and skirted it. She wasn't sure how to intercede. Harry carried a leather sap, but otherwise they didn't have any real weapons. She'd never allowed them to carry guns or knives. It was a point of pride she was deeply regretting. Each carried a Maglite flashlight. The lights and whatever surprise they could muster would have to suffice.

When she was twenty feet away, she sank down and waited. The night closed around her. The wind whistled through the bushes, biting at her cheek. In a minute, her joints began to ache.

Alone in the dark, Bobby Stillman's mind was flooded with memories of the day she had left her son.

They were coming!

She saw him fleeing down the hallway of her apartment in the Village. He was just a boy, and gripped by a child's unspeakable panic. She was at his back, exhorting him to hurry. At the end of the hall, he flung open a closet door. She crouched at his side and lifted up the floorboards to reveal a neat rectangular space dug into the earth.

'Jump in,' she said.

Little Jack dropped into the hole and lay down in a single fluid motion, just as they'd practiced so many times before. She stared at him, her thin, anxious son with his mop of curly hair. He was a good boy, so eager to please, so obedient, yet the tears always so near. It was because of her, she knew. He had adopted her paranoia, her anxieties, her everlasting fear of the world.

'I'll be back for you,' she said.

'When?' he asked.

She didn't answer. She couldn't bring herself to lie to him again. How could she say 'never'?

Working quickly, she replaced the floorboards. He remained still, his arms pressed to his sides. Sensing his fear, she bent to him. The flyaway strands of her unruly red hair tickled his cheek. She smiled and his eyes widened and he looked as if everything would be all right. But a moment later, he was lost in his waking nightmare. He knew his mother was leaving and she had said nothing to make him think differently. The tears streamed from his eyes. Silent tears. Obedient tears.

And then, he pressed his lips together and forced a fragile smile. He wanted her to know that he was strong. That her Jacky Jo would be all right.

She laid the last plank into place and rushed from the house.

They were coming!

Only afterwards had she realized that she hadn't told her son she loved him.

She hoped she would be given one more chance.

Somewhere ahead, a hard voice said, 'On your knees.'

Bobby Stillman's heart stopped. She looked to her left and right. She was waiting for a signal from Harry. Darkness stared back. Squinting, she made out shadows, phantoms born of her imagination. She moved forward a step, and then another. She spotted Thomas on his knees in the center of a small clearing. Jenny was next to him.

She stepped closer and a stick snapped. All heads turned toward her. Bobby froze. Dressed in black pants, a long-sleeved black shirt, her hair dyed a widow's black, she blended into the night. They saw nothing.

She could not take her eyes off her Jacky Jo.

A shimmer of metal caught her eye. Someone moved closer to Jack . . . no, to *Thomas*. She must call him by the name he'd lived his life by. A man stood close to her son, his arm stiff, outstretched. Squinting, she could tell that he held a gun.

Harry, where are you? she wanted to shout. *What are you waiting for? Walter?* Then she realized it was her they were waiting for. She was their leader.

'No!' she screamed, turning on her flashlight, running wildly through the bushes. Around her, two other lights illuminated the scene.

A gunshot blistered the night.

John Franciscus lay still, his eyes half-open and glazed, his breath coming in shallow, undetectable sips. *Closer*, he urged the two guards. *Just a little closer.*

'Hurry up,' said the man nearest to him. 'Find out if we should get EMS.'

From the corner of his eye, he saw one of the men rush out of the shack. The other bent over him, ear pressed to his chest. Franciscus rolled his eye to the left. The butt of the pistol was there. Inches from his fingers. The holster was unsnapped, the pistol's safety on.

The guard raised his head, staring toward the open door. 'Get a move on it!' he yelled.

Just then, Franciscus sat up and yanked the pistol from the holster. It was a clean clear. The guard shouted with surprise, too startled to immediately react. Franciscus notched the safety and fired into his chest. The man toppled to one side, grunting. Franciscus placed the pistol against his forehead and pulled the trigger. Rolling to one side, he pushed himself to his feet.

'Frankie, what gives?'

The second guard ran through the door. Franciscus staggered toward him, firing once, twice, the man collapsing to the ground, his head striking the concrete, thudding like a cannonball. Franciscus leaned against the wall, gathering his breath. His injuries were more severe than he'd imagined. The busted cheek was killing him. Worse, his vision was royally fucked, the light shattering into thousands of shards like he was looking at the world through a kaleidoscope. He took a step, looking out the door and down the barn. The stables were deserted.

This is it, babe, he said to himself. The voice was strong and it gave him hope. *Whaddaya know? I just might make it.* For a moment he thought of Vicki Vasquez. He hoped she'd give him a chance. Just listen to him . . .

He started down the center of the barn. He kept the gun in front of him, his finger tugging at the trigger. With each step, his entire body rocked this way and that, searching for balance. He was rickety as a condemned building. Vicki would love him now. She might take an older guy with a weak heart. A half-blind cripple with a face that had lost the demolition derby was another story.

He needed to get outside. Ten steps and he would be there. He'd fire off a few shots, shout for help. A crowd would show up in no time. He dropped a hand to his back pocket and felt the outline of his badge holder. He wanted to smile, but his face was too wrecked. For a moment, he felt warm, and oddly satisfied with himself.

He reached for the barn door, but something was wrong. The door was opening inward toward him. He tried to step back, but he was too slow, and the door slammed into him. He stumbled backward. A figure rushed at him. It was hard to see who. Damned eye. A detached retina. That's what the problem was. He aimed wildly and fired. Before he could squeeze the trigger again, something hot, blazingly hot, crashed into his chest and knocked him to the floor.

He stared up, looking at the hurricane lamp swaying above him. The light in the barn was fading fast, as if someone were dousing the wick. His mouth was very dry; his breath running from him.

Guilfoyle leaned over him, clutching Franciscus's badge holder in his hand. He flipped it open and dug a thumb into the crease between the badge and the leather. Finding nothing, he swore and dropped it on the floor. 'That's the one place I'd forgotten to look,' he said. 'Been bothering me for twenty-five years. So, where are they? What did you do with Jacklin's fingerprints?'

Franciscus tried to open his mouth, but his body no longer obeyed him. The prints were safe, he wanted to say. He'd sent them where they might do some good. Away from men like Guilfoyle and Jacklin.

'Where are the prints?' Guilfoyle asked again. 'Dammit, I need to know.'

But Franciscus could no longer hear him. He was floating. Above the stables and the pine forest, high into the sky.

Thomas Bolden jerked at the sound of gunfire. The pistol left his neck. Suddenly, the clearing was illuminated by light. An agitated voice shrieked, 'No!' Lashing out, Bolden spun and kicked Wolf's feet out from beneath him. Bolden jumped on top of him, pummeling him in the face, about the head. The pain in his chest, his body, was immense, a roaring brushfire that had engulfed him. It no longer mattered. His rage was fiercer still. All that mattered was that he kept up the assault. Again and again, he raised his fists and brought them down on his assassin's face.

Wolf freed a hand and rocketed a fist into

Bolden's jaw, knocking him to the ground. The Scanlon operative rolled to his feet, his face bruised, blood dangling in cords from his nose. Bolden stood. The two circled each other, the gun on the ground between them.

Other figures were running around him. A tall, gray-haired man wielding a heavy Maglite clubbed Irish. Jenny wrapped her arm around the blond man's neck and held him in a headlock. Somewhere there came the spit of a silenced gunshot, followed by the crunch of a hard object striking someone's skull.

Wolf spat out a gob of blood. Carelessly, he wiped at his face. Bolden waited, gathering his breath. Wolf charged. This time it was Bolden who went with the attack, following the blow, grasping the man's wrist, twisting it and pulling him over his shoulder. Wolf hit the ground. Bolden landed on his chest, driving his knee into the sternum, his hand cupped around his neck, fingers digging into the soft flesh. He found the windpipe. His fingers closed in on it, crushing it. Wolf thrashed on the ground, his hand clawing at Bolden's face, seeking to gouge his eyes. Bolden brought all his weight onto his hands. The band of cartilage began to give . . .

'No, Thomas, don't . . .'

Bolden didn't hear the words. He increased the pressure, forcing his thumb deep into the tissue. He stared into the burning brown eyes, wanting to extinguish their hateful fire for ever.

'Stop!'

Hands grabbed Bolden's shoulders and pried him off the Scanlon operative. Wolf pushed himself up. A figure stepped over Bolden and struck Wolf across the face with the Maglite. Wolf fell to the ground and was still.

Bolden lay on his back, sucking in the air. Stunned, he looked up at his mother.

Bobby Stillman stood above him, the flashlight in her hand. 'I don't want my son to be a killer.'

Chapter 67

The floor of the Jeep Wagoneer was rusted through, holes the size of a grenade chewed away by corrosion, rock salt, and years of abusive wear. Bolden sat in the rear seat, a wool blanket wrapped around his shoulders. He could see the icy path rushing beneath them, hear the clatter of gravel striking the undercarriage. Every bump, every turn, every acceleration made him wince. Adrenaline and emotion did something to combat the pain, but not enough. Jenny sat beside him and, next to her, his mother, Bobby Stillman. The vehicle turned violently, fishtailing on the slick pavement. Bolden caught the cry deep in his throat and stifled it with an iron fist.

'They still down?' asked the driver. His name was Harry. Bolden recognized him as the rangy, gray-haired man who'd come to the rescue in Union Square.

'No one's moving yet,' answered Walter, seated in the lookout's seat, shorter, paunchier, in need of a shave and a shower. He was studying a rectangular object similar to a Palm personal assistant. A topographic map was brightly illuminated on its screen. At its edge, a triangle of dots remained motionless. 'Satellite tracking device,' he explained. 'You familiar with Lojack? Works just like that. Just on people, not cars. Looks like all the other goons have headed home for some shut-eye.'

'People with transmitters?' asked Jenny.

'They're "chipped",' said Harry. 'Don't look so surprised. The Army's been using the technology for years. Only way they could find our Delta operators in Afghanistan.' He glanced over his shoulder. 'How you doin', my man? Think you can hold out till we can get you to a hospital? Have a doctor clean you up?'

'He's not going to a hospital,' said Bobby Stillman. 'Not yet. He's a wanted murderer, for Christ's sake. You think a man walking into the emergency room with a cross carved on his chest isn't going to raise a lot of questions?' She leaned forward and tapped Harry on the shoulder. 'Stop at an all-night supermarket when you get into DC. We can pick up some lidocaine spray, antibiotic cream, and bandages there. That'll have to do for now.'

Bolden pulled the blanket around him, unable to keep his gaze from Bobby Stillman. He was hoping to spot a hint of resemblance between the two of them, something to prove to him that she was his mother. Something other than the 'change of name' form that Marty Kravitz had dug up in the Albany county clerk's office stating that John Joseph Stillman would now and for ever be known as Thomas Franklin Bolden.

'Wondering if you're really mine?' Bobby Stillman asked, catching him staring at her. 'Surgery. Nose, cheeks, my hair's dyed. After twenty-five years, I'd be surprised if you still recognized me . . . even if I hadn't changed a wink.'

'You were there,' he whispered hoarsely. 'Last night. I saw you.'

'At the dinner?' asked Jenny, looking between them.

'She was outside watching.'

'Yes. I was there,' said Bobby Stillman.

'How long were you watching me?'

'Your whole life.'

Bolden considered her words. 'I never called you,' he said.

'No, you didn't.'

'What are you talking about?' asked Jenny.

'That's what set them off,' Bolden explained, going slowly. 'Guilfoyle had come across a few indicators, minor things that they could have written off to business. But it was the phone calls that convinced them. Three nights in a row, someone placed a call from my apartment to her house. But I was in Milwaukee last week. It couldn't have been me.' He looked back at Bobby Stillman. 'You didn't want them to miss it.'

Bobby Stillman nodded, but in the rearview mirror, Bolden caught Walter's smile. It was his handiwork. Jefferson could hack into his bank accounts. Walter could tamper with his phone records. Three cheers for personal privacy. 'Why didn't you just shoot up a flare?' he asked.

'You have to understand how important it was for us to get inside Jefferson. We'd tried so many times and failed. The security was just too tight.'

'Why not just ask me?'

'And say what? "Hi. I'm your mom. Sorry I've been gone for twenty-five years. Now that I'm back, I've got some bad news. You're in business with a world-class sneak, a murderer, and a threat to the entire country. I've come to ask you to risk your career and everything else you've busted your butt to earn, to help me bring him down." ' Bobby Stillman looked into her son's eyes. 'I don't think that would have worked. No, Thomas, we had to show you what they were capable of. We had to make you feel it.'

'What did you expect me to do?'

'We knew that Jacklin would make the first move. It wasn't Guilfoyle who came across the indicators. It was Cerberus. Cerberus is what they call their all-knowing, all-seeing data mining system. What's that company you're about to sell Jefferson? Trendrite. Yeah, well, it's like Trendrite on steroids. Anyway, Cerberus picked you up. We imagined they'd question you, maybe cause some problems at work. Discreetly at first, just enough so you'd realize they'd compromised your privacy.'

'And then?'

'And then, we were going to contact you and tell you what was what. Point you in the right direction. It was just a matter of letting you be yourself. You would push right back.'

Bolden held her eyes, damning her. 'I guess I didn't push hard enough.'

'I . . . I didn't . . .' Words formed on Bobby Stillman's lips, but she didn't continue.

'What?' said Bolden. 'You didn't expect them to do this to me? You said it yourself. You wanted me to "feel it". You know something? It worked.'

'I had no idea they were so desperate. I—'

'You knew damn well this is what they'd do. This, or something like it. You pushed me into the line of fire without a prayer.'

Bobby Stillman swallowed, her face taut. 'No. This time was different. They went farther. Too far.'

'It's Crown,' said Jenny. 'I saw it in the minutes.'

'What minutes?' asked Bobby Stillman.

'The club's,' said Jenny. 'I found them upstairs in Jacklin's house. It's what they call themselves. The Patriots' Club. Von Arx from the FBI, Edward Logsdon, Jacklin, Gordon Ramser, Charles Connolly, and Mickey Schiff.'

Jenny went on: 'They're going to do something

to Senator McCoy. She won't join their group. They're waiting to hear from President Ramser if he could convince her.'

'They're going to assassinate her,' said Bobby Stillman. 'It's all set for this morning. At the inauguration.'

'You know about this, too?' Bolden asked.

His mother nodded. 'We got it out of the Scanlon operative we nabbed at Union Square. That's the good news. The bad news is that he didn't know the when and how. Only the where.'

Crown. Bobby Stillman. Bolden put a hand to his forehead. It all fit now.

'Have you called the police or the Secret Service?' asked Jenny.

Bobby Stillman frowned. 'And say what? Should I mention who I am? Or, that I'm shielding a suspect wanted for murder in the state of New York? That makes two killers. Why not call the FBI while we're at it? Put me through to Director Von Arx. Oh, I forgot, he's part of the club, too.'

Jenny stared at her, aghast. 'And so . . . we do nothing to stop it.'

Bobby Stillman lowered her head. 'I don't know what we can do.'

They drove in silence. Snow fell steadily, a white wilderness illuminated by the headlights. They turned onto George Washington Parkway. Here and there, the Potomac peeked from the trees, wide and flat and dark. Bolden peered at the water, wanting answers.

'You have no idea what it took to walk away.'

The words were so hushed that Bolden thought that they might have come from inside him. He looked across the seat at his mother. 'I was your son. You'd already seen fit to dump my father. You shouldn't have dumped me, too.'

'I was on the run. I couldn't take you with me.'

'Why not? What was the worst that could happen? You get caught, they take me away. Same difference.'

Bobby Stillman couldn't hold his gaze. 'Because you slowed me down.'

'Ah, the truth.'

'But I didn't want *them* to take you. I had some friends in mind, people I thought I could trust. I hid you, but . . . but they let me down.'

'The left-wing fringe,' said Bolden. 'Dependable as ever.'

A shadow passed over his mother's face. Sighing with anger, desperation, even hope, she began to talk about the past. About bombing Sentinel Microsystems and David Bernstein's murder, about Jacklin framing her. About spending her life moving from one town to the next, always scrounging for money. And finally, about her mission to expose Jefferson, to unravel their fraud, and put an end to their meddling.

'How can you understand?' she asked. 'It was a crazy time. We were so impassioned, so angry. We believed. Does anyone believe in anything any more?'

'But you never came back,' said Jenny. 'You never wrote Tom a single letter.'

'It was better for him to forget me.'

'You didn't leave when I was two,' said Bolden. 'I was six. You were all I had.'

'And do you think you would have understood? Do you think a six-year-old can grasp the concept of sacrifice? All kids think about are themselves. Well, wise up, sonny boy, some things are more important than having a Coke and a smile.'

Bolden shook his head. He felt no loss, no sorrow or self-pity. That part of him had died a long time ago. He was surprised when he heard her gasp and saw tears running down his mother's face. She looked away, wiping her cheeks.

'Oh, Lord.' She laughed achingly, her chin unsteady. 'I was terrible. I know that. It was my choice and I'd make it again today. I couldn't let Jacklin steal the people's voice. That's what he does. He doesn't trust us. Any of us. So there. Now you know it. I was a bad mother. I've had to live with that every day. But I did what I had to do.'

Bolden reached out his hand. His mother looked down at it. Her eyes rose to him. Lacing her fingers through his, she took his hand and held on to her son tightly.

Chapter 68

Agent Ellington Fiske of the United States Secret Service strode through the front door of the White House and addressed the assembly of men and women standing inside. 'Mr President. Senator McCoy. We're ready for you.'

It was ten o'clock in the morning, Thursday, January 20. Inauguration Day by vote of Congress. Standing in the vestibule were the President and First Lady, their three grown children and two grandchildren, Senator McCoy, her father, her sister, and two nieces. At Fiske's announcement, the group hastily set their cups and saucers on the table and headed to the door.

Four limousines waited outside: heavily armored black stretch Cadillacs, the Stars and Stripes flying from the hood like a cavalry unit's guidons. Only the second and third in line, however, were outfitted to transport the President of the United States. These carried extra armor sufficient to withstand a direct strike from a rocket-propelled grenade, bulletproof glass capable of stopping a .30-caliber round fired at point-blank range, and puncture-proof tires.

President Gordon Ramser and Senator Megan McCoy climbed into the second limousine in line. Their family members and guests trooped into the third and fourth. Though the inauguration would not begin until twelve o'clock, protocol dictated that the incoming and outgoing President visit the Hill for morning tea with congressional leadership inside the Capitol rotunda. Fiske checked that all doors were properly closed before walking to the head of the motorcade and climbing into the command car, a navy blue Chevrolet Suburban with no armor, no bulletproof glass, and a set of standard steel-belted radials. Secret Service agents were expendable.

'Tomahawk to Braves. We are go to the Capitol. Move 'em out.' Fiske put down the two-way radio and looked at Larry Kennedy, his number two. 'This is it. The big day.'

'You da man, chief,' said Kennedy. He nodded confidently. 'Everything's gonna go smooth as silk.'

'Your mouth to God's ear.'

For twelve months, Fiske had worked tirelessly to ensure that nothing would mar this day. Success was measured in how quickly the average American would forget it. Fiske wanted four minutes on the evening news and not a second more. Larry Kennedy put out his hand. Fiske shook it firmly. 'Let's do it.'

The motorcade departed 1600 Pennsylvania Avenue, turning right, then right again at the end of the block and continuing down Fifteenth Street. Fiske stared out the window with suspicious eyes. The snow had stopped. The clouds had broken. A sky of frosted blue peeked from behind the curtain of white fleece. The next instant, the sun hit the ground, gilding the newly fallen snow and sending spirals of reflected light shooting off the wet streets. Fiske nodded grudgingly. About time the Lord got with the program.

The spectators were taking up positions along the parade route, staking out spots on the sidewalk and filling the bleachers. Clusters of eight magnetometers governed entrance to each fenced-in, three-block perimeter. It was simple mathematics. Three thousand people an hour could pass through each checkpoint. There were twenty checkpoints in total. Sixty thousand people an hour could gain access to the parade route and National Mall. Last time the crowd had numbered an estimated three hundred thousand, between the Mall and the parade route. But now ... Fiske grimaced. The change in weather would bring them out in droves. A steady stream of men and women passed through each choke point along the route. So far, so good.

His eyes rose to the roof of the Reagan Building. A shadow flitted above the parapet. Sharpshooters were in place at seventeen strategic locations along the route. Anti-aircraft batteries had been erected at eight others. To his right, a K-9 team conducted a final check for explosives beneath the bleachers.

Two thousand uniformed police.

Two hundred of his own agents.

A thousand volunteers.

Everyone was in place.

Fiske sat back. All he could do was wait.

Thomas Bolden tramped awkwardly across the snow, his arm draped over Jenny's shoulder. Despite the bandages wrapping his chest and the heavy dose of over-the-counter lidocaine spray-on painkiller, his chest throbbed ferociously. He'd just have to take it for a while. The National Mall was crowded to bursting with spectators. From the steps of the Capitol building to the sloped foothills leading up to the Washington Monument, it was a sea of bobbing heads with more arriving every minute. Bobby Stillman led the way, not afraid to push, squeeze, or plain shove her way through the grinding crowd. For over an hour, Bolden had argued that he should find a Secret Service agent and inform him of their fears. His mother wouldn't hear of it. One mention of a threat to the President-elect, and he would be whisked off to a holding cell where he could be interrogated. The first thing they would do was ask for his driver's license, or social security number, and run him through their computers. Word would come back that he was wanted for murder, and that would be the end of that. Case closed. Innocent or not, he was a fugitive whose word had lost its value.

They had come to keep watch. To pray that they'd spot the attempt on Senator McCoy's life in time to warn her.

They stopped at a spot beneath the television tower. The strains of the Marine Band reached their ears. All brass and drums, a chest-thumping call to arms.

'Nothing like a Sousa march to get the blood flowing,' said Harry. 'Makes me want to straighten up and fire off a salute.'

'Makes me want to run in the other direction,' said Walter.

The presidential stand was two hundred feet away. The seats behind it were nearly full. Bolden spotted Von Arx of the FBI, and Edward Logsdon, Charles Connolly, the author, and of course, James J. Jacklin. The Scoundrels' Club. Only Ramser and Schiff were missing.

Bolden checked his watch. Eleven fifty-five. The inauguration would begin in five minutes. He glanced over his shoulder and surveyed the crowd. There were uniformed police everywhere. He'd read in the morning's paper that an additional fourteen hundred officers had been brought in to provide adequate security. According to his mother, Scanlon had been hired to enhance perimeter security and provide a 'secure but porous event environment'. He knew what that meant. They would be dressed in plainclothes, but armed and with a mandate to intervene when necessary. Some, he knew, would be looking for him.

'Walter,' he said. 'Got your little radar kit?'

The short, paunchy man fished the device out of his back pocket. 'You having the same thought I am?'

'Just curious to see how many of our buddies are hanging around.'

Walter switched on the device. A stable black dot indicated the base unit. Flashing Xs identified RFID transmissions, or, in this instance, Scanlon men who were 'chipped'.

'Nothing,' he said. 'Let me run through some bandwidth.'

Abruptly, the Marine Band stopped playing. All heads lifted to the Capitol steps. The air was quiet except for the distant thumping of the Blackhawk helicopters hovering at a thousand feet to maintain air security. The President and First Lady descended the stairs, followed by Senator McCoy, and the vice president and vice president-elect.

'Holy shit,' blurted Walter, bringing the tracking device closer to his eyes. 'Man, they are everywhere. I'm counting eighteen at least within a hundred yards of us.'

'Just doing their job, right?' said Bolden.

James Jacklin took his seat on the reviewing stand next to the two men who had preceded him as Secretary of Defense. It was no coincidence that both were employees of Jefferson Partners. He pushed his hands deep into the cashmere-lined pockets of his overcoat. The vice president had been sworn in a few minutes earlier. Now it was time for the main event. He looked around him. It was hard not to be awed by all the pomp and ceremony, the gold piping and crenellated bunting and the long, red carpets, symbols since Caesar's time, of majesty. The flags hanging on the Capitol building were as big as city blocks. It was the Roman Empire all over. Christ, he loved it. What a party this was. He remembered his first inauguration, thirty years ago. Back then, it had been on the east side of the Capitol, where the winds howled at you across the Anacostia plains. In 1841, 'Old Tippecanoe', William Henry Harrison, had braved the fierce cold for ninety minutes to shout his inauguration speech. A month later he was dead from pneumonia. It took 'the Gipper' to change things. Ronnie wanted to face west when he took the Oath of Office. West toward the open country. West toward opportunity. Manifest Destiny wasn't dead. No, thought Jacklin, his chest expanding, it was just beginning. People talked about the American Century. It would be the American millennium. This country was born to rule. And he planned on being at its helm. Oh, not in office. Never. The real power was behind the throne. No truer words had ever been spoken. The French had the right word for it. An *éminence grise*. A gray eminence. He would rule from the shadows.

Catching Director Von Arx's eye, he nodded. Von Arx looked away without the slightest indication he'd seen him. Charles Connolly sat behind the First Lady, her very own lapdog. Chief Justice Logsdon stood on the reviewing stand, the drab black jurist's robes making him look more like a squat, dyspeptic funeral attendant than the nation's ranking interpreter of the Constitution. For an instant their eyes met. Logsdon ducked his head, as if he were shaking off a bee.

They were wrong. All of them. McCoy would not join them. Not now. Not ever. She was the renegade. Her gall enraged him. Who did she think she was to turn down an offer to join the club? In six months, she would just be worse. Their only chance was now. Why was he the only one to see it?

Jacklin smiled smugly. He knew they were forming against him, whispering to one another, planning his ouster. None of it bothered him a whit. On this chill morning with the wind out of the east snapping the American flag and the sky as blue as faded denim, he felt supremely secure. In control. Jacklin had his own plans.

'They're leaving,' said Walter.

'What do you mean?' Bolden stood at his shoulder. 'Who's leaving?'

'The Scanlon men. They're taking a hike.' Walter held out the electronic device for Bolden to see. The Xs that denoted the Scanlon operatives moved steadily toward the perimeter of the screen. He looked around him, knowing it was hopeless in this crowd to try to spot them, but doing it nonetheless.

Bobby Stillman yanked the handheld tracking device out of Walter's hands. 'This is it,' she said. 'It's happening now. He's pulling them out!'

The loudspeakers broadcast Senator McCoy taking her oath of office.

'I do solemnly swear that I will faithfully execute the Office of President of the United States, and will to the best of my ability, preserve, protect, and defend the Constitution of the United States.'

Bolden searched the rows of seats behind the President. It took him a moment to find Jacklin. The chairman of Jefferson Partners sat idly, his eyes on Senator McCoy as she took the Oath of Office. It made no sense that the Scanlon men were deserting their posts. Bolden was no expert on security, but he knew the goons didn't leave until the President had left the podium and the event was officially over. Even then, there was the parade that would pass adjacent to the Mall.

'Are they meeting up somewhere?' he asked. 'Maybe it's a security briefing.'

'They're headed to all points of the compass,' said Walter. 'Off to hell and gone.'.

McCoy's voice died off and a great roar rose up from the crowd. The applause spread over Bolden, enveloping him in its enthusiasm, a wild, unfettered cry for democracy. It was done. The nation had its next President. The men and women behind the new President were on their feet, applauding, patting each other, some hugging. Bolden looked back toward Jacklin. His seat was empty.

Chapter 69

Bolden collared the first police officer he saw. 'Sir, I need to speak to a Secret Service agent. It's urgent. It concerns the President's welfare.'

The others were behind him watching, swallowed by the crowd. He didn't care if he was risking arrest. There was no other way. If only he didn't say the words 'assassinate' or 'murder', maybe he could get his message through without being carted away.

The police officer was short and tubby, with two chins hanging over his collar. He took a long look at Bolden. 'What about her welfare?'

'It's imperative that I speak to a member of the Secret Service.'

The policeman shifted his weight. 'You got something to say, say it to me.'

'I have some information that I think a Secret Service agent should hear. It's very urgent.'

'And it concerns the President?'

'Yes.' It was difficult not to shout. Bolden wanted to grab this fat, badly shaven cop by his shoulders and shake some sense into him. He wanted to rip off his own shirt and say, 'Look at my chest. This is what they're capable of. They're going to kill the President and we have to stop them.'

The cop unclipped his radio and brought it to his mouth. But instead of calling for backup, he said, 'When's shift change?'

'One o'clock,' a voice squawked.

'Roger that.' The policeman stared dully at Bolden, as if saying, 'You still here?'

Bolden stared right back, reading the cop's mind. He was thinking, *What can this wired, uptight fool possibly tell me that might in any way affect the President? If I don't pay any attention to him, maybe he'll just get lost.*

President Megan McCoy was delivering her inauguration address. Her strong, vibrant voice carried through the air, offering a message of renewal and hope. Around him, all faces were raised toward the reviewing stand. Bolden spun away, sighing, the desperation rising in him. The sudden motion made him wince and he knew he'd opened up his chest again. He stepped toward the street. The nearest checkpoint was two blocks away. He would have to run.

'Sir, how can I help?'

Bolden looked over his shoulder. The man was dressed in a navy suit and overcoat, and wore the dark sunglasses and earpiece that had become the Secret Service's uniform. 'Something strange is going on,' Bolden said slowly, as if delivering a report. 'All the men who work for Scanlon are leaving the area. They're just getting the hell out of here. Moving off in every direction. I need to speak to the director of security. The guy who's running the show.'

'How do you know this?'

'It doesn't really matter right now. What's important is that these men are leaving the area nearest the President's podium. I believe they were hired to provide close perimeter security. They're leaving. What does that tell you?'

'I don't know, sir. What are you implying?'

Bolden looked away in frustration. 'You tell me,'

he said, too loudly. His calm was slipping away, fleeing as surely and quickly as the last sands in an hourglass. 'What would make you want to get away from where the President of the United States is standing? Figure it out.'

The agent stared at him for a moment, then grabbed him by the lapel of his jacket and dragged him ten feet away. 'You stay here. What's your name?'

'Thomas Bolden.'

'All right then, Mr Bolden. You will not move one step. Understood?'

Bolden nodded.

The agent spoke into his microphone, relaying to his superior everything that Bolden had just told him. 'Mr Fiske's on his way.'

Barely two minutes passed before a blue Chevy Suburban screeched to a halt, and a trim African-American man leaped to the ground. 'You Bolden?'

'Yes sir.'

'What's this garbage you're spouting about Scanlon leaving the area?'

'Are you the agent in charge?'

'Ellington Fiske. This is my show.'

'Have you asked the Scanlon guys why they're all taking a hike?'

Fiske's mouth tightened. 'We haven't been able to raise them.'

Just then, a tall, red-faced agent ran up to them. 'Thomas Bolden is wanted by the NYPD for murder. He popped some guy on Wall Street yesterday.'

'His name was Sol Weiss,' said Bolden. 'I didn't kill him. It was an accident. Another man shot him, a security guard working for my firm, Harrington Weiss, but actually, I think he works for Scanlon, too. Look, I'm turning myself in to tell you guys this. You've got to listen to me. There is going to be an attempt on the President's life. And I mean now! Would you get off your asses and do something?'

The red-faced agent grabbed Bolden and spun him around, throwing cuffs on his wrist. 'You bet we're going to do something, mister.'

'Hold it,' ordered Fiske. He stepped toward Bolden. 'How do you know this?'

'I just know.' He held the Secret Service agent's eyes. 'Can you afford to find out if I'm lying?'

Fiske looked away, the muscles in his jaw working overtime. 'Okay, Mr Bolden. You've got two minutes to convince me. Larry, take off the cuffs. Bolden, get in the car. You're coming with me.'

Thirty-one pounds of RDX lined the hollow interior walls of the Triton Industries-manufactured podium. RDX, or Research Department Explosive, was as deadly an explosive as was currently manufactured, and used primarily in the destruction of nuclear warheads. In fact, so tightly controlled was the material that its chemical signature was not among those regularly screened for by the United States Secret Service. It was manufactured by the Olney Corporation of Towson, Maryland. Two years earlier, Olney had been purchased by Jefferson Partners.

James Jacklin took a last look at Senator McCoy as she began to deliver her inauguration address, then rose from his seat and scooted to the outside aisle. All eyes were on the President, as he walked up the stairs and crossed the Capitol esplanade. He'd been told it was necessary to be at least five hundred yards from the blast site. The RDX had an effective kill radius of two hundred feet. It was not so much the force of the blast that made RDX so effective, but the tremendous heat it generated. At the time of detonation, temperatures at the core of the bomb would exceed three thousand degrees. Everyone on the reviewing stand would be cooked as crisply as a Christmas goose.

Jacklin checked his watch. He had two minutes to distance himself from the bomb. In reality, he was already safe. The stairs behind the podium would deflect the blast upward and back toward the crowd of spectators. Still, he wanted to make sure.

He had reached the steps leading to the Dirksen building when President McCoy broke off her speech in midsentence. A hushed roar passed through the crowd. A siren began to wail, then another, and soon, it sounded to him as if every police car in the city were heading toward the presidential reviewing stand. He looked at his watch again. It was too late.

The time was twenty minutes past twelve. Ellington Fiske kept his foot on the accelerator as he turned the corner of Constitution Avenue and Second Street. 'Goddamm it, would somebody get me one of those motherfuckers from Scanlon on the horn!'

'Their receivers are jammed,' said Larry Kennedy, his number two. 'Probably just a short, boss.'

'Like the one that knocked out the microphone on the podium,' said Fiske.

'Do we clear the area, sir?' asked Kennedy.

Fiske shot Bolden a damning glance. 'Go on,' he said.

'And so, we got the information out of a Scanlon operative,' said Bolden. 'It's called Crown. They're killing her because she won't join the club.'

'Jacklin is?'

'Yes sir.'

'The billionaire? The guy who runs Jefferson Partners? You're making it hard on me, Bolden. Very hard.'

The Suburban rocked to the left as it came around the back of the Capitol building. They passed through a cordon of police cars and emergency vehicles, Fiske bringing the car to a violent halt. 'Get out.'

Bolden opened the door and climbed out of the car, wincing and grunting. Fiske eyed him warily. 'What's up with you?'

Bolden didn't think there was any point in answering the question. 'Has anything out of the ordinary taken place in the last day or two? Anything near the President? Special guests, some new equipment that was put into place in the last twenty-four hours, something that could make a very big bang?'

'Just a podium.' Fiske walked briskly across the esplanade. Ahead, nearly a dozen policemen blocked the way to the top of the reviewing stand. Looking west toward the Washington Monument, the Mall was a sea of humans. Everywhere, there were American flags. Lining the snow-covered fields, gracing the government buildings, waving from the hands of thousands of spectators. A shower of red, white, and blue.

'A podium,' said Bolden, working to keep up. 'Where'd it come from?'

'Virginia,' said Fiske.

'From Triton Aerospace?'

Fiske stopped in his tracks. 'How do you know that?'

'Triton's owned by the same group that owns Scanlon. Jefferson Partners. It's Jacklin's company. I'd say you have a problem on your hands.'

Fiske raised a hand to his forehead and

mumbled, 'Shit.' He looked at Kennedy. 'Anyone raise Scanlon?'

'Negative, sir.'

Fiske looked down, a cloud of anguish passing over his face. As suddenly, it was gone. 'We have a code red,' he barked into his lapel. 'Clear Eagle. I repeat, Clear Eagle.' He looked at Bolden. 'Mister. You had better not be wrong.'

Bolden followed Fiske through the line of policemen to the top of the stairs. President McCoy was surrounded by a flock of Secret Service agents, all but invisible inside a sea of navy blue and black. The tight knot moved quickly off the stage and began a pained march up the stairs. Fiske ran down to meet them, shouting, 'Hurry!' The crowd watched, no one moving, a sentiment of anxious horror playing on their faces.

She's safe, Bolden said to himself.

The light was tremendous, a blinding torrent of oranges and blacks brighter than a thousand suns. An unseen hammer struck his body, lifting him into the air. Bolden lay on his back. Folding chairs clattered to the ground. He looked to his right. A man's leg, naked except for a sock and shoe, lay next to him. He sat up and waited for his vision to clear. There was something in his eyes. He wiped at his face and his hand came away streaked with blood. Kennedy was on his back nearby, his face blackened, a gash laying open his cheek. He muttered something, then scrambled to his feet and ran down the stairs.

Bolden stood up unsteadily. The reviewing stand was in ruins. A pall of smoke hung in the air. The first few rows of seats no longer existed. A craggy, black crater dug out of the Capitol stairs was all that was left. The blast had vaporized the stage. The podium. It had been the Triton podium. An

American flag hung in tatters off to one side, flames devouring the red and white stripes.

Everywhere there were bodies, torn and rent and bleeding. Moans drifted through the air. Shouts for help, at first timid, then louder, strident. He staggered down a few stairs. The President of the United States pulled herself from the pile of Secret Service agents. Except for a scrape on her shin, she appeared unhurt. Immediately, two agents grabbed her arms and basically carried her bodily past Bolden up the stairs. Ellington Fiske lay crumpled over a row of chairs, his face a mask of blood, his head turned at an unnatural angle.

Bolden sat down and buried his head in his hands.

It was over.

The President was alive.

Chapter 70

James Jacklin threw a last shirt into his suitcase and zipped it up. Walking to the dresser, he picked up his passport, his billfold, and an envelope stuffed with fifty thousand dollars and slipped them into the pockets of his blazer. It was just four-thirty. He should relax. He had plenty of time to make the eight o'clock flight to Zürich. Stopping in front of the mirror, he combed his hair, taking a moment to cut the part razor-sharp, then tighten the knot of his tie. He had an appointment with his banker on the Bahnhofstrasse the following morning at nine, and he wasn't sure if he'd make it to the Baur au Lac in time to freshen up.

From the window, he saw the limousine pull into the driveway and advance slowly toward the portico. Dusk was falling. A crescent moon hung low in the sky. It was time to get out of Dodge. The investigation into the bombing had tied down the explosives used three days earlier as RDX. They'd even come up with a batch number. Ramser and Connolly were dead, but Logsdon and Von Arx had survived the blast, though Von Arx had lost his right leg at the hip. Jacklin hadn't spoken with any of them since the incident. The news about the RDX would do it. They'd know beyond a doubt that he was behind it, and he knew what action they would take. He was not the President. The club's legitimacy didn't rest on his shoulders.

As Jacklin walked downstairs, he shook off one set of worries for another. His spies at the Securities and Exchange Commission had informed him that the head of enforcement had received certain confidential documents outlining massive payoffs from Jefferson Partners to a dozen former government officials, including the recently retired head of the FCC and a prominent four-star general. There was no indication of who had supplied the documents, but Jacklin knew well enough. It was Bolden. He had managed to fire off some copies to his friends, after all. Jacklin's attorneys would handle the matter. In the meantime, Jacklin would repair to his private island. From there, he would direct the usual overtures. Promises would be made. Money would change hands. He was worth eight billion dollars, give or take. That kind of wealth bought lots of friends. Jefferson was too big to kill. It had too many secrets. In the meantime, he would see what he could do about Logsdon and Von Arx. It was just a matter of time before he was back.

Jacklin opened the front door. The chauffeur stood waiting, cap drawn low over his eyes. Jacklin noticed he had a strange scar on his cheek.

'Just the one bag,' Jacklin said. 'I'll be right there.'

'Take your time, sir. We're in no hurry.'

Jacklin placed the note he'd written to his wife on the kitchen counter, then set the alarm and locked the door behind him. He took a last look at the house. Everything was secured. The journals had been packed up and sent to a safe place. Somewhere away from prying eyes. The heirlooms of Washington and Hamilton, likewise. He didn't want them rotting in a museum. They were meant for privileged eyes only.

He took a breath of his beloved Virginia air –

American air – and climbed into the back seat of the limousine. It was only when he sat back that he noticed the figure at the far end of the passenger compartment. A big man with dark skin and narrow, hate-filled brown eyes.

'That you, Wolf?'

'I came to wish you bon voyage, Mr Jacklin.'

Jacklin's hand flew to the door. He pulled at the handle repeatedly.

'Locked,' said Wolf.

'Who told you? What exactly is going on? Hold it right there! That's an order.'

Wolf advanced across the compartment at a crouch. He held something sharp and angular in his hand. 'Change of management, sir. The President sends her regards.'

The sun's dying rays flashed off the knife's honed blade.

Epilogue

Spring had arrived in a spray of vibrant greens. The air had warmed, and a wandering breeze swept across Central Park. Hand in hand, Thomas Bolden and Jennifer Dance sat on a bench next to an empty baseball diamond.

'Mexico City?' Jennifer said. 'But you don't even speak the language.'

'I can learn,' said Bolden. 'It will be the biggest Boys' Club in the country. They need someone to run the place. Mostly someone who can help them raise the money to keep it going.'

'Isn't it dangerous down there?'

Bolden shrugged. 'I think we can look after ourselves.'

Jenny nodded. 'It's just so far away . . .'

'I'm not going without you.'

'You're not?'

'Wouldn't think of it.'

'What about your mother?' Jenny asked.

'Bobby? I figure she can visit once every couple of months. I think that's enough, don't you?'

Three days after the attempt on President Megan McCoy's life, Bolden had received an envelope from the New York Police Department containing a copy of the fingerprints found on the gun that had killed two Albany police officers twenty-five years earlier. A note stated that the fingerprints had been identified by the NCIC as belonging to James J.

Jacklin. It was signed Detective John Franciscus. With the new evidence and a lack of eyewitnesses, all charges were dropped against Bobby Stillman.

'You're probably right,' said Jenny. She narrowed her eyes. 'Mexico, huh? You expect me just to pack up and move to a foreign country with you. I don't know if I'm that kind of girl. I mean, we haven't even lived together yet.'

Bolden got up off the bench and led her to home plate. Kneeling, he took her hand. 'Jennifer Dance. I love you. I want to live my life at your side. Will you—'

Bolden stopped midsentence, distracted by a black Lincoln Town Car that had pulled up on the road directly beside them. The door opened and a squat, older man emerged, dressed in a funereal black suit. Bolden recognized him immediately. 'Um, just a second, Jenny.'

Bolden rose and jogged over to the man. 'Mr Chief Justice,' he said.

'Catch you at a bad time?' asked Edward Logsdon. 'The worst.'

'I'm sorry, son. Important matters.' Logsdon laid a hand on Bolden's shoulder and guided him away from the baseball diamond. 'I need to discuss something with you.'

Bolden nodded, glancing behind him. Jenny remained by home plate, arms crossed over her chest. 'What exactly do you want?' he asked.

Logsdon stopped walking and turned to face him. 'I've come to speak to you about the club. You didn't think we went away, did you?'

Bolden shook his head. 'I guess not.'

'We owe you an apology, as well as a debt of gratitude.'

'Look, whatever it is, I'm not interested. That's over. I'm just trying to get on with my life.'

'At least, hear us out.'

Bolden looked toward Jenny, then sighed and said, 'Okay.'

Logsdon stepped closer. 'Actually, Tom, I've come here to ask you to join us.'

'To join you? The club?'

'Yes.'

'Are you kidding? I mean, why me? Aren't I a little young?'

'To be honest, yes. But in this case, age isn't a qualifying factor.'

Bolden waited, not saying a word.

'There has always been a Pendleton in the Patriots' Club,' Logsdon continued. 'I'm obligated by our covenants to ask you to join us.'

Bolden swallowed. 'James Jacklin . . .' he began.

'Your father.'

'What was that about?' Jenny asked, when Bolden returned.

'He wanted me to join a club.'

'*The club?* What did you tell him?'

'I told him I'd think about it. I had something more important to take care of first.' Thomas Bolden took a knee. 'Now, where was I?'

The Devil's Banker

Christopher Reich

'Reich does for finance what John Grisham does for the law' *San Francisco Chronicle*

In Pakistan, the man with the money is being tailed by Sarah Churchill, British MI6 agent. She has a microdigital camera embedded in her sunglasses and a machine pistol concealed in her waistband. She's in the crazy smuggler's bazaar in Peshawar and very soon everything is going to explode all around her.

In Paris, Adam Chapel, a US treasury agent, has his eyes on a man carrying a scuffed briefcase. There is half a million dollars of terrorist cash in that case but before Adam can get his hands on it, four government agents will be dead.

We are in a new era of the war against terrorism. It's a war against terrorist money. Dirty money. Christopher Reich's new thriller is his most brilliant, most gripping, most bang-up-to-date yet.

'The plot is so suspenseful, the dialogue so believable and the characters so finely drawn' *New York Times*

0 7553 2370 X

headline

Now you can buy any of these other bestselling Headline books from your bookshop or *direct from the publisher*.

FREE P&P AND UK DELIVERY
(Overseas and Ireland £3.50 per book)

The Devil's Banker	Christopher Reich	£6.99
Straight into Darkness	Faye Kellerman	£6.99
Flint	Paul Eddy	£6.99
Last Rights	Barbara Nadel	£6.99
Miracle on the 17th Green	James Patterson and Peter de Jonge	£7.99
After Midnight	Robert Ryan	£6.99
The Graft	Martina Cole	£6.99
Alarm Call	Quintin Jardine	£6.99
Double Homicide	Faye and Jonathan Kellerman	£6.99
Jacquot and the Waterman	Martin O'Brien	£6.99
Thorn	Vena Cork	£6.99
Mixing With Murder	Ann Granger	£6.99

TO ORDER SIMPLY CALL THIS NUMBER

01235 400 414

or visit our website: www.madaboutbooks.com

Prices and availability subject to change without notice.

Christopher Reich was born in Tokyo and grew up in Los Angeles. He worked in the private banking department of a major Swiss bank in Geneva before joining the bank's department of mergers and acquisitions in Zurich. In 1995 he decided to pursue writing full-time. He lives in California and Switzerland and is the author of four previous bestselling thrillers, *Numbered Account*, *The Runner*, *The First Billion* and *The Devil's Banker*.

Also by Christopher Reich

Numbered Account
The Runner
The First Billion
The Devil's Banker